"Gnarr's finest accomplishment in this boo
the absolute immediacy of the childhood experience...
emotions—all the emotions of childhood—to their context, adding the
suffering of learning them, finding new restrictions, fearing ones you don't
know, and we relate to them once again. This is the gift of *The Indian*, the way
that it makes the child, our child-self, alive, close to heart and mind, in all his
pain and his happiness. The Indian is brave in this gift, and dares me to be
brave too, enough to find the child of my past and make him present."
—P.T. Smith, *Three Percent*

"By turns funny and despairing (Gnarr had ADHD and severe dyslexia as
a child), as well as providing a glimpse into Icelandic culture beyond Björk,
The Indian is entertaining and enlightening." —Cary Darling, *Fort Worth Star-
Telegram* Critic's Pick

"A novel about self-discovery in a world where being different is of no good.
It is an ingenious and bleak book, cleverly exploring the life of a ginger
misfit, with writing that seamlessly blends Jón Gnarr's comedic abilities with
an emotional connection that results in a need to learn everything there is to
know about the boy who didn't fit in his surroundings and wanted to become
an Indian." —Denis Barbov, *Graphic Policy*

"*The Indian* is refreshingly original because it not only speaks to a very specific
subset of people who have learned to cope with, or are learning to cope
with their learning disabilities, but also anyone who has ever experienced
feeling like an outcast or alone in their childhood, aka: Everyone. Gnarr's
story is incredibly relevant to all our lives and this is a book that needed to
be written...this story of Jón Gnarr, similarly to how it was necessary to
write, is a book that must be read." —Eilidh, via Young Adults Book Central

"As a Psychiatrist I found this book to be amazing. I loved the juxtaposition
between his experience and the excerpts before each chapter from various
Psychiatrists. This is the best first-person account of the real neuro-biological
differences that children with serious learning differences have. This is a
bittersweet story but Gnarr's genius is in how he keeps the tone victorious.
I loved this book." —Adam Rekerdres, via Goodreads

Thank you
for reading!

— Jon Gnarr

THE OUTLAW

—

Jón Gnarr

TRANSLATED FROM THE ICELANDIC BY
LYTTON SMITH

DEEP VELLUM PUBLISHING
DALLAS, TEXAS

Deep Vellum Publishing
3000 Commerce St., Dallas, Texas 75226
deepvellum.org · @deepvellum

Deep Vellum Publishing is a 501c3
nonprofit literary arts organization founded in 2013.

ISBN: 978-1-941920-52-7 (paperback) · 978-1-941920-53-4 (ebook)
LIBRARY OF CONGRESS CONTROL NUMBER: 2016959430
—

This book has been translated with financial support from the Icelandic Literature Center.

—

Cover design & typesetting by Anna Zylicz · annazylicz.com

Text set in Bembo, a typeface modeled on typefaces cut by Francesco Griffo
for Aldo Manuzio's printing of *De Aetna* in 1495 in Venice.

Distributed by Consortium Book Sales & Distribution · (800) 283-3572 · cbsd.com

Printed in the United States of America on acid-free paper.

THE OUTLAW

The aircraft lifted itself from the ground at Reykjavík Airport. It was only the second time I'd been on a plane. I'd gone to Norway with my mother and father. I'd never been to Reykjavík Airport—never flown domestically. I had a limited understanding of Iceland in my mind, and was exceedingly oblivious as to its character. I'd taken a road trip around the country with my parents, but everything seemed so utterly identical I couldn't work out where I was at any given moment. The country felt somehow alien to me. I could conjure up a picture of Iceland but I couldn't place myself within that picture. I'd gone all the way to Akureyri, but didn't have a clue where to find it on a map. And now I was headed to Ísafjörður. I knew nothing about the place and was struggling to imagine what it would be like. I guessed the town would be some podunk place like Búðardalur; given the name, it was safe to assume it must always be freezing cold there in "ice fjord." I bet people had gardens full of dockweed.

All kinds of folks were on the plane, adults and children alike. I didn't know anyone. An older woman was sitting beside me.

"What's taking you to Ísafjörður?"

"I'm going to Núpur."

"The boarding school?

"Uuuuh..."

Núpur at Dýrafjörður, to give it its full name? What was it, exactly? I hadn't seen a picture of the location and had no idea

3

what a boarding school was. I'd never been to such a place. I'd heard stories, though, about kids who'd gone to the boarding school at Laugarvatn, and it sure sounded fun. A mix of being in school and living in a commune. You had a fair amount of freedom, everyone was good friends, and there was plenty of booze. I hoped it'd be like that at Núpur at Dýrafjörður. But Núpur was probably some storage depot for delinquents, some sort of care home that primarily catered to troubled souls. I didn't quite know if I was a delinquent, but I was close to being one, at least. Delinquents were like me. Although we might not see ourselves as troubled youths, others did. Núpur at Dýrafjörður…the name itself sounded ancient—almost like a foreign language.

I found it fascinating to fly over Iceland and see it from the air. The skies were clear that day so I could see right across the country. Snow-packed mountain slopes, fjords, and then some black blots that were definitely wildernesses…or highlands. I'd never been to the highlands but I'd sometimes heard about people in the news who got lost there. The highlands were dangerous places. Especially in winter. One time, I went camping with Mom and Dad and the family of a man who worked with my father in the police. I had no clue where we were and we had to spend the night in tents and the adults drank alcohol. One guy was really funny; he told me a story about the time he and my father headed to a spring up in the highlands to retrieve the body of a man who'd gotten stuck there over winter. The man was lying face down, and when they arrived they saw that ravens had pecked his ass clean off. The guy told the story like it was the funniest thing. He said it was a good thing the corpse was face down or the ravens would have gotten his face, taken his eyes, nose, and lips. I totally agreed: the lesser of two evils would be to have ravens eat my asshole and not my eyes. It seemed a bit nicer to let ravens peck at your ass than your eyes. They guy burst out laughing and called out:

"Kristinn, remember how much trouble we had getting that body into the car? He was frozen stiff, solid as a rock."

Dad nodded, smiled faintly, and didn't laugh. He clearly didn't find it as amusing as his friend did. Perhaps he felt uncomfortable that I was hearing the story. The highlands were no-man's land, a place no one should go. From the air, they struck me as desolate, black, bereft of humans as far as the eye could see. The friendly lady sitting next to me told me she had not been to Ísafjörður in a long time. She was headed to visit her family. She talked about some places and mentioned some names I didn't know. The woman tried to explain to me where her family lived and I nodded my head at regular intervals and uttered the occasional "oh, yeah, got it" like I was able to put it all together in my head and follow what she was saying. Önundarfjörður? I had no idea whether it was the name of a fjord or a company. I let the situation keep going this way, nodding as though I knew what the hell she was talking about.

We landed at Ísafjörður. Everything there looked just as I'd imagined: nowheresville buried under snow. Ísafjörður was a coastal town surrounded by high mountains. On top of the houses were snowdrifts as high as a person. The mountains astounded me. They were daunting as they towered above, covered in snow, glinting with rocks and scree. I found the place unpleasant and glaringly inconsistent with what the woman had said when she described the lovely town of Ísafjörður and how nice it was. She'd even gone so far as to say that Ísafjörður was the most beautiful place in the world. I, on the other hand, felt like I'd come to hell. To my mind, it was undoubtedly the ugliest place I'd ever been. Ugly, cold, and buried under snow.

People disembarked. The weather was still but cold. As always, I was wearing a t-shirt, jeans and a leather jacket. I pulled the jacket tighter, crossed my arms, and walked into the terminal along with a bunch of kids. We shyly glanced at each other out the corners of our eyes. Suddenly a man turned up and called:

"All aboard the bus for Núpur at Dýrafjörður."

He was a total country bumpkin. I'd seen this sort of hick before. They didn't wear normal men's clothes but silly stuff—some weird country version of menswear. Their pants never fit. They were always just that bit wider than necessary. These guys didn't wear dress shoes like men in Reykjavík but rubber shoes instead. This guy was wearing rubber boots. No one in Reykjavík wore rubber boots unless he was doing work on his house or going fishing. We kids shook ourselves, picked up our bags, and walked out to the bus. I discreetly examined the other kids to see if any of them might secretly be punks. I didn't see anyone that fit the bill; I was apparently the only punk in the group. Most of them were just ordinary. There seemed to be no jocks, or, at least, no one wearing sports gear. Some wore leather jackets like heavy metal rockers—boys and girls. Leather jackets aside, these metalheads were recognizable by their AC/DC patches. Metalheads listened to AC/DC, Saxon, and Iron Maiden. One of the girls had a picture of Eddie on the back of her jacket. Eddie was depicted like some kind of monster; there was also an Iron Maiden logo.

I thought heavy metal music was really dull. And yet I knew some heavy metal fans who weren't dull. They wore leather jackets and were like punks in many ways, strapping spikes on their arms and wearing band logos. It was just the music that was boring. Heavy metal relied chiefly on guitar solos and song lyrics that weren't about anything especially important: just people running around or pulling pranks. The refrains were catchy, though. In my mind, heavy metal was just bad punk. Some people confused heavy metal bands with punk bands and I often had to explain to someone or other why a particular heavy metal band wasn't punk. I noticed several kids with the Rolling Stones logo, the one that looked like a giant tongue. I'd never seen kids with Rolling Stones logos before; it looked kind of hippie. The Rolling Stones were some old guys who sang about girls all the time.

The only kid I knew in the group was Gaddi the Fists. Our paths had crossed back at Rétto School, where he'd once helped me beat up a kid who was bullying me. We'd been in the same scout troop together, but I still didn't know him very well. In truth, no one did. Gaddi didn't share anything about himself with other people and it was very difficult to have a conversation with him. Gaddi somehow wasn't interested in anything, wasn't into any particular brand of music, and was absolutely indifferent to soccer. He was just Gaddi. He was called Gaddi the Fists because he was always up in someone's face. Rumor had it Gaddi had been sent to Núpur because he hit his mother. Who beats his own Mom? Was it even possible to hit your Mom in the mouth? I couldn't imagine how that could happen. Siggi the Punk was rude to his mother, told her to shut up, yelled at her: "Leave me in peace, you old hag." But I would never have imagined Siggi the Punk hitting his mother. Gaddi was slim; he made these fast little twitching movements and his gaze darted all around. He reminded me primarily of a cowboy from a Western. Clint Eastwood. Silent, unpredictable, entirely unafraid of violence—a thing of which I was absolutely petrified.

I didn't recognize anyone else. Some of them knew one another; they sat together and chatted on the bus. Some kid sat next to me and said,

"I'm from Hafnarfjörður."

"I'm from Reykjavík…"

I felt sure Hafnarfjörður was somewhere near Reykjavík, more or less. I thought it might be in a similar direction to Kópavogur—maybe it was even part of Kópavogur? I couldn't remember whether I'd ever been there. For a while, my grandmother had definitely lived in Hafnarfjörður. I hadn't any idea, though, what she did there or why she was living there or whether I'd visited her house ever. Back home in Kúrland, there was a picture hanging on the wall of some old woman standing in front of a turf house. Perhaps it was a picture of grandmother; maybe it was taken at Hafnarfjörður?

The bus set off and we drove through town. Along the way we drove past a shop called Hamraborg. Kids were hanging about outside. I reckoned it might be possible to get punk posters there. Perhaps you could walk from Núpur to Hamraborg and buy punk posters. That'd be great. I had no idea how far from Ísafjörður Núpur would be. The bus stopped at a gas station; the driver filled the tank.

While we waited, we looked around us in the meantime and I tried to be nonchalant. I gave a nod to Gaddi, who responded in kind. The kids all seemed to be my age. Possibly some were a little older, but definitely no more than 1-2 years. I also saw a few who looked like they were morons who might start picking on me.

Ísafjörður didn't seem quite as hopeless a place as I first thought. There was a restaurant called Moon Coffee and some people who weren't in rural get-up, but in what might pass for trendy clothes. And there were no sheep in town. Maybe they were being kept inside for winter? Maybe the town was full of sheep during the summer? I scrutinized the people walking among the snowdrifts and saw a few girls in disco clothes. That strongly suggested there was a nightclub in Ísafjörður. And if there was a nightclub, maybe there was a movie theater, too. Then I noticed a bank. Ísafjörður was actually quite like Akureyri. Just a little smaller and colder and with more snow.

The driver climbed back into the bus and we drove off. We left Ísafjörður behind and drove up into the mountains. The higher we drove, the deeper the snow got. At a certain point, you could look up into the snow because the drifts were taller than the bus. The road meandered through drifts; it was like we were inside a snow-tunnel. It reminded me of when I went driving with my parents in Norway. That time, it had felt like we were in a hall of trees. This time, there was nothing but snow. No houses and no sheep. Only wilderness and coldness. When we finally found our way out the snow-tunnel, Núpur loomed.

The school consisted of four large buildings on a desolate mountainside. A short distance from the building was a church and a small graveyard. I immediately felt the place was extremely lonely, remote, and awful. Above it towered a coal-black mountain. That must be Dýrafjörður. There were no blades of grass shooting up and no trees save for the odd Christmas fir. The bus stopped in the parking lot and kids tumbled out. Outside one of the buildings stood some men who were there to meet us. They were taking snuff.

"Welcome to Núpur! I am Ingólfur Björnsson and I am the principal here."

Ingólfur seemed like a fairly ordinary guy. He wasn't some hill-billy and didn't seem to be some kind of freak like the principal at Rétto had been. He reminded me mostly of Kári, the principal at Fossvogur elementary school. Beside him stood an old guy, clearly a country type. He looked like one of the outdoorsmen in Reykjavík who Dad had shown me pictures of: Óli Maggadon, Ástarbrand, and Odd the Strong from Skagan. In Reykjavík, they were crazy; out here they were possibly entirely normal.

"This is Zakaraías Jónsson, head of maintenance. He's going to show you to your dormitory."

Dormitory? What was that? We fetched our bags and trooped after the old guy, along a sidewalk, up some stairs, and into the largest building.

"That corridor is the girls' one," the man said, pointing. Some-one came and led the girls along the corridor.

"The second and third stories are for the boys," he added and pointed up the stairs. He walked up and we piled after him, dis-oriented, half-afraid, flashing glances around us. There were a few kids who'd gathered and caught our eyes. They either stood in doorways or by the stairs and stared at us. I didn't like the look of things. I didn't know anything about these kids. Some had wild hair and others didn't have any at all. It was like their hair had grown madly in all directions and they never cut it. Some were obviously country kids; they were wearing stereotypically rural get-ups. Zakaraías Jónsson read names and room numbers off a sheet.

"Jón Gunnar Kristinsson, two hundred and eleven. Elvar Örn Birgisson, two hundred and eleven."

We were two to a room. I nodded at Elvar Örn and we went into our room. It was small and held two cots, two wardrobes and two desks. Between the desks was a sink. We would primarily use it to piss in. I put my bag on one bed and Elvar Örn put his on the other. We had chosen our beds.

"We're sharing a room," I said, just to say something.

"Yes," muttered Elvar Örn.

"I'm from Reykjavík."

"Huh. I'm from Reykjavík, too."

He wasn't a punk, a jock, a disco freak, or a metalhead. There was nothing remarkable about his appearance. He didn't have any particular haircut or long hair, like many metalheads have. He didn't have any patches. While I studied him, he studied me.

"You a punk?"

"Yes!!!" I said proudly. There was no doubt! I was in my Sid Vicious t-shirt and a rugged leather jacket with all kinds of punk logos. Elvar Örn answered straight off, "Yeah, punk is the only way."

This was my deeply held belief. I was so relieved. Elvar Örn added, "My favorite band is Purrkur Pillnikk."

Purrkur Pillnikk was an Icelandic punk band. I thought they

were cool. Their songs were short and had clever lyrics. They played about with the language and created all sorts of new phrases. Instead of saying "it's right in front of your eyes" they sang, "it lies under your eyes." The singer was also insane and did all kinds of crazy things on stage. He also worked at the record store Gramo and I'd met him. I avoided asking him anything about any of the albums because he simply messed about with your words, made fun of you.

Elvar said, "I'm called Purrkur."

Purrkur. I wouldn't ever call Elvar Örn anything else. Purrkur. Cool.

The walls were painted white and there was a single window with nylon blinds. One of the panes opened, but had bars across it. The window had a view over the fjord. I thought it was ugly. Nothing but endless mountains, sea, and snow. Cold and chilly.

"Hmm, bars across the window?" I said and laughed throatily.

"Yes, this is a detention center, after all."

"Yeah…"

Detention center? Wasn't this a boarding school? But why were there bars over the windows? What did they expect you were going to do? Crawl out the window and go where? Somewhere up the mountain? Down to the sea? There was nothing there! I picked up the bag, stuffed my clothes in the closet and then hung up the punk posters I'd brought with me. They were mostly pictures I'd got from *Bravo* magazine. I also had my Crass albums, *Stations* and *Feeding of the 5000*, and lots of assorted singles. The album covers were all posters, too. I fixed one of them to a wall with sticky tack. The poster was a picture of a withered male hand on barbed wire. Underneath it was "your country needs you." Then I put my cassette player on the windowsill. Crass was all I had. I'd stopped listening to all other bands. I was no longer just a punk: I was a Crass punk, an anarcho-punk. Punk was dead. Crass had said so in their song "Punk is dead." Those who listened to anything but Crass were fake punks who didn't know punk was dead. Punk had become a fad like disco. Logos and patches you bought in a store like 1001 Nights had become fashion merchandise. But not Crass. It was okay to listen to Crass and it was okay to have a Sid Vicious t-shirt because Sid Vicious was a legend. He was dead, too. He'd died of a huge drug overdose. That was very cool.

We sat on our beds, silent and staring ahead. Purrkur stood up, walked to the sink, turned on the tap and let the water flow to see if it worked.

"A sink?" he said, and smiled weakly.

"Yeah…"

A sink in the room…why would you need a sink in your room? I wondered what life awaited me at Núpur. I had no idea, but I imagined that we were gathered there, a bunch of kids always in school, one way or another. Sometimes we'd be allowed to eat. Perhaps there would also be gangs of boys who ruled the place. I had noticed some pretty well-built guys. But some of the kids had smiled and said hello. I'd smiled back and said hi. But maybe they were a bit…special. The teachers' special idiots. I was both excited and anxious to see what would happen when I left my room.

You weren't allowed to smoke in the rooms and the residence hall, but you could smoke in the Smoker, a room at the end of the girls' corridor. Cigarettes were one of the things my mom had bought me before I left. One carton of Winston Lights. I actually smoked Winston but Mom wished I smoked Winston Lights. She smoked Winston. The difference between Winston and Winston Lights was that the latter had a ring with little holes on the filter. I was quick to fix that: I cut the filter off at the ring. If I didn't have scissors on hand I just broke the cigarette. It sucked to smoke Lights. Only jerks and dumbasses smoked Lights. Salems were girls' cigarettes, like all menthol cigarettes. I smoked Winston like Mom and Siggi the Punk. It was cool. It was also cool to smoke Marlboro and Camel; the toughest and trendiest of all was smoking filterless Camels. But they were also the most dangerous.

I hadn't brought much stuff with me. I had very specific opinions about clothing and didn't just wear any old thing. Mom had gotten incapable of buying clothes for me and I didn't have a lot of them. I had two pairs of jeans, two t-shirts, and a sweater. And, of course, I had my army jacket, my army boots, and my canvas shoes. If I needed fancier clothes, I had an elastic-waisted leather jacket. I also had a single pair of sports shorts and some sneakers for gym. No outerwear. I wasn't a dork. I had a few books and some small things, underwear, two pairs of socks. Nothing else.

The first day I tried to get my bearings and work out how the land lay, looking out the window and studying what was around me. Figuring out where the Smoker was and where the dining room was. The building I was in was divided into two three-story wings. At the end of each corridor was a teacher's apartment. The smoking room was at the end of the lowest corridor. The front door was next to the stairs. Opposite it was a big lounge with sofas, tables, and a TV. If you went through the lounge you were in the other wing. There was a dining room and the kitchen off of it. In the basement under the dining room there were classrooms. When I had gotten my bearings inside the building, I explored the other buildings. Next to the big building I was in, there was a smaller building: the apartment of the principal and his family. It also housed a girls' dormitory. Farther up the hill was another, bigger structure. In it were classrooms, storage areas, a workshop, and a gym. In the basement were a small swimming pool and a sauna. In the attic was a little shop where you could buy candy and cigarettes. The gym had a handball court and basketball baskets. Along the sides were bleachers and, at the far end, a stage. The space was clearly intended to be a sort of multiple-use space where you could do exercise but also have entertainment and concerts.

I examined a sheet of paper that had been stuck up on the wall. It listed the things you ought to buy in the bookstore down in the basement. The store sold various study books and other school necessities. They'd been pre-purchased for me, so I went down and took delivery of a stack of books and magazines, some pencils and erasers, a ruler, and a little card box containing watercolor paints.

On the whole the kids seemed mostly harmless and everyone I met was friendly or just kept quiet. But I was scared I was going to run into someone who would hassle me for being a punk. I worked out that the population consisted of extremely wholesome rural kids on the one hand and, on the other, kids who seemed just as troubled as me. There was no in-between. I was pretty quick to chat to other students, to ask them where they were from and what kind of music they listened to. There was a group of kids from Hafnarfjörður who were all part of the Rolling Stones gang. I'd never heard of that gang. I knew all about the Breiðholt gang and Brutal World. The Hafnarfjörður gang went around in leather jackets and they had the Stones logo on their jackets and t-shirts. The logo was nothing but a giant tongue. I thought it sucked. It didn't tell you anything; there was no message. It was just froth. It was much more important to have something to say than to just spew stuff. There were several kids from Reykjavík and Akureyri and finally kids from the fishing villages and the surrounding countryside, from Flateyri, Þingeyri, Suðureyri, Bolungarvík, and Ísafjörður.

The first few days I spent mostly getting a feel for the environment and coming to accept this new situation. Most of the time I was in a classroom under the canteen or in the building that housed the sports hall. The Hafnarfjörðurs had formed the group. Everyone else seemed to be more or less on their own but gradually got to know one another and form small groups and cliques. Even though Purrkur was my roommate, I didn't really know him. He was peculiar and unsociable. It was hard to eke out a conversation with him; he rarely spoke up first. He answered questions "yes" or "no" and then didn't elaborate.

"Things seem good here."

"Yes."

"Aren't you feeling it?"

"Sure."

"The food's pretty nice…"

"Yes."

Purrkur was an oddball. I tried to be in our room only when he wasn't. It wasn't as if there was a good reason to hang out inside your room.

The main place to hang out was the Smoker; there wasn't really any other place to go. It was the only place you could smoke. The Smoker was a miniscule room; along the walls were handmade benches to sit on, and a table in the center. There wasn't anything else there except a huge old oil-barrel, which contained cigarette butts and other trash. Sometimes the trash caught fire from a still-burning cigarette stub, and you just hocked up phlegm into it. The room had no window and a door on one side only. The walls were covered in graffiti and a few band posters hung here and there. Sometimes teachers and other employees came to find us and droned on about how we should be doing something other than smoking; often, they left the door open. In fact, that was about the only time the door *was* open. You were never alone in the Smoker, where there was always someone there who was willing to hang out for long stretches and smoke.

Purrkur and I amused ourselves by vomiting and pissing in milk cartons and keeping them in our room for a while. We thought this was hilarious and clever, but perhaps we somewhat unconsciously did it defensively, in case, one day, a group of bullies invaded our room. Everyone knew we had lots of milk cartons with fetid pee and puke on a shelf in our room. No one hassled us.

One of the things I entertained people with in the Smoker was belching. I could say words and even whole sentences by belching. And when I was belching sometimes I was able to get bile or even vomit in my throat. I'd learned how to throw up when I wanted to and didn't even need to belch in order to do it. I'd started this back at Rétto school when the Morons were teasing me. I simply vomited on the street in front of them.

Most of them would then hurry away fast. I also did this trick after I came to Núpur to ensure that everyone knew that if someone hassled me I would puke on him. I was like a fulmar on a cliff. I was Jónsi Punk, Jónsi Rotten. And I felt respected for this and was sometimes even asked to vomit. I would either vomit into the cigarette barrel or else open the door and spew up just as casually as others would spit. This always earned a big response and a lot of laughter. One time, I even went so far as to vomit in my hand and wiped it in my hair. The kids screamed and rolled about in disgusted admiration. I quickly stopped doing this, though, when I realized that it could greatly reduce the possibility of my ever getting to feel up any girl's breasts. Girls would definitely not let some boy who might potentially throw up on them fondle their breasts.

Around the cluster of buildings at Núpur, there was nothing. The surroundings were simply rocks and snowdrifts. Above Núpur were mountains; below was the sea. A whole lot of nothing. I was extremely frustrated and spent the first nights lying awake. Nights, loneliness and anxiety poured over me. Thoughts and feelings came to me that I had managed to push away during the day. Sometimes, when Purrkur was asleep, I cried a bit. I felt so alone in the world. I wonder if I'd leaped from the frying pan into the fire. I missed Hlemmur and my friends there. I missed being able to look out the window and see something other than mountains and boulders. The emptiness of Dýrafjörður filled me and I felt alone and neglected and far from everything. It was also weird because everyone around me was a kid. When I was in my room, I listened to "So What" by Crass over and over. I had my knife, but I no longer felt like I needed to carry it with me. There were no threats against me. I went to class in the morning and had my regular seat. In the dining room, I had my own seat at a table that had somehow been selected for me. I didn't sit with the Rolling Stones gang or the metalheads. I had no desire to sit with the country kids, so I sat at a table with Purrkur and the other oddballs from Reykjavík.

When I watch movies that show people meeting on their first day in prison, it always makes me think of Núpur. In they come, holding a blanket and a toothbrush. First they are shown their cell and then they go into a public area full of men looking at them. Some mutter things; you can read into the gazes and see all kinds of looks between people. Then the newcomer sits down some place and that's where he'll always sit. And those sitting around him will become his friends. That's how it was in Núpur, too.

In class, I chose to sit at the back. It was convenient because it was far away from the teacher, so he bothered us less. That's where you'd find those with a similar level of motivation as me—those who'd come to relax and hide, rather than because they had some great interest in the lesson. Those sitting up front were just idiots or teachers' pets.

When the dormitory had been locked for the evening, a fun atmosphere would break out in the communal corridors. There was no longer anyone about to stick their nose in so we boys came out of our shells. We began to get to know each other and as friendships grew my confidence began to increase. I stopped crying myself to sleep at night. More and more I realized that I had no choice and simply had to reconcile myself to my situation and do my best. I'd called home a number of times and raised the idea of coming home with Mom. It was a dead end. I was having second thoughts about having come to Núpur and did my best to get her to understand how badly I wanted to come home. It all came to nothing and I always got the same answer.

"End of debate, Jón. You can't come back home. We've discussed this time and again. You yourself wanted to go to boarding school."

I'd had no desire to go to boarding school. In my mind, I'd just made a suggestion.

"Yeeeeah, but I really wanted to go to Laugarvatn and you wouldn't let me."

"End of debate, Jón; it's out of the question for you to come back to town. You finish this, and then we'll see what happens."

That was how it was. There was no arguing with my mother. When she'd decided something she couldn't be deterred. It was a lost battle. I had to accept it, even though it sucked.

There was no snow in Reykjavík when I left, but Núpur was entirely submerged. The weather conditions I encountered were, however, only a taste of what was to come. I'd never experienced this kind of weather. It was like I'd never experienced winter before. In Reykjavík it snowed for maybe one or two days. At Núpur, on the other hand, a huge snowstorm raged for days and even weeks. There were nonstop storms. The snowblindness was so bad you could usually only see one or two steps in front of you. Cables were strung between the buildings so that students could get between them by feeling their way along the rope. It snowed and snowed and the snow never melted and drifts grew and grew. On Dýrafjörður there was an endless supply of snow. The splashes of rock on the mountainside soon disappeared in the snow and dazzling white blankets stretched from the beach up to the mountain peaks. When I looked out of the window it was like I lived all alone in a house up on the Vatnajökull glacier. Nothing but damn snow as far as the eye could see and freezing cold. Often we couldn't get out in the morning because it had snowed so much in the night and the drifts were so high they towered above the windows and blocked the front door. The landscape had vanished. And, unlike Reykjavík, it never rained at Núpur. Every morning we had to dig ourselves out with metal shovels, find the cable, and dig our way along it. The path we dug one day could be gone by the next. For most of the winter we clambered along in snow two or three meters deep. And it was always cold. I didn't have any clothes for such conditions. I had lost my socks and was always barefoot. I was usually wearing torn jeans and a t-shirt, a leather jacket or my military jacket. I always had a cold, always coughing and sniffing. Colds were simply the norm.

After I got to know the kids in the school better and they got to know me, I became part of a particular community. Society shapes the individual just as the individual shapes society. I got to know the boys because I was on a corridor with them. I especially got to know those who hung out in the Smoker. I became friends with the kids who sat at the back of class. Kibba sat beside me. She was very tall, with long, curly, blond hair. Kibba was from Akureyri. I thought all the girls were cute. Some of the boys talked about how one girl was cute and another was ugly. I just felt all the girls were very beautiful. I'd never seen a girl I found ugly. Girls were like flowers. There are no flowers that are obviously ugly; they're just not equally beautiful. But Kibba was one of those girls who was more cool than cute. She wasn't a punk but still utterly cool and she cussed a lot. Kibba was the leader of her own gang; a group of girls followed her everywhere. She reminded me of the girls in Reykjavík. The ones who were hard as nails. Kibba was also hard as nails. She had a leather jacket. We became great friends immediately. We spent our time in the classroom talking and giving the teachers crap when they bothered us. They showed us a varied amount of respect.

At Núpur, none of the teachers were qualified. Most were itinerant folk with college degrees; the others had somehow washed up at Núpur. Some had even followed some woman there. She'd have left but they'd stayed on. I think that a few hadn't been able to cope with jobs at sea and instead had decided to become teachers at Núpur. One of the greatest teachers was Valdi from Mýrum. He taught math. Valdi was an old farmer from the nearby farm. He was very smart and knew a lot of math. He had a strict sense of discipline and you behaved yourself in his classes. Valdi was lucid and resolute, but it was quite a different story with other teachers. The teachers at Núpur were totally unlike those at Rétto, who at least had been teachers of a sort. The ones at Núpur were burnt out. They weren't real teachers. They were just pretending.

Örnólfur taught Icelandic. We felt like he was as old as the hills, but he can't have been older than thirty. Örnólfur was a corpulent, jovial man, but somewhat nervous. He was peculiar in his ways, always wet around his mouth and he sweated so profusely that the sweat pearled constantly on his forehead. Perhaps he was that nervous. No doubt he was scared of us. The way hungry wolves chase the scent of a wounded and frightened animal, we chased Örnólfur's scent. I think he never got to fully enjoy the benefits of being a teacher at Núpur because we pursued him in a single-minded, unceasing persecution. There was no one person who decided to harass Örnólfur, it just happened. In fact, it was strange, because he was a very lovable person and treated us really well. We just didn't care for his attention. If he asked us questions, we mocked them, even replied with other questions. He got even more nervous, began to quake and raised his voice. Goal achieved! Then Kibba and I would go to the front of the class and shine with joy at our earnest, insistent harassment of him. We sat back down alongside Purrkur and Klikka, tilted back our chairs and put our feet on the table. Kibba was a genius at expressing herself. When

Örnólfur ordered us, for example, to take our feet down from the desk, Kibba simply told him to shut his mouth.

"Shut your mouth and do what you're told!"

"Kristbjörg!" yelped Örnólfur, shocked. He tried to sound like a resolute police officer but his nervous tension and fear rendered his impression a comical mewl.

"You don't teach manners. You teach Icelandic. And I'm not Kristbjörg! I'm Kibba."

"You're called Kristbjörg," screeched and stuttered Örnólfur.

"Shut up! I know what I'm called."

Örnólfur evidently didn't know how to reply and always said:

"Listen, my dear…"

We imitated him:

"Listen, my dear. Listen, my dear…"

We were good at mimicking him; the whole class would laugh. I sometimes dragged my legs off the table because I felt sorry for him, stuttering and quivering. But because Kibba didn't budge, I usually put them back right away. And so we formed a sort of solidarity and friendship and it led to a sense of purpose and diversion in my otherwise uneventful life. Örnólfur feared us, especially Kibba, and so he avoided us. We were the perpetrators in the situation, not just victims who did what they were told to do. With this growing freedom, we were quick to get more and more pushy. We stopped sitting at desk height like the others and instead sat on the floor at the back of the room and jabbered together while the lesson went on. Örnólfur didn't challenge us, preferring to have peace to teach the minority who had some interest in grammar and spelling. He made a few futile attempts to restore discipline, ordering us to sit in chairs and pay attention. But we responded by retaliating, and soon things were back to normal.

We sometimes took toilet paper to class with us. Örnólfur often turned his back to the class as he wrote on the board, trying to explain different declensions of nouns. The word *horse* in the nominative, accusative, dative, and genitive; singular and plural. He wrote neatly and eventually filled the entire board. When he wasn't looking we snuck two or three sheets of toilet paper out and chewed them thoroughly so they were well-moistened with saliva. Then we flung the drenched paper blots at the board with enough power to make a real smack. The wetter the blots, the louder the percussion. We really enjoyed seeing how strongly Örnólfur reacted. He screeched and startled. Then he got really angry. He knew that it was me, Kibba, Klikka, and Purrkur who were responsible. We denied it, though; we suggested it had come from the mountains. Kibba always answered him back at the top of her voice.

"I know you threw this!"

"Errr, no…" I muttered, as innocently as possible.

"Prove it!" said Klikki.

"I don't need proof."

Kibba looked right into his eyes and said:

"Of course you have to prove it!"

"I don't need to prove anything at all, Kristbjörg."

"You can't accuse people of things without being able to prove what you're saying! Prove it! Prove it!"

"Kristbjörg!"

"This is just something you believe…" I added. Örnólfur looked at us, entirely confused, shook even more and faltered.

He was no match for Kibba. She could talk anyone into a corner. With Kibba, I was safe. And once Örnólfur let us alone, we sat down again and started playing Solitaire.

Lessons with Örnólfur always followed a certain pattern. It was great to hang out with Kibba, hassle Örnólfur, and play Solitaire. But sometimes we took it a bit too far. And sometimes it meant that he completely lost control of his temper and started screaming and raging at us. And when he yelled at us, phlegm went in all directions and all over us.

"I won't accept this kind of behavior!"

"Are you spitting on me, you disgusting pig?!"

"You will not talk to me that way, Kristbjörg!"

"She's already made it clear she wants to be called Kibba," I said, admonishingly.

"I'll talk to you as I see fit. You talk to me as you see fit, right? What gives you that right?"

"Er…Kristbjörg, I'm a teacher!"

We all laughed at once.

"You're no teacher! Leave us alone and stop bothering us!"

"You won't talk back like this, Kristbjörg."

"Why won't you call her Kibba? Are you mentally challenged?"

Occasionally he tried to throw some of us out of the class, but in return he got a severe flurry of well-chewed toilet paper onto the board and back of his head from where we sat. When he tried to avoid the paper spitballs, we tried to throw them directly at him. The goal was to get him right in the back of his head and preferably for the spitball to be as wet and cold as possible. Those were particularly disgusting. Örnólfur did his utmost to not to let anything ruffle him, and to show us that he was not bothered. But the quaking, sweating, and stuttering were unmistakable.

Although I had a great deal of fun teasing Örnólfur, I still thought he was a good man. And though I was so troublesome to him in class, he was still attentive and courteous to me. I felt like he had a decent opinion of me. He had every reason to simply hate us, but he didn't. He never gave up hope that we would at some point discover an interest in grammar. The rumor around school was that he was mentally disabled, but I was sure that was only because he shook and sweated so much. He ended up with the nickname Spittle. I felt for him. Örnólfur was sweet natured. Sometimes I went to him because I needed something, whether to borrow some books or for information. He always treated me well and got really cheerful when I showed an interest in something. And eventually a kind of truce developed between us. He left us in peace as much as possible, and we stopped teasing him and even paid attention if we found something interesting. Örnólfur also taught literature and poetry and occasionally even discussed things I actually wanted to talk about. I was really into poetry, for example; I knew a lot of poets, and had written some poetry. Poetry wasn't that different from punk lyrics. Örnólfur taught me about rhyme, rhythm, and alliteration; he encouraged me and sometimes even congratulated me.

We all had a lot of enthusiasm for learning English and were rarely a problem in those lessons. English was the key to the mysteries that lay in song lyrics and articles written about bands, whether the Rolling Stones, Iron Maiden, or Crass. We sometimes tried to read English books because most of us thought English was cool.

English lessons were met with definite respect and everyone paid close attention. Our English teacher was called William Douglas Wilson. He was Scottish and spoke with a strong Scottish accent. He was ruddy and fairly freckled, balding but with a lot of red hair on the sides of his head, and a great big red beard. He was the image of the Scottish janitor in *The Simpsons*. Douglas had come to Iceland because of his love of the outdoors and nature. He'd traveled around the Westfjords and somehow settled here. I thought he was especially admirable because all kinds of particular British accents were impossibly cool. I tried to speak English with an accent. Instead of saying "My name is" I said, for example, "Moy naim is." The lion's share of my English had, of course, come from punk music, which was usually spoken and sung in a Cockney accent. Douglas's Scottish accent had the effect that we ended up speaking English with an evidently Scottish accent. No doubt it would have been funny to watch Douglas's lessons as we took great pains to mimic his accent. I needed continual guidance and explanation for punk lyrics, and he was obliging enough to help me translate stuff and put things in context.

Danish lessons were entirely unremarkable. None of us saw any particular reason for learning Danish. It was just an obligation. Not I, nor Kibba, Klikka, or Purrkur saw any purpose in partaking of what went on there and we had strong contempt for all things Danish. The Danish teacher didn't even speak Danish himself. He wasn't a teacher and only taught Danish because he'd lived in Sweden for several years. He was called Björn Sjöberg; he was an itinerant worker from Flateyri. In the first class, he wrote on the blackboard "Andrés And," so we were clearly going to learn something about Donald Duck. As a loyal fan of the Danish Donald comic strip my whole childhood, I knew full well that this was a mistake: the Danish is "Anders And."

"You don't know Danish! You can't even write 'Anders And' right!"

We all laughed. But I was totally right. He didn't know Danish any better than us. He no doubt expected that through our lessons Danish would somehow permeate us and at the end of the winter we'd all speak fluent Danish. We weren't into it. Klikka, Purrkur, Kibba, and I gave him the same treatment as Örnólfur. Every lesson was a nightmare for Björn, who maintained an unceasing war against us, especially with Kibba. We quarreled and cursed continually. We chewed toilet paper and threw it at him when he couldn't see. He was sturdier than Örnólfur so it was not so easy to knock him off track. Sometimes whole lessons were nothing but an argument between him and us.

"Shut up! Stop talking at once!"

"Are you telling me to shut up?! Shut up yourself!"

"You don't tell me to shut up, Kristbjörg!"

"I say what the hell I want, pig!"

"Kristbjörg!"

"Shut your mouth, jerkface, and leave me alone!"

Björn didn't put up with that and walked across the room, took Kibba by the shoulder, and shook her violently.

"Are you feeling me up, you pig?"

Björn became embarrassed, blushed, and looked around.

"You were feeling her up," I said.

The class all agreed, but Björn shook his head.

"I was not feeling you up, Kristbjörg. Kristbjörg!"

"Yes, you were feeling me up! Fondling my breasts, you pervert. Are you a pervert?!"

"No! No! I didn't fondle you! You're vulgar and uncouth."

"Oh? Isn't it vulgar to fondle kids?"

He was totally backed into a corner and didn't know what else to say, so he repeated Kibba's name a few times with an accusing tone.

"Kristbjörg…Kristbjörg…Kristbjörg…"

We drew caricatures that exaggerated him into a large baldhead with even bigger round glasses. There was an earnest competition among the students as to who could draw the funniest cartoon. Those who got to class first would draw a picture of him on the board. Björn started every class erasing cartoons of himself. We regularly put drawing pins on his chair and often loosened the legs, so that Björn fell clumsily onto the floor when he tried to take a seat. Sometimes we also stuck drawing pins into holes on the chair seat and filled sponges of water that slowly leaked water as he sat. Kibba didn't let any opportunity pass.

"You've got piss all over your ass!"

"Om du vil sige noget skal du sige det på dansk."

"Did you pee yourself?!"

The whole class laughed.

"Do you enjoy Danish so much that you don't have the heart to go to the bathroom and pee? Are you a retard?!"

"Who did this?"

No one ever knew, and that's how Danish lessons went up until winter. Not entirely unlike Icelandic class. We even left

the classroom in the middle of the lesson to smoke. Sometimes
we went back to class, sometimes we didn't. It didn't make any
difference.

With the drop in temperature came head colds. I was constantly sick with bronchitis and kept coughing up yellow mucus. I didn't understand and didn't connect the illnesses to the fact that I wandered about in the Dýrafjörður winter storms in my Sid Vicious t-shirt and canvas shoes. Sid Vicious loved it out on Dýrafjörður. Sometimes at night when I was coughing in my sleep, the suspicion crept up on me that I might have lung cancer. I knew that smoking was carcinogenic. There was cancer in my family. Everyone who died seemed to die from cancer. When my mother went to visit them they didn't look good. When she came home from the hospital she would say, exhaling, "It's horrific to see him. He looks like a concentration camp prisoner."

I suspected that if I kept smoking I was certain to get lung cancer. But I loved to smoke. It passed the time and was an important part of my social life. The Smoker was like a youth club. Smoking gave me joy and pleasure. Apart from the looming shadow of cancer, everything about smoking was great. Everyone who was cool smoked. Only the hick dumbasses didn't. All famous people smoked. Smoking was sophisticated, and trendy, too. And smoking was also bound up with being a rebel and being independent. To smoke was to be adult. Maybe I'd get cancer. But what else did I have to look forward to? I was well aware I wasn't going to excel in the study of anything. I desperately wanted not to have to learn any of the stuff I was forced to learn. I wanted to know more about anarchism and I wanted to know everything about Mikhail Bakunin. None of the teachers at Núpur knew who he was.

"He's the most famous anarchist in the world!"

The teachers nodded their heads but had nothing to add. I longed to learn more English. I imagined that the English were generally more knowledgeable about Bakunin than Icelanders were. Maybe it was a mistake to speak Icelandic. Perhaps it's not possible to take anyone who speaks Icelandic seriously. Perhaps people don't listen to you unless you speak English.

I didn't think the future looked too bright. I wasn't sure how long I would be there. A few years, maybe? Then I would probably end up back in town and would doubtlessly come to a similar stage as the winos at Hlemmur. They weren't punks. They weren't disco freaks. They didn't seem to have any particular musical interests and had no interest in punk. Sometimes when they were in high spirits they sang drinking songs like *Det was brændevin i flasken da vi kom* to amuse themselves. I knew two of them well, Svabbi and Red Stjána. I would definitely end up like Red Stjána. I could talk to them and they sometimes went to the liquor store for me. I could scrounge sips from Svabbi if he wasn't already too loaded. When he was drunk, he was unpredictable and might try to punch you, totally out of the blue. Svabbi was a bruiser. He was strong and quick. Sometimes he hit the other winos. I didn't know why exactly, but there was definitely bad blood. Svabbi simply punched them until they fell to the floor unconscious. He kept kicking them and shouted that they should not be such great idiots.

"So you think you can just cuss me out, you damn idiots?!"

Sometimes the cops came and dealt with him. But more often

than not, no one came. It was just some winos in Reykjavík. It didn't matter that they were beating each other up so long as they didn't beat up ordinary folk. Once I saw Svabbi smash his hand to bits. I was sitting at Hlemmur on the bench in the corner where I always sat and chatting with some winos. On the left, I saw Svabbi come walking up. He was clearly out of it and very wild. The guy sitting next to me didn't care much for him and stared with angry eyes. He was also out of it and he didn't care for Svabbi.

"There's nothing that should prevent a fella from becoming a sailor."

"No, no…"

"You can't cheat someone afterwards."

"No, no."

"That's just fraud. They aren't men of their word!"

"No…" I said, nodding. Svabbi approached. He was clearly struggling to keep his balance but he prowled like a cat after its prey.

"Look, it's Svabbi!" I said, pointing out this sudden arrival to the wino.

"I will never go back to sea!" the wino said, not seeming to notice anything.

"Isn't it too cold out there anyway?"

"Yes, that fucking crew is just bastards and traitors."

I could see how that might be the case. I'd never been to sea but imagined it would be like being in the military or at war. Always a terrible panic, always bad weather, and always someone screaming at you. Svabbi walked up to the wino. I tried to smile and nod to him, but he didn't notice me. He lifted his shoulders, clenched his fists, and swung his arm back. I moved discreetly to one side.

"Ha, hey there, Svabbi, pal," said the wino cheerfully. The blow struck. But instead of punching the wino in the mouth like he planned, Svabbi swung full force against an iron pillar next to him. At that, the wino sprang to his feet and scarpered. Svabbi stood there confused and did not quite understand what had happened. I made myself scarce.

Next time I saw Svabbi he had a cast on his hand. He had no memory of what had happened.

"I think I fell."

In the future, I would probably be one of them. Still, I would not be like Svabbi. If he wasn't dead by the time I was a wino, I was going to keep away from him. I would be more like Red Stjáni. I would be the next generation after him. Red Jónsi. I would hang about town and drink booze. I would break in places and steal stuff. And then I would go to jail. But that wasn't horrible. It would probably be just fine to go to Litla-Hraun, the prison. Red Stjáni had been in prison and had only good memories of his time there. Everyone I met who'd been there said it was totally fine. I had never been but I imagined it wouldn't be that different from Núpur. The only difference would be that everyone there was an adult. Otherwise, it was just the same. Litla-Hraun was definitely really quite like Núpur. Some place far out in the ass-end of nowhere, surrounded by mountains and buried under snow. Still, it must be better to be in prison because you didn't have to learn things or go to school. There were also definitely more porno mags than at Núpur and probably VCRs and you could watch real porn.

Red Stjáni never needed to go to school. When I was done serving my prison sentence I would go back to town. I didn't know how long the sentence would be, but it couldn't be more than a few months. You only got a long sentence for hitting people or for murder. I wouldn't do such things. I would just do break-ins. But I wouldn't steal from poor people. I would just steal from the shops and from rich people. Mostly, I would just party and relax.

In my wandering around Reykjavík, I'd often seen places that would definitely be very easy to break into. Some of them I discovered out of sheer coincidence. Like when I went behind a house to take a piss, I sometimes noticed that at the back of some store there was a narrow window that a guy like me could crawl into. No one would notice. I would steal everything from the store and then sell the stuff on the black market. I knew several people who bought all kinds of stuff others had stolen. You could take whatever you had to them. Albums, electronics, jewelry, wristwatches. Even, believe it or not, stamps. Or one could also, of course, steal something in one shop and then take it to another store and return it and get a refund or store credit. There were several ways to convert things to money. In second-hand bookstores you could sell books, magazines, and albums. I'd managed to sell all my albums and books. I still had the records by Crass and all the albums that Southern Studios, Crass's label, had put out. I didn't enjoy much of it, though. Crass released singles by a bunch of bands. I really only liked Flux of Pink Indians and Zoundz. But if Crass saw a reason to publish it, it must be noteworthy. The only book I kept was the *Tao Te Ching*. It was reassuring to have the book with me and to be able to open it at random.

I wondered sometimes if Crass had read the *Tao Te Ching*. Someday, I was going to go to London and meet Crass and I'd ask them. I'd also sold all the stamps I collected as a kid. When I was little, I was excited about stamps and proud of my collection. Now I couldn't care less. It was just dorks who collected stamps. Crass didn't collect stamps.

One thing that I did to while away the time was cutting myself. I had no idea why. I had taken my knife with me to Núpur just in case I had to defend myself against some morons. Lots of people at Hlemmur had a knife, and when we had nothing to do we sometimes tried them against our wrists, cutting them. The girls started it. They often cut themselves. I tried cutting myself with a knife. I was curious and wanted to know how sharp it was. It started off as just fiddling about but little by little became a hobby and a pastime and I began to do it regularly. I cut myself on my hands and feet. Sometimes I even looked forward to going to my room so I could cut myself. It was a bad thing to do, but all the same it gave me an outlet. I also began to fiddle about by burning myself with a lighter. That gave me a similar relief but the pain was different. At times I would light the flame of the lighter and let it lick against the metal until it became scalding hot. Then I closed my eyes and immediately pressed the metal anywhere on my skin. It was very painful but also offered me a strange release. It felt good afterwards and I felt happier and much more relaxed. It became a sort of habit or addiction and gave me pleasure. I was also beginning to get interested in sex and had started masturbating. All the boys masturbated. And so the days turned into weeks. I smoked, masturbated, and cut myself or burned myself to pass the time.

I wanted to get high, feel euphoric. Any kind of high. And I thought a lot about how someone might get high and why. Could you masturbate constantly and get a really powerful orgasm? If I could get ahold of nitrous oxide, I huffed that. The same applied to petrol and paint thinner. Sometimes it lasted several days. I sniffed on my own and with others. When I was high in school, I wasn't full of myself. I was tranquil inside. When I was high, I didn't find anything dull. I even managed to pretend to learn. Just to get some peace and not be lectured at. I was waiting, however, the whole time for class to end so I could get back to the bathroom or my bedroom to masturbate, burn myself, smoke, and possibly sniff more. I've no idea how long these periods lasted. Sometimes days, sometimes weeks. This was my daily bread and that's how time passed.

When I wasn't in class, I mostly hung out in the Smoker or inside my room. At Núpur there were lots of organized social activities, sports teams, various clubs. I never took part in anything sports-related but sometimes dawdled about with whatever others were up to. I had no particular friends. Everyone and no one was my friend. Sometimes kids went hiking around Núpur. I had little interest in that, and to be honest there was little to see except snow and mountains. The only place that I was at all interested in was down at the shore. Perhaps there was something fun happening there. That must be the reason we were forbidden from going there. One day Gaddi and Gisli came and found me as I sat inside the Smoker and asked if I wanted to come on a hike with them.

"A hike?"

Gaddi said, firmly:

"Yeah, it'll be a blast. A stroll up the mountain."

I thought about it.

"Isn't it shit cold?

"No, no, it's fine out. Hardly cold at all."

I decided to go along with them, thinking it was a great chance to get to know Gaddi better, and ran up to my room, changed from my canvas shoes into my military boots, a ripped long-sleeved shirt, and put a leather jacket over the top. I reckoned I was ready for an Arctic expedition. The weather was still and not too cold. We walked up the slope, over the hill and into some valley that lay behind it. I had no idea what this valley was called. It never occurred once to me that it had a name at all. Everything was underneath snow and the only thing you could see was an unusual stone that poked out from the snow. While we walked, we chatted about the day and the path. We talked about life at Núpur and told stories about teachers. It was really Gisli who talked, because Gaddi said almost nothing.

"Fucking milk worker's strike…"

Gaddi nodded. Just nodded.

"I'm not bothered. I hate milk," said Gisli.

"Well, I do too, really," I added. "I only use milk to pour on my cornflakes. I don't put milk in my coffee…"

"You take your coffee black like your women," said Gisli, in English, and laughed loudly.

"Yah…" I said, and laughed. I had no idea what that meant or what he was getting at. I was used to Gisli saying weird things to me that I didn't understand. Gaddi had completely dropped out of the milk conversation. Suddenly he said:

"Hey! Shall we have a competition?"

"Competition?"

"Yes! Who can run the fastest up the mountain?"

Gaddi pointed up the mountainside. It was quite exciting. Without discussing it any further, he ran off up the mountainside. The slope was long and gradual but seemed to get steeper the higher it went. Gisli and I ran after him immediately. The snow was deep and soft so we sank up to our crotches with every step. It was difficult to run but we hammered away at it, moving forward through the snow. It was exciting and fun. Gaddi maintained his lead and Gisli tried to keep up with him. But Gaddi was a sports freak and in better shape than Gisli, who was a self-declared anti-sport star. And gradually we moved higher. As we got higher, the snow became thinner and harder so we didn't sink so deep. We came to a stop high up on the slope in front of a vertical snow wall that was frozen on the outside but soft on the inside. It reminded me of chocolate-coated cream puffs. You could punch and kick your way through the outer crust. Without any explanation, Gaddi began to make holes in the snow and to climb up using them. He didn't say anything. I looked uncertainly at Gisli. He shook his head and called to Gaddi:

"Isn't that dangerous?"

"Anything fun is dangerous," Gaddi said quickly and kept on going.

"No... I don't dare."

Gaddi looked sharply at Gisli and said:

"Jónsi and I would totally dare!"

Gisli looked questioningly at me. I was between a rock and a hard place. I couldn't admit I didn't dare. I wanted to be as cool as Gaddi. I also wanted to get to know him better. Gaddi interpreted my silence as agreement and said:

"Go back home, Gisli. Off you go to sleep!"

I nodded my head, not wanting to be as weak as Gisli. I was going to be tough like Gaddi. Gaddi did not wait for an answer and kept pressing on, punching and kicking into the snow wall to get a foothold or a grip. Gaddi had a good punch and I wanted to be good at that, too. I didn't want to punch or hurt anyone, but I wanted to learn self-defense so I could protect myself if someone threatened to attack me. And if people knew I could punch, they would definitely leave me alone. It was also good fun. I kicked and punched my way up the snow wall next to Gaddi. Gradually we made progress upwards. Soon Gaddi was quite a bit ahead of me. Suddenly I realized I was already pretty high and if I fell it would be some drop. That scared me. How was I going to get back? How would I find the holes I'd made in the snow wall? Should I make new holds? I didn't dare continue. I wanted to turn back, but didn't dare do that either. I slowed down but tried not to lag too far behind Gaddi, who was tearing up the wall like some snow spider. I had great difficulty looking below me; I felt dizzy and my stomach churned due to my fear of heights. We were ridiculously high, probably twenty to thirty meters, and Gaddi was probably ten to fifteen meters above me. Suddenly the snow gave way under him and he fell. I saw him try to catch his balance in the snow, but he grabbed nothing. The ice and snow swirled in all directions. Gaddi rushed past me. He didn't seem afraid, but instead had a determined expression on his face as he tried to stop himself. Terrified, I started to retrace my steps.

"Are you all right? Are you all right?" I heard Gisli cry, standing there in the same place we'd left him. My heart beat in my breast with fatigue and nervous agitation. When I reached the bottom Gisli grabbed me. We looked down the slope. Far in the distance we finally caught a glimpse of Gaddi, buried in snow.

"Shit, man," whispered Gisli.

"He just fell headlong," I said.

"Do you think he's dead?" Gisli asked, worried.

I suspected as much. No one could survive falling down an entire mountain.

"Gaddi? Gaddi?"

No answer. We ran as fast as our legs could go down the hillside. Ran, rolled and slipped in the snow and occasionally called:

"Gaddi? Gaddi?"

He did not answer since he was, indeed, dead. I tumbled down the slope, thought to myself that I was going to become like my father because he had so often seen dead people and gone to where they had fallen in the wilderness or died from exposure. Perhaps it would change me. Maybe this would be a shared experience that joined Dad and me. Maybe we could talk about it and Dad would tell me how he felt when he came on this sort of thing and then I could say something like:

"Yes, that's how I felt, too, when it happened to me."

Perhaps we would then somehow be equal. And alongside it, the certain anticipation of seeing a friend dead. This was a turning point; I was becoming more of a man. And I knew it. I could get a sip of liquor from someone and describe how Gaddi had looked after he was dead. I imagined his face being monstrous, like in a horror movie, his hands bent.

Gaddi was not dead. He was banged up and confused. When we got to him he turned his head towards us and it was obvious he wasn't quite sure what had happened; it was like he didn't know who Gisli and I were.

"Are you all right?" asked Gisli loudly.

"Yes," he answered, distracted.

"You just fell from the mountain," I said, as if for clarification.

"Yessssss…" replied Gaddi like it wasn't important and he didn't remember. We helped him free himself from the snow and scramble to his feet. He looked around surprised. It was like he had no idea where he was.

"It was horrible. We were sickeningly high up."

"Yes."

We looked up at the mountain and I pointed out the path we'd taken down the whole of it.

"We thought you were dead," Gisli muttered and smiled faintly.

"Yes, I thought I was going to die. I was just trying to make sure not to fall on the rocks."

"Yeah."

I looked about at the stone roots that rose up from the snow here and there. Gaddi could not put his weight on one of his legs and we had to support him.

"You think maybe you've broken a leg?" Gisli asked.

"Yes, reckon," said Gaddi, slowly.

"Or just a sprain?" I added, encouragingly.

I was glad Gaddi wasn't dead and ashamed to have let myself even think about it. But I felt glad it had happened because I wouldn't have dared go much higher. It was fortunate in that we could both easily have died. We didn't get back to Núpur until late in the evening. At the dormitory there was chaos and uproar because we were missing and no one knew where we were. Gaddi was taken to the district hospital in town. He had broken his leg and returned the following day with a cast. The evening after, the entertainment in the Smoker was especially fascinating because we told a theatrical and dramatic story about how we climbed the mountain.

"We thought he was dead for sure!"

I didn't tell anyone that I had half hoped it.

There was nothing to fear. I was no longer afraid when I went out of my room. I did not need to peek out and check who was in the hallway before I left. I did not have to sneak along walls or take detours between houses. I could just walk proud and unafraid like everyone else. No one teased me for being a punk. Jónsi Punk was just a top guy and everyone seemed happy with him. At Núpur, no one beat up Jónsi Punk. Some of the kids were nice, others were interesting. So I was usually in a pretty good mood. I was also glad that no one was going to hit me.

Yet at the same time I also felt a sense of melancholy, one that was often associated with music. Sometimes I heard some music echoing along the hallway out of someone's room and didn't need to hear more than a single sentence or even a certain tone, and I was suddenly stricken with grief. I felt a great surge in my breast.

Although my brain didn't always understand it, my heart perceived it in some way. Sometimes I couldn't control the tears that broke out and often I'd have to return to my room to recover. For a long time, I'd sit alone in my room, listening to music and weeping. It broke out suddenly and spontaneously and instead of trying to suppress it, I let my feelings flow through me. Boys shouldn't cry. Boys who cry are women. Girls cry. But I couldn't control it. Sometimes I sobbed or whined and other times I cried out of my eyes. I cried from sadness, disappointment, self-pity. I wept over what had happened and how miserable things were. I wept, disappointed with myself. I cried about Mom and Dad. I cried from anger, too. Anger about this hellish hell. This damn system that had everything all planned out in advance and seemed designed to place limitations on me. The system was designed to build up a labyrinth where everyone was trying to go along organized narrow corridors. No other options available. In the maze you couldn't pause or stop because then you were back to square one. The system treated people like a puppeteer treats his mindless dolls. I knew I would never be able to find a way out of this building. And just as some people feel uncomfortable being in an elevator or locked in a narrow space, I detested the system. I had so often tried to find my way, but strayed from the path and given up. To get ahead in the maze you had to solve riddles at certain intervals. The riddles became increasingly complex the further along one got. I found myself thinking that I could solve it if I only wanted to, but I just didn't want to. I didn't care about winning this game. I found the puzzles pointless and boring. I wanted, however, to solve many other puzzles, but they were all outside the maze and lay there like garbage.

I wanted to know all about anarchism. But nothing was taught about it. No one seemed interested in it or knew anything about it. But it was a high priority for me to memorize verbs in Danish. I found that a ridiculous task. I was certain that knowing about anarchism would benefit me far better than Danish verbs. And I was only able to solve these boring puzzles once I agreed that they were, after all, remarkable, fair, and useful. I had so often heard adults say that you should follow your heart. I thought about that a lot. I reckoned I knew that if I dragged myself through the maze and labored through the puzzles I would eventually become boring. I would be unhappy. Because I had not made the effort for myself, but to please someone else. And I would have betrayed my heart and pursued powerlessness and sadness. I also found it terribly dismaying and unfair that there was only one path. Why weren't there many ways out of the maze? Why only one? To hell with these stupid puzzles. They are dull and you are dull. I will not become a slave like you. Fuck the system!

I could always take shelter in Crass. The band was my family when I had no family. Crass was a friend who accepted me as I was, showed me respect and understanding, and answered my questions. I was in hell. I was at Dýrafjörður. I was buried inside a snowdrift. But at the same time I was in heaven. I was in a small kingdom of heaven that existed inside the middle of hell. Although I made many friends, these friendships rarely reached the depths I wanted. It was because no one listened to Crass. No one could understand me properly unless they understood Crass. I was always ready and willing to educate people about Crass if they showed any interest. That seldom happened, however.

Crass had done so much for me and helped me understand so much that I desperately wanted to help others by introducing them Crass. Núpur was full of gangs and I dreamed of creating a little Crass-punk gang. Admission was simple: it only involved listening to no other music than Crass. I went so far as to write a tour-de-force article for the school paper about the band, in which I did my utmost best to inform and educate my classmates about the importance and excellence of Crass. I concluded my article by telling all interested readers that they could come directly to me if they wanted to learn more. I expected the result would be a grand flood of wonderful questions and I mentally prepared answers. I was going to be totally ready when these burning questions came. I was certain it was only a matter of time until there was a tap on my shoulder and someone said:

"Hey, Jónsi. Really neat article you wrote about Crass. They're clearly a very special band. Though the songs might not be that good, the lyrics are great! I really, really want to know more about Crass…"

Even if people didn't like the music, it didn't matter because Crass was so much more than just music. Crass was a lifestyle. In the first days after the paper came out, I waited, excited and ready. Time passed and when no one had come up and talked to me, I began nudging people and asked if they'd read the article. Some had, and most agreed it was pretty good.

"But the music is so tedious. They don't know how to play instruments."

"But Crass is more than just a band. Crass is a lifestyle!"

"I like music far too much to listen to them."

I didn't like such arguments.

Life at Núpur revolved around music and kids were divided into groups by musical taste. A few kids had good stereos. Most, like me, just had an old cassette player. Often a bunch of us gathered and listened to music. Everyone listened to some type of rock. No one listened to disco—at least no one was willing to admit it. Disco wasn't welcome at Núpur and had never been tolerated. There were many, many people who hated disco. I had written in large letters on the wall in the Smoker: *Death Before Disco*. We were rockers. Cool, tough guys who lived in a world where the Rolling Stones, heavy metal or punk ruled the world. The Rolling Stones-gang only listened to the Rolling Stones. To their mind, everything else was drek. The metalheads had a bit broader tastes and their favorite bands were groups like AC/DC, Saxon, Scorpions, Iron Maiden, Uriah Heep, and Motorhead. There were several punks, including Purrkur, but they weren't real punks and they didn't listen to Crass. They usually just listened to new wave, not punk. Punk was dead. Crass had been saying so for a long time. It was no longer around. Today's punk was just run-down new wave. There was only Crass. Punks listened to anything from Sex Pistols to The Cure. I never listened to the Sex Pistols. They were traitors. Except Sid Vicious. He was a legend because he died while punk was still going. Johnny Rotten was, however, the greatest traitor. A punk for sale. Public Image Ltd was a junk band. Pretentious, arty, new wave trash. Sometimes I listened to The Cure. But I never told anyone, and did so in secret. The Cure helped me to cry. But I would never admit it.

Sometimes we had album presentations. Any student could hold a presentation and hang an advertisement on a board in front of the dining hall. He named the proposed time for the presentation, the band name, and the place.

> There will be an album presentation in the room below the dining hall after school today at five. The album is *Stand and Deliver* by Adam and the Ants. Look forward to seeing you! Bjössi.

Since the weather meant we rarely left the dormitories, we had to be quite self-sufficient about social activities. Outside, it was freezing and moreover, it snowed constantly so there was no point shoveling or you ended up with slippery ice. You couldn't even play soccer outdoors. And there was nowhere to go. You couldn't walk to Dýrafjörður, and Þingeyri was on the other side of the fjord. No matter where you looked, snow, mountains and waste-land loomed; nothing else. Not counting the times we had in the Smoker, there weren't a lot of surprises. The album presentations were therefore welcome and popular. I went to most, even if I found the albums and music boring. Most of the presentations dealt with some heavy metal bullshit or guitar solos. I still enjoyed going to the presentations of crappy bands, making fun of the music and saying funny things. I also corrected facts and defended punk from prejudice and misrepresentation.

"Adam Ant is not punk! This is jokey new wave. Punks don't wear Indian gear!"

My remarks and humor were never badly received. Everyone liked Jónsi Punk. Jónsi Punk was always fun. He was witty and always jovial. And though he was a prankster, he was a good one. I often

parodied popular songs and got lots of laughter, even from those
who liked the songs. I was somehow able to make fun of things that
others couldn't. If someone else had, for example, mimicked the
Scorpions's vocals, they'd have been beaten up. But not Jónsi Punk.

Since the response to my article had been considerably smaller
than I expected, with no requests for additional information on
Crass, I decided to hold my own album presentation. I thought the
article in the school paper hadn't been the right way to introduce
Crass since Crass relied to such a degree on the figurative. Their
album covers, for example, were not just typical covers but also
posters and the pictures contained incredibly important messages.
The article was probably just the spark that would ignite the bon-
fire that would result from the presentation. I had planted the idea,
but now I had to follow up. People seemed to see their music as an
obstacle. And maybe it didn't always show off the lyrics because the
singer often spoke so fast and screamed. After careful deliberation,
I decided to hold the album presentation in the room below the
dining hall. I made a poster where I drew the anarchy sign and
the Crass logo and wrote some basic Crass slogans.

> Album Presentation! An album presentation in the
> classroom under the dining hall. The Feeding of
> the 5000 and Stations by Crass! Also some singles.
> Dying to see you. Jónsi Punk.

I dedicated myself diligently to making the poster, and especially
to writing Crass exactly the way the band did. I spent many hours
on it. I put the paper over the album cover and traced letters and

went over them. When I was satisfied with the ad, I walked into the dining room and hung the paper on the board. I arrived an hour before the presentation to prepare everything very carefully. I had taken down all the posters from the walls of my room, folded them up very carefully and gently cleaned them of sticky tack. I then decorated the classroom with posters and album covers from *The Feeding of the 5000* and *Stations*. I also added the posters of several singles like "Nagasaki Nightmare," "Reality Asylum," "Merry Crassmass," and "Bloody Revolutions." I had already written a speech, a kind of introduction, which built in important ways on the article I wrote for the school paper, in which I went over the history of the band. I suspected most people would already have read it, perhaps more than once. I decided to proceed directly to talk about anarchism, as that was such a big part of Crass. I had written down the major misstatements about anarchism and then corrected them, and also some declarations about the point of anarchism. This was all done purposefully and the idea was that I would strike down any misunderstandings and prejudices before the real enlightenment began. Breaking down and building up. That way, questions and discussion would be factual and meaningful. I was aware some of Crass's songs were not as engaging as others, but that didn't matter because the lyrics were always great. People had to understand that the genius of Crass lay in the lyrics. The music was basically irrelevant. I had created a playlist, but also had photocopied some of the texts in the staffroom so that I could share them for the attendees to read as they listened to the songs and so they could follow the lyrics even if they didn't understand the singer. The content of the lyrics wouldn't escape anyone.

The presentation was to start at five exactly. I had also prepared a discussion of Poison Girls, the sister band to Crass, given how interesting Crass were and what they stood for. It would be good to be able to discuss other bands that shared the message. Poison Girls was, in my judgment, far from reaching the same heights as Crass, of course, but still an important part of what Crass stood for. I myself didn't enjoy Poison Girls. The lead singer was an old lady, the music was boring and I didn't get the lyrics. But Poison Girls was connected to Crass and so I respected the band.

I was ready for action. The clock struck five. I had decided to start the Crass-tour with *The Feeding of the 5000*, their first album. I'd start with "Reality Asylum." It was an exceptionally strong song and well suited to start a good presentation. There was also a funny story behind the song because it was banned and not on the first version of the album but released on single. Technically, "Reality Asylum" wasn't really a song but talking and noise. It has little in the way of lyrics; it's less sung than spoken. But I'd still start with it because of how effective the end is when Crass's singer, Joy De Vivre, says loudly, "Jesus died for his own sins not mine!" I thought that line was both innovative and cool and totally set the tone. After listening to this song, people would definitely be ready for songs like "So What" which are more lively. That was one of my favorite songs, too.

By quarter past five, no one had come. Slowly the horrible suspicion crept up to me: no one was going to attend. Could it really be that there was no interest at all in an album presentation about Crass? It couldn't be. I decided to wait patiently. I would take it calmly and be at peace with people coming and going during the presentation. I could simply jump around with my points and even play the same song over and over, for example, "Reality Asylum," if someone missed something while he went to the Smoker or something like that. No problem. But I would have *Stations of the Crass* handy because it was more of a rock album than *The Feeding of the 5000.* The album was more melodic and musical, less spoken than the latter. If people wanted, however, to dip directly into it, I would be happy to play, for example, "White Punks On Hope" or "Heard Too Much About," melodic songs. They would certainly work well for those who were primarily thinking about music.

When the clock reached five thirty and still no one had come, I decided to stroll over to the Smoker at the other end of the building and see why. Was there something else going on? Unlikely. There really wasn't much happening at Núpur. Had everyone failed to notice the album presentation, perhaps? It would be unusual: stuff on the board usually didn't pass anyone by. Maybe the kids had just mixed up the time? Or, worse, I had written the wrong time on the ad? I decided to check and left the room. On the table hung the poster I had made with such painstaking work. It clearly said "begins at five o'clock." It shouldn't have confused anyone. But maybe there was something else going on. There was, for example, a soccer game being held in the gymnasium? I usually never knew because I paid extremely little attention to what went on there. Maybe that was it. Maybe everyone was at soccer? Maybe it was some sporting final taking place? When I got to the Smoker I saw, however, it was packed. There was clearly nothing going on. I went in and said, questioningly, "Hi?"

Everyone returned the greeting: "Hi," as if everything were normal. What were they thinking? Surely they knew I was doing an album presentation?!

"Errr, I've got this album presentation…" I said, pointing back toward the dining room.

"Yes," said some, smiling; others kept quiet, looking ahead. They were apparently all aware that I had a presentation happening now.

"Crass…" I added, proudly.

"Yeah, I saw it on the board!" replied Gisli. I watched the crowd—my friends—either sitting or lying on the benches. I looked searchingly at each of them.

"And…no one wants to come?"

I tried to sound as relaxed as I could.

"I've got *The Feeding of the 5000* and *Stations*… and some singles!"

"Oh, Crass are so dull," someone said.

"It's not even music," muttered another.

I'd heard this before. I lit my cigarette, took a good drag, blew out the smoke and said so, quite deliberately.

"Crass, of course, is about much more than just music…their lyrics are crazy good. Crass is a lifestyle!"

"You can't understand the lyrics."

"I've photocopied them so you can read along while you listen to the songs."

Some of the group nodded; clearly, that was a step in the right direction. I felt sure the kids in the Rolling Stones-clique were beyond saving. They were totally fascinated by Mick Jagger and his compatriots, and cared for nothing and no one else.

I thought, however, that some of the metalheads would have been interested in Crass because they would enjoy the lyrics. For example, I went to Robbi's presentation on Iron Maiden. He had also copied lyrics and we were able to both listen to and read the words of the song "Run to the Hills." Robbi told us that the lyrics dealt with the story of when the white man came to America and how happy the Indians were to meet him—at first. The joy, however, quickly turned to fear and sorrow since the white man had guns and since he forced the Indians to flee to the mountains, or else they got shot. I kept the sheet with the lyrics because I thought they were good and I would even read aloud the first stanza and sing it from time to time. It could have been a Crass lyric: "White man came across the sea. Brought us pain and misery." Misery even rhymes with "anarchy" so Crass might have just added that and said "White man came across the sea. Brought us pain and misery. Then we discovered anarchy and now we are free."

I concluded that, although the music was terrible, the lyrics were fine. But with Crass (and only with Crass) you got music and lyrics that went together really well. What limited metal was mainly the guitar solos. Who wanted to listen to someone scrape his guitar for ten minutes? When I'd taken the last drag of my cigarette and no one had got up, it became blindingly obvious to me why no one had come to my album presentation. They simply found Crass boring. I didn't understand. Even kids who listened to punk found Crass boring. They'd rather listen to The Stranglers and the Sex Pistols. Some were even happy to listen to Stiff Little Fingers. You could almost say they made it a point of principle not to listen to Crass.

"Just forget it, Jónsi," said Robbi, after some deliberation. "No one wants to think about it."

"Why not?"

"Because the music is absolutely terrible!"

"Yes, but the lyrics are so good!"

"Oh, Jónsi, come on, no one listens to music to hear the lyrics." Several kids nodded their heads.

"People listen to music because of the music, not for any other reason."

I'd gone to his album presentation! Why couldn't he come to my Crass presentation?!

"Sure, like anyone wants to listen to some guitar solo…gvanggg gvaaang. Stupid!"

"There's nothing stupid about guitar solos, Jónsi."

"Of course they're stupid. Listening to some guy in flower pants screeching a guitar solo! It's pathetic."

"Oh, you just have zero taste in music, Jónsi."

Everyone in the Smoker agreed. I was devastated. This wasn't just unfair. It was downright wrong. I had great taste in music!

"Well! Of course I have great taste in music. I listen to punk."

"Jeez, Jónsi, the punk you listen to isn't any good."

"The Sex Pistols are a good band…" someone said.

"Sex Pistols are not punk!" I said, loudly.

"Aren't the Sex Pistols punk?!"

"No! The Sex Pistols are bubblegum punk! They're traitors. And punk is dead, too!"

"Then why do you listen to punk?"

"Because I only listen to Crass!"

"Wait, you're not a punk?"

"Sure, I'm a Crass-punk. That's totally different from ordinary punk. Anarcho-punk!"

"Oh, Jónsi, you make it all so complicated," said Gerður. "Can't you just listen to Class if you enjoy it and let us listen to what we like?"

"They're called Crass, not Class!"

Gerður shook her head and giggled. What was so funny? I narrowed my eyes accusingly at Robbi.

"I went to your album presentation!"

"Yes, sure. I wasn't really bothered about it."

Robbi was apparently indifferent. There had been a room full of people at his presentation. It was evident no one had any interest in Crass. Perhaps that was okay. Maybe I had to keep Crass just for myself. Maybe that was the right thing. I lit another cigarette with the embers of the last one, which I threw into the stub barrel.

"I put up posters and got everything ready."

The album presentation was dead in the water. I decided to hang in the Smoker with the other kids until the food bell rang. While they were crowding into the dining hall, I walked back down to the classroom, took the posters gently down from the walls, eased the sticky tack off them, and rolled them up carefully. Then I gathered up the sheets with lyrics on and took everything to my room. Maybe I could give them to some people who were curious about Crass another time. Then I went into the dining hall and had dinner.

As the winter days got increasingly shorter, the nights grew longer and the mountains seemed higher. It was always cold and it always seemed to snow. It snowed for days and weeks. And with the snow came horniness. I'd heard of horniness, but I'd no idea she would visit me or that I'd have anything to do with her. She was totally uninvited. She didn't arrive suddenly, but stole over me like a disease. Like a small midge bite which leads to a rash: it seems innocent at first, but soon you get obsessed with it. Horniness is like itching; it doesn't affect the skin alone, but also your soul and nervous system. After taking over your nervous system, it spreads to your brain and comes to live in your prick. I'd sometimes woken up with a hard-on in the morning and it was because I needed to pee. I was piss-hard. But now it happened every morning and it wasn't because I needed to pee. It wasn't piss-stress. It was like my prick had a life of its own, a free will. My hard-ons weren't thoughtful or predetermined. They just happened. Until now, I hadn't paid my prick any particular attention. I was quite fond of it and found it quite funny, since I was able to do amazing things with it. I could piss with it and that meant I could take part in all kinds of piss competitions that revolved around who could piss the farthest. I could also write in the snow and urinate both letters and pictures. I had also shown it off several times, eliciting a range of reactions. Some found it hilarious, but others found it weird and awkward.

Mom called my prick "Shortie." She sometimes would ask if Shortie was okay or whether there was any problem with him. I also used that name when I thought about my prick. Shortie was nothing but good, innocent fun. I peed with him and sometimes fiddled with him. Otherwise, I didn't think about him particularly. Shortie was never a conversation topic. No one ever spoke to me about Shortie. Now Shortie had changed and basically wasn't Shortie any longer.

What happened to Shortie was like what happens to many kids: they have a cute nickname that fits them while they're little. But when they grow up, they don't want to be called that anymore. It doesn't suit them. Like when Little Siggi becomes Sigurður.

There are various names for prick in Icelandic and most of them seemed rather disagreeable to me, like knob, pecker, or dick. I found the scholarly term "member" too distant and impersonal. Cock didn't feel like a good word, an injustice to this remarkable organ. Some called their prick "friend," like it was a good pal they often hung out with. I didn't think it a good choice. I thought that prick was a decent word. It was about right. Neither too academic, nor too belittling. Somewhat neutral. Girls also had all kinds of words for their genitals: hoo-hoo, purse, bud. Some of them just referred to their crotch. I didn't like that term. I'd sometimes seen words like vagina and vulva in books and magazines. I thought they weren't right, either. Pussy is probably the best word. It's flexible enough to be full of meaning, yet it's free of pretense. Not academic like vagina or demeaning like slit or cunt. Those are really ugly words. Gash and twat, too. Pussy is better than twat. Of all the words in this long list, I think the prick and pussy are the best.

Shortie was all grown up and no longer wanted to be called "Shortie." He'd become a prick. It was also like he'd expanded. Not just when I had an erection, but all the time. He was full of new feeling. One sensation I'd previously experienced was needing to pee badly. Shortie knew that feeling well. But he didn't recognize this new sensation. Only a prick can understand such feelings. And the prick was ready to do something other than peeing. It was like a virus had infected me. I began to dream strange dreams.

Even when I had to pee badly, the prick wasn't interested. It was always about to burst up into the air in response to some strange stimulus. It called attention to itself incessantly. You wanted it to disappear, but it came back. It wanted playing with. I finally decided to let it have what it wanted. I took it under the covers and stroked it. I realized at once that the prick enjoyed that. The feeling was woven through with curiosity and amazement. It was like I'd got something completely new between my legs where Shortie had been before. I stroked myself back and forth, tugged and pulled. Suddenly it was like an earthquake had occurred. The whole universe pumped inside my head and my cock exploded everywhere! And then I was writhing about as heavenly pleasures spread throughout my body. The virus that had consumed my body exploded out the tip of my prick. The explosion blossomed then descended into my testicles. From there, up into the stomach and from the stomach to my spine, an electric heatwave that finally shot all the way up into my brain where the joy shattered into a trillion pieces which sprinkled like PCP inside my head. I had never experienced such happiness before. This was possibly the greatest happiness I could have imagined. My newly acquired prick was the key to this divine feeling. I had had my first orgasm.

Never in my life had I experienced anything like this. But as quickly as the joy had come, it was gone. After came uncertainty, fear, and desperate shame. I had a vague idea of what had happened. I knew I had come somehow, but I didn't know quite what that was. Coming was something I'd often heard about, although I'd never experienced it myself until now. It all had to do with the prick.

It was also called an orgasm. It further fueled my despair, discovering that this part of me wouldn't bend to my will, but was instead a mysterious force that drew me forward. My curiosity outweighed my fear and I peeked under the covers. My heart fought in my chest. The whole while my ecstasy had lasted, substantial amounts of sticky fluid had pumped from the penis. I'd never seen this before but I knew what it was. This was sperm. The stickiness was warm to the touch, but cooled rapidly and soon got stickier still. I felt deep shame. I was certain I'd done something ugly. I'd done something to myself. Perhaps it would be visible on me, on my face, even. Maybe I'd get sperm-acne on my forehead. I had heard somewhere that if boys masturbated, they would probably go blind. I couldn't stand to have even less vision. The blanket, my stomach, the sheet, and my underwear were soiled. Happiness and joy gave way to despair. What had I done? Had I been masturbating? The shame! Mortification poured over me. This was probably ugly and wrong. No one, however, had explicitly told me so. It was one of those things no one talks about. Sperm is like crap. You don't say anything about that sort of thing to anyone. I'd done something very wrong and shameful.

Purrkur was out. I jumped up and locked the door quietly. I felt like a murderer trying to cover up his crime. I soaked the towel in the sink and did my best to clean the semen, which seemed to be limitless in quantity; it stuck to everything. It was disgusting and I was amazed that this abomination was any part of me. I felt like I had shit myself while sleeping. I washed my underwear under hot water and hung them to dry. There was nothing unusual about this; Purrkur and I washed our clothes like this all the time.

I wouldn't tell anyone. If someone noticed acne on my face or my ears grew bigger, I was going to play the innocent and steadfastly deny it. No, it's not sperm-acne, just acne. If my sight deteriorated I wasn't going to tell the ophthalmologist anything. I wouldn't admit that I had done anything. Also, I was never going to do it again, ever. I didn't want to go blind.

I didn't have to worry about Purrkur. We never really talked. And, despite the shame, I experienced a great release of stress. What happened had somehow eased things. It had put an end to the infection in my nervous system. It was like the prick had retired and gone on vacation to Mallorca. It no longer had any need to swagger about.

This gentle feeling of ease couldn't, however, quash my shame and fear. I thought of my grandmother. Amma had been blind so I knew exactly what that entailed. I didn't want to go blind. I had myopia and wore glasses. Maybe that meant I was at greater risk than others. I started examining my surroundings carefully. I didn't think I was seeing any worse than before. But maybe it happened so slowly you never noticed. I had, for example, not noticed when I started to lose my sight. I comforted myself with the most likely idea, that nothing happened the first time since it was just fiddling about and not intentional. But if I did it again, I would definitely experience deterioration in my vision. I'd also heard that boys who masturbated got red noses. I didn't want that either. I was absolutely not going to end up a blind, defaced cripple. It was probably best to just try to forget it.

Yet I was overcome by shame. I didn't know where it came from. No one had ever talked to me about any of this. And maybe the shame stemmed precisely from that silence. No one had talked to me about diarrhea, either, or the difference between the trots and the runs. I'd learned that from Þórbergur, the author. The trots were more watery and granular; the runs were diarrhea plus bad wind. I'd had diarrhea. But it wasn't as shameful as this. No one had told me it was inappropriate to shit myself and crap all over myself. That was just something you don't do. It'd be rude and disgusting. And that's how it was with this. I decided never to do it again.

I felt better. I'd tried it but had learned my lesson. I would never do that again. Never! I could breathe easy and go to school.

Addiction is a remarkable phenomenon. When people are in the grip of an addiction, they're led to do things that go against their own will. We know smoking is unhealthy and dangerous, but we still smoke. People drink more wine than they mean to drink. They don't feel good about it, but do it anyway because the pleasure they get from wine is usually stronger than their shame. Their shame and joy struggle constantly. And people are always just about to quit. The addicted gambler believes he isn't addicted. He's always just going to put one more coin in the machine and then he'll take the kids to the zoo. The road to perdition is full of promises and good intentions. This virus had come to me and taken root in my whole being, body and soul. Innocent and ordinary dreams took on new shapes and I began to dream all kinds of new things. The virus that had taken up residence in my prick was now occupying me entirely; it had changed my whole worldview and my way of life. What had previously mattered was now insignificant and I now had another vision. And what changed most were girls.

Almost overnight, I'd started to see girls in a different light. I'd always categorized them as either interesting or annoying, and seen them as a strange sort of creature. Some were especially cute and others not as cute, but that had never especially preoccupied me. I felt it was more important that they be engaging or be interested in anarchism. Now I started for the first time to fully notice that they had breasts. And I thought more about their breasts than whether they were funny or had any interest in anarchism. I thought constantly about how they looked and what it would be like to go out with them. And I thought about their pussies. It wasn't a passing interest or something that I thought every once in a while: I had a deep and abiding curiosity and thought of almost nothing else. I would have been perfectly happy being surrounded by the most annoying girls day and night so long as I could see their pussies and breasts. In a flash, all girls, and women too, had turned into sexual beings. And when I looked at them I undressed them with my eyes. It was not even me who did it, but the virus that had occupied me. It made me do it. Certainly, they were people, but above all they were people who walked around with breasts and a pussy. It took over my whole perspective. At night, I dreamed about breasts and pussy and my prick. I was so obsessed with the speculation that it took my whole being to think about anything else. Even anarchism was defeated. I had a new obsession. I didn't even care any more about talking anarchism with girls.

Every day I had to force myself to be disciplined and not to stare constantly at the breasts of the girls who were sitting with us in the Smoker. Before, I'd been really interested in what was outside the t-shirt: pictures of bands, for example. Now I was totally indifferent to that, and only thought about what was under the t-shirt. If the girls wore tight pants, I peeked sideways to try and get a glimpse of their pussy. And when they talked to me, I was so aroused I did not hear a word they said. My thoughts were completely occupied imagining how they looked naked. If I saw the hint of a nipple shape, I was hypnotized. The result was a nonstop erection. It was like my prick was trying to blast its way out of prison and I wondered how it would be to stick my prick into the pussy of a particular woman. It was like I wasn't even the perpetrator of these thoughts. The virus and the prick were driving things; I was just a passenger. I was more like a servant accompanying the master of the house. I wondered about all the possible ways to make it happen; I went over them again and again in my mind.

These thoughts weren't confined to girls but to all women, no matter whether the person was a classmate or one of the women who worked at the school. The only requirement for entering my imagination was having a pussy and breasts. Even the women I'd previously thought of as old crones. Like the fat woman who worked in the cafeteria. Now this woman had turned into a Divine Being with a pussy and breasts I constantly wanted to see and to touch. I stared at her in the queue for food as she shoveled meatballs onto plates from a large pot. She was corpulent, and so had large breasts. Not all breasts were the same size. I wondered whether women with large breasts also had big pussies?

She wore white close-cut work clothes that were a bit tight on her and cleaved to her butt, which accentuated her butt cheeks. Instantly my prick stood to attention, and I covered it with my food tray. While she put sausage meat and cabbage on my plate I wondered whether there was any chance of going out back with her. Could I possibly put my prick in her pussy? Could I possibly get to see her tits? These were not complex thoughts; I was totally open to everything. And then came the shame.

"Are you going to stand there all day!?"

I came to.

"What?"

"You're a bit of a sheep," said the middle-aged woman, smiling in a friendly way. "You're standing there like some old imbecile."

I blushed and took my tray and made myself scarce. I looked sneakily around me to see whether anyone had noticed. Could people read my thoughts? I rubbed my hand across my forehead and exhaled. I did not seem to have any sperm-acne.

Was I going crazy? Was this the life awaiting me? Would I now have to deal with this for the rest of my life? Was I stuck with these ungoverned thoughts? Was I a pervert? Some men are perverts. They don't intend to be. It just happens. They can't control themselves. I'd been cursed. I was cursed as a child, always in trouble, constantly having a "wobble," as Mom put it. Was this new wobble here to stay? This wobble was the strongest of all. I knew well the impulse to tear something apart to see it, to break into something or break it apart, but I could usually stop myself. This was different. This wobble had taken over. Increasingly, I speculated constantly: what possibilities might exist for this or that woman to be willing to allow me to fuck her? That's what it was called: putting your prick into some woman's pussy was fucking. Fuck... I thought it the most beautiful word in the world. I savored it in my mind like some delicious candy. My eyes grew still; delightful chills went through my body and once again I had a hard-on. If any of my friends smiled at me, I wondered immediately whether there was something more implied. Was she giving me a sign that I might possibly fuck her? Maybe not now, but maybe some other time? This uncultivated thought and expectation always gave way to shame. Afterwards, I felt like I was a pervert staring at people with a hard-on. I was embarrassed, especially for thinking that way about my female friends. But I could not control myself.

"He always claims he's told us something he never did. He's not even a teacher! 'Why haven't you done this?' 'You never told us we should!' No one in the class had done it. He never said to!"

"Exactly."

And while they were talking, my mind wandered to their breasts and pussy. Wouldn't it be great if they suddenly decided to throw off their clothes and say: "You're allowed to fondle all our breasts and play with our pussies and fuck us if you want?"

The shame was absolute. I was deeply disturbed. I felt like an addict who injects himself in secret and hopes that no one will discover, that no one can see the wine in his eyes or the injection marks on his arm. What if the bulge in my pants was visible? Would the girls know what I was thinking? Hopefully not. I made sure to sit cross-legged. Perhaps this was also part of some game I didn't understand. How did it work? Since all this was happening to me, was something similar happening to the girls?

Were they potentially in the same position as I was? Were they, perhaps, equally fascinated by breasts as me? Were they possibly thinking about me the way I was thinking about them? With watchful eyes I searched constantly for lustful looks from some girl. But despite a thorough search, I found nothing. No girl seemed to have any discernable interest in mentally undressing me, stripping off my Sid Vicious t-shirt. I saw no hint of lasciviousness in their glances. It was quite obvious that things were somehow different for girls. Maybe they thought differently about these things than I did. Maybe they didn't think about it at all. That was a scary thought. I couldn't, however, ask them. There was no way. I didn't even dare ask the guys.

All day long I was preoccupied with these thoughts. And this was not just a wobble; it was a profound desire, a demanding requirement. I wanted. I'd never wanted anything so much. Sometimes I wanted a cigarette when I hadn't smoked for a while and felt like stabbing myself if it meant getting to go outside to smoke. I'd happily walk two or three hours for a cigarette. But I wasn't willing to walk three hours in the shitty cold for a cigarette. If I knew, however, there would be a chance of meeting some completely naked woman, without thinking about it I would gladly walk through a snowstorm for two days. Nothing could stop me. I'd climb the mountain Gaddi had fallen off the top of, if I only knew that on the other side a naked woman awaited me. I wouldn't actually walk through a snowstorm—I'd run. I'd never experienced such burning desire. I recalled the excitement and desire that came with tearing open Christmas presents when I was little and knew the package hid a castle for my toy soldiers that I was incredibly looking forward to playing with. My mind was aroused, and I felt jittery with excitement. But this newfound desire was a thousand times stronger than all the desires I'd experienced before.

Girls are different from boys. They think differently, have other interests, and talk more than boys. Girls could talk about things boys would never usually talk about. Girls, for example, were always talking about how they felt. They said, for example, when they were afraid. Boys were unlikely to talk about that. Girls could admit that they were fragile and could cry in front of others. And the girls didn't only cry if they were regretful or sad; they could also cry if they were brilliantly angry. And all the other girls understood them, talked to them, and looked after them.

Boys weren't like that. No guy would console another guy if he cried. It was simply silly. Boys shouldn't cry like some old woman. It was something you did when you were alone and made sure no one could see. Boys had more difficulty talking about feelings. They seemed not to have so much interest in each other as the girls did. I didn't talk with the other boys about pricks. I felt it would be awkward and inappropriate. Some things boys simply don't discuss.

Yet I was clearly not alone. Most of the boys were fascinated and preoccupied with their pricks. Sometimes a few of them got together in a room, took out their pricks, and measured the length with a ruler. But you measured your own prick. No one went and measured someone else's prick. Anyone who did that would be gay. He was judged gay and given a gay nickname. Gay Árni. It didn't matter whether he was actually gay. It was just gay to so much as look at another's prick. As much as I wanted to show girls my prick, I had no interest in showing other guys. I measured my prick in private. Pricks were carefully measured with a ruler and most seemed to be of similar size. I tried a few times to measure my prick in private. But it was difficult because the ruler was straight but the prick curved. I really needed a tape measure. After that, I decided for myself that my prick was close to the expected size. Maybe girls could talk about their breasts with other girls in ways boys couldn't. Perhaps boys can only talk about certain things with girls. I didn't dare.

I wasn't prepared in any way for these thoughts. But I knew it was just a matter of time before you got to fuck. It was something that happened sooner or later. I knew that first you had to get a girlfriend. Couples definitely fucked all the time. But I was not aiming for any girl in particular. I was aiming at all the girls, though I couldn't have a girlfriend who wasn't punk. I could totally imagine having a girlfriend who was also a good friend. But how did you get a girlfriend? I had no idea. Just choose some girl out of the crowd and talk to her?

"Hi."

"Hi."

"Would you be my girlfriend?"

"Sure."

Then we'd just go into a room and start kissing. I'd never kissed anyone but I'd seen others do it. But then what? Did people slowly take off their clothes? Did you say something about it or not? It was an incredibly complex process with numerous obstacles. I doubted there would come a time when it would happen for me.

The most beautiful words in the Icelandic language were "pussy" and "fuck." Pussy was such an amazing word that I didn't even dare say it out loud. I could say fuck but only if it was part of some joke. I couldn't even say "breasts." I was in my own boat, sealed tight in my own world, unable to take the initiative, and felt it was unlikely any girl would. It was just something I had to achieve for myself.

One time, a female friend of mine asked me to go to her room. I was sitting in the Smoker, smoking and speculating and deliberating the mysteries of the female body. I startled.

"Jónsi?"

"Yes."

"Come on," she said, and gestured with her finger. What was going on? She wanted me to come to her room to fuck?

"What?"

"Come, I'll show you a little something."

A little something? That could only mean one thing. There was no mistake. She was going to show me her breasts. It was that simple after all. I jumped up, threw my half-smoked cigarette away from me, confused and upset. I smiled awkwardly at her.

"Yes, I'm right here…sorry…just thinking something, I was just…"

She led me to her room and shut the door. She was alone in the room. I looked at her bed. She didn't lock the door behind us. Wasn't it customary to lock the door? You don't want some fool padding in while you were fucking. But I dare not say anything. We would kiss first, then I would fondle her breasts. When I'd fondled them sufficiently we'd get into bed and fuck. It'd be great.

She looked shyly at me, but I reckoned she was as excited as I was.

"Well," I murmured.

"Want to hear a song?"

"Uhh, yes, sure…"

I hadn't expected this. She nodded, smiled excitedly and turned on her tape player.

"I've been listening to this song on repeat all day. It's awesome!"

Yes, of course. Naturally, music was an important element. Of course girls wanted to listen to some romantic music before they fucked. I knew that from romantic scenes in movies. I had never done this before and had no idea how it went, but I was taking pains: I didn't want to screw it up. She was pretty and interesting. She wasn't a punk, but almost. She was a new wave freak. That was okay if you were a girl. New wave was a girly version of punk. We would just listen to the song and then we would start kissing. It felt like my prick was going to break the seams of my pants. My eyes clouded and I could feel a heavy throbbing in my groin.

I strove, however, as well as I could, to not let anything happen and to show sincere interest in the track. The music began to play.

"This is OMD."

I knew OMD. Orchestral Manoeuvres in the Dark. New wave. Actually, New Romantic. Romantic music. The song began with a drum machine and electric keyboards. Instruments I despised above all others.

"Enola Gay you should have stayed home yesterday."

We stood frozen and listened to the song. She looked at me, excited and curious. Should I perhaps try to kiss her? I pretended to listen to the song and nodded and smiled reassuringly.

To me, the song was sentimental and dull, but I was prepared to tell her how great I thought it was. When the song finished, she immediately rewound the cassette.

"Want to hear it again?"

"Uh, sure."

"Isn't this an awesome song?"

"Oh, it's just fantastic."

I decided to show some initiative: I sat on her bed. If she'd only sit next to me, we could get to the kissing. She must be coming on to me. The song started up again. Her face shone, and this time she sang along with the song. She didn't seem likely to sit next to me. While I nodded, pretending to listen to the song, I wondered what her breasts were like.

"Listen. This is my favorite section."

I pretended to listen to the singer scream something I didn't understand.

"This is insane!"

"Yes," I replied, nodding. When the song was over, doubt started to creep up on me. Perhaps she didn't have any interest in kissing me or letting me fondle her breasts? Perhaps the song wasn't simply an excuse to get me into her room? Could it be she was really more interested in the song than me?

"What do you think?"

"Er, well, it's good!"

"The song is called 'Enola Gay.'"

A question hung in the air.

"Don't you know what that is?"

"Uh, no."

"It's the name of the atomic bomb that was dropped on Hiroshima."

Although I'd always had an enormous interest in any history to do with the Americans dropping nuclear bombs on Japan, that all seemed extremely remote right now. "Nagasaki Nightmare" was one of my favorite songs. This was disappointing. Her breasts, which a moment before had seemed steaming towards me with a swift wind, were now fast disappearing. They'd previously been trying to break out of her shirt towards me; now they were trying to hide under it. At this moment, it was exactly like when the Americans dropped nuclear bombs on Japan. That event was certainly horrible, but not nearly so terrible as what I was experiencing at this moment. Had she really only dragged me into her room to listen to this miserable song? Was there really no secret agenda? What a damned idiot I was. I was pissed off at her, but mostly angry at myself. And I felt ashamed. Why did I think like that in the first place? Did I really believe that any girl would invite me into her room in the afternoon to fondle her breasts? I didn't give any indication I was thinking any of this; I smiled awkwardly, apologetically, and encouragingly, all at the same time.

"Wow, that's really cool."

"Yes, it's the best song I've ever heard! Think about naming an atomic bomb with a woman's name."

I didn't think that was so far off. Girls were walking nuclear bombs ready to explode at any moment. I hoped they'd explode on me. I wanted to get in their way.

"Do you want to listen to it again?"

"No, I want to digest it a bit first."

"Think about how great an injustice it is!"

"Umm," I replied, distracted.

"Think about being unable to help."

"Yeah…"

"Dropping an atomic bomb on an entire city…"

"Yes," I answered and snuck a glance at her breasts. It was hopeless. It wasn't going to happen. She hadn't even locked the door. She had no interest in me. I was both ugly and stupid. Yet, even so, I still had a faint hope the night wouldn't end there. Maybe she'd ask me, "Should we cuddle?"

"Let's listen to it once more," she said, pleading.

"Yes, why not just do it?"

The song began again, and all my romantic and erotic chances flew out of the window, all the way down to the shore. I focused on the track and this time I thought it was a pretty cool song. Enola Gay was not the name of the bomb, but the plane that dropped the bomb. The song talked about how she never should have taken off. The idea behind it was absurd and destructive and it should never have happened. Just as we weren't going to kiss and nothing was going to happen between us.

"Isn't that a completely insane song?"

"Yes, though it's a bit new wave…"

She laughed like I'd made a joke. I wasn't kidding.

"But it's still cool?"

I nodded.

"Yes, really cool, really."

We stood up, she opened the door, and we went back to the Smoker. Once there she said to everyone:

"We were listening to an insanely cool song."

Maybe she said it so no one thought we'd been inside the room getting fresh.

"What song?" asked Robbi.

"'Enola Gay', by Orchestral Manoeuvres in the Dark."

"Yes, OMD…" someone said, and I nodded, blushed, and muttered:

"It was only a bit cool…"

It was horrible. We could just as well have listened to the song and cuddled a bit.

Little by little, Crass became less important to me and with that my fastidious attention to, and burning interest in, bands declined. I'd acquired a new hobby, which had changed everything. It wasn't just me that had changed, but the whole world. Girls had changed, but so had my attitude towards them. And everything had changed for the boys too. Conversations about sex and hard-ons were getting common, something everyone was interested in. There was lots of talk about masturbation, sexual fantasies and similar stories.

"Damn! I badly want to fuck Ásta," someone said out of nowhere. We all laughed. Everyone wanted to fuck Ásta. I followed these conversations with great fascination, but was too shy to be at all forward. Though I agreed with most of what was said.

I had started masturbating every morning before I got up. Sometimes I even woke up having come in my dreams. I had, of course, never seen a pussy with my naked eye, but I knew quite a bit about what they looked like. I had seen some pictures at school and in a book by Alex Comfort at my cousin's house called *Sjafnaryndi*. Those were, however, only illustrations, not photos. Several times, I'd seen naked women in pornographic magazines but, at the time, had had very little interest in such things. Back then I'd found it unpleasant and disgusting. I'd had little sex education in school. We learned about how children grow up, but we weren't shown any three-dimensional images. I got no education from my parents about these things because it was taboo and never discussed in my home. And I was confident that my parents were altogether sexless. I didn't discuss it with my siblings. They were much older than me and I didn't know them well. I had lots of friends and acquaintances but they knew nothing more about these issues than I did. Also, I had never seen real breasts except in *Sjafnaryndi* or porn mags. I had actually occasionally seen my cousins' breasts when they sunbathed, but when I tried to think back I barely remembered what they looked like. Now everything had changed and I was overtaken by sexual thoughts from morning until night.

Self-pleasure wasn't time consuming or complicated. My prick was always about to explode and I barely had to touch it. I came immediately. That morning satisfaction lasted about until noon, when I'd get restless again. There was nothing to do but to go somewhere remote or back to my room. The sensation was like being thirsty and needing to get a glass of water. Like a growing itch. The only solution was to take your prick and solve the problem, almost like squeezing a ball. Sometimes I woke up in soaked underwear after coming in my sleep during the night, but I still had an erection that insisted on being answered. This went on all day too. If I couldn't go to my room I just went to a toilet. Sometimes I needed to urinate badly, but couldn't because I had such a huge erection and needed to masturbate in order to piss. Afternoons began with my prick back under control. I could pleasure myself after dinner and then again before I went to sleep. Gradually this became a habit and I often masturbated almost automatically. It was good, of course, but more important, however, was the relief that followed. It was like my prick had taken charge of my head.

It had broken ranks on its own power and ruled my thoughts and feelings. If I didn't respond to it, it caused me to feel bad.

I had experienced a similar aggression in my head before. Like when you get some great ideas that simply have to be executed. I had often gotten obsessed with some idea, like anarchism. But I had never felt it affect my flesh this way. I had never lost control of my limbs before and never sensed that my hand or leg had its own independence. I knew the sensation of hunger. It was like your whole activity was centered on your belly, which dictated what you should do: my feet carried me somewhere, my hand picked up food to put into my mouth, and my stomach quieted down. But I couldn't see my stomach inside my body. My prick, however, was a visible, external organ. I examined its nooks and crannies often, trying to understand it better. It was part of me, similar to my feet, but it still seemed to possess an independent will. My prick seemed to have all kinds of ambitions that were not necessarily my ambitions. But since it was a part of me, I was forced to follow it. I felt as if I had suddenly acquired a conjoined twin that I was suddenly forced to take into account. Before, I was just one; now I was split in two. And I felt like things weren't about what I wanted. I myself was second in line. When my brain and prick banded together, I felt a bit like a spectator standing at a distance, watching. Forced to participate.

In the boys' dorm there was an exchange of porno mags and pictures between rooms. Those who were fortunate enough to have such treasures lent them to others. I considered porno mags a holy relic to be handled with great respect. I was struck with humility and shyness in the face of these treasures and couldn't bring myself to try to obtain them. When an acquaintance offered one night to lend me a dirty magazine, joy poured out of me. Delight and excitement, anticipation and curiosity entirely enmeshed me. I was timidly beginning to pore over the holy object when he said, "Just to borrow," as if that wasn't self-explanatory. I tried to rein myself in and was careful not to disclose my heartfelt joy. I wanted to leap into the kid's arms, embrace him, thank him and tell him I was going to go straight to my room to examine the pussies and breasts. But I played it cool. I took the mag like I was distracted, quickly flipping through it and saying, calmly:

"Yeah…I might."

But I felt my voice shake and there was a definite crack of excitement. I tried to make it look like it was a matter I might get around to if I had nothing else to do that was more important. I gave a big yawn:

"Well, I'm headed to sleep," I said slowly, and stood up. I snuck the mag in between my school books and yawned again so no one doubted I was going to do anything but sleep. I would perhaps peek at it a little later, if I remembered.

"Good night."

"Yes, good night," my schoolmate said, and smiled faintly. I had lost all sense of time, and didn't realize that it was barely past nine.

Purrkur was, happily, not inside the room. He usually hung out down in the Smoker until everyone was kicked out at ten. I still locked the door as a security in case he or someone else came. My hands trembled as I took the schoolbooks from on top of the porno mag and eyed the cover. This was the Scripture containing the truth about what really mattered in life and in the universe. A magic writing surrounded by charms. I was about to take a new step in my spiritual development. With quivering hands, I carefully turned the pages. The main feature in the magazine was pictures of totally naked women, the focus being their genitals. The women were not what mattered; it was their pussies that were the focal point. Very much in keeping with my ideas. Sometimes their faces weren't even in the photo; it was just their breasts and pussies. There were all kinds of images of all kinds of pussies of all sizes. So that was a pussy! The pictures had such a profound impact on me that I started to suffocate. It was magic and I had to close my eyes to catch my breath. I had never in my life been so influenced by any publication. It was as if I had entered the door of heaven. I scrutinized the magazine again. There were also pictures of people fucking. Prick in pussy, a close-up of a prick and a pussy together. Sometimes you couldn't see any of the prick at all because it was so deep inside the pussy. I imagined myself in a similar situation: I mentally slipped my prick into all these pussies. I tried to make myself imagine how that would feel. I took out my prick, but this time I didn't even need to tug at it; I came just by looking at the pictures. It wasn't over before I was already hard again. My prick had never before experienced such delicacies.

After examining every possible pussy carefully and committing it to memory, I looked at my prick. I had never thought that pricks were especially interesting, except my own. Other men's pricks didn't concern me. But I noticed that the pricks in the mag were different than mine and I examined them carefully. The men in the paper seemed cheerful and happy. No big surprise, since they must be the happiest and luckiest men in the world. They got to fuck all kinds of women all through the day. Maybe it was just their job. Could it be that they did it for a job? They were fuckers. It had to be the most desirable job in the world, certainly something I could see myself working as. I'd wake up happy every morning, get breakfast, and then go straight to work to fuck all day. And none of it would be embarrassing or uncomfortable. You didn't have to talk to these women first, or listen to some romantic new wave; it was the women's work, too. They waited cheerfully and naked in bed until the man started to fuck them. I'd never realized such a job existed. All my other ideas about possible future careers vanished like dew in the morning sun, replaced by this dream job.

It caught my attention, however, that most of the pricks in the magazine were either rigidly straight or else turned slightly upward. Not so with my penis. Mine bent not up but down and sideways. Was that normal? Could it possibly be a hindrance to me? Of all those happy guys in this wonderful job, none had a prick like mine. Could it be that my prick was bent out of shape in the wrong direction? And what did that mean? I recalled three-dimensional illustrations I had seen at school of human genitalia and people fucking. One illustration was particularly memorable for me: a man lying on top of woman with his prick inside her pussy. The man's prick went into the vagina, which belonged to the woman and seemed to curve slightly upwards, like a tunnel. They seemed to fit quite perfectly. The parts must be designed with a shape that fit together, like a jigsaw or Lego. If the vagina curved upwards, it would be natural to expect the prick did the same. But my prick bent not up but down. I was appalled. I, who had been so happy in heaven, was now thrown out. Could it be that my cock wouldn't fit into any pussy? I wasn't just a strange, odd, ugly, truly very horny pervert (like a movie-ticket seller or a priest), but I also had a faulty prick. I closed the mag quickly and covered it with my biology book. My prick shied away and escaped into its shell.

After the dormitory was locked at night and we got together inside our rooms, the conversations more or less revolved around girls, sex and porn. Different boys expressed themselves in singular ways on these matters. Some had heaps of confidence while others mostly listened. I'd always positioned myself more as a listener than a direct participant in such forums. I was rather ashamed, too, for thinking as I did. Crass was against pornography. They placed great importance on showing respect for women in these ways and others. And if Crass said it, I considered it right. But I still wanted to do it.

Some of the boys had already had some sexual experiences with girls, though it was very uneven. And you didn't always know what was true and what made up. Some kids had seen a girl totally naked; others had fondled their breasts, kissed them and cuddled with them, or done oral. Some said that they'd slept with a girl. It was difficult to distinguish between reality and fiction. And sometimes it didn't matter. If the stories were good, they were fun to listen to. It seemed, however, that when boys had claimed to have had sex, they didn't have much to say about it. Gaddi was the only boy I was certain had had sex. He never talked about it, however. He never talked about anything, actually.

The most credible stories dealt with petting and fondling. They were also usually the best stories. Most kids, however, just told stupid stories that were clearly taken from porn mags, in which the boy hit the jackpot big time with some extraordinarily sexy woman.

I was usually silent, watching closely and listening carefully to everything that took place. I found all the speculation about whether girls could get horny very interesting. I'd wondered a lot about that. I greatly doubted it, but I was keeping an open mind. There were various theories about the matter. One of the most popular was that girls were designed so that they needed preparing: you had to somehow "warm them up," which you did mainly with music, candles, and massage their breasts. If you did all of this right, they would automatically be massively horny, even hornier than you were. That struck me in every way as an extremely tempting situation. I also learned that some women were "nymphos." They didn't need their breasts massaged. These women couldn't get enough sex and were always unsatisfied. The women in pornos were definitely nymphos. I had never met any of these women, as far I knew, but thought that they must be absolute goddesses and the most wonderful women in the world. There was, however, no way to see from outside if they were nymphos, and it could be that virtually any woman was. They concealed it. But when you were alone with them they transformed into sex-crazy, wild animals. I often wondered whether I was ever going to be lucky enough to be alone with a nympho-woman who would tear my and her clothes off, leap at me, and let me fuck her as much as I wanted. I wouldn't exactly bat her away. Another theory was that women got hornier with age.

Girls were generally not as horny as older women. They had managed to work out what was fun and wanted it more and more. Older women were often very vulnerable to young, horny men. That seemed a compelling, logical theory.

Klikki was full of fantastical stories. He was small, a weakling of a boy, really ugly, but by his own account had gotten an enormous amount of sexual experience. I didn't believe him, but enjoyed listening to him tell the class revealing stories about his imaginary experiences. He seemed surrounded by man-crazy women who saw him as some kind of hunk in ways that were a complete mystery to us, his schoolmates. Once, he said, he'd been standing at a bus stop waiting for the bus when a drunk older woman came up to him and tried it on with him. The woman didn't say much, but went straight to work touching him. Klikki, ladies' man that he was, didn't pull away from her, but responded in kind. They got to kissing; he fondled her breasts under her blouse. She moaned loudly when he touched her breasts. She got so excited she asked if he was in a rush somewhere or whether he wouldn't rather take her home to fuck instead of taking the bus he was waiting for. Klikki was reluctant at first and said he was in a bit of a hurry, but when she begged him, he relented. He took her home and fucked her over and over again all night. Although I was almost totally sure that this was an empty lie, I thought it was a good story. I really wanted to believe it. It was possible and if it could possibly happen to Klikki, then maybe it could happen to me. When I was in Reykjavík, I was always waiting for the bus, more or less. Sometimes I even hung out for hours at a bus stop because the bus had stopped running. It would be quite possible some drunk lady would come up at some point or other and start touching me.

Because I did not openly admit to masturbating and pretended not to have any particular interest in it; too afraid and shy, I found something else to talk about. I told stories and made jokes while people lay there listening, looking at porno mags, even masturbating a bit. It didn't disturb me because I was so obsessed with my own story telling that I didn't lose my rhythm. Masturbating was simply a part of life in the boys' dorm.

Although most kids at Núpur were good friends, and we shared friendship and trust, there was admittedly still bullying; it surfaced mostly at night after the dorm had been locked. We had little to keep ourselves busy, so to entertain ourselves we wandered from bedroom to bedroom. If we weren't looking at porno mags, we chatted or even hassled each other. Some enjoyed hassling others. It was so much fun to hassle Sprelli, for example. He was small and fat and hadn't started puberty. He had a reedy, childish voice. He never directly hurt anyone, but he was given stick all the time. Boys often went into his room, tampered with his stuff and messed him about.

"What's in your closet? You got any porno mags, Sprelli?"

"No."

"Sprelli's got no porn mags?"

"Leave me alone," said Sprelli in his child-like voice.

"Leave me alone, leave me alone," they would mimic while they rummaged in the closet and emptied his schoolbag on the floor.

"Leave my stuff be, don't do this," said Sprelli in his reedy voice, trying to sound authoritative. But it didn't matter because everything he said drew laughter and hilarity.

"Listen to you! Can't I just look at your things?"

"No, I'd rather not," Sprelli would answer pitifully. Usually the visit reached its peak when someone took some stuff from him that he tried get back. The boys started throwing it between themselves, usually over his head.

"Give me it!" Sprelli cried in his screeching voice.

"Give me it, give me it," mimicked the boys in response, adopting even screechier voices, laughing even more. The game went on until Sprelli gave up. We thought this was great. We were just teasing. Sprelli never got angry and he never started to cry. The funniest was when Gisli jumped at Sprelli as he stood there, dead tired and sweaty, grasped him firmly by the baby fat on his belly, shook him, and said: "Oooohhh, you're so fat and soft, Sprelli, love."

Sprelli wriggled away, shrieking like a little girl, and we all laughed. I was never directly involved in this, but I never felt there was anything wrong with it. It was just teasing. At the same time, I was also enormously grateful they were hassling Sprelli and not me. And though I wasn't directly involved, I always watched, and got entertained. I got on really well with Sprelli and often liked talking with him. He had had hard times in his life and I felt sorry for him. His mother and father died in a car accident a few years ago. Since then he had been roaming between foster homes and never settling. He had a brother who was a drug dealer and lived in Reykjavík. Sprelli looked up to his brother a lot. He wanted more than anything to live with his brother, but "damn child services," as he put it, wouldn't let him. I was sure it would be better for Sprelli to be with his brother than at Núpur, no contest. Although his brother might well be a drug dealer, he would certainly not tease and humiliate him constantly.

One thing we did sometime with boys was to do the pissed ghost. Lots of things could lead to someone being made a pissed ghost. You might have sworn at someone or said something bad about someone to someone else. Sometimes there wasn't even a reason.

Sometimes we just did pissed ghost to someone because it was fun. But it was usually decided in advance; we planned who should get got. Few kids in the dormitory locked their rooms, so it was always possible to crowd into whichever room. If the person had locked their room it called attention to it, and led to a group of boys hanging on the knob, knocking on the door and hollering. When the person finally opened up, the crowd rushed in and he had to explain why he'd had the door locked. Ideally, he had to admit that he'd locked himself in to masturbate, and then he was a manic masturbator. The punishment was a pissed ghost so that he'd learn his lesson. Often, there were three or four perpetrators working together. They held down the victim's limbs while someone from behind took hold of the waistband of his underwear, lifted it up and tried to pull it as high as possible. Ideally, the aim was to stretch them above his head. This was both extremely uncomfortable and humiliating; it could be painful and it always ended with the underwear ripped. That meant goal achieved. The victim stood there angry and upset, torn underwear hanging out his waistband for others to laugh at.

Another thing that was done to resolve disputes or disagreements was two or three boys holding another one down and striking him rhythmically in the same place on his chest with their knuckles. They didn't strike hard but regularly and fast until they get the desired howl of pain, or even tears. It could be pretty painful. The reason could be anything: for example, leaving a stink in the bathroom. The consequences could well involve a sizeable bruise on the chest.

Sometimes, someone was grabbed and given a hickey. It was

very shameful to have to show-off a hickey given this way because everyone knew it was from a boy, not a girl. Getting a hickey from a girl was cool. A hickey from a boy was not cool. When a girl gave her boyfriend a hickey, she was marking him; it was romantic and sweet for couples to give each other hickeys. It was a great honor and a sign of true love. Similarly, it was equally humiliating if a guy got a hickey from another boy. It was like saying he was miserable, gay and a dumbass. Hickeys lasted a long time, and usually they were in a prominent place on the neck, clearly visible. But not everyone suffered. Often it was the same kids that got endlessly repeated harassments: bruises on their chest, hickeys on their neck, being made into a pissed ghost. Sometimes I thought the joke went too far and sometimes asked them to show the victims mercy. I stopped laughing and spoke up: "Oh, leave him alone" or "Enough teasing Sprelli now, he's got to go to sleep." They usually listened to me and stopped. I didn't want to change positions with Sprelli; I felt great that the tormentors were leaving me alone. At the same time, I was one of them. Just as I was one of the masturbation crowd. Yet this was still bullying. Repeated harassment, bullying, and always directed against the same people.

The most tormented of all was Biggi. He was from Hafnarfjörður; he was an extremely eccentric kid who no doubt had developmental problems. He was peculiar in his mannerisms and dress and had odd hobbies. One of them was studying Serbo-Croatian. He always had a Serbo-Croatian dictionary or children's book under his arm. In good moments, he'd show off Serbo-Croatian phrases. No one knew why; for some reason, it was his greatest desire to learn this language. Most kids thought he was just a freak.

He didn't have a hairstyle or haircut, but grew his hair wild in untidy tufts that went in any direction. Biggi got bullied constantly, every day, from everyone. In lessons, in the dining hall, in the Smoker. He was one of the few kids you could tease in the Smoker. Normally, the Smoker was a place of immunity. Usually, everyone in there was on peaceful terms and rarely got into conflict. The girls made sure the Smoker was free from teasing; they usually nipped any trouble in the bud. Some kids would try to impress some girl by giving another kid trouble, but that wasn't allowed in the Smoker. The girls made sure.

But when the dormitory was locked at night, there were no caring girls around. There were also no adults. It happened, fortunately for the bullies, that Biggi's room was the farthest from the teachers' apartment, right at the other end of the corridor. What happened in there couldn't be heard in the teachers' apartment. We were quite aware of how sounds carried to the apartment and how loud we could be while being mean. Evening after evening, boys piled into Biggi's room in groups to tease him. Biggi seemed not to have any personal ambition, and it was almost possible to do anything you wanted to him. He was often kidnapped, his clothes torn off, and he'd be tossed onto the hallway where he was made to run back and forth naked. Someone put the stopper in the sink and turned on so water flooded his room. Meanwhile, others went through his stuff and threw it on the floor, with Biggi jumping back and forth across the room to try to save what he could. Books, magazines, and clothes. His pillows and blankets were on the floor and got extremely wet. He'd so often had pissed ghost done to him that he had no underwear left and had long ago stopped wearing any. Biggi's reactions always aroused a hearty laugh. He was incredibly funny as he sat there like a thundercloud, staring dead ahead, clinging on to his Serbo-Croatian books, waiting for it to be over.

"How do you say 'I'm Biggi and an idiot' in Serbo-Croatian?"

He didn't answer but looked angrily straight ahead. Someone ran ice-cold water in a glass, sneaked up behind him, and poured the glass down his back. Biggi angrily sprang to his feet; we fell about laughing. Biggi and I were actually quite good friends. I was probably his only friend at Núpur. He was very shortsighted, like me. It was funny if someone snatched his glasses. Biggi was hilarious as he squinted and fumbled, half-blind, looking for his glasses while boys threw them among themselves, put them on, and impersonated him. Biggi was a little portly and when he scrambled to his feet and tried to catch his glasses they poked his stomach: "Potbelly, potbelly."

He was often held down while someone fetched a black marker and drew on his face. They'd draw glasses and a mustache on him. And then Biggi went around for days with traces of colored marker on his face. When the color finally disappeared, the game was repeated. And if Biggi was harsh to someone scratched at them, boys rushed over and held him down while they knocked their knuckles on his chest until he began to cry. He worked out pretty quickly that there was nothing he could do. He was fighting a losing battle. Inside Biggi's room, a competition took place in which the aim was to humiliate him in the most original, but effective, way. I never took part in it and wasn't always present, but I knew about it. Like everyone else, I liked to hear stories about what had happened inside Biggi's room. And I never said anything.

I felt like Biggi only had himself to blame. It was his fault for being so ridiculous. His fault for being so weird. If he didn't want to be teased, why not stop learning Serbo-Croatian? When I watch movies that take place in prison, I think of Núpur and know many of my classmates think the same way. Especially during scenes where guards rush into someone's cell on the pretext of looking for something. Then I think of Biggi. The guards are rarely looking for something but use it as an excuse to throw stuff back and forth and rummage through everything. The ritual is a humiliation in which the strong show the weak their superiority and power and the victim experiences utter powerlessness. Guards treat prisoners the way we treated Biggi.

At the beginning of winter, we had to buy all kinds of school stuff, including watercolors in a little cardboard box. One time, Klikki shat in the cardboard box and took it with him the next time he went into Biggi's room. His stuff was thrown on the floor and out into the hall. Someone tore off his glasses and ran out into the hall with them. While Biggi ran after the glasses, Klikki used the opportunity to stuff the box of human shit behind the radiator near Biggi's bed. He made a shush sign to us with his index finger. Not that he really needed to, since none of us were about to shoot our mouths off. No one would mention it, least of all to Biggi. After that, we rarely went into Biggi's room. The shit stench was unbearably oppressive. Biggi, however, wasn't aware of anything. He was impervious to the stink. The smell intensified and emanated into the corridor. You had to hold your breath when you walked past Biggi's room. The teachers noticed the smell too, but did not understand what it was.

"Do you know what this smell in the hallway is from, Jón?"

I shook my head.

"No, no idea," I replied innocently. Zakariás the janitor came and checked the toilet but found nothing wrong.

As bizarre as it sounds, I was, despite everything, Biggi's friend and found him both a fascinating and fun kid. He was extremely knowledgeable about lots of things, especially the occult, which I enjoyed discussing with him. Ghosts, hauntings, monsters, and images that people had taken of ghosts fascinated me. He was a subscriber to the magazine *Unexplained*. It considered many aspects of this topic and it intrigued us both. We were both especially fascinated by spontaneous combustion. In each installment of *Unexplained*, there was coverage of someone who had burst into flames and burned to ashes out of nowhere. An old man had sat in his armchair at home after dinner and lit a pipe. When his wife brought him coffee there was just an ash heap in the chair. This was an utterly bizarre case and no one knew how it happened. I had a theory that the devil was behind it all. Biggi was skeptical. He argued instead that there had been flammable material in the food the old man had eaten. I found Biggi not just knowledgeable and interesting, but also a hoot. I especially thought his extraordinary interest in the Serbo-Croatian language was both fascinating and amusing and I liked to listen to him speak Serbo-Croatian. But though he was my friend, I still never let him know there was human shit behind the radiator in his room. That was another matter and did not concern our friendship. It was a common joke for everyone in the dorm and a daily source of comedy.

"Hell, there's a disgusting smell emanating from you, Biggi."

"Yes? I don't know what it is."

We couldn't keep our laughter in check and cracked up.

"It makes people sick when you open the door to your room."

"I think it's coming from the toilet," said Biggi. We howled with laughter.

"Fuck, you're disgusting, Biggi!"

Poor Biggi couldn't smell, but he knew something was wrong: "Yes, I just don't understand."

It took several weeks for Biggi to find the cardboard box; he threw the contents out the window. It was still a long time before the smell disappeared.

Biggi not only had to go around school with marker-pen glasses and a mustache; sometimes his face was covered in black spots. Someone had taken it on themselves to draw a hundred little dots with a marker. Often, he was wearing clothes on which had been written, "Hello, I'm an idiot" or "Kick here" with an arrow pointing to his ass. Biggi was at the bottom of a pyramid of power and I wasn't and for that I was grateful. I wasn't on top. I was somewhere in the bottom third. I wasn't part of the regular kids, not part of the teasing bullies, but not part of the fools. I'd managed to create my own image and role. I was the funny, strange Jónsi Punk. My only role was to be a prankster and funny, and so I gained popularity and even respect. I put myself out there to meet expectations and was up for endless clowning around. I didn't have much else interesting to offer.

The food at Núpur was notoriously terrible. I have never in all my life, as long as I've lived, had food so gross and terrible. We had to eat it three times a day: breakfast, lunch, and dinner. For breakfast we always got porridge or cornflakes. That was okay. The lunch was hot food, almost always meat. It was usually cut into slices, beaten with a meat hammer and fried in a pan. The meat was gray and ragged, and not unlike a floor cloth in appearance. It was seasoned with herbs, but behind the seasoning you could detect a strong oily taste. If we were lucky, we got fries and ketchup. Sometimes, we got mincemeat or meatballs, spaghetti in tomato sauce, or the so-called "trainwreck." That was either whale or seal meat. Very rarely we got roast lamb, known as drawer steak. It was soup-meat that had been allowed to cook in the oven for a very long time. Dinner was various mushroom soups or rice pudding and bread.

The raw ingredients were extremely poor. And although we were young and naïve, we realized fairly quickly that they were treating us stingily. There was whale in everything, once in a while fish or a trash plate, corned beef and spaghetti with tomato sauce. The meals all had promising names like goulash, sausages, minute steak, or squash. It didn't really matter what you were having because it was all equally bad. Drawer steak was a little better. On Fridays, we sometimes got pizza. The pizza admittedly looked nothing like a pizza but it was called that on the menu. Pizza was made up of the week's menu. Pizza with goulash, pizza with sliced hot dog and spaghetti, and pizza with whale meatballs drowned in lots of cheese to hide the evidence. Often the food was so terrible and tasted so bad you realized something had gone off. Sometimes it was terrible enough that we couldn't possibly stomach it. The mince whale meat had putrefied or somehow gone moldy. Then you just filled yourself up with the bread and butter that were brought out with the food. But the bread might also be moldy and the butter rotten.

"Holy crap, this tastes disgusting. Is this awful taste from the butter or bread?" I said as I sat eating with my schoolmates.

"I think it's a mixture of both," said Sprelli's screeching voice.

"Uh, no, it's just butter gone rancid," said Biggi.

"Rancid—isn't it rotten?"

"It's okay to eat rancid butter, it just tastes stronger," said Biggi and stuffed another slice of toast in his mouth. I'd never heard the words "gone rancid" before and had never had to eat rancid butter. But it meant that the butter was either rotten or moldy in some way. At best, it was past its expiration date; the bread too, for sure. Dry and hard. One often had to hunt through the slices of bread to find some bread that was not moldy or just a little moldy so you didn't notice it.

Sometimes, several kids would get an unexplained stomach bug. It was treated as though someone had got a contagious fever, something that was going around. We strongly suspected that we had diarrhea and stomach pain because of the food we had to eat. But we couldn't prove anything. Often we were just so hungry we clean forced food into ourselves to have something to eat. But often the food was so bad that it was impossible to force yourself to eat it.

We regularly skipped meals and many times went hungry. Sometimes the food was also so disgusting to see that we did not have to taste it to know that it was unhealthy. It was "goulash" on the menu by the door, but it actually resembled puke. Then we'd head straight to the Smoker and satiate our hunger with cigarettes. And we weren't able to complain to the cook, who responded badly to any criticism.

"What is this?"

"It's food, kid!"

If you didn't want his food, you were ungrateful and picky.

Sometimes the fish didn't even look like fish since the pieces were so dry, shriveled, and hard. The taste was somewhere between water and spices. Some peculiarly inscrutable added flavor that no one could identify. The fish was always redbelly, lumpfish, or gill. To my mind, that wasn't food. Occasionally, however, we got breaded fish fried with onions. It was usually possible to cram it down your throat because it was made with breadcrumbs, and cheese was used to cover up what was inside.

It was not until much later that I learned the cook at Núpur was not a real chef any more than the teachers were real teachers. He was a fat, old Faroese sailor who had fled his tax responsibilities in the Faroe Islands and got himself hired as a cook at Dýrafjörður, somewhere no one would find him. It was also hard to ask him what was in the food because he only spoke Faroese and I understood little or nothing of what he was saying. He spoke extremely fast and probably would rather not explain in detail the contents of the food. He also wasn't concerned about our welfare and nutrition. He was there to cut and fry whale meat and wait for his tax liabilities to expire so he could go back to the Faroe Islands and the sea.

When you were simply starving, you could often steal a slice of bread or a cookie to take to the dorm. By the entrance to the dorm was a room with a payphone. There was also a small side table and a toaster; you could make popcorn if you were fortunate enough to have some. The student association ran the school shop and sometimes you could buy Coke, Prince Polo, Tópas licorice, Mars, and popcorn. But it was practically impossible to reach Núpur all winter, and massive demand at the shop meant many long periods when it stood empty. Perhaps the student association wasn't exactly holding its own in management. Sometimes there would be a period where there wasn't even bread at Núpur. I would sneak cornflakes from breakfast up to my room. For a time, I lay in bed at night, reading and munching on dry cornflakes out of my trouser pockets. We often discussed the situation. It was unacceptable. The student association had repeatedly made clear to the school board and the principal that we students were unhappy with the food. Their meetings always ended with the principal assuring the student representative that he would talk to the chef, that it was a temporary situation and things would improve. Sometimes the meat improved as a result, like getting lamb instead of seal meat. But it only lasted briefly and then whale meat began to reappear in unexpected dishes.

Our discontent escalated. It grew to a climax. We were eating goulash with spaghetti. Served with moldy bread and rancid butter. The goulash featured cuts of whale meat. It, too, had gone off and the fish taste was even worse than usual. It wasn't just the meat but also the spaghetti, which tasted like someone had spilled oil over it. We'd had enough. There was a murmuring in the dining hall and we spat out our food. The atmosphere was freighted with stress. This was the last straw. We had put up with bad food for far too long. We wouldn't eat awful, moldy, fetid food any more. We caught each other's eyes, said what we thought about the food and nodded.

"This is an abomination!"

Everyone nodded.

"A fucking abomination!"

The tension mounted. Someone swashed water around their mouth and spewed it onto their plate. Dissatisfaction spread; everywhere there was the sound of spewing, spitting, and people swearing. Then things really burst to life. The chef and the serving woman stood behind the counter in the dining room and watched in silence. They didn't know what was happening, but felt that things were not quite right. Suddenly, someone stood up with his plate and shouted loudly:

"Pig food is for pigs!"

Then he threw his plate in their direction. The uprising had begun. The plate hit the wall above the counter and shattered; glass shards rained down. A second person gathered up his dishes, screamed, and threw them towards the two. More grabbed plates and glasses and threw them in the same direction. Scraps, broken dishes, rotten whale meat, and spaghetti splattered all over the counter; the chef and the serving lady had to make a break for it. They ran into the kitchen and locked it behind them. Furious kids rolled the tables over, throwing them hither and thither across the room, kicking chairs back and forth. The result was nothing short of chaos. Chairs, bowls, tables, anything loose flew this way and that. It started with a lot of screaming and cursing that changed to laughter. We screamed and laughed and had fun. The tension and frustration that had been building inside us finally got an outlet. We'd done something people usually don't dare to. Of course, not everyone got involved. Some were afraid and sloped off, but most kids stayed to take part. Before long we were standing, shaking, amid food scraps, overturned tables and broken chairs. And we laughed in each other's faces. The teachers came running; they stood in the doorway and looked over the battlefield. They were so surprised that they couldn't control their faces. Their gaping expressions made us laugh still more.

"What the devil is going on here?!" shouted the principal, Hilmar, across the room. We stood frozen in our traces. No one uttered a word. It seemed no one was going to come forward and explain things and so become a sort of revolutionary leader. No one person had thought this up. We all did. Some looked down at the floor, others right at the teachers. We caught each other's eyes and breathed fast and hard.

"They were trying to kill us!" the chef's assistant said from behind the kitchen door. We shook our heads.

Without delay, we were driven into the dormitory and locked in. We were interrogated: the principal and the teachers went room to room asking the kids about the source of the riots and who was involved. No one admitted having thrown anything or seen who threw things. No one remembered who instigated the protests. No one remembered who said "pig food is for pigs." I knew they would try to pin it on me. I discussed it with Purrkur and he agreed.

"They'll definitely try to blame me and force me to tell them something."

Purrkur said nothing but nodded decidedly. He was convinced.

"To hell with them! To hell with them all! I'm not going to tell them shit."

When the interrogation party came into our room, I bowed my head and stayed silent. They were going to try to blame me for this, even though I was innocent. Many had done much more than I.

"Well, Jón," said the principal, powerfully. "That was rather an ugly sight in the dining hall tonight."

I nodded.

"And it occurs to me to suspect you had a role."

That wasn't right. I had thrown my plate but took care to throw it against the wall where it shattered. I didn't hurt anybody with it. I threw some chairs around and rolled some tables, but didn't damage anything. I just had fun. It was also unfair to give us such disgusting food.

"I didn't do anything," I murmured. They shook their heads in disbelief.

"I find that extremely difficult to believe."

"I don't give a shit what you believe."

"Are you swearing out of that mouth of yours, boy?!" shouted Hilmar.

"I've not done anything."

"Do you want me to call your parents and tell them about this?"

I really didn't want that. I looked up and stared right at them all.

"I didn't do anything."

The teachers sighed. It was obvious they didn't believe me.

"The food is so disgusting…" said Purrkur, as if to explain.

"Who was the instigator of this?" asked the principal, firmly.

"Not me," I said, firmly.

"Who was it then?"

"I don't know. It was just someone who threw his dishes all of a sudden and then some others threw their dishes too, but I didn't do anything."

Purrkur nodded supportively. The group of teachers looked skeptically at me. They didn't believe me, but also had nothing on me. I had done something, but I wasn't at the forefront. I was just one along with the others.

"But didn't you see who was throwing dishes?"

We both shook our heads.

"No. It all happened so fast, you see."

"You must have seen someone?"

"No, I didn't see anyone…"

I looked at Purrkur, who shook his head and shrugged his shoulders.

"And you two didn't leave, but didn't do anything."

"We were probably not really thinking about it."

"It's like talking to halfwits," the principal said, wearily, to the teachers. He looked back at me thoughtfully.

"Well, whether you admit it or not, you're strongly suspected of taking an active part, and of being a moving spirit in the whole thing."

"That's not fair, I'm always trying to watch out."

These words fell on rocky soil. I saw that the principal could hardly keep from smiling. They hadn't a shred of belief in what I was saying. But it was true! I was trying to keep out of trouble, trying not to get expelled from Núpur. I had friends, I was left alone, and, in addition, I had, for the first time in a long time, created a niche for myself in society. I was the entertaining kid. I was a witty guy. I was Jónsi Punk and I liked being him. Other people also liked Jónsi Punk; he was part of the group. For all these reasons, I'd never dare instigate riots or shout "pig food is for pigs."

The inquisition never found an instigator. No one was ever kicked out for it. Probably they knew the food was inedible and the greatest wonder was that this hadn't happened earlier. I, however, was reprimanded, placed on probation and told that the slightest fault or breach of discipline would cause me to be immediately expelled from the school without further warning. The principal told me that whether I confessed or not, whether it was proven or not, it looked to him like I was the root of the problem. He also said he would expel me immediately if he could prove anything. We were made to clean the dining hall. It took us a long time to pick up the broken glass and goulash with spaghetti, which was all up the walls. The Student Association had to pay for the damage. But the riots had been a success and the food improved a little after them. Whether it was dead seal or flotsam whale in goulash that fateful day, we weren't served it again.

Whales sometimes ran aground on the beach below Núpur; porpoises especially. Sometimes they weren't quite dead when they reached land and lay there dying on the sands of the beach. Some kids had seen live whales and gone up to one. The whales were so fat and heavy they couldn't move. They just lay there powerless, only able to blink their eyes. Some kids had looked into a live whale's eye. The girls found them beautiful and adorable, but the boys found them funny and ridiculous. Obese invalids with intensely beautiful eyes. Sometimes the whales disappeared as quickly as they appeared, swept back out on the next big flood. Later, a carcass would float up elsewhere on the beach. Perhaps it was often the same carcass, traveling up and down the beach.

It was about a half-hour hike along the trail to the beach from Núpur. Since we were strictly forbidden from going there, we found it absolutely necessary to go from time to time. When we took a beach trip, we snuck out, walked away from the school, behind the hill and down it, then down to the shore, invisible from the school. We'd invented a game we called "Stormy Seas." We went to this place there was a gravel beach; the game was to chase the undertow. When it ebbed, we ran after the waves. When they turned, the knack lay in finding the exactly right moment to run away without having them catch up. It was awesome. The waves were large and the noise against the rocks so huge you couldn't understand a single word. The noise was so huge you had to scream in the ear of the person right next to you to beat the sound of sea and stone. This was disturbing and dangerous but at the same time exciting and fun. The breakers were so strong we knew that if they caught us they would drag us out to sea.

The beach was full of unexpected mysteries. Driftwood, flotsam, plastic bottles, and other debris. You could also often find dead birds, animal bones, seals, and whales. I had never seen a live whale but really wanted to. I wanted to lock eyes with a whale. If I could find a whale, I would try to save him. I would try to roll the whale back out to sea. If I managed that, I was sure the whale would always be grateful to me. He would reward me with provisions for life, following me wherever I went; whenever I came down to the sea, my whale would swim gracefully past and greet me by blowing a jet of water high into the air. If I ever were to fall into the sea, the whale would rescue me. He would allow me to climb up on his back and swim with me to land. I would pat him gently and talk to him. There would even be an article about it in the paper. I would be interviewed and there would be a picture of me pointing out to sea. "Punk and whale are best friends." There would even be something about it on TV. People would watch and they'd understand punks aren't evil or dangerous. Punks can be useful and help animals.

But all I saw was a dead whale, once. A porpoise. The skin was coarse and the porpoise had no eyes; the gulls and ravens had eaten them out. The eye sockets stood empty. We examined the whale from top to bottom, kicked it, climbed on it and slid down. We got rocks and used them to break out of some of its teeth. The teeth were rather small, not much bigger than horses' teeth. Then Gisli said:

"I wonder what whales eat?"

We weren't sure.

"Definitely fish…"

"And octopus," added someone.

"Octopus? There are no octopuses in Iceland."

Maybe they ate seals, too. We had sometimes seen half a seal on the beach, like they had been cut in two. Maybe porpoises eat seals.

"Why don't we check out what's in its stomach?" Gisli asked.

"Yes, let's do it."

This was exciting. Gisli found a sharp stick and came running over. The whale lay on its side, stomach turned to us. Gisli poked the belly of the whale with the stick. Some instinct made me retreat as Gisli drew the stick back and aimed it deep into the belly of the whale. And it was just as well I escaped because the stomach exploded and the innards gushed over Gisli. Rotting intestines, shit, oil, water, and other abominations covered him at once. Even worse was the terrible smell that followed. Gisli stood frozen, still with the stick in his hand; he gagged and puked. I laughed out loud then gagged too. Gisli retreated from the whale and vomited again. He was quite shaken. He was also drenched from head to toe and it was cold, so we went back to Núpur. I kept myself away from him because of the smell, but only had to look at him to burst out laughing. He was soiled in meat-shreds and grease-splatter, but put up with it well, walking through the snow completely soaked.

"Jesus, that was a fucking shock!" said Gisli, his teeth clinking from the cold. I laughed so much that I got tears in my eyes and had to wipe them in order to see. It was fun being there. It was good to be at Núpur. It was great seeing a whale explode over Gisli.

Although I liked everyone and everyone liked me, I didn't have any real friends at Núpur. Everyone was an acquaintance. I knew I'd have no connection with them beyond Núpur. I wasn't headed down the same path as any of them, most likely. I'd taken on the role that best suited me: that of a clown. My role was extremely well received amid the relatively uneventful daily life of Núpur. I was always a willing servant with my antics and silly talk. Some kids spent their spare time with sports, playing Parcheesi, or hanging out in their rooms. The main social activities, however, took place in the Smoker. There was always a nonstop traffic of people; it didn't matter whether you smoked or not. Kids came to the Smoker for entertainment. It was well known that smokers tended to be more fun than non-smokers. I was the life and soul of every gathering in the Smoker, a kind of ringmaster. When no one had anything to say, I always found something to bring up or talk about. I asked questions and aroused people's curiosity.

I had excellent relations with everyone, but better with the boys than the girls. I didn't want it that way, but I was so shy around girls. I found them fascinating and entertaining, but was soon so plagued by sexual thoughts that it interfered with further communication. I felt ashamed for watching their breasts and thinking about them in that way.

There were always a few couples. Kids were constantly getting together and splitting up. And then starting up with someone else.

I felt like it was generally the same kids. All that stuff was very removed from me. I thought it equally likely that I'd get with a girl as get an A on a Danish test. I felt ugly and stupid, and besides, I was a punk. I was Jónsi Punk and Jónsi Punk was fun. That said, no one wanted to kiss him or get physical with him. I simultaneously yearned for girls and was afraid of them. The fear was the stronger of the two. I came off as somehow sexless towards girls, pretending not to share the huge interest the other boys had. I found I didn't always share the other boys' humor, especially when it came to girls. For example, I found dirty jokes not funny; they were rather uncomfortable. It was all so tortured and complicated. My feelings and thoughts were fighting each other inside me.

"Can you give me a cigarette?"

"Sure, if I can see your breasts."

"Oh, come on, Stebbi. Give me a cigarette."

"If I can see your breasts!"

"Are you a retard? Do I have to show you my breasts to get a cigarette?"

"No, hey, I was just kidding."

I sat silent in such conversations. They weren't funny but awkward. I wanted to see her breasts but there was nothing funny about it. If she had come into the Smoker and lit a cigarette and suddenly said, "Hey, guys, want to see my breasts?" I would have been totally into it. But I couldn't pull it off. I could only let someone else do it and then follow along: "Sure, exactly."

I felt I needed to understand more and know more before I could explore this territory further. There was nothing funny about breasts and pricks and sex. Jónsi Punk never thought about things like that; he was just amusing. And though I had an abiding interest in girls, I was certain they had no interest at all in me. I was different. I wasn't one of the guys they couldn't bear and said thought with their pricks. Girls didn't find it funny or cute when boys thought with their pricks. I'd often heard them speak moralizingly about boys who did. I wouldn't be one of them, even though I actually was.

I studied couples from a distance and carefully watched what they did and said to each other. Sometimes, especially at night in the lounge, the boys put their hands under their partner's shirt and fondled their breasts. They generally seemed to find that uncomfortable, and asked them to stop or turned away. That didn't quite click with what others had said about how you should fondle a woman's breasts, get them into a sort of trance. And I wondered a lot about how couples got started, but didn't want to ask anyone. I'd heard of guys who asked some girl to go out with them. When and how did one do this? Would you just go to her room, knock on the door:

"Hi."

"Hi."

"Do you want to go out with me?"

"Sure."

"Great. Why don't we get physical tonight?"

"Sure, once I've finished studying."

"Yeah, me too."

How does petting start exactly? Is it predetermined or is it just like in the movies where people are suddenly looking at each other very intently, like hypnosis? Then a long silence and then they start slowly approaching each other and it finishes with their eyes growing very still, then passionate kissing. Should I perhaps try to stop telling jokes some time, just shut up and look at some girl, walk really calmly over to her and kiss her? I dare not. The ultimate aim, naturally, was getting to fuck. That was the goal. I couldn't do that. I was deformed.

I still had a few decent female friends. Among them was one who was a bit of a punk. She was not a real punk, but she enjoyed punk and shot her mouth off a lot and was a good laugh. We talked to each other a lot, usually sat together in class, and were together for most meals. And I sometimes wondered whether we might perhaps become a couple but I just had no idea how. Boys definitely had to take the initiative. Girls want to be chased. But while I was pondering all of this, she one day found herself a boyfriend.

Sometimes it was like the girls might be showing some interest but I was never quite sure. No one said anything clearly and definitely to me. Sometimes some girl said something to me I did not quite understand. Maybe they were beating about the bush, or maybe it was some girl joke. Maybe they were just teasing me, or making me make a fool of myself. I had no idea. If any girl said something to me that I did not get, then I replied by saying something to her that she did not get. One girl invited me into her room. She wasn't considered one of the cute girls, but she was still not ugly. Many of the boys had a system for rating girls according to set rules. An ugly girl was a three, an ordinary girl was a six, and the cutest girls were tens. I thought very few girls were a one; most girls were a ten. This girl was not punk but also not a rocker. She was just a girl. So six, or even seven. We went into her room and as soon as she closed the door, I was gripped by an enormous tension, my mouth dried up, and my palms sweat furiously. I didn't let it show, acted totally normal, and tried to be as casual as I could. She sat on her bed and I stood there awkwardly in the middle of the floor. I tried to keep breathing regularly and hoped she couldn't hear the heartbeat inside me, which sounded like a drum beating rhythmically.

"Uhh, did you want to talk to me about something?" I muttered awkwardly. She giggled and smiled. What was going on? Was this a prank? Was she trying to make a fool of me? Had she got some girlfriends maybe hiding somewhere? Would they suddenly burst into the room and laugh at me?

"I just wanted to chat to you."

Chat to me? About what? Perhaps she wasn't making fun of me? Maybe she really wanted to chat with me. It happens. Of course! People begin chatting then suddenly that stops and they start kissing. And once you start kissing it's okay to fondle breasts. And I had also heard that if girls let you fondle their breasts then they are willing to go all the way. But I didn't need to do that. I would just be happy to start kissing and to fondle her breasts. These thoughts trampled uncontrollably back and forth in my head like a bouncing ball in a gym. I felt like I was about to burst all over the air at any moment, like the whale on the beach. My hands were ice cold, but my face was on fire. I was so dry in the mouth that I swallowed repeatedly and tried to wet my lips. She stopped smiling and looked worried.

"Is everything okay, Jónsi?"

"Oh, well…" I murmured but did not manage to continue or explain.

She looked at me curiously. What was she really thinking? Why was she looking at me like that?

"What kind of music do you listen to?" I asked finally, just to say something.

"All kinds. I just enjoy all music."

She smiled again. That was good. At least better than she was worried about me. I didn't have to explain my musical tastes because everyone knew. I was silent. Why didn't she say something? What was she waiting for? Was it here that I had to show some initiative? Should I just walk up to her and sit with her? Then we'd look into each other's eyes and fall into kissing. Then I'd fondle her breasts and she would take her shirt off and let me see them. But we weren't together. I wasn't about to ask her to go steady with me. You can only fondle the breasts of a girl who's your girlfriend. I couldn't ask her out now. That was ridiculous. But if she would ask me then I would say yes. This was embarrassing and uncomfortable and maybe she was just messing with me. Maybe it was just some plan she'd made with her friends to pick on Jónsi Punk. I did nothing. Stood there, clammy, in the middle of the floor, swallowed repeatedly, cleared my throat. She looked shyly at me. As time went by it became even more awkward. Why didn't she speak? Why did she just sit there and smile at me? When the excitement was so unbearable that I thought I would die, I muttered:

"So I do really have to meet Gísli, I promised…"

"Yes, okay," she said. I couldn't tell whether she was disappointed or else simply relaxed. I quickly tore open the door, expecting a group of girls to be eavesdropping.

"Okeydokey," she said, quietly.

"Yes," I answered and dove out. "Nice chatting with you…"

Then I rushed to shut the door behind me. I sighed in relief. I just couldn't manage this. Was this real or just my imagination? What was going on? I felt pangs of extreme regret as soon as I'd left. I wasn't headed to meet Gísli. I was curious to know what she would have liked to talk about me. Perhaps she didn't have a crush on me and perhaps she wasn't trying to tease me either. Maybe she wanted to ask me something or maybe she just wanted to talk to me because she was worried about one of her friends. Girls could talk endlessly about issues like that. Or did she have a crush on me and wanted to do some kissing? Or maybe she simply didn't want that? I had no idea at all and fled to my room, sat on the bed and tried to calm my mind and balance my breathing. It was probably best not to think about it and to try to forget it. It was just awkward. After that I avoided her. I only went to the Smoker if she wasn't there and I left as soon as she arrived. If I met her in the hallway, I seemed to be in a hurry to meet someone.

"I'm coming!" I called in the direction of the gym and ran off.

One time I listened to the conversations of some girls as they sat in the Smoker, discussing a girl who had just begun going out with a boy. I pretended I was distracted and not listening to them. They talked quietly and even half-whispered.

"He's a complete idiot."

They giggled.

"But you know why she's with him…?"

I pricked up my ears.

"No?"

"Because he has such a big prick!"

They giggled even more.

"You're kidding?"

"No! She said so."

This was among the most important information I'd heard in a long time. They were talking about some girl who was with some guy just because he had a big prick. Girls clearly thought it mattered even though they didn't speak about it much. They had views about pricks. According to the information I had gotten, I reckoned I had neither a small nor large prick. It just seemed to be a fairly normal size. But my prick was bent and crooked and stupid. It seemed clear to me that I had to end all this. It would ultimately drive me insane thinking about it. Anyway, I could never manage being with a girl and knew it was better not to try to achieve it. It had become obvious that I couldn't cope with such situations. I lost all control and became an idiot. The thoughts and physical effects were too strong for me. No girl would kiss someone who was so dry in the mouth. And she'd tell her friends about it, and they would laugh at me.

"Don't you know why she broke up with him?"

"No?"

"His mouth was so dry it was impossible to kiss him."

"Seriously?"

"Yes. And he was deformed, too."

"Seriously?"

"Yes, he has a deformed penis."

I just had to accept this, forget it, stop thinking about it. I didn't need more trouble in my life.

I had found my niche. I could nowadays, in a few good ways, avoid getting myself thrown out of class, except once in a while. I even sometimes thought it was fun to learn. I enjoyed learning English. I liked reading poetry books in Icelandic and I read the *Saga of Gísli Súrsson*. I loved it. It was the first Icelandic saga I'd read. Sagas were available at home, but because they were written in the ancient Icelandic language, I couldn't read them. There were many words I didn't understand. It was harder to read Icelandic sagas than English, but the book we were reading was a modern version. What was most remarkable about Gísli's story was that it happened on the same Dýrafjörður where I now was. The story discussed love and destiny and honor. Gísli had to escape because so many people who wanted to kill him. He was an outlaw. I was an outlaw, too. We were both exiles in Dýrafjörður. I was quite sure if Gísli lived in our time and we met on the beach, we would really be able to have a good conversation and no doubt we'd become good friends. We'd meet up and smoke together and talk about how miserable things were and how everyone was a bunch of idiots. Gísli would listen to punk. Crass, mostly.

I also really liked my room and the dormitory and found it awesome to hang out in the Smoker and lark about and talk nonsense and shoot the breeze with the other kids. My sexual tension I handled through regular masturbation. And I tried to find a solution. I tried simply not thinking about women stuff and drove all such thoughts from me. I tried to send out the message that I was asexual. I was just Jónsi Punk. My worldview was characterized by Crass who had many remarkable views on women. The two main singers of Crass, Eve Libertine and Joy De Vivre, had much to say about relations between men and women. They said that women should enjoy as much respect as men and that men should not employ their bodily advantage or gain some male power over women. Crass were feminists who put great emphasis on women's rights, gender equality, and respect for women. And I shouldn't think anything that was inconsistent with that. I took Crass really seriously and had steadfast faith in everything they had to offer. And when they sang: "Fuck is women's money, we pay with our bodies. There's no purity in our love, no beauty, just bribery," I took it very seriously. Although I was quite open to the idea of kissing some girl and fondling her breasts, yet I didn't talk about getting to have sex with her, and I knew it wasn't right. I couldn't lie that I had a crush on her just to get her to sleep with me. I had to put off all this girl business until I understood it better and could cope with it. Maybe I would one day meet someone who could guide me and to whom I could talk.

There was no alcohol to be had at Núpur. No one had any liquor or could see to getting some. From time to time, other drugs were available. I was really interested in getting to experience all possible drugs and get high. I really enjoyed doing that and felt better when I was high. The intoxication did away with my distress and anxiety, and helped me to forget all the unpleasant thoughts. The easiest way was sniffing. Sometimes it was possible to get hold of gasoline, thinners, or other solvents. When we succeeded, Purrkur and I lay inside our room as time passed and sniffed until we lost consciousness. When we came to, we went back to sniffing. We poured petrol on a cloth we put in front of our mouths and noses and breathed in. In the school supply store, they sold UHU brand glue.

We emptied the tube into a little sandwich bag and breathed it in. It was also possible to buy Butane at the shop. We pumped gas inside ourselves, breathing it in whenever the opportunity allowed. But Butane and glue cost money, and I rarely had any. Once a month, a nurse came from Þingeyri for visiting hours. I'd affect a cough to get some Norwegian cough syrup. I'd drink the whole bottle at once to get high. I also got others to affect a cough for me and get some cough syrup. Sometimes I managed to get hold of several bottles and drank them all at once.

In the summer, Núpur was a meeting place for people in the surrounding countryside and things like weddings, birthdays, and country balls took place. The trash containers had whole bags of empty wine bottles. The bottles were mostly totally empty, but in a few of them you could find a tiny drop, and we gathered all the drops in a single bottle. It was difficult and time-consuming work, requiring great caution, because no one could know about it. We took turns standing on guard. It was generally a tiny yield, no more than one sip per person. We had got hold of syringes from a class-mate who was diabetic. He injected himself every day and taught us the key points about doing it. We filled syringes with alcohol and injected the wine into our arms. It only worked occasionally. We had to ensure that there was no air in the syringe because then we could die. Then we had to make sure to find the vein, because if you injected into the muscle you got a swollen hand. Some-times it was successful and we got high and were pretty drunk. But sometimes nothing happened. We experimented with different dosages and methods. When Gísli fell ill after I had injected him in the hand, we stopped for good. His hand swelled almost to twice its size, and Gísli became seriously ill. He protected me and just said he had been fiddling about alone. Zakarías the janitor came and removed all the bottles.

When we couldn't get hold of anything, we resorted to suffocating each other until we got high. We did it by leaning forwards, breathing really quickly for about one minute, getting up really fast, and making someone else grab us around the neck from behind. This way you stopped the blood flow to the brain and lost consciousness, getting a kind of rush that was like being high. I didn't care what I did. I stopped at nothing to get one high or other and it didn't matter whether it was moonshine, Norwegian cough syrup, glue, lighter gas, pills, or something else. I was willing to try anything.

Some of the kids had various medicines because of something that ailed them. When I heard about this, I immediately went and spoke to the kid. If he wouldn't let me to try the pills, I simply stole them. I never thought about whether it could be dangerous, harmful or have consequences. If I overdosed, I'd just go to the hospital in town. There would be a lot of people to attend to me and it would definitely be a refreshing change from Núpur. As long as I could get high. That was everything.

On the few occasions hash came to Núpur it was through Sprelli. His big brother was a drug dealer in Reykjavík. Sprelli stayed with him during the holidays and generally came back with a few grams of hash. His brother sometimes sent Sprelli back with hash hidden in his underwear and candy. Then it was a good time to be Sprelli's friend. He didn't smoke hash himself, but used it to buy friendship and respect. It was his way of getting recognition.

Hash was the epitome of all the drugs I had tried. You just had to smoke a single pipe and you were high for hours, unlike huffing, which lasted just a few minutes. Being stoned was awesome fun. Everything was enormously enjoyable at Núpur. I even looked forward to going to class because I found it so incredibly nice to just sit, relax, and listen to the teacher's crap. When I was high on hash, nothing they did got on my nerves. I felt a great affection for them. Life was so much fun and so wonderful. Even turning on the water taps was funny. I locked myself in the toilets, jerked myself off, then turned on the faucet, closed my eyes, and listened to the water stream. I felt like I was lying in a boat somewhere in a distant land, passing along a huge and exotic river. I also found it hilarious and enjoyable to pee in the sink and collapsed laughing alone in the toilets when it occurred to me to do that. Hash changed everything for the better. All this dull everyday life was funny and a great adventure.

The teacher who lived in the apartment in the dormitory had the task of watching over the dorm, keeping an eye on us, and being there in case something came up. The teachers divided this responsibility between them so the inhabitant of the apartment often changed. Sometimes there was also someone in the apartment who didn't work at the school and whose identity we didn't know. And sometimes it housed someone who was working at Núpur temporarily. Once, a substitute teacher lived in the apartment. He was different from the other teachers and extremely well liked by us kids. His classes were enjoyable. He showed some interest in us and even sometimes came to the Smoker to chat with us and smoke. He listened to similar music as us and seemed to have a great deal of sense. It was fun to talk to him. It wasn't common knowledge, but rumor had it this teacher would some-times invite boys into his apartment in the evenings and even give them a drink. I found that very exciting and I sincerely hoped that he would invite me one night. I'd never been in the teacher's apartment and also longed to have a drink. I was more than willing to sit in the kitchen with him and drink. But he never asked me.

Later I learned that he chiefly invited Sprelli. This was a surprise to me and I didn't understand. Why was he inviting Sprelli? Sprelli? He hadn't even started drinking! He didn't even like music! He was just sort of... a gimp. Why didn't he invite me? I was totally shocked. Since the teacher was so likeable and wise, I debated talking to him about it. I wanted to tell him that he would much prefer to have me over than Sprelli. I was cool, but Sprelli was a geek. But it was some sort of secret that no one talked about and I never got the opportunity to discuss it. But it nagged at me and eventually I asked Sprelli:

"Is it true you've been invited to the teacher's apartment over the weekend?"

Sprelli got embarrassed and began avoiding the subject, but I could tell it must be true.

"And? Did he give you a drink and so on?"

He looked down at the floor.

"I really don't want to talk about it," he replied in his childish voice. "Can't we just talk about something else?"

I was insulted and wounded that the teacher hadn't invited me. I kept waiting for him to knock on my door and ask whether we couldn't go to his apartment and have a drink, listen to music, and talk. But he never came. And one day he was just gone, as suddenly as he arrived.

I didn't understand time. People said I had no sense of time. What did that mean? Was it like having no sense of smell or taste? Some people had no sense of taste and didn't care what they ate because they couldn't taste food. I'd never met anyone like this, but I'd heard about it. I had a sense of taste and found all the food at Núpur disgusting. But I didn't have a sense of time. The nuances of time went entirely over my head. I perceived time, but did not really feel it was real; it made no difference to me. The world was out there and what happened in it didn't matter to me. I wasn't even properly a part of this world and would probably never get admitted into it.

Suddenly, there was no milk. Everyone seemed to know why, but I had no idea. I just knew I couldn't eat cornflakes in the morning like I was used to. I had no idea where milk came from. I knew that it came from a cow; I had been to the country and knew how to milk a cow, but knew nothing about how the milk got from there to Núpur. People said that the milk processors were on strike. I had never met anyone who was a milk processor. I didn't know how people had such information. Was it on the news? The news was never about Crass or Bakunin. All the news was boring. It was just people like my father who were interested in it. But it wasn't cows that had gone on strike, but dairy scientists. Maybe the milk processors were people who were super sharp at milking. What happened to all the milk? Was it poured away?

I just felt sad not being able to put milk on my cornflakes. If there had been a cow near Núpur, I would no doubt have put cornflakes in a bowl, run with it to the nearest cow, and milked it. But there were no cows at Núpur.

I was fourteen years old and I did not know the seasons properly. I knew that after winter came spring and summer and autumn. But I did not know how long each period was or what the months were called. I just found it either cold or freezing cold. On rare occasions, it wasn't that cold. Sometimes there was sun and it was rather warm. Like when I was in the country-side and it was so warm outside that we bathed in the river. I also didn't know when the major holidays were. They seemed to simply come according to a system that was an utter mystery to me. Christmas was in the winter around the same time as New Year. Easter was uncertain. It came all of a sudden like a bolt from the blue. At Easter you weren't required to cele-brate anything, but everyone got Easter eggs. Sometimes Easter came in the summer, sometimes in winter. One day, it was just Easter. And Easter wasn't connected to God and Jesus at all. Per-haps this was just something people had done in the old days. Maybe people had no eggs to eat and made themselves eggs out of chocolate. I didn't know where chocolate came from. Maybe it came from a tree? Perhaps it was made from honey? It was just a weird festival that came suddenly and all at once it was Easter Break from school.

The bus came to Núpur. We took the bus, drove to Flateyri, and flew home for Easter break. Everyone looked forward to getting

Easter eggs and we talked about what size we would get. I hoped I'd get a really big Easter egg. When I was little, my mom always hid my Easter egg and I looked for it. It was a game I had invented.

Mom and Dad didn't seem particularly happy to see me. But not for any particular reason. I hadn't done anything. I felt weird coming home and wondered if I shouldn't be staying at home any more. Was my room no longer my room? Was my room at Núpur now my room? The Easter holiday lasted a few days. I mostly hung out inside my room and listened to Crass. Occasionally, I snuck up to the attic where I sniffed fabric glue through a sponge stub. Fabric glue was a strong and refreshing change from the gas and Butane at Núpur. I started the day by masturbating. I woke up every morning with a hard-on and usually had been dreaming something sexual. Often sexual thoughts poured over me, sometimes completely out of nowhere, but often inspired by something I saw. I was transfixed by underwear advertisements. Sometimes there was a picture of a woman in a bra in a magazine. And such a simple picture elicited an erection. I went into my room or the bathroom and masturbated.

I got Easter eggs from mom and dad. Three of them. It was weird because I used to get four. Sometimes I chatted with them while we ate, but otherwise we didn't have a lot to talk about. They never asked me anything about Núpur. Dad waffled as always about things that no one was interested in. It didn't matter who he was waffling to.

"It has been raining in Trondheim for a month!"

Mom and I nodded our heads.

"There is flooding in the streets! I spoke to Anna yesterday and she said Gunnar had not traveled to work because the streets are flooded."

Dad laughed and hit his thigh. His waffling had stopped getting on my nerves. It was just like any other ambient noise. Usually, I didn't even hear what he was saying. It was just like the sound of a car driving past.

My mother complained that I was dirty. She felt I was always dirty. I took a daily bath. As I lay there for hours, listening to music and fiddling with my prick. I didn't even bother to go down to Hlemmur to see my old friends. I was tired and disinterested. After a few days, Dad drove me back to the airport. Mom sneaked me a carton of Winston Lights without Dad seeing and kissed me goodbye. It was odd to say goodbye to Dad at the airport.

"Goodbye, son." I thought he was talking like he was acting in some crappy film. The aircraft flew us back to Flateyri where the bus was waiting to drive us back to Núpur. Easter was over.

At Núpur there were many oddballs and you had to really excel in strange behavior to be considered something special. In the dormitory was a kid who was considerably older than the rest of us. He had to have been eighteen, nineteen. He never cleaned or cut his hair and was so filthy that a bad smell accompanied him. His hair sat like a haystack on top of his head, uncut, unkempt, and dirty. He was called Lubbi. He was from the countryside. He was tall, a real muscleman. His eyes were hidden behind his long hair. But Lubbi always had cigarettes and pipe tobacco, so that when you were out of cigarettes you could go talk to him. Lubbi answered everything in a misleading way, twisted things around, even answered your question with another question. It was hard to have a real conversation with him. Still, he wasn't hostile. He was just confused and possibly crazy. Once, we sat inside his room and smoked a pipe.

"Have you had sex ever?" he asked suddenly, totally out of the blue.

"No."

"Why not?"

"I just don't have much interest in it."

"Have you got hair on your balls?"

"Yeah…"

"I've fucked often."

"Yes?"

"I get it regularly in the country."

"So, you've got a girlfriend?"

"Noooo," he said with a mysterious expression. "But I still get to fuck."

"Huh, who?"

"I just fuck the sheep."

I had never heard of this. It had never occurred to me.

"Is it possible to fuck a sheep?"

He smiled his friendly, insane smile.

"Sure, sheep have pussies."

I nodded.

"A hole is a hole."

My face dropped, I simply stared at him and nothing came into my mind to say. What could I possibly say? I didn't want to know any more. But Lubbi was thrilled and pleased with himself and persevered with his bragging.

"Sheep have better pussies than old women do."

I nodded.

"And they don't give you any grief or lecture you like a wife would."

I'd been to the countryside and had plenty of contact with animals like horses, sheep, and cows. I knew they had genitalia: I'd seen a bull mount a cow, a stallion a mare. I'd never imagined someone would fuck an animal. I felt really uncomfortable; in my mind, Lubbi had gotten even more disgusting. He wasn't just dirty outside, but inside, too. I wondered if he was just lying about it to make himself sound good like other boys did, especially when it came to sex. I waited for him to start laughing and say he was just teasing me.

But he wasn't making it up. He was telling the truth. Lubbi fucked sheep. He'd survived sex with animals, and had no problem with it. I thought of all the animal species I knew, but none of them gave me any kind of sexual thrill. Animals aren't sexy. You can have affection for animals, you can enjoy touching and caressing them, but there's nothing sexual about animals. Udders are not breasts. There's nothing stimulating about seeing udders. To do something like that, you'd have to be cracked, which was certainly true of Lubbi. He was crazy. Lubbi had no friends, and you avoided talking to him or interacting in any way. I only talked to him if I needed to smoke.

The farmer in the next town hired him one time as a day laborer. One day, Lubbi turned up with a cast. He'd broken his leg and didn't have to come to class. Gísli and I went to his room to find out what had happened. He was lying in his nest of a bed with one leg up on a pillow. He had a plaster cast from mid-calf to groin.

"What happened?"

"Nothing much."

"You fall?"

"No."

He didn't want to talk about it, which made it even more intriguing.

"Oh, come on. Tell us!"

"You promise to shut your mouths if I do!"

"Of course!"

"I was shoveling shit in the cowshed… there was a cow there who was showing off and waggling her pussy in my face. This real randy heifer…"

Gísli and I snuck a look at each other and held back our laughter.

"And what happened?"

"I went over to the milking stool… and when I was fucking her, she suddenly kicked the stool away and I fell down. Damn pussy."

We burst out laughing, and ran out.

"Keep your mouths shut," he called after us. I never went back into Lubbi's room after that.

Sometimes unexpected things happen that change people's lives. Incidents that mark you for life. Lena's birthday was one of them. They say the brain has the ability to make people forget horrible things. But some things are so awful that you cannot forget.

It was Sunday and I was inside my room. I lay in bed, reading. That's how it usually went when there was no school. I mostly hung about inside my room and read, occasionally going to the Smoker to get a cigarette and talk nonsense with someone. I'd talk some crap, have a laugh, and go back to my room to hang and read.

I'd learned to never go about with a pack of cigarettes. Everyone automatically asked to borrow a cigarette. As much as it was nice to have a whole pack of cigarettes and consequently be a popular guy, it was simply too expensive. Everyone wanted a "loan" of a cigarette.

"Can you lend me a cigarette, Jónsi?"

"Uhh…"

I felt I couldn't say no; when I offered people the pack, they'd even take two.

"One for now and one for later."

I always forgot immediately who I'd lent cigarettes. And though I was willing to share, not everyone was as willing to share with me. I always seemed to have no cigarettes, even though I had a lot of cigarettes. I loosened the skirting at the base of the wardrobe in my room and hid my cigarette packages there. I didn't even tell Purrkur.

JÓN GNARR

He was so ruthless that he had stolen whole packs from me, sold them, and denied having done it. I snuck into the hiding place regularly, got a single cigarette, and went down to the Smoker. Every cigarette was my last cigarette. People couldn't ever get a smoke from me.

This Sunday was no different. I loosened the floorboard, got myself a cigarette, opened the door, and started off towards the Smoker. As soon as I came out into the corridor, I felt that the atmosphere was electric. There was something going on. There was an unusual amount of boys in the hallway. They whispered in giggles and snuck about. I looked at one; from his face shone some previously unknown joy and excitement. It was like the circus had come to Núpur. It was certainly something really very fun and unexpected. Something everyone would like. I hesitated.

"What? What's going on?"

The boys looked at each other and giggled. Villi, who was in the room next to me, walked over and whispered, low, "Haven't you heard?"

Villi smiled excitedly and pursed his lips.

"What?"

I looked at the guys around me. What exactly was happening at Núpur that had never happened before? What was so great? Had a band come to the area? Were the Outsiders here? Was Bubbi Morthens perhaps sitting down in the dining room drinking coffee?

"What?"

I demanded an answer.

"You really haven't heard?!"

"No, no, what? What's going on?"

I was bursting with curiosity and excitement.

"It's Lena's birthday," whispered Villi low into my ear between his clenched lips. I looked into his eyes.

"And?"

He leaned back into my ear.

"Everyone has to fuck her a happy birthday."

"For real?"

I exhaled involuntarily. "Fuck her a happy birthday?" Just the word "fuck" immediately had my undivided attention. How was it possible to fuck Lena a happy birthday? Could it be done? Was it really possible? Was it all in order? Do girls allow boys to fuck them when it's their birthday? Is that how it's done? Was there some sort of custom or something that everyone followed? That'd be magnificent. It had completely escaped me, if so. I was going to keep an eye on the girls' birthdays. If I knew it was a girl's birthday, I could walk up to her and say:

"Hey, well, happy birthday. Aren't I meant to fuck you a happy birthday?"

"Yes, absolutely!"

This was the most amazing tradition in Iceland, by far. And I hadn't even known about it! I tensed up, elated by this good news. "Fuck Lena a happy birthday." Yes, of course!

"Where is it that everyone is…?"

This I had to see.

"Downstairs in Conan's room."

I didn't hesitate, and Villi followed a short distance behind me. We went down the boy's corridor. I was emotionally in turmoil, thoughts wheeling sharply in my head. Was I about to lose my virginity? Was I going to fuck Lena? I had never had any particular interest in her. She wasn't pretty but wasn't especially ugly. But she was a country girl and didn't even have long hair. Her hair was pixie short, kinda like a boy's head. But she was still a girl, and she had breasts and a pussy. I didn't demand more than that. I was incredibly excited. Outside Conan's room stood a crowd of guys. Conan himself was in front of the door like a bouncer. I noticed that the pile of boys had formed a queue. Everyone exuded fervent joy and anticipation. Like right before heading into the premiere of a great movie. I trundled up to Conan.

"Is it true?"

Conan nodded his head with a sardonic expression.

"Can I see?"

"Uh, okay…"

He spoke a little hesitantly and his eyes wandered to the guys in line. Then he opened the door carefully, his face stealthy. I felt my heart fighting in my chest. I set one foot in and peeked.

It's said that when you run into a trauma or accident, you perceive differently than usual. The brain responds differently; even when people get into a car accident at high speed, they think that everything happens more slowly, like in slow motion. People have sufficient time to take in all kinds of details they generally wouldn't notice.

There were three guys in the room. Two stood at the window, grinning ear to ear. They were naked and their pricks stood up into the air like spears. In one of the beds, there was Lena. She was also naked. She lay on her back with her knees up and her legs apart.

I immediately noticed her breasts. They were convex, as large as two halved handballs. Her nipples were small, almost as small as mine, but around them were dark circles. I had never seen breasts before and stared at them. On top of her was a boy. He held himself up with his hands and had his legs between her legs. I felt like he wasn't fucking her so much as having some kind of difficulty. He looked at me and smiled friendly. I smiled awkwardly back. I looked at Lena. She looked at me and smiled back faintly. Half embarrassed and really half-apologetic. Now's your opportunity, whispered a voice within me, she's enjoying it. She's having a birthday and it just feels enjoyable to fuck. I stood there like lead. Now was my opportunity! I could shut the door, undress like the boys, and it would all be fine. Just like that, I could be standing there naked with them, watching and waiting for my turn. And certainly no one would be pissed even though I had managed to jump the line. When these kids were done fucking her, I could get some. It was even okay that my cock was bent, because it was all in service of a birthday.

But it wasn't right, despite this. None of this was right. As much as I wanted to with all my life and strength of my soul take this opportunity, I couldn't. And though it seemed right in some ways, it was absolutely wrong. Instead of undressing, I left. I felt dizzy; everyone immediately turned their eyes towards me. I was having trouble breathing and I gasped to catch my breath. I looked apologetically at the guys who were waiting and they looked back full of expectation as though they were waiting for me to say something. I smiled foolishly, laughed slightly and muttered something incomprehensible that even I didn't understand, yawned, and stole away.

My feelings and thoughts trampled powerfully up and down my body. Are you going? Are you an absolute idiot? Why didn't you take the plunge? This isn't right. This is just pathetic. Why didn't you go right into the room to see her pussy? I'd found it embarrassing. But she smiled! It was still awful. She thought it was just some fun and she thought it was really great. But it wasn't right. I didn't want to do it. As much as I really wanted to try it, I wouldn't do it this way.

I went back up to my room and sat on the bed. I wiped the sweat from my forehead. I was so hot it was like there was a fire kindled inside me. My head was like a huge bustling beehive. Should I go back? No. Why not? For sure, everyone was done fucking her now. Maybe she's all alone in her room. Maybe she feels sad that I've not returned. I can go back down, knock and ask her if she wants me to fuck her…that's ridiculous. What if she says no? Then I'm just standing like an idiot in front of everyone. There's no way to ask girls if they want to fuck. They just want a guy to be resolute and to say that you want to fuck them. No, I don't believe that. Of course you have to ask. You shouldn't have to do anything to someone if you don't want. I didn't tease anyone who didn't want teasing. I didn't tease Biggi. It was ugly if you did so. He hadn't done anything to anyone. And I never hurt anyone. While the boys sometimes hurt Biggi, I didn't. You don't do something to another person if you're not sure they want it—no matter how much you'd like to.

The more I thought about it, the more I realized what was so wrong about this. Lena was a little bit weird. Perhaps she was a little challenged. She didn't usually say much and when she was in the Smoker she sometimes giggled and laughed a bit at jokes, but rarely said anything. She was more than a little bit weird. She was weird like Selma in the book about Jón Oddur and Jón Bjarni. I would never fuck Selma to wish her happy birthday. And it definitely wasn't a tradition. I'd never heard of it before. This tradition in all likelihood didn't exist. I thought back to the other girls at Núpur who'd had birthdays; I was sure there'd been no hubbub in the corridor. If it was a real thing, I'd have heard about it by now. I was pretty aware of all the likely and unlikely opportunities for getting to fuck. The boys were just taking advantage of Lena. I wasn't that sort of person and I wouldn't be like that. I thought about the future, too. If I were to do something I wasn't totally sure was right, how would I feel about it in the future? I would definitely feel guilty and feel awful about it. Maybe Lena would also realize and get angry. I would be ashamed. No, there is no such tradition. A person does not and cannot do something with someone he isn't sure wants to. I'm not Lubbi. I'm not an idiot. And though Lena was involved in this of her own free will, it was still wrong. She's a person and much more interesting than this. And though she was allowing the boys to fuck her, they would never be grateful to her. In their eyes, she was just the world's best hooker. If she was doing this to gain popularity among the boys, she was just like Sprelli. And for everyone who participated in it, it was an insignificant accomplishment. Like stealing or lying. It's easy to lie to yourself that it's okay to steal. But it's still wrong.

The days went pretty smoothly. It was rare for something to happen. Very rarely there was some conflict; arguments were peacefully resolved, on the whole. People sometimes quarreled a bit spitefully, had a spat, settled things, were friends again, went to the Smoker, and laughed at it all. I never felt at risk of being punched or hit.

There was only one person that everyone had to beware of: Gaddi. He was totally unpredictable. He spoke so little that you never really knew what he was thinking, but he enjoyed fighting. In Reykjavík he went by the nickname Gaddi the Fists. While others tried to avoid conflict, Gaddi tended to seek it out. He couldn't care less about the majority of things others thought mattered. He did not seem interested in anything except fighting and maybe soccer, and he was never willing to talk to anyone. He was very handsome and always had a girlfriend but he was also always changing girlfriends. They were always cute. I still don't quite know how anyone could be Gaddi's girlfriend. Though he was handsome and attractive, I didn't think he was much fun; he said very, very little. He was this mysterious character. Handsome and mysterious. Maybe his girlfriends fell for that.

There was talk that he wasn't always kind to them. Sometimes I heard a whisper that he had punched his girlfriend or threatened to do so. It felt really very ugly. Only losers hit girls. It's like beating up people weaker than you. Girls are not as strong as the boys and I'd never heard of a girl who liked to fight.

Some boys liked to scuffle and I could even understand that some boys enjoyed punching each other on the mouth. But who liked punching girls? Girls didn't even seem to know how to punch. And they rarely fought, just scratched or tore each other's hair. Girls were more vulnerable than boys. They were tender and could begin crying for so many reasons. But you still ought to treat them with respect. There had to be equality between boys and girls, not just because Crass said so, but because girls could do a lot of things better than boys. I felt that girls were usually both smarter and more mature. I thought all the girls were awesome, more or less. I was often totally fascinated with how they thought, and it was almost like they came from another world. Exotic angels or goddesses. If not in the spiritual sense, then certainly in the physical. I thought all the girls were somehow beautiful. Their bodies were certainly more beautiful than boys' bodies. Some of them were dog-boring and could be dumb as oxen or really pretentious, but their bodies were always beautiful and it didn't matter whether they were small, large, fat, or thin. I couldn't imagine how anyone could bring themselves to damage such a divine body. I found it a disgusting thought, like hitting and punching children. But Gaddi, of course, had punched his mother, and if you who could hit your mom, you could hit anyone.

Sometimes there was evening entertainment inside the lounge. A movie was shown or there was even homemade entertainment. These events were usually organized by the student association. The student association appointed a coordinator from among the students. He had to ensure that everything worked out and everyone left after the entertainment. By the door, in a corner of the room, there was a large painted iron bucket where everyone had to throw their trash. When the evening entertainment was officially over, the coordinator turned off the lights. Then people went to their rooms or to the Smoker, though the couples were often left in the dark cuddling. The next day you could often see jackets, shoes, and socks that lay scattered here and there around the lounge.

The teachers complained, which led to Kristinn, the coordinator, deciding to start a crusade against this. He hung up a notice in the lounge, which said that leaving clothes, trash, and other stuff was forbidden. Kristinn was a conscientious coordinator and before the evening festivities began, he stressed that we all had to throw away our trash and take our clothes with us. Most obeyed the rule. I had very few clothes and usually no money for candy so rarely left any mess. But others often forgot things. Girl stuff. Girls seemed to have endless kinds of stuff. They had all manner of clothes, scarves, fingerless mitts, leggings, scrunchies, and cosmetics even: lipgloss, lip balm. There was always something left behind. One evening, Kristinn announced that anything left behind from now on would be considered junk and he would throw it in the trash with the other stuff. After that, most people stopped leaving things. The girls just needed to look for their stuff one time in the trash and they stopped leaving it.

Then one time a red Millet-brand jacket was left behind. Kristinn threw it in the trash and there it lay when we walked along the corridor on the way to the dining hall. It was Gaddi's girlfriend's coat. When Kristinn came into the dining hall, Gaddi rushed over to him, slammed him against the wall and screamed at him:

"Did you throw that jacket in the trash, you worthless piece of shit?"

Kristinn was a well-brought up farm boy: diligent, efficient, a true gentleman.

"I've told you many times that everything left behind goes into the trash."

"Do you want me to beat you up, you fucking idiot?!" said Gaddi and raised his clenched fists in a threatening manner. Everyone was silent and watched. You didn't see this often. Before anything more could happen a teacher came over unexpectedly and broke things up. Gaddi let go of Kristinn and stepped back. No one had any idea what he was going to do. He was just as likely to beat them both up.

"What's all this about?" the teacher asked.

"This idiot throws people's coats in the trash!"

"I am just getting you all to stop leaving clothes in the lounge. I've said it many times; it's also on the notice board."

"Yes, isn't that just how it is?" the teacher asked Gaddi.

He said nothing, shook his head and walked off into the hall. I thought that's where it ended. But after school, a rumor spread among the students that a fight had been proposed for after dinner, in the gym. A huge excitement—the whole school was going to gather, though of course the news couldn't reach the teachers or other staff. After dinner we snuck unseen and via roundabout routes into the gym. It was built so that the hall was more or less like a pit with a spectator gallery above. The platforms were so high it was impossible to jump down to the floor of the gym. We assembled there together.

Gaddi was already there and stood tall in the middle of the space. Kristinn came into the room, calm and controlled. He was strongly built and played both football and handball. He was a healthy farm boy who neither smoked nor drank, and in my mind was the image of bravery. Gaddi, however, was thin as a reed, a jerky, gangling guy who smoked like a chimney, and didn't play sports. They were of similar height. When I looked at them I thought Kristinn would be quick to finish off Gaddi and knock him down like some kitten. But I knew Gaddi was unpredictable. This would be a thrilling fight; there was a lot of tension in the crowd. We sincerely hoped no teacher had seen us sneak into the gym and that no one would come to interrupt the fun.

The boys set up facing each other, with a few meters between them. I was expecting some sort of tussle and that they would grab and pull each other and the one who won would be the last to give up. Maybe someone would get punched in the mouth, but nothing serious. I had never seen such an organized fight before. There was no judge present or anyone who ran the fight. Kristinn was the first to step forward. He held out his hand as if to greet Gaddi in a brotherly manner. Gaddi did not shake his hand, but leapt forward and struck Kristinn a blow to the face. Within seconds, he rained several blows in Kristinn's face, flailing with both hands. Kristinn couldn't offer any resistance. He tried to bring his hands to his face to defend himself, but Gaddi hopped around him and punched and struck. His lips cracked and bled. He was buffeted on the nose and blood sprayed like a jet of water. Kristinn fell to his knees and held his head. He had lost but Gaddi continued to beat him about the head and body until Kristinn fell prone against the floor. He no longer held his head, but his hands fumbled in the air while Gaddi kicked him repeatedly in the head and body. Kristinn lost consciousness and stopped moving. A pool of blood began to form around his head. Bloodstains were all over the floor. Gaddi had stunned Kristinn, but continued to kick him.

"Motherfucker! This is what happens to a fucker who throws other people's clothes in the trash!"

The audience stood there petrified. The pool of blood around Kristin grew and grew. We looked fearfully at each other and started crying at Gaddi to stop.

"Stop Gaddi, he's out cold!"

Gaddi pretended he couldn't hear us. He slipped in the blood and fell to the floor. Group of kids were running down the stairs in the gym. At the same moment several teachers came running. Gaddi scrambled to his feet. He was covered in blood but grinning ear to ear. He fell over onto his back and I noticed that his shoes were so bloody they'd left a shoeprint behind. A bloody Adidas shoeprint. We were all ordered to the dormitory; we didn't need telling twice. Most of us were in total shock. No one expected that this would happen and we wondered whether Kristinn would survive. Had Gaddi killed him? I thought it quite possible. Maybe Gaddi had beaten Kristinn to death.

"He totally hammered him!"

"Yes, it was horrible..."

"Did you see the blood?"

"He's definitely dead."

No one had ever seen anything like this. I knew that deep down this was the way Gaddi was. He simply enjoyed to the fullest beating and hurting people. He had fun and he felt he was within his rights. When he came to the dormitory later in that evening after being questioned by the principal, he was victorious and happy. We boys all stood with a lump in our throats and asked for news.

"Is Kristinn okay?"

"Who gives a shit about idiots!"

"It was horrible what happened…"

"What happened had to happen! This fucking idiot won't throw any more coats in the trash!"

"You thrashed him until he was bleeding."

"I had to," said Gaddi with conviction. "That's the only thing idiots understand."

Gaddi wasn't interested in discussing it further. It was as though he thought it wasn't remarkable or unnatural. He took a shower, headed to his room, and went to sleep. Other kids sat up sleepless with the tension. Kristinn wasn't dead, but he was severely injured and was sent to the hospital in Ísafjörður. A few days later, Gaddi was expelled from Núpur. Kristinn was in the hospital a whole week. He was still swollen, bruised, and wrapped in bandages when he came back. He had been knocked out and gotten a concussion. His skull was fractured. It wasn't talked about much, but everyone was thinking about it. No one knew what to say. After this incident, I often thought about how fortunate and necessary it was no one had a grudge against me. I would be kind and decent to everyone so no one would hurt me.

Kids sometimes went home on free weekends. Especially those who lived in the surrounding towns like Ísafjörður, Þingeyri, Flateyri, Súðavík, and Suðureyri. Kids who had relatives in these places often visited them on weekends. Those of us from the south generally stuck around. When they came back, they always had stories to tell because these places had shops, discos, and even movie theaters. To get weekend leave, your relative had to call the principal and tell him you could come and stay that weekend. Then your parents had to call and give permission too. If these conditions were met, you got to go. I didn't know whether I had relatives in these towns. It didn't matter because Mom would never have given me permission to go anywhere. She didn't trust me. There was no point me ringing her and trying to tell her some lie. She knew I was just trying to go on a bender. Some of the kids played the system, however, and had developed a way of cheating themselves a free weekend. They called the principal from a phone in the dormitory. First some girl called, altering her voice, and introducing herself as some old woman from Ísafjörður or Þingeyri.

"Yes, good morning. Is this Núpur at Dýrafjörður?"

"Yes, this is Ingólfur Björnsson, the schoolmaster."

"Yes, hello and good day. I'm Gudrun Ólafsdóttir from Ísafjörður. I am Egil's aunt."

"Yes, good morning."

"I'm calling to let you know that he is welcome to come and stay with us for the weekend."

"Yes. Thanks for calling."

"But of course. Goodbye."

"Yes, goodbye."

Kibba was especially sought after for such calls because she could play an old lady very convincingly. Then, some other boy or girl rang and claimed to be the mom or dad of the student who was going on weekend leave, saying that he had full permission to go. It was so well done and organized the headmaster never suspected anything. I decided to try it, but was still hesitant because I knew that the principal had so often talked to my mom and dad about me. But it couldn't hurt to try.

A weekend came around where something amazing was happening in Ísafjörður and a group of kids was planning to go. There was a famous band playing a gig at Sjallinn nightclub; it was going to be awesome fun. I had been to Ísafjörður a few times on my way to and from Núpur. Ísafjörður was like Akureyri. There was a downtown, shops, a burger place, Sjallinn, a movie theater. I asked Kibba if she was willing to play some old lady in Ísafjörður who was going to let me stay. Kibba was going herself; she was so cool and confident that she was always up for calling. I, however, had no one in mind to pretend to be my dad—except Lubbi because he was older than the others. He also had a similar voice and spoke a similarly formal language to Dad. After school, Kibba and I went to the lounge where the pay phone was. We leafed through the phone book and chose some woman who lived in town. Kibba called the principal and I held my breath.

"Good day. Sigrún Magnúsdóttir is my name and I live in Ísafjörður."

She peeked a look at the phone book.

"My house is number 6 Mánastræti."

"Yes, good day."

"I am calling because my nephew is a student of yours at Núpur, Jón Gunnar Kristinsson."

"Yes, indeed, that's correct."

"Yes, and he has asked to come and stay with me for the weekend and therefore needs weekend leave."

"Yes, exactly."

"He informed me that I would need to call and grant my permission."

"Yes, that's absolutely correct, that's the rule here at the school."

"Yes, very good. He told me to say that he has, as requested, my permission."

"Yes, thank you."

I was so excited that I shook and trembled. It seemed astronomically odd that principal Ingólfur couldn't tell what was up; I had to hold my mouth to keep from laughing out loud. I didn't want to mess with Kibba's concentration.

"Yes, that was all."

"Yes, thank you."

"Yes, and thank you and goodbye."

"Goodbye."

Kibba smiled at me and we looked into each other's eyes mischievously."

"I fucking cannot believe this!"

"No problem. He believed it entirely."

"You totally sounded like some old woman."

"I just speak the way it makes sense. It's not hard. Instead of saying 'hi' you just say 'Good day,' and, you know, speak the way only adults speak."

"You were absolutely terrific."

"Yes, nothing to it."

"Thanks!"

"No problem."

Kibba thought it was just some fun, a laugh, to trick the principal. "Dad" was up next. I knocked on Lubbi's door and asked him if he'd be up for it. Lubbi was totally in. I explained as best I could how Dad would likely speak to principal Ingólfur; I knew that we needed to think more carefully about what my dad would say than we did about some old woman in Ísafjörður. I described my father as best as I could.

"He speaks in a small voice, and very slowly."

I mimicked Dad:

"Goooood daaay. Is evvverything alriggght with the boy? Haaaas he donnne something else wrong? Weeee haaaaave connnnstant connnncerns about hhhhhim."

Lubbi mimicked me and said:

"Goooood daaay. Thhhhis is Kristinn, the faaather of Jón Guuuuunnnnnarrrr."

After school the next day Lubbi and I went to the pay phone. I had written Dad's name on paper, along with a few key words so Lubbi definitely wouldn't mess up.

"Hello, and good day, Ingólfur. Kristinn Óskarsson here, the father of Jón Gunnar."

"Yes, good day, Kristinn."

I held my breath. It had started well.

"Jón is planning to go on weekend leave and stay with his great aunt, Sigrún. She used to work with me in Bjarkarlundur."

"Yes, indeed. She rang me yesterday and told me that she was expecting him."

"Yes, she is a very good relative of ours who would like to see the boy."

"Yes, indeed."

That was it, and I gave Lubbi a sign to end the conversation. But Lubbi was having so much fun playing my father he kept talking.

"Is everything else going well, or no?" Lubbi asked, grinning.

"Yes, he has done quite well lately. He has improved his behavior since that other incident."

Lubbi smiled. I was becoming nervous and indicated he should stop.

"That's good to hear. We his parents are always very concerned about him."

I glared at Lubbi. He just grinned even more. Ingólfur answered: "That is understandable."

"He will hopefully continue on this path."

"Yes, let's hope so; if not, I will be in touch with you."

I pushed Lubbi hard and gave him a really clear and angry signal to stop.

"Yes, please do not hesitate. But the boy has, as I said, our consent."

"Thank you for ringing."

"Not a problem. I just enjoy making calls."

Ingólfur hesitated a moment. I looked questioningly at Lubbi.

"Yes, thank you for now. A very good day to you."

"Good day."

Lubbi hung up. I couldn't believe it. I was so excited that my palms were sweating. Principal Ingólfur was such an idiot that he believed Lubbi was my dad. Lubbi had gotten into the role a little too much and gone too far, but it didn't matter. I was headed for my first weekend trip. When the bus came on Friday, I'd get on it because I was going to stay with my "aunt Sigrún" on some road called Mánastræti and I had permission from my "Dad."

I didn't prepare myself especially for the trip; just took off my canvas shoes and put on military boots. Those were safer if it turned very cold. I wore torn jeans, my Sid Vicious t-shirt and pleather-leather jacket. I felt ready to take anything on and ready to deal with whatever awaited me in Ísafjörður. I had brought along markers, half a pack of cigarettes, a lighter, and a little spare change. I was looking forward to this so much, though at the same time I was also afraid something would come up. It was too good to be true. I imagined Principal Ingólfur running across the yard as I was about to step onto the bus. After school on Friday a little transit van came to pick up the kids who were headed off for the weekend. They'd packed stuff into small bags and had this and that stuff with them. I loitered around in my t-shirt and leather jacket. It had gone around the kids that Lubbi and Kibba had helped me and I hoped no one would rat me out. I was expecting that any moment my shoulder would be grabbed and a loud voice would say, "Where the hell do you think you are going, boy?!" But nothing happened. There wasn't even a teacher to monitor who was getting on board the bus. I got on undismayed and wished the bus driver a cheerful morning. No one came, the door closed, and the bus set off. I didn't breathe a sigh of relief until Núpur had vanished into the sea and we were on a route surrounded by snow. I had no idea where we were, but sometimes the bus stopped and passengers tumbled one by one out of the bus and into various cars that were waiting for them on the roadside. Then the bus went on again.

Finally, we came to Ísafjörður. The weather was calm, with cloudless skies, but cold. We stepped down from the bus and kids disappeared into the arms of those who'd come to fetch them. I was left alone. There was no one coming to pick me up. Kibba and the others had gone off by car earlier in the day. There was always some boy there to meet the girls. There was no one to meet me. I knew that there was a party in town that evening and I had a piece of paper from Kibba with the address on it. Now I just had to wait. Ísafjörður was not a big town, but it was still a town. I wandered about armed with marker pens and wrote "Runny Nose" on bus stops and in alleyways. The guys in the band would be in stitches to hear that our name now adorned nooks and crannies around Ísafjörður.

The town had one restaurant that sold hamburgers, pizza, candy, soda, and alcohol; it was called Mánabar. It also had a billiards table. I went inside, bought a coke and hung out. I looked carefully about and scanned for other punks. Who knew, maybe there were some punks in Ísafjörður? As time passed I noticed people paying attention to me, even looking right at me. I concluded that it wasn't very likely. These people seemed to have never seen a punk with their own eyes. Close to Mánabar was a shop called Hamraborg;

after hanging around for a considerable time in Mánabar, I decided to stroll over to the store and see if anything was going on. There were some teenagers, some of whom I knew from Núpur. Robbi was particularly glad to see me.

"Hi."

"Hi."

"How are you finding Ísafjörður?"

"Good."

"What have you been up to?"

"Uhhh, I was in Mánabar."

"Yeah, it's a cool place."

"Yeah, right, almost cool enough to be in Reykjavík."

"Have you managed to get any booze?"

"No."

"Okay. I got myself a bottle."

"Seriously?"

"Yes!"

"Shall we have a drink?"

"Okay."

We walked behind Hamraborg and he took a bottle out of his pocket. We both had a decent drink. The fun was about to begin! I was going to get booze. Soon the town would be full of kids with liquor bottles and I could sneak a sip here and there. I was on the way to scrounging a bender. I had no money for booze. I was cheerful and chatty thanks to my sips of liquor. I chatted with all the kids and had the courage to ask the sales clerk if there were any punks in Ísafjörður.

"Punks? What's that?"

"Kids who listen to punk music—especially Crass."

She burst out laughing.

"I don't know!"

She was probably just a country girl who didn't have a clue what punk was. Country girls like that read magazines such as *The Time* and *Youth*, and books by Jón Trausti and Guðrún from Lund. I hung out with the Núpur crowd in Hamraborg until we'd had enough and wandered back over to Mánabar. Along the way, we slipped into an alley to have a drink. That's how the day passed. We hung about inside then slipped out for a drink. After the trips out and the drinking had gotten more frequent, I began to more strongly feel the influence of the alcohol. It not only made me cheerful, carefree, and relaxed, but also warded off the cold and warmed my body. I was no longer chilly. Booze not only warmed my body but my soul, too. Everything was brighter and better. Ísafjörður was a great place! Fascinating kids and shops and Mánabar. And not that cold, after all.

Sjallinn opened at eight p.m. There was a dance night. There was supposed to be a concert where some band was going to play up a storm. Probably just some country-dancing rubbish, but still worth going to and a chance to bum some liquor. So later that evening I went to queue up at Sjallinn. I was getting quite drunk. I was fourteen years old, so I had never been to a nightclub. I'd seen these places from afar when I hung out at Hallærisplan and downtown, but absolutely knew I'd never get admitted. But perhaps it wasn't so strict in Ísafjörður. Perhaps they were all dumbasses and wouldn't know how old I was, or else thought it was cool to let in punks from Reykjavík. The line was full of men in suits with liquor bottles.

The bottles passed among them in line and they gave each other drinks. I muscled in among them and looked longingly at a liquor bottle. To my astonishment, a guy extended me a bottle. I grabbed it, took a gulp of a sip, and gave him back the bottle. Maybe they weren't all men. Perhaps they were just kids who looked like men because they were in suits. I felt so good I decided to sing.

"Do they owe us a living? Of course they do, of course they do. Owe us a living? OF COURSE THEY FUCKING DO."

I even thought that maybe someone would recognize the song and ask over the din:

"Hey, Crass! Who was singing Crass?"

"Do they owe us a living? Of course they do, of course they do. Owe us a living? OF COURSE THEY FUCKING DO."

"Shut up!"

I didn't see who spoke, but it was definitely some disco freak who hated Crass.

"Shut up yourself, disco shit!"

I was so happy that I laughed out loud.

"Death before disco!" I shouted loudly. Suddenly I got a blow to the head and fell back. What had happened? My jaw ached. I had been punched on the mouth. I didn't see who had hit me. But this was no problem. I shook it off, scrambled to my feet, and tried to squeeze back into the line. I cast my eyes around and tried to work out who had punched me. Why I had been punched? Because I'd been singing Crass? I saw a liquor bottle floating in the air and my worries vanished like dew in the morning sun. I asked the guy with the liquor bottle if I could have a swig. He stared me down and I recognized immediately the animosity in his gaze.

"Are you a punk?"

"Yes."

"What do you think you doing here?"

"What, I'm not allowed be here?"

"No, you shouldn't be here. Punk idiots are banned! Didn't you know?"

Someone laughed.

"No, no one told me."

"Fuck off!"

"No, I'm allowed to stay. I have the same right as you."

"You have no fucking right!"

More guys from the line now turned their attention to me.

"Don't you understand Icelandic? You don't speak Icelandic down south?"

I could tell there was something uncomfortable in the offing and suddenly became afraid. They were all older, bigger, and stronger than me. And I was obviously not welcome.

"Are you cruising for a bruising?!"

"No."

"Do you want to get kicked in?!"

"No."

"What are you doing hanging out here and stealing drinks, punk idiot? Want one in the kisser?!"

"No."

I tried to shake off my intoxication. Suddenly I was punched again on the mouth, and I jumped back. The men laughed. I didn't know what to do so I sidled away. I wanted to try to get into the club, but I did not want to let them beat me up.

Suddenly one man jumped over to me and pushed me, hard, so I fell back into the street. A car braked sharply and honked.

I was clearly not getting into Sjallinn. As much as I wanted to, I wasn't going to let them beat me. These men were clearly not going to just talk or just shove me. They were prepared to beat the shit out of me. I went back to Mánabar, bought a coke, and hung out by the window. People came and went. Some folk were sitting at tables drinking alcohol. When they stood up and went off, sometimes they left something in the bottle. In a flash I was quick to switch my glass and theirs without anyone noticing. Brennivín for coke. I finished the glass and switched back glasses. I played this game again and again, until I was caught and someone called:

"What! Were you drinking from my glass, kid?!"

I seemed totally at a loss, lifted my glass and said:

"I've just got a coke…"

They guy looked angrily at me:

"Did you drink from my glass?"

"Uhh, no. I don't drink, I'm only fourteen years old."

I moved to the other end of the bar. I continued to play the same game, but was careful now to make sure that people had definitely left. Before I knew it, I was getting shit-faced and staggering. Things spun around in front of my eyes. I got up and was going to go to the bathroom, but I stumbled and fell onto some people sitting at a table. There was a commotion and they pushed me away. I mumbled something and someone shouted. My hand was firmly seized, the door opened, I was thrown out and it closed behind me.

It was getting late into the evening and Hamraborg had closed.

I didn't have a watch, but I guessed it was gone twelve. Now it was time for a plan. I couldn't go to Sjallinn nor to Mánabar. But where was the party? I couldn't find the piece of paper with the address on but thought that if I just walked around I would probably hear the sound. Ísafjörður was not a big town. I decided to just wander aimlessly around the place. I was drunk. With every step I mis-stepped and fell. The streets were covered in snow and I did not know what was sidewalk and what was road. Suddenly I was grabbed firmly by my shoulder. I looked behind. Had those older guys come to beat me up? It was a police officer. Where had he come from? The policeman dragged me through a door. Suddenly we were inside a police station. It reminded me of the police station in the Toll House back home. That's where the police often took me when they picked me up downtown. There was a large room with benches and a counter.

"He was wandering about out here, this one. Dead drunk," said the officer to another man who was sitting at the counter.

"Name?!"

"Jón…"

Now it was time for a plan. They would certainly call Mom and Dad. I tried to carry myself manfully and did my best to conceal how drunk I was.

"And what's your name other than Jón?"

"Jón Gunnar Kristinsson."

The police wrote down the name.

"Where are you from?"

"I'm from Reykjavík."

"And what are you doing here in Ísafjörður?"

I decided to use the ruse of Aunt Sigrún.

"I'm here to visit my aunt."

"Well, what's her name?"

"Sigrún Magnúsdóttir."

I hoped it wasn't his wife or sister. I even had the address, so I added that.

"And you're staying with her?"

"Yes."

He looked at the policeman who was standing next to me.

"Just put him in the cell."

The policeman grabbed my shoulder again and led me to the jail cell and shut the door behind me. I had been in a prison cell before. In Reykjavík, they were concrete, painted green, and had a bench. This was different. It was made of wood and there was also a window. I wondered if I should try to climb up and out the window. But I didn't dare. I just hung about inside the cell and waited for something to happen. After an hour or two it was suddenly opened and the policeman stood in the doorway.

"Get out."

I followed him. What now? Had something come up? Had they rung Núpur? All of a sudden three cops rushed passed with an evidently mad guy between them. The man fought tooth and nail and the cops were clearly having difficulty attempting to restrain him. The policeman accompanying me joined his fellows trying to subdue the guy. There was screaming and panic. They threw the man into the prison cell I had just been in and slammed it locked. The man raised hell inside, kicking and banging the door.

"Let me out! Let me out you bastards! Let me out!"

The cops walked away and I realized no one was paying attention to me. I snuck out and went back to the street. I was going to find the party. It had started to snow. I was freezing and I was getting cold to the bone. The alcohol was beginning to lose its magical powers. I was beginning to sober up and feel the soreness in my jaw and how bad my body hurt. I felt like a bus had run over me. I went to a garage, grabbed the handle, and opened the garage door partway, slipped under, and closed it behind me. It was warm and cozy inside the garage. It was full of cardboard boxes, bric-a-brac, and camping stuff. I found a rolled-up camping mat and a sleeping bag. I spread the blanket on the floor, crawled into the sleeping bag and slept deeply.

I started the following day by going to Hamraborg to get myself something to eat. I bought a Mars bar and some chocolate milk and hung out there until Mánabar opened at noon. As the day went on, kids dropped by. We talked about what our yesterdays had brought. Everyone seemed to have enjoyed themselves quite a bit more than I had. My story was the most interesting, though. A fight outside Sjallinn, getting detained by the police, overnight accommodation in a garage. There was another party that evening. Some girl was home alone while her parents were abroad. She had turned the house into a temporary nightclub with total party gear; some kids had been at her house the night before. According to the stories, this house was sheer heaven. Booze flowed freely everywhere and people got up to all kinds of things. It sounded like an oasis in the freezing, snow-packed wilderness. Like the day before, I had no alcohol and stole sips from those who had some and so was no more than tipsy. I told stories about my adventures from the night and got sips as payment. The day passed in Mánabar where I smoked, drank chocolate milk, and got some more sips of booze. Everyone was waiting for the night.

When night fell, it was time for the party. It was important you had a condom. Some girls were absolutely certain to sleep with you if only you had a condom. Most boys showed the foresight to have a condom in their wallet or back pocket. I didn't. You could only get them in drugstores and I couldn't for the life of me imagine walking into a drugstore and asking for a condom. I'd once been walking with my friend in Reykjavík when he said he needed to go the East Town Drugstore on Réttarholtsvegur. I innocently walked there with him; he went directly to the counter and said loudly and clearly:

"I'd like a pack of Durex condoms."

I was so shocked I jerked back. I hadn't expected that! I wouldn't have been more astonished if I'd been slapped with a wet rag. I wanted to disappear into the ground. I turned my face down towards the counter and pretended to be deeply absorbed looking at lipsticks. My friend made his purchase, and we didn't talk about it anymore. If I acted like this happened all the time, he might get the idea I did it regularly myself. I admired him, however, for daring to do it. I didn't even dare say the word "condom" aloud, let alone talk about it with someone. I couldn't imagine asking the boys from Núpur who were hanging out at Mánabar with me whether they were willing to lend me a condom. But I really wanted to have one. I was, however, completely certain that if the opportunity arose then I wouldn't know how to use it and wouldn't dare to, or be able to, cuddle up with a girl. But it's all right to let yourself dream.

A party is always an uncertain journey. You never know what's going to happen. You only know it will be fun. When evening came, we set off to paradise. The party was in Hnífsdalur. I gathered that this was a suburb of Ísafjörður, but it felt like a really odd name for a suburb: "Valley of the Knives." Perhaps it wasn't any weirder than my suburb back home, Fossvogur. We set off for paradise. It was a hell of a long walk. We seemed to walk out of town and then there was nothing and we were walking out into the wilderness. It was a stretch to call Hnífsdalur a suburb. When we finally found the neighborhood, we couldn't find the house. We walked up and down through Hnífsdalur. Someone reckoned it was the last house in one of the cul-de-sacs so we walked there. The house wasn't there. Someone had misunderstood or miscalculated and we went somewhere else. The house wasn't there. And so we promenaded through Hnífsdalur, inside and out.

Belatedly, we finally arrived at the right house. It wasn't exactly paradise. It was a ranch high up on the mountain. Everything inside had been completely destroyed. Chairs lay on their sides, there were broken bookshelves, and broken glass and shattered picture frames lay on the floor. Bottles of booze, glasses, and other garbage were strewn around the house. Among it all lay drunk or alcohol-dazed youths like driftwood discarded here and there. The house smelled of smoke, like porridge had burned in the pan or on a blanket been set on fire. Through the burning smell you could still clearly make out the smell of puke. I immediately went to look for booze. There was no wine cellar and no room bursting with liquor, as someone had said. I found some worthwhile scraps here and there. I took some sips from some of them then grabbed a half-empty bottle from a boy who was asleep in the hallway. While I was on my scrap hunt, I saw that the kids had managed to lug some guy up onto a chair in the living room. They weren't seating him in a chair, but placing him over the back so his ass faced up in the air. When they were done placing him over this saddle, they pulled his pants down so his bare butt was exposed. Then they drew a face on his butt with lipstick. This attracted a lot of laughter and merriment. Someone took a burning cigarette and positioned it between the ass cheeks. That got even more approval. This was sick funny. A smoking ass-hole. Someone brought a camera and took pictures of everything.

"Kodak moment!"

Apart from this lone smoking asshole, the party was pretty miserable. There were a small number of girls, and a ton of guys. This house was not the paradise we had been promised. If it was right that the mom and dad were abroad and the girl alone at home, she'd totally managed to destroy the house. It would be impossible for her parents to come home to. I didn't feel like being there any longer and decided to go and try to find another party. I had gotten pretty drunk on scraps and was ready to embrace a spirit of adventure.

"Do you know of any other parties?" I asked one boy.

"There are lots of parties in Ísafjörður."

"Aren't we in Ísafjörður?"

"Are you from Reykjavík?"

"Yes, and?"

He grinned.

"No, we are in Hnífsdalur."

"Hnífsdalur? Isn't it the same? Isn't this Ísafjörður?" I asked, pointing out to the fjord. The boy giggled.

"No, this is Deep Ísafjörður.

"Isn't that still Ísafjörður?"

"No, not really, Ísafjörður is more on Skutulsfjörður."

"Where's that?"

"Look, the town of Ísafjörður is on Skutulsfjörður."

"But where is the Ísa fjord itself?"

"There is no Ísa fjord."

It was too complicated. I didn't feel like talking to him any longer.

I told the Núpurs I was going to walk to downtown. They had all made themselves comfortable in the room and couldn't be bothered to come with me, so I just took off alone. I thought that if I just walked around, maybe some horny lady would run over and ask me to come home with her. Maybe I would also find a party where there would be plenty to drink and possibly some more girls.

It was late at night and definitely close to three or four. Everything seemed dead and silent. Hardly anyone was about, just the occasional car in the distance. There was no proper street lighting and everything was in semi-twilight. If any nymphomaniac wives were inside the houses, they would definitely have a lot of trouble spotting me in the dark. It was a hopeless hell.

I heard faint sounds of music in the distance and walked towards the sound. Little by little I drifted away from the buildings and before I knew it I was down by the sea. I was a long way from town and could only see lights in the distance. The house

JÓN GNARR

from which the music was coming stood alone and abandoned somewhere out in the countryside. It was coal-black dark and I was drunk enough to be both slurring and sick. I felt my way towards the house. Suddenly I fell down. I managed to touch the house before I fell down. I got a blow to my face and felt pain in my hand. I lay on the gravel. I felt around me and realized that I had fallen into a ditch that had been dug around the house. I felt the taste of blood in my mouth but did not know where it came from. I had either scraped my face or split my lip. Maybe both. I crawled out of the ditch. It was like a fortress moat around a castle. But somewhere there had to be a bridge into this party castle. The music resounded. Icelandic country ball music. I fell back again and down into the moat. I couldn't move. I was exhausted. Inside the castle, Þorgeir Ástvaldsson was playing a concert. "Summer Fun" or some other sort of rubbish.

The lights on the shore shine bright
the ship moves closer still to light
this sea voyage ends tonight
I'm done with drudge and toil,
a deck to clean and my bag to haul.
Torn I stand on the prow right here
As soon as the land is coming near
I get my things and go from here.
I go on holiday.
I go on holiday.
I go on holiday.
And what I want for is nothing more.

165

When I woke up I was lying in bed in some apartment. I was beaten-up and hungover. I felt nauseous, I had a headache, and my body was sore everywhere. Terror seized me. What had happened? I was hazy about the evening. I remembered leaving the party, but little after that. How did I get here and end up in this bed? I vaguely recalled going to a concert by Þorgeir Ástvaldsson somewhere out in the middle of nowhere. But it had been cold and coal-black dark. I looked at my hands and saw that they were all scraped and scratched. My face was sore, my headache was intensifying and my heart was beating in my chest because of the hangover, but also because of my fear. I scrambled to my feet and looked for my clothes but couldn't find them. I opened the door to the room and looked out. It seemed to be an ordinary home. Certainly not a farm. I called out:

"Hello? Hello?"

Suddenly Aunt Helga came round the corner. Helga had sometimes looked after me when I was little. Had I returned to Reykjavík? She looked like thunder and stared angrily at me.

"What are you doing in Ísafjörður?!"

"Errr, errr just… well… I'm here for the weekend."

"Do your parents know you're here?"

"Uh, yes, they totally know," I said as convincingly as I could. I did not want her to go and call them. "Why are you in Ísafjörður?" I asked her.

"I live here, Jón."

"Are we in Ísafjörður?"

"Are you still drunk?"

"No!"

I wasn't drunk. I was just deathly ill.

"It was sheer luck those people found you! And you were so drunk you didn't recognize me."

"Yes," I said, and agreed with her, as if knew that very well. I was afraid to admit to her that I couldn't remember anything and nodded as convincingly as I could and agreed that it had been a stroke of great fortune that we had come across each other. I had no memory of the people. How did they find Aunt Helga? As much as I wanted to know, I dare not ask and acted as if I recalled the whole thing. She was silent and looked angrily at me. I smiled back, encouragingly.

"Yes, thanks for allowing me to stay."

She didn't answer, looked at me, and shook her head.

"Where is the bathroom?"

She pointed to the door. I went into the bathroom and locked it. I opened the toilet and fell to my knees in front of it and vomited. Spurts of puke shot out of me. I went to the sink, got some water and vomited some more. I went back out and went into the kitchen where Helga sat at the kitchen table.

"Where are my clothes?"

She pointed to a table where the clothes lay folded.

"I washed them. They were an absolute abomination!"

"Yes, thanks for that."

"Did you come all the way here alone?"

"Uh, no… we were just on a class… a crowd of us from class… we're on weekend leave, you see."

"Indeed. Would you like something to eat?"

"Er, yes, please."

She stood up, fetched some bread and cold cuts, cereal and milk. I got dressed and dived in to eating. It was the first meal I had eaten in days.

"Are you going to call your Mom or do you want me to?"

Good God. I couldn't imagine talking to Mom.

"Uhhh, just call her. She knows I'm here."

I was afraid to talk to my mom. I knew for sure that she would figure it all out and start screaming at me. I would have to recover before I spoke to her.

My aunt was silent and looked angrily at me while I ate.

"Do you know what time it is?" I asked innocently.

"Nearly two."

"Yes, okay," I responded as though that meant something to me. She lifted her eyebrows questioningly.

"I need to go to Mánabar and meet the other kids, you see…"

I sucked loudly up my nose.

"We are going to take the bus together."

"When is the bus?"

"Err, I think at six."

"What possessed you to do this? You could have died from exposure!"

"Yes, I know. I was just going to a concert…"

A concert? You were in the industrial area. There are no concerts there."

"No, I got lost somehow… I've never been to Ísafjörður before really."

"You were in Hnífsdalur!"

"Yes, I know…," I replied, nodding as though I was fully aware of the fact.

"You were nothing but dead-drunk!"

"Yes... I had been to another party and some kids there had some liquor, so... they were giving it to everyone."

She shook her head.

"A fourteen-year-old drunk in the middle of the wilderness. You could have died! Do you realize that?"

"Yes."

I had no idea what she was talking about. My head was exploding and I remembered only a fraction of what had happened. I looked out the window and saw that we were in an apartment block. It was some distance from the town, which I could see out the window. I looked at the place and wondered how I would get there.

"Here... are there any buses here or anything?"

"I need to go to work and I'll drive you downtown on the way."

"Yeah, excellent!"

I didn't know my aunt well. I knew that she had sometimes looked after me when I was little and I had met her a few times at family events. I didn't know how she was related to me exactly. I never knew how anyone was related to me. Sometimes strangers greeted me and asked me if I didn't recognize them. I never knew.

"I'm your cousin!"

"Yes, of course!" I replied, always pretending to fully recognize the person.

We got in the car. Helga drove me Mánabar where I had told her all the kids were going to meet. I thanked her and she drove away.

Mánabar was closed. I walked over to Hamraborg to see if I

could find anyone there. Several teenagers were inside, but none from Núpur. I did not have my cigarettes on me. I hadn't dared to ask my aunt for them.

"Uhh, can you lend me a cigarette?"

The kids looked at me without answering. I had noticed that kids in Ísafjörður looked strangely at me. I was a punk, I was different. But now it was as if something else was going on. They looked at me differently, whispered and muttered. There was clearly something going on. I paused while I tried to find out what was happening. It was no longer just curiosity in their eyes; now I sensed anger. I had become very good at sensing when I posed a danger to people and when it would be good to disappear before someone attacked me. Could it be that I had done something I couldn't remember? What had really happened yesterday? What had I done? Suddenly one kid from the group came up to me and said:

"Are you insane?!"

"Uhh, nah… why?"

"You destroyed my friend's house!" said one girl loudly.

"Err, I? Uh, no, I didn't!" I said, and shook my head.

"Well, it was full of people who saw you do it!"

Had I destroyed a house? I had really ruined a house? I didn't remember though it wasn't like me. I went through what little I remembered from the night before. I didn't recall having ruined anything. The house had been destroyed when we got there. But I didn't do it! I was just looking for booze and had no interest in destroying anything at all. I didn't do anything. I didn't even paint anything on that kid's butt. But I had laughed a lot at it.

"You should just get going or you'll get a beating!"

"Yes, but I didn't do anything!" I replied, desperate. The boy rolled his eyes and turned away. "You'll get a beating" resounded in my head.

"Well, there's a whole group of boys looking for you and they'll all beat you up!" said a girl.

I was terrified. My god! I was scared of nothing more than getting beaten up. What should I do? Where could I go? Where were my friends? I was like a wingless goose. If some kids were looking for me, they would surely sooner or later come to Hamraborg. I had to hide. I hurried out, leaving Hamraborg behind, heading in the direction of the pier and watching carefully all around me. I slipped past houses and snuck about and checked round corners. Suddenly someone shouted:

"There he is! There he is!"

I heard the sound of a motorcycle and ran away into the blue beyond. Ran as fast as my feet would go between the houses, jumping over fences and gardens, and threw myself down behind some cars. I heard the shouts and cries of kids who were obviously looking for me.

"He ran that way!" called some girl. The motorcycle approached and I buried myself into pieces of trash and wood lying next to the cars. I lay perfectly still and the motorcycle and kids went away. There was silence around me. I thought that I really ought to talk to someone, to connect with the others. I snuck up and ran as fast as I could to Mánabar. It had opened and I ran straight in. To my relief there were some guys from Núpur sitting together at a table. The kids sprang to their feet. They were clearly terrified too.

"Do you know what's going on, Jónsi?"

"No, but there were some kids saying they were going to beat me up."

"That they'll beat us all up. They blame everyone from Núpur for ruining the house!"

"Yes, but we didn't. It was already trashed when we arrived."

"Yeah, but they're blaming us anyway."

We were all scared. A few of our group were missing and we wondered whether they were being beaten up. It was horrible. We sat there and waited for whatever would happen next. It was not long until the group found us. The group consisted not only of teenagers, but also adults, men, similar to those that had repeatedly hit me in the nightclub line. This was a large group, ten to fifteen men and two boys on motorcycles.

This was definitely an Ísafjörður gang. They set themselves up in front of Mánabar. The gangly ringleader came to the door and looked in at us.

"Come out and talk."

"No, we're just sitting here."

"Scared to talk to us?"

"We didn't do anything!"

"Fucking drag yourself out, you pieces of shit!"

We didn't stir. I was so scared I wanted to cry. I had a headache and I felt sick. I was going to have to call my mom and now I was going to be beaten up, too. Everything awful that could happen in life was happening at the same time. I turned to the person working there who was watching curiously.

"They're accusing us of damaging a girl's house but we didn't."

He went out and spoke to the crowd.

"There won't be any fighting here!" he called in a loud voice and commanding tone.

"Just send them out, Gaui!!"

"Go away or I'll call the cops."

"They totally trashed a house. They're vandals. Vandals from Reykjavík who trash houses!"

"They're just some poor kids. Leave them alone."

We held our breath and watched out the window. I wasn't going to go out there and let them beat me up. I looked around me and skimmed my eyes over the range and other fixtures to see if there was anything I might grab onto if the group pushed its way inside. I wasn't going to let myself be pulled out. The man came back in.

"You are some odd birds."

The group outside had started to dissolve. A few kids came up to the window and smeared their faces frightfully against the glass. They spat on the glass and gave us the finger. I wanted to give them the finger back but daren't; I tried to look elsewhere.

Then something unthinkable and magnificent happened. The principal of Núpur himself came into Mánabar. I had never been glad to see him before. He slammed the door behind him and looked at us.

"What the hell is going on here?!"

"Uhh, nothing. We were just waiting for the bus. And these guys were bugging us."

"They were spitting at the window," I added.

"Is this true what I hear you've been up to?"

"No, it's a total lie. We didn't trash that house."

The principal borrowed the bar phone and made a call.

He spoke to someone on the other end and had a questioning expression when he came back.

"Núpur is cut off. They won't have it cleared until the morning."

I thought with horror about having to stay a minute longer in Ísafjörður. We would sooner or later have to leave Mánabar and then we would be beaten up by a mob for sure.

"And what should we do until then?"

"There will be a plan. You all wait here."

He went out. After an hour, a snow truck drove up and parked outside Mánabar. A teacher stepped out of the cab, exchanged some words with the kids outside, and came in. He opened the door and told us to leave.

"Come on."

We scrambled to our feet, walked hesitantly out to the snow truck. The kids stood around watching us with hateful eyes and clenched their fists or gave us the finger. Some tried to spit on us.

"Vandals! Bloody Reykjavík rabble! You'll be beaten up, you punk shits!" someone shouted. "You'll all get beaten up!"

We were, however, totally innocent and hadn't done anything. Later, we learned the whole thing had been blamed on us. Someone had gone berserk in the house and claimed it was us.

I didn't know how it would go with my mother, but perhaps she would call. And maybe I would be told off. But it was okay because at least I wouldn't be beaten up. Not this time. The snow truck made its way across the mountain and wilderness like an Arctic tank. Suddenly Núpur was right ahead and I all at once I found it beautiful to look at. I knew every corner and all my friends were there. And I was filled with joy and anticipation.

My heart grew warm and I looked forward to being back at Núpur. It was my home, my family. I wasn't ever going on any damn weekend leave again and I would never go back to shitty Ísafjörður.

All humans are the same. Humans are like sheep. No sheep is entirely the same as any other sheep. No sheep is any better or more interesting than any other sheep. But, still, each one is a unique part of the whole. To live and to exist is an experience, from the time you're born until the time you die. Everyone experiences similar things, but they are so complex that no one is exactly the same as someone else. But we are all similar. It doesn't matter what language we speak, what country we're from, whether we are have light or dark skin, are men or women. I often sat in the Smoker and wondered at the other kids. I sometimes imagined myself being someone else. I imagined myself as Sprelli. How I would feel and what I would think. I also wondered what it would be like to be a girl.

There's no need to trample over other people, and no need to force others to do things they don't want to. And so you should never use violence. You should never hit anyone, not even if the person specifically asks for it. But violence is not just physical. You can hit people without ever lifting a finger. I thought about how my Dad would come over and talk to me. Sometimes, I felt really very queasy after talking to him. Dad never hit me, but it felt like he had. Like I'd been harmed and humiliated. He forced me to listen to him. Maybe he thought he was a remarkable person who really mattered and that I was an unexceptional person who was less important. But nothing gives you the right to be disrespectful to others. And nothing gives you permission to exploit others. So says the *Tao Te Ching*, and Crass said so too. And that's not because it's a rule some God made, but because it makes perfect sense. And if everyone understood that, there would be far fewer problems in the world. Most problems are caused by the fact that people think they're more important and better than others and reckon they have the right to manipulate others. If someone is kind to a person, he must be kind in return. If someone is an annoying person, you don't have to be annoying back. Instead, just stop talking to him.

I know how it feels to have a mean nickname and I know how it feels to be looked at with contempt. I know, too, what it's like to force yourself to listen to something you don't want to hear. Like when I'm forced to learn something I don't want to learn in school, or when Dad holds me fast and waffles on. It hurts and wounds and makes me feel bad. I won't cause someone else to feel like that. And people feel bad enough about all kinds of things already. Life is full of various kinds of unpleasantness and it can be an utter shit-fest. People are much better off supporting each other than pulling each other down. And I don't want to be a person who drags others down. I want to be a team-builder, helping people and urging them on. People are basically just imitations of each other, like branches on a tree. A white guy in Iceland and a black guy in Africa have more in common than not. Like Icelandic and African dogs. No one would think there was any difference between these fabulous animals. They may not be identical, but they're basically similar. Both are, at heart, dogs.

What you do in life and how you treat others gives rise to the reputation that shapes you. I had read the ancient poem "Hávamál" in school and learned the opening lines by heart.

Cattle die,
kin die,
the self itself dies;
but fame
never dies
when one does good.

You're always creating your reputation and it's linked to your name. I want to shape a good reputation for myself. I want to try to understand others and think beautifully about them so that they will do the same for me. What's more, you're judged by your reputation. If everyone has heard you're an idiot, they judge you as being one before they meet you. And if you're not an idiot, you constantly need to prove you aren't. A reputation is something valuable and you yourself create and shape it. To be kind and decent to others is not just cute and nice. It is, simply, right. You get more out of life this way. Taking advantage of others is like stealing. Abusing others is like being a slob. It's not good manners.

And girls are people. They have pussies, yes, and breasts. And although I notice that intensely when I look at them, I can imagine they don't think the same way. Deep inside girls are the same parts, more or less, as inside me. They're humans; they think and feel. You cannot be nice to some people and hate others. That's a misunderstanding of how all this works.

You can't divide people into categories without there being unpleasant consequences. People are different and have varying abilities. And I think everyone feels bad at some time, whether they're a boy at Núpur, a woman in Germany, or a man in Brazil: we all feel pretty much the same.

You can't do whatever you want; you have to accept that. Sometimes you get to choose. Like when people are going steady. You stop thinking about everyone else, and just think about yourselves instead. I want people to be interesting and not dead dull. I want people to show me respect and understanding because I'm not like most people. That's what most people want. And no one is like most people. People need to learn this, just as they learn manners.

Sometimes people give you something, not because they care about you or want to please you, but perhaps because they're afraid or trying to buy friendship. Like Sprelli. He buys friendship with weed. I sometimes get weed off him, but that's different because I care about Sprelli. I feel sorry for him. I'm not manipulating him. We're friends.

I was glad not to have taken part in fucking Lena a happy birthday. And I imagined that in the future when people talked about it, it might not be as fun as it first seemed. I didn't understand that exactly, but I felt it somehow. It was like going into some room and eating all the sweets in front of you without being sure everything was okay. Maybe Lena will regret this in the future. Maybe she'll become a murderer. Maybe she'll make a list of all the guys who fucked her a happy birthday and kill them all. Poison them. They'd all get sick and die, one after the other, and no one would know why. I'd like not to be on that list.

Maybe I think this way because I'm an anarchist. In anarchism, you can do what you want as long as it doesn't detract from others. You allow others to do what they want as long as it doesn't detract from you. This means that you also recognize and accept that you don't own other people. Parents don't own their children. A man doesn't own his wife. People simply work together and help each other. Diplomacy and unions are just types of cooperation. There's no chance of cooperation, however, if someone thinks he rules over everyone else.

I thought about all this when I was at Rétto and boys were teasing me.

"Are you a punk?"

"Yes."

"Can I spit on you?"

"Nooooo."

"What! Aren't you a punk? Or just a pseudo punk?"

"Nooooooo."

"If you're a real punk, you can be spat on!"

"Uhhhh…"

It wasn't always easy to understand or explain anarchism. Especially not if people were hassling you and trying to spit on you. Sometimes other kids came and tried to intervene.

"Oh, leave him alone."

Often, the answer went:

"What? He wants it. He wants to be spit on, he's a punk."

Did I want that? Maybe they really thought they could spit on punks. But if they wanted to spit on me and really thought they could spit on punks and it'd be fun, like Lena found it fun to be fucked happy birthday, they would have been polite and asked me:

"Hi there, good day, Jón."

"Hi, good to see you, friends."

"We really want to spit on someone."

"I see."

"We're always thinking and talking about it. We often spit in the sink at home, but we really want to spit on someone."

"You do?"

"And we were thinking, since you're a punk, couldn't we spit on you?"

"No, guys. You may not."

"But spitting on punks, any punk, is okay, isn't it?"

"No, guys. It's just an excuse used by people who want to spit on other people."

Often when other kids were bothering me, I didn't know how to respond. Sometimes I looked angrily at them, but that just incited them. Usually I looked at the floor and stayed silent, though sometimes I smiled and tried to hold myself together. It didn't matter because they weren't really thinking about me. They were using me to suit themselves. Maybe Lena felt the same on her birthday. Maybe she didn't know what to say and just tried to smile and hold herself together and pretend there wasn't a problem.

People react differently to things—take Biggi, for example. When boys invaded his room, messed about with him, and threw the contents of his closet on the floor, Biggi often smiled. It was not because he enjoyed having these kids in his room humiliating him and trashing things, but because he was nervous and didn't know what to do. Sometimes people smile because they're nervous and scared.

Perhaps, too, they hope people will stop messing with them. Biggi often asked the boys to leave his stuff alone. But as soon as he said that, he could be quite certain that more attention would be placed on destroying certain things. So people often act like they don't care about things that are actually tremendously important. Sometimes a person acts that way about themselves.

People who victimize others never admit they're villains. They always claim that others enjoy the treatment. Kids have often asked me if I wanted to get beat up.

"Are you asking to be thumped?"

If it was something I wanted, that was their excuse to hit me. But no one wants to be hit.

I remember all the guys who spat at me. I remember every sputum, their expressions, and what they said. I don't want anyone to have memories like me. They definitely came back to haunt me later. I don't fully know where I learned to think like that, maybe from experience. I learned some stuff from my mother, some from the *Tao Te Ching*, and other stuff from Crass. But perhaps I just knew this deep inside, but didn't always know it, so I needed an explanation or reminder from outside myself. It benefits others if I don't fight and steal. People can be relaxed around me. And if I show everyone consideration, attention, and respect, then I'll most likely get the same treatment. So in some mysterious way, by being decent and kind to others, a person is to themselves.

The *Tao Te Ching* also says:

"I repay good with good; evil I repay with good, too. This fosters goodness. I make trust meet trust, and faced with mistrust, I trust. That fosters trust."

Crass say the same thing in many places in their lyrics, which I've memorized. In the song "Big A, Little A," they sing:

> Be exactly who you want to be, do what you want to do
> I am he and she is she but you're the only you
> No one else has got your eyes, can see the things you see
> It's up to you to change your life and my life's up to me
> The problems that you are suffer from are problems that
>   you can make
> The shit we have to climb through is the shit we choose
>   to take
> If you don't like the life you live, change it now it's yours

I am the only Jónsi Punk in the world. There are many people like me, but no one exactly me. Biggi is the only Biggi in the world and Lena the only Lena. And that's why we're all unique, valuable, and interesting. We mostly want the same things, enjoy the same things and are, in principle, agreed on what's good and what is bad. Most people enjoy music, though not everyone likes the same music. Some listen to disco and others listen to punk. Some like to listen to guitar solos, while others like to listen to lyrics.

Respect and consideration are necessary. Anarchists have morals. Many people think that anarchists are against the rules and respect nothing. I'd read so much about anarchism that I knew that wasn't quite right. An anarchist is a person who is free but responsible. Being accountable and responsible for yourself and not harming others with your behavior proves you don't need rules. The *Tao Te Ching* discusses that a lot: "The more laws there are, the poorer people will be." Rules are established because people aren't responsible and honest. If everyone was kind and good, conscientious and responsible, we'd have no rules. They'd be totally unnecessary. You don't have rules or laws about things that are natural and normal. There's no law about how to walk. No specific Walking Regulations:

"When you walk, you're required to put one foot forward and place the weight of your body on that foot. Once your body weight is on that leg you are to move the other foot forward, a decent way past the first leg, but so that you can still balance. Those who fail to do this must pay a fine and may face prison."

Such rules would be silly and unnecessary. And so should it be with all human relations. Peace, respect, and consideration should be as natural as walking; something we do instinctively and without thinking much about it. But that's not how it is, and that's why we have rules and laws. Human relations are also much more complex than walking. And sometimes there are situations where a person lets himself down. You get angry or act rashly or even go on a bender. Laws and regulations are crutches; we must not become dependent on them. We should always aim to learn to walk unsupported, by ourselves. That's way I found Crass much more interesting than God. God is like a crutch. The Bible is full of rules and commandments that forbid most things and allow others. And the reason is always that God decided it. And there's nothing to explain to us why we're to do this or that. It's just "the will of God." I hate that adults make you do things without explaining why you should.

"Why should I do that?"

"Because I tell you to do it, child!"

God was like an adult, to my mind. The Bible says it's forbidden to kill. But you're not told why. The Bible also says that if you think something, it's as bad as doing it. Jesus said so. I had often dreamed of killing someone. I had many times thought about how I wanted to kill the Morons at Rétto. I had also often said so out loud.

"Damn, how much I want to kill that idiot!"

But I would never do it. I would never kill anyone. But not because the Bible forbid it or because I'd go to jail. I was under-age and wouldn't actually go to jail. But I wouldn't do it because it didn't solve a problem. It only created more problems. I didn't want anyone to kill me. I didn't want to be on Lena's list. And if you're a murderer, that's your reputation. I wanted to be Jónsi Punk and not Jónsi Killer. If it was considered all right for everyone to simply kill other people, then surely you'd always be terrified you were going to be killed. Fortunately, it's very rare that someone is killed, and when it happens it's not because someone had forgotten to read the Bible or the section where it states you're forbidden to kill. It happens because someone loses control. Crass explained that to me. They say that violence never solves anything. The *Tao Te Ching* says it too. And I agree.

I had not been at Núpur long when I was expelled from school for the first time. The reason for my expulsion was misconduct in class, rudeness, and bad behavior towards teachers. As a result, I was temporarily removed from school. I was summoned to the principal's office.

"You were thrown out of class yesterday."

"Er, yes."

I knew for sure that I had been messing with the teacher's words and talking and not listening to his instructions; he finally gave up on me and kicked me out. I didn't think it was an issue, just more fun because I could go to the Smoker and smoke. I enjoyed being alone in the Smoker sometimes, having a leisurely cigarette, thinking things through, and waiting for the next class to begin.

"It has also come to our attention that you've missed several classes."

"Er, yes, I just sometimes forget that it's class."

"I've talked to your parents."

I froze. Talked to my parents? Why talked to my parents? What came of it? I hadn't thought about them for a while and didn't see how they were relevant.

"Uhhh, yes?"

"Yes, I and your teachers have agreed, due to repeated disciplinary violations, poor attendance, and behavioral problems in class, as well as your general conduct in the dormitory, to dismiss you temporarily from school."

Dismiss me temporarily from school? I had no idea what that meant.

"Uhhh…am I being fired?"

"Yes, you will be suspended from school and cannot attend again until next week at the earliest."

"And where will I be?"

"Back home."

"Can I come back?"

"Talk to your parents and then they can take the next steps."

Though I was sad to leave Núpur, it was also a little bit exciting. Apart from Mom being angry, this was just like a little holiday. I didn't even know it was possible. I thought it was impossible to get away, except in spring. I was startled, but soon I was excited and happy. Mom would definitely be angry, but for just two days or so. Zakariás the janitor drove me to Þingeyrar. I flew from there to Reykjavík in a tiny plane. I was the only passenger. Dad greeted me at the domestic airport and drove me home. We were silent the whole way. I walked hesitantly inside. My mother sat thoughtfully at the kitchen table and smoked. Dad took off his coat and hung it up; it was heavy and brown.

"Hey," I said to my mother, trying to sound cheerful. She didn't return the greeting and said in a certain voice:

"Come here and sit down."

There wasn't to be any pretense. I knew exactly how to react. Mom was angry and when Mom was angry you didn't object.

"We talked to the schoolmaster. He called us."

"Yes, indeed. He told me about it."

"He didn't exactly tell a good story."

"Eh, nooo. That's his side of things, of course…"

"He says you don't show up for class, make disruptive comments, blather and jabber the whole time. He says you behave badly and never clean yourself. Have you stopped washing, child?"

"No!"

I tried to sound like I was totally shocked and did not know what could have made the principal say such a thing. But it was entirely right. I very seldom took a bath.

"He tells us that you neither clean your room nor yourself and are generally quarrelsome and clownish."

"Well, it's not just me, really. There's lot of others, too."

Mom sighed.

"What do the kids who are there with you say? Do they think it's okay?"

"Er, yes. They think it's a bit of fun."

"They think so, do they? They think you're clever?"

"Uh, right. Everyone thinks I'm clever."

"Not the schoolmaster! He can't see anything clever about it."

"Yes, but he's got no sense of humor, so…"

Mom shook her head and rolled her eyes. Dad sighed loudly as he stood and watched.

"I don't really know what to do with you, child."

She looked at me searchingly. I nodded. I understood her concern.

"No… how about I just try to do better?"

I tried to look shamefaced and optimistic. Mom took a big

drag on her cigarette, blew away the smoke, and sighed. She was indeed totally out of confidence that I could improve. I had so often promised her that before. She asked my father:

"What should we do with him? What can we do with him?"

My father said nothing, but shook his head, disappointed.

"Go to your room. Stay there and think about things."

I nodded. She added:

"Once you have decided what you want to do with your affairs, please come back down and tell me."

"Yes."

I was very cheerful. But I tried to let my answer sound like I thought it was a wise suggestion and right for the situation. It was by far the best course of action for me to go to my room and think long and carefully about all this. I would write down what was going on and what I was going to change and how. I nodded repeatedly like someone who is really thinking things through. Maybe I could establish principles in the style of Þorbergur Þórðarson. He was always writing newer and newer principles to live by. Maybe that was something I could do. I had no principles in life and the days just passed in one continual loiter. Now I would draw up some principles regarding what I would and wouldn't do. Ten rules for what I was going to do; ten rules for what I wouldn't do.

I was going to be a new man. I was going to quit smoking. That was unhealthy, especially smoking filterless cigarettes. I'd learned a lot about smoking and cancer. All smokers got cancer. Cancer was the scariest disease in all the world. Everyone who died in my family died of cancer. Gaddi, my mothers' brother, had died of cancer.

He smoked. When I was in the country with Gaddi, I stole cigarettes from him. Filterless Camels. If you smoked filterless cigarettes, you'd definitely get lung cancer. It was the most disgusting type of the most disgusting disease. Your lungs blackened like an ashtray and you suffocated. I remembered when my mother came home after visiting Uncle Gaddi in hospital. When Dad asked her the news, she sighed and aspirated the words:

"It's a horror to see him. He's wasted away. Looks like a concentration camp prisoner."

Dad shook his head helplessly. Mom gave me Winston Lights because she didn't want me to get lung cancer. She cared for me and I thought that was beautiful. But she didn't know I always tore the filter off the cigarettes she sent me with. I smoked them filter-free like Uncle Gaddi.

It was nice to be back in my room. I knew it well, but it was still somehow alien and unreal. This was no longer just my room. But it was full of stuff I had missed, like the Fisheries Game. There was also all kinds of stuff in there from when I was a kid that I liked seeing. It was amazing to think how things had changed. It was as if it had been my room in another life. I lit a cigarette and smoked out the window. I flicked the butt far, far out into the garden. I sat on the floor in front of the closet and went through my old stuff. I found my Action Man figure and my Lone Ranger. I examined them carefully and I played with them a little. Lone Ranger was in danger. He sat on the top shelf in the closet. Suddenly Action Man came running up to him and kicked him off the edge of the shelf. Action Man got to him as he lay on the floor.

"You were sitting too close to the edge. I've told you time and again you shouldn't do that. You don't have my muscles. Are you just going to keep on doing this?"

Lone Ranger didn't answer. He didn't know what he was meant to say. Action Man headlocked him.

"Give up? Give up?"

Lone Ranger tried to break free and shake Action Man off but was no match for him. I took Lone Ranger and put him back into the box.

"Let him just lie there and think about his future!" Action Man said and laughed. I enjoyed my play but nevertheless thought to myself that maybe I was too old to be playing with Action Man. It was fun, but at the same time, a little shameful. I would never admit to anyone that I enjoyed playing with Action Man or playing the Fisheries Game all by myself. The boys at Núpur played poker or solitaire. I threw Action Man into the closet, went to the window and lit my second cigarette. At Núpur you could only smoke in the Smoker; smoking in the dorm was forbidden. But sometimes I smoked out the window of my room when no one could see. I had gotten some incense from one of my female friends and lit it when I smoked so there was no smell. If a teacher came into my room and asked me if I'd been smoking, I flatly denied it and showed him the incense.

"It's just this incense, see…"

I'd never been allowed to smoke at home but since Mom had given me cigarettes, I was therefore allowed to. Dad didn't know I smoked. I was quite certain my mom hadn't told him she was giving me cigarettes. If he knew that, he would constantly talk about it. He was often going on about how he didn't want me to smoke and making me promise him I would never fiddle about with tobacco, as he put it.

"Will you promise me that, dear boy?"

"Yes!"

I nodded and smiled encouragingly, waiting for him to get lost.

"Is that a promise?" he whispered.

"Yes!"

I watched the neighborhood out of the window. It would be fun to go seek out Óli. It was decent weather out, calm and bright. I put on a leather jacket and put my pack of cigarettes and matches in the pocket and went out. Mom was still sitting at the kitchen table.

"Where do you think you're going?"

"I was thinking I'd check things out and take a walk."

Mom turned stinging eyes towards me, like she wanted to impale me with just a flick of her pupils.

"You're not going anywhere! Get the hell back to your room."

I obeyed immediately, went back into my room and shut the door behind me. Now I needed a plan. I had to stay home for a week. A week is seven days. Mom would be angry for about two days. After three days, things would be all right. Dad would be annoying the whole time. He was always there.

It would probably be best to write down my principles for living and show them to Mom. But what was it in my behavior I wanted to change? I would stop getting thrown out of class. It wasn't like at Rétto. At Núpur, a note was made and I got minuses on the register. I also sometimes answered back.

But I was not annoying or mean to anyone. When the teachers walked into my room, came over to me and said they smelled smoke, Purrkur and I would say it was nonsense. There was no cigarette smell in the room; we'd just been striking matches, or some incense. Maybe I could change that. But I was not ready to stop being a punk and start being neat. That wasn't me. Steve Ignorant, the lead singer of Crass, was not neat. I was a punk and I had a right to be a punk. I was totally not going to change myself into some neat idiot. I was not going to stop being a laugh but I could perhaps do less of that in class. I was going to be quiet in class and stop talking nonsense and fooling around and getting thrown out. And I was going to stop biting my nails. That wasn't tough. I got out the Fisheries Game, sat on the floor and played it on my own. I lost myself in it until it was dark out. I heard my mom call out:

"Dinner time."

I walked out and went into the kitchen. The radio was on. News. Dad sat and listened. Dinner was liver and rice pudding. I wondered if I should say something, if I should tell my mom my life principles. But she was clearly still too angry and needed more time to recover. Perhaps it would be best to talk to her tomorrow. Then it would be more likely that she'd believe me. I didn't feel like talking about this in front of my dad. He would just hold my hand, tears in his eyes, stroking the back of my hand with his thumb and saying things that would make me feel bad and sick. We ate in silence. I felt my mother watching me. I feared her and thought she could see through me. She was always somehow a step ahead of me in everything. I'd tried a million times to lie to her, but it never really succeeded. I didn't know if my dad was angry or sad or just listening to the news. He simply got on my nerves like always. He always talked to me like I was a bit simple and five years old. I didn't feel like saying anything to him. He was just a person between me and my mother. And when Dad went to work tomorrow, I could talk to her.

When I woke up the next day, it was after ten. I was home alone. The fridge was full of food boxes from the City Hospital. I got some asparagus soup and a fruit cocktail and sandwich bread with cucumber. The trays were labeled A+ and A-, B+ and B-. When I'd finished eating, I went out on the balcony and smoked. I had no idea where my mom was. Perhaps she was working at the hospital and perhaps she was in town. Maybe she'd stepped out to the store and would come home at any moment. I hadn't got permission to go anywhere so I didn't dare go out. I knew I needed to talk things through with Mom before I could do anything else. I stayed home all day, killing time by playing the Fisheries Game alone. It was past five when she came home. I had already decided what I was going to say to her. I was going to tell her that I had been really thinking a lot about things and I was very upset about it all and I was going to stop acting like I was doing. I was going to be polite and calmer in class. And I was quite serious about this. These were my new principles. I hadn't managed to write them down, but I was pretty much decided on them. I peeked out. My mother had a coat on.

"Hi?" I said, searchingly, and tried to sense her mood. She did not look at me.

"Hello," she said, wearily. I knew that if she was really very angry she wouldn't answer me. Now she was more tired than angry. I was safe to come out.

"How was work?" I asked, trying to sound interested. Mom sighed sadly. She realized I wasn't interested in knowing how things had been at her work.

"I've just been here at home…"

"Yes, as well you ought to be!"

I sat at the kitchen table while Mom went and poured herself coffee. Then she sat at the table with me and her cup of coffee.

"Well, did you think about things?"

I was somewhat relieved.

"Yes, I've been thinking about it a great deal."

"Really?"

"I find it all quite frustrating."

"Yes, as do I."

"I know it's not good to behave like this and I want to change."

"How? How are you going to change?"

"Uhhh, just by… by not getting thrown out of lessons and stuff."

"And what are you doing that they're dismissing you all the time?"

"Uhhh, it's really often just something someone else is doing and I get blamed."

Mom sighed and blew out some smoke.

"But when I do something, I'm only joking about and saying something funny, nothing more."

"You're running you mouth rudely, that's what you're doing!"

"No, I'm not running my mouth…"

"You're running your mouth, Jón, and talking back to people!"

I knew it wouldn't mean anything to discuss this with her.

It would be more profitable to accept the blame. I nodded.

"Yes, exactly."

"And you have to stop. Stop always running your mouth and making disruptive comments. Why can't you just do what you're told to do! And be silent!"

"Yes, that is definitely what I'm going to do."

She lit a second cigarette from the embers of the first. I wanted a cigarette, too. I wanted to sit and smoke and talk with my mom. But I wasn't meant to smoke at home.

"I was also thinking about maybe trying to compose some life rules…"

"Life rules."

"Yes, like Þórbergur did… like ten principles. Ten things I'll stop doing and ten I'll do better."

"Foolish nonsense."

She sighed loudly.

"You don't need any damn principles. You chiefly need to stop running your mouth and then start doing what you are told to do. Just start behaving like a man!"

I nodded my assent.

"Yes."

Principles were clearly nonsense. What could I possibly include in my life principles? To smoke less? To huff less? I knew well that it was dangerous to huff. I knew of a boy who had huffed solvents and become mentally handicapped. Now he was brainless and in a hospital. I really didn't want to end up like him. But it was good to sniff. Maybe I could cut down on it. Maybe I could just huff on the weekend? Or maybe just at night? Sort of like when people go on a bender.

Perhaps I could also masturbate less. That was definitely dangerous. I also felt ashamed about it. Perhaps it would be best to do that just on the weekends, too? I really intended to be calmer and obedient and not run my mouth to anyone. And I was going to try to smoke less. Just one cigarette in the morning and one in the long recess, one at lunch and one before the dorm was closed for the night. And I was going to quit smoking in my room. And I would just masturbate and huff on weekends.

I contemplated my mom. She was tired. She looked like someone who spends all day digging ditches. She had circles under her eyes. Mom was always tired. She was tired of everything. She was tired of me, tired of work, and tired of my dad. Dad was simply the most annoying man in all the world. He was certainly very glad to have got rid of me to Núpur. Mom knew nothing about Núpur. She never asked me anything about the place or how things were Núpur, how I felt or what I was doing. I was just not to run my mouth.

"I was thinking about poking around outside later," I said hopefully. She looked into my eyes.

"You're not going anywhere! Is that understood?"

"Yes, it was just an idea…"

She was still angry but not as angry as she had been the day before. But now I had told her I was going to stop running my mouth and I had been thinking about things. I would obviously need to stay in today but tomorrow I would definitely be allowed out.

As soon as I woke up the next day I decided to take the bus and go down to Hlemmur. There was no one at home. My parents were both working. I had no money, so I just waited for the bus drivers I knew and bummed a ride. It was nice to visit Hlemmur and meet the kids. I hung out there all day and met old friends, told stories about Núpur, and got the news. There were now several new punks. I felt like they looked up to me and had heard stories about me. It was nice to know that people talked about me. I made sure to be home for dinner to avoid making my mother even angrier. I wanted to show her I was working on being a new and better man. I was being responsible. I wasn't running my mouth. I'd changed. I'd become stiller and calmer and quieter and now showed people more consideration. I was punctual. Mom was in the kitchen.

"Where have you been?"

"Yes, I went for a walk."

"Walk? So you spent the whole day walking?"

"Uhhh, no. I also went to visit Óli."

"Mmmm."

"He asked how you were," I said cheerfully. Mom didn't answer except to roll her eyes.

"What's for dinner?" I asked, interested. I was a new and changed man. I was interested in what was for dinner.

"Goulash."

It was goulash from City Hospital. B+. Mom had brought it home with her. She was no longer angry. Now everything would be better and I would go back to Núpur.

"This is really good," I said, and shoveled down goulash. She nodded.

"Is it okay to pop back round to Óli's after dinner?"

"Yes, I don't see why not."

I was very relieved. It was done. Dad was nowhere in sight. He was probably working a double shift. After dinner I went to Óli's and talked to him. I told him stories about Núpur and asked him for news of kids from the neighborhood. Óli was playing in several bands. He was a guitarist in one and a bassist in another. He had also gotten quite a bit of a studio in the basement so he could lay down tracks himself. He was a wizard with gadgets. He had a record player and amplifier and also something called an equalizer. With it he could modify the sound, set whether he wanted to hear the bass most or the other instruments. He also had huge, cool speakers. Cables didn't run into them but were clamped behind. One was red and the other was black; you pinched the wires into the speakers from behind. It was fun to be around Óli. I also saw his mother and chatted a lot with her. She was interested in Núpur and life there. I told her that there were bars across the windows and it was very remarkable.

"Seriously! There are bars across the windows? Why? So that you don't run off?"

"Yes, exactly."

"Where would you go, though?"

"Eh, I think it's mainly to stop the boys sneaking into the girls' dorm."

"Sure, I get that. Bars are the only way to keep young men from the women."

"Yeah."

She laughed, and I tried to laugh.

I did everything I could to avoid talking to Dad the whole time I was at home. When he knocked on my room door at night

I pretended to be asleep. I could not imagine sitting down with him to talk. He would just hold fast my hand and mutter that I should be a good boy. The thought sickened me.

"Were you naughty at school?"

"Yeah."

"Huh?" he'd say, like he didn't believe his ears. Then he would tell me the story of when he was in school half the winter. Only half the winter. He only had one sheep and gave it to the teacher as payment, but one sheep was only enough for half the winter. His mom and dad had no more sheep, so he didn't attend school any longer. Then he would tell me about all the wonderful grades he'd achieved and how he had always been grateful and happy to go to school. I didn't appreciate it. I didn't give a shit whether he'd been there. When he came home, I made myself scarce or took a bath or didn't go anywhere except when he was sleeping in front of the TV. We didn't talk to one another until he was driving me to the airport. I knew I had to have a conversation with him in the car, so we would not get into it in the middle of the airport in front of everyone.

"I have discussed things with Mom and I'm going to change."

"Yes, yes. That's what I like to hear."

"I'm going to stop running my mouth and just be calm."

"Yes, that's good. Did you discuss it already with your mother?"

"Yes, we discussed it thoroughly."

"And it's a promise?"

"Yes, it's a promise."

He couldn't hold my hand or look at me while he was driving. That was good. It was alright to sit behind him when you were talking to him. Dad was glad to hear the matter had been resolved so successfully. It was possible to tell him any lie because he believed everything.

"So you promise me you'll change your behavior, stop running your mouth, and be diligent in your studies?"

"Yes, I promise!" I said solemnly.

When we arrived at the airport he took my bag from the trunk and handed it to me. He took my hand and looked deep into my eyes. I tried to appear as relaxed as I could to send him a calming message that everything was okay and that he would not have to worry about me, hoping that we could finish this quickly.

"Is everything all right, Jón?" he asked, shaking my hand and squeezing.

"Yes, everything is all right," I said, and shook his hand back.

"And you promised?"

"Yes, I promised."

He squeezed my hand and now dramatically pulled me to him, looking more deeply into my eyes and said:

"You remember what you promised me."

"Yep."

Now it was about to be over and done with.

"Is it confirmed, then?"

"Yes, it's confirmed."

"Goodbye and Godspeed."

"Yes, bye."

He didn't let go and kept looking into my eyes. I smiled encouragingly to him as I fought myself free and lost myself in the terminal. It was done. I was returning to Núpur.

I had not felt well for a while. In general, things were fun. It was easy to forget yourself with the kids in the Smoker, following along with their banter, being entertaining in some way. I was the funny guy, the clown, the source of endless entertainments. I made up new scenes or was asked to repeat old skits. "Jónsate" was very popular. It was my own version of karate. Jónsate consisted mainly of grimaces. I got someone to stand up and gave him some relevant orders about how he should behave. He would then pretend to attack me while I defended myself with Jónsate. I told the person to punch me but only very slowly. He punched me in slow motion. I grimaced and screamed tremendously and acrobatically evaded the blow or stopped it with both my index fingers around his fist and aimed it back at him. The blow and that trick weren't the only things that could be stopped by Jónsate. The only requirement was that everything was done in slow motion. When others tried Jónsate, I stood over them and corrected their movements like a veteran kung fu champion. It was not enough to show them the correct moves because the expressions were of paramount importance. My students always forgot something, whether it was to yell or to bare their teeth. Jónsate was a source of great joy and merriment among the kids, like most of my skits. I was happy and lost myself in the task. I got a lot out of hearing the kids laughing and managing to shape something unexpected from things I'd boiled up in my head. And with this I gained respect and goodwill. To a certain extent I was playing a role, but that suited me and I felt good about it.

But when I was alone, I was far from joyful. Then anxiety and loneliness washed over me. I avoided being alone. I sought out company and was happy to go to the Smoker. When no pills could be had and there was nothing to huff, there was little else for me to do but read *Tao Te Ching* and listen to Crass. I fared badly when alone, getting restless and miserable. In class, I experienced powerlessness. I found the material inaccessible and distant. It was basically only in the Smoker that I felt joy and a sense of purpose. It was the one time I said and did something important. Playing the fool was good for me and I laughed heartily at my shenanigans. No one shared my interest in Crass or anarchism. I had time and again tried to get kids to understand their importance, but without success. It had been put to the test. On the other hand, they all enjoyed Jónsate or hearing fun stories. I was a good storyteller. I could even make trivial things interesting and fun. The kids often asked me to tell the same stories again and again. I told them about when I got lost at sea on a raft and I did impersonations. I mimicked the teachers and weird people I had come across in town, telling stories of Hlemmur and the kids there.

But I was bored inside my room. Sometimes I sat for hours in bed gnawing my nails. I didn't feel the future looked bright. I feared it and worried. I didn't know anything or understand anything. Everything was an empty tangle. I was tangled up, Reykjavík was tangled up, other people were tangled up and I was confident that I would never be able to tease out all these twists. I drew Crass logos in Visual Arts and put them in my window so I would not see the bleak, lonely landscape all about. It was as though I saw myself in that landscape. When I walked into the gymnasium, I tried to look down in front of me. If I looked around, anxiety and distress immediately poured over me. I was no longer safe in my room but solitary and abandoned somewhere at the ends of the universe. The weight naturally rested like a nightmare on my soul. The cliffs and the sea and the snow. I got a lump in my throat and a heavy chest.

I had a poor sense of time. I didn't get days or months. I was never sure what month it was or where it came in the sequence. I just wandered about timelessly and then jumped suddenly when someone said:

"Oh, I'm so glad it's Friday."

Then I was sure it was Friday. Otherwise, I had no idea what day it was and didn't feel it made a difference. They all somehow ran together as one.

One day there was a loud noise in the distance which seemed to come from somewhere above the mountains. A sort of mix of thunder and an earthquake. I felt the floor tremble beneath me like it was an earthquake. I had previously experienced an earthquake, but it hadn't been accompanied by this noise. We looked questioningly at the teacher.

"An avalanche," he said, casually. Avalanche? I'd never heard of avalanches.

"It's just a sign of spring," he added as an explanation. I had no idea how the avalanche and its noise were associated with spring. In the following weeks, it began to warm up and to rain; the snow was melting and you could glimpse stones here and there. One day someone said:

"Now it's just a week until we go home."

Go home? I hadn't even begun to think about that. Go home?

And do what?

"Why?" I asked. The other kids laughed like I was joking. I laughed like I was. But I wasn't. I didn't get what was happening.

"Summer holiday!"

Summer holiday. It dawned on me that I was leaving Núpur. It was an exciting but anxious feeling. So much had changed and such a long time had passed. I felt sure I wouldn't recognize my old friends and was also not sure whether they would recognize the me I'd become. There were now many new kids at Hlemmur and I didn't know anything about them; most of them were younger than me. Besides, I didn't belong to any particular group at Núpur. I was not in any gang and not from Hafnarfjörður. I probably wouldn't visit or hang out with any Núpurs in Reykjavík. Although Purrkur was my roommate, we weren't friends. I would absolutely have met up with Gisli, but knew he was going to be in the country all summer. I was definitely not going to meet the kids in the Rolling Stones gang and hang out with them some place in Hafnarfjörður. That was just lame. Punks didn't hang with Rolling Stones fans. I looked forward to seeing my mother and my sister Rúna and perhaps also the kids in my street. I could tell them about Núpur. But I wasn't going to tell them anything boring, just the fun stuff. It didn't get you anything thinking about the annoying stuff. It was better to focus on what was fun. It was fun at Núpur, everyone was lovely and always happy.

The last day of school arrived. We had to empty our rooms, clean and scrub them. I threw my stuff in my bag, took down the posters and rolled them carefully. It wasn't certain I would have the same room after summer and I had also heard that I wouldn't know who was going to be my roommate. I had no particular preference. I didn't really care, but knew that I really didn't want to be in Lubbi's room. But it would be better if no one was in there, and Lubbi got a room to himself. It wasn't possible to assign anyone to his room. No wonder: he was insane and smelled disgusting. I would be totally happy rooming again with Purrkur. Despite sharing a room with him for a whole year, I knew little or nothing about him. Purrkur usually said nothing of his own accord, but as a result we never particularly got into conflicts. He was a good roommate and not much trouble. He didn't masturbate in front of me like some boys and just kept it to himself.

The same bus as drove us to Núpur suddenly appeared from within some snow banks ready to drive us back the same way. We crowded on, singing happily as it drove away. I was going to town. Summer was here and it would soon be warm.

"It's shocking to see you! You've become horribly thin!" Mom said when I got home. I mumbled something. Mom always said this. It was always shocking to see people. Either they were too thin or too fat. Sometimes it was the same people who grew fatter or got skinny. No matter who it was, Mom found it simply shocking to see people.

I stopped dead when I saw my room. All my stuff had gone, and the wallpaper; the carpet had been replaced, and the entire room painted.

"What happened to my room?"

"Nothing. We just fixed it up and used it as a guest room."

My room had become a guest room? It was no longer my room?

"And who's been in my room?"

"Just some visitors. Anna and Gunnar stayed here when they visited."

Anna Stína was my Norwegian sister and Gunnar was her husband. I didn't really know them. I had only met them once when I was little, but I'd forgotten them by now. I didn't feel this was my room any longer, but some guest room. I no longer lived there. I was just a guest in the guest room.

"What did you do with my pictures?"

"I threw all that stuff out," Mom replied briefly.

"You threw out my pictures?"

"Oh, it was just such a nasty mess."

I knew there was no point discussing it with her, but I was seething. She had taken all the photos I had collected for years and worked hard to cut out of magazines. Worse, I had traipsed all over town searching for Stiff Little Fingers and Nina Hagen and Crass and the punks in Poland and Camilla, the punks in Sweden. All gone! Rubbish that my mom had to throw out. I had no home. I didn't even have a room. My room at Núpur was no longer my room and my room with Mom and Dad was no longer my room, either. I was an outlaw.

I didn't find work that summer. It was too late to apply for Youth Pay and most businesses had already hired their summer help so I didn't do a lot, simply stayed home. It was like I was between two worlds, life at Núpur and the life I had away from Núpur. From time to time, I got money from my mom to buy cigarettes and sweets, and I also got money for babysitting my sister Rúna's child up in Kjalarnes. I enjoyed being around her in Kjalarnes. When I wasn't babysitting, I went for a walk down to the sea and played on the beach. I sometimes went down to Hlemmur, but many of my friends were no longer around, were working somewhere, or had gone to the country. Hlemmur was full of new faces that I didn't recognize. I also often went up to Rúna's even if I wasn't babysitting. I walked up to the headland and hitchhiked the rest of the way. It felt relaxing and enjoyable to get to Kjalarnes. It was peaceful. There was nothing to do in town and the days were all alike. I stayed home, took a bath, or went to the attic to huff. But Kjalarnes had nature. I was drawn to nature; she pulled me in. I went down to the shore, lit a campfire out of driftwood and debris and sat there at leisure and smoked. I walked the length and breadth of the beach. Saltvík was the next town to Mói, where Rúna lived. The town was deserted but the houses were being used as a summer school for kids and teens. In Saltvík there were several houses, one old apartment, and several cottages.

To while away the time, I'd break into houses in Saltvík.

I was careful never to damage anything. Often I found an open window to crawl in through, and occasionally I came across an unlocked door. Breaking in was a release, often accompanied by a little excitement. When I was lugging myself back and forth from Kjalarnes, there were times no cars came or else none stopped for me. So I often walked long distances along the highway. Sometimes I saw cottages and amused myself breaking into them. It was always exciting. Especially when it was starting to get dark. I always had a small flashlight with me and while I looked for an entry into the home, I put cloth over the aperture so the light couldn't be seen from afar. Somehow I always got in. Once there, I didn't do anything but sneak around and look. Open drawers, look in chests, and dig into closets. It was enjoyable and I tried my hardest to look for the secret places where people would possibly store things of value. Often, these were small spaces or bedrooms in cottages that had some kind of storage, with cardboard boxes containing papers and other junk. There were also often books, paintings, and statues that I really enjoyed looking at with my flashlight.

I never sought to steal anything. The aim of the tour consisted primarily of entering the home, finding stored stuff, and looking. While I examined the stuff I imagined who owned this sort of thing and what they were like. And why they kept hold of all this. For example, this particular painting. Why this painting: who was this man in it? The same went for photos. Peering with flashlight in arms, I could have lost myself for hours looking at pictures of people I did not know anything about. I'd wonder what the people in the pictures were called. The men were always called Hannes or Einar and they were either truck drivers or fishermen.

This woman was certainly his wife. Her name was surely Sigrún or Valdís. She was clearly not called Ásta because all Ástas are blond. This woman was dark-haired and obviously not an Ásta. However, she was possibly called Berglind. Dark-haired women were often called Berglind. The man facing her, however, was very much a Hannes. Boorish guys were called Svenni.

I surely broke into every holiday home between Reykjavík and Kjalarnes one or more times. I was repeatedly in the same home. I never stole anything or damaged anything, not even to break in. It was all part of the game, finding a way in without doing any damage. I was a master burglar like the guys in the movies. Sometimes I spent long periods outside the cottages where I snuck around and looked at everything very carefully and tried to find a way in. I'd examine every board, try to force every window, and look for weak spots. Often, however, I had to back off. But I put this house in my memory and continued wondering about possible entry routes. There was always a weak spot, somewhere, I could enter. It was just a case of persistence and patience. Sometimes, bungalows were locked tight front and back. Then the solution was a hidden key. People often actually hid keys to their cottages somewhere around about then. They never wanted to have driven all the way to their cottage and find they'd left their key at home. I pretended I was a detective who had to solve the mystery of "Where is the key?" I had the image of the cottage and its surroundings in mind and I set up a scene in my head where I was standing with the people who owned the bungalow and we were going out. We were done tidying up and had locked it and were ready to go.

As we were getting in the car and driving away, someone hid the key. It wouldn't be too far away, but it couldn't be too close. I saw several places that were an option and, after much deliberation, I went back, often at night, and checked out potential hiding spots. And more often than not I found the key. It was quite a victory and I felt smart and good at something.

I was good at breaking and entering because I was smart. I also made me realize that because I was good at breaking in, I would probably sometime in the future land in jail. But I also imagined that the prison wouldn't hold me captive; I would always be able to escape. I'd always find the weak link. I'd seen many movies about men who fled from prisons, for example, a film about the Colditz Concentration Camp. I would do all sorts of things in order to escape that no one had previously thought about. When the prisoners on TV were escaping, I considered why they did this or that a certain way, and didn't go the other way or do something else. That is, I saw all kinds of possibilities that hadn't even occurred to them. I felt I possessed a remarkable talent. I was good at breaking in and at breaking out. Maybe my life would in the future be characterized by burglaries. Maybe I would be known across the country as a master burglar people said could get into wherever he wanted. No one would know my real name, but the papers would call me Black Shadow or Specter. "The master thief Specter broke into yet another jewelry shop in the night." I could break into a bank or into shops and steal things no one else could steal. I'd be tough like the toughest burglars in the movies. I was slick and resourceful and tried to avoid breaking down doors and windows, but went up to the roof and found open skylights.

Then I'd rappel down by rope, take the diamonds, climb up the rope again with the jewelry, and shut the skylight behind me. All other burglars would wonder how the diamond was stolen. I was going to be a burglar. Burglary would be an art form to me, and I would even be world famous. The Master Thief Skuggi (The Shadow, to the British media). I might be known as The Phantom. While the police were looking for me, I'd be alone in my house surrounded by diamonds and money, reading the paper laughing at everyone who couldn't tell up from down and who wondered what genius had stolen all the things.

Finally, though, my number would be up and I'd have to go to jail. The detective who caught me would be world-famous for that. But it was okay because the prison would be just like Núpur. It would definitely be nothing but fun being there. Yet I would still escape. Always in such way that no one would understand how I could have done it. I was suddenly gone. One day when the guards opened my cell, they'd find it empty and no one could realize how and when The Shadow was gone. And while the guards were looking for me, and descriptions of me were in all the papers, I would just come home, read the news, and laugh at everyone. Unless the prison was somewhere far away like Núpur. It wasn't possible to escape from Núpur: it was a snowdrift out nowhere and always freezing. But Little Hraun was in the immediate vicinity of Reykjavík, so I did not have to worry about it; it would be no problem. And if I did not go to Little Hraun, most of the prisons were in Reykjavík, on Síðumúli, or Skólavörðustígur. If I was sitting in jail on Skólavörðustígur I would plan and prepare for the escape carefully. Then I would run away and go directly to Hlemmur and sit around, carefree. There'd be a description of me in the papers and the police would announce that the master thief Jón Gunnar, better known as The Shadow, had fled from prison. Everyone was looking for me and the cops would drive past Hlemmur and see me sitting, calm as could be, smoking. They would come running into Hlemmur and catch me before I evaporated or walked through the wall like a fairy king.

"What the hell are you doing here?!" the cop would ask, surprised. I would just laugh and not say a word because master thieves never reveal anything, especially not how they burgle or escape. That's why they are master thieves.

To break in but steal nothing was not just a hobby, but a passion. I often dreamed at night that I had to break in or out. I dreamed that I was in Colditz and was going to lead all the captives to freedom. And when the Nazis were about to catch me, I'd flee. Just flee the livid Nazis. Whether I was breaking in or out I always managed to find a weak link. By finding it, I was smarter than everyone else. I was smarter than the warden, smarter than the cottage owner.

I sometimes do things that are completely pointless and I don't know why I do them. For example, I bite my nails. I bite them down so far they bleed. I don't know why I do it. I get ashamed and try to hide my hands. You shouldn't bite your nails. It's disgusting and stupid and pointless. Mom says it's ill-mannered and Dad has repeatedly made me promise to stop. Every single time, I promise him I'll stop. I've often tried, but I keep forgetting. Often I forget even while I'm in his presence and I start biting. Then he tilts his head and says:

"Are you still biting your nails, Jón?"

I pull my finger out immediately.

"Uhhh, yes, but only very occasionally."

"Let me see."

I really don't want to extend him my hand but I know I have to. He takes it and looks carefully at my nails. He shakes his head and begins to look all distressed. The ugly nails make him sad. A feeling of discomfort takes over all my thoughts and sensations. Pain gathers in my stomach, like rocks are in there; I feel sick. I want a way to vent and to rid myself of this unease. I want to scream at him or throw up. But I also want to be able to stop biting my nails. I do it just instinctively. I want to tear myself free and yell at him:

"Let me be, you damn pain!"

But I say nothing; I keep quiet and wait. He examines each

finger carefully. Then he looks at me, still holding fast to my hand, squeezes it, and looks into my eyes. His face shows he is both surprised and wounded.

"Didn't you promise me you'd stop biting your nails?"

I feel humiliated. I'm disgusting and I bite my nails. My hands are disgusting and I bite my nails even though I promised to stop. I'm a disgusting liar who betrays and hurts others. I nod, ashamed. He squeezes my hand even harder.

"Then you must make good on your promises. Do you like betraying your father?" he whispers.

"No!"

My chest feels so heavy I can't breathe.

"Would you do that for me—stop? I find it so irritating."

"Yes!" I say immediately and nod my head in agreement. This time I will stick to it. He grabs really hard onto my hand and I flinch.

"You promise?"

I nod and nod my head in a compelling way and mutter:
"Yes."

Then he puts one hand behind his ear and smiles impishly like he can't hear exactly what I'm saying because I'm not speaking loud enough.

"Yes, I promise," I say louder and nod my head again convincingly. He stares ahead and looks thoughtfully to one side as if he is wondering whether to believe me. This is to be expected. Then he nods his head too, as though he's come to the conclusion that he will try to believe me this time and give me one more chance. Then, finally, he releases me. I smile weakly at him, stand up, walk to my room and sit on the bed. Emotions wash over me: I get tears in my eyes, sob, and whisper quietly to myself over and over:

"Fucking shitty damn asshole!"

Tears run down my cheeks and before I know it, I've started biting my nails.

One of the places I always enjoyed going was the library. I loved sitting there and browsing newspapers or books. The library had been my second home when I was a kid; all the staff know my name. I got books to take home and lay in my room, smoking and reading. Occasionally I'd nip up to the attic and huff a little.

The intoxication was convenient in that it affected me only while I was sniffing, but as soon as I stopped it left me immediately. There was no smell so my mom never realized—unlike what happened when I drank booze or took pills. I could be weird for a long time after that. But when I sniffed I could just sneak off, huff, and come back as if nothing had happened.

Sometimes I went to see Óli. He wasn't a punk, but he was a childhood friend. I thought Óli was a good person and enjoyed being around him. He'd always been good to me. He never judged me, never looked down at me and was never angry with me, even when I threw dirt at his house. He wasn't pissed at me even though I turned up uninvited to his birthday when we were little. His mother had told him not to play with me. But he was always happy to see me, even when I hadn't been invited. Óli cared about me and wanted to help me and educate me. He was always ready and willing to assist me and I could always turn to him. I spoke to Óli when I wanted to learn a musical instrument. So, too, when I wanted to learn to dance. And when I was ready to give up, as often happened, he urged me on and congratulated me on my progress.

Óli didn't look at me the same way others did. When he looked at me, I knew for sure that he wasn't thinking about how strange I was or wondering if I was somehow mentally handicapped or even a bit dangerous. Óli knew well that I was neither. He was interested in music and had a large record collection. His album collection included quite a few punk albums and it was he who introduced me for the first time to punk and its significance.

Óli was knowledgeable about many topics; he usually knew something about everything. I enjoyed talking to him and never felt embarrassed or uncomfortable, but relaxed, fun, and engaged. If I had a brother of similar age, I would have wished he was like Óli. Good, helpful, and fun.

"Are there any cute girls at Núpur?"

"Eh, I don't know. I'm not really into girls, really."

"No! You really don't enjoy looking at cute girls?"

I absolutely did. I enjoyed looking at the girls and sometimes I found them quite enchantingly beautiful. How they looked, moved, and spoke. But I didn't admit it to anyone. Not even Óli.

"Nooo, not really, not. I mostly just listen to music and read."

Óli tilted his head.

"You think you might be gay?"

I jumped right in and said firmly:

"No! I just don't think about girls much."

I saw Óli struggling to believe me. All boys thought about girls. I wanted, but just did not dare, to talk about these things with someone. I was a failure and wasn't able to do anything about it. When we were small, Óli was called Óli the Stud because he was always kissing girls. He had had a series of girlfriends and had definitely had sex.

He was the sort of guy who was the first to have sex. He was cute, fun, smart, and decent. Moreover, he was outgoing and knew both how to play guitar and how to dance. When we were around other kids, Óli was always the one who could hold a fun conversation and notice all kinds of things that seemed to others, especially me, entirely hidden. He listened to people and remembered what they had said before; he also remembered what everyone was called and who they were. I was just unclear about people.

The girls in the neighborhood appreciated boys like Óli. Everyone liked him. They weren't really into me, however. I felt they'd become distant, almost unrecognizable. It was like I'd known them in some other life. Now they'd changed, got mature and had breasts. I'd often played with Ásta, who lived in the same street as me, when we were kids. But she was no longer the Ásta I once knew. Now I was shy when I met her and afraid to talk to her. We no longer played ball games or pick-up-sticks. And when I looked at her I also couldn't help seeing her breasts and then I got an erection. I found that awkward. We were clearly not going to play ball games. I usually never said anything to anyone.

I also didn't especially want to speak to anyone. If people didn't know anything about Crass or anarchism, I had nothing to talk to them about. I didn't want to answer questions about how things were at Núpur. I didn't want to answer questions like:

"What's new with you, Jónsi?"

What could I possibly say? There was nothing new for me. I was just at Núpur and I'd begun to masturbate. Could I say that?

"I'm at Núpur and I'm always huffing and masturbating."

"Yes, isn't that fun?"

"Indeed, a lot of fun. I would be happy, though, to try fucking. You've grown a wonderful pair of breasts. Can I see them? Can I perhaps fuck you?"

I couldn't talk to anyone and I didn't want to. Except Óli.

But I still couldn't talk about all this with him. I couldn't talk to anyone about it. I found these thoughts so unpleasant. I felt uncomfortable looking at my female friends and getting erections. Sometimes I dreamed of them at night and they were showing me their breasts. I woke up sometimes having had a wet dream and filled with shame. I was ashamed of myself for thinking that way. I felt ashamed of my hard-ons like I was ashamed at myself for biting my nails. I considered myself a disgusting pervert and feared that the situation would get worse and worse and eventually lead to insanity. I wouldn't tell anyone about this because I was afraid the news would spread and I'd be sent to the madhouse at Kleppur. I was Jónsi Punk. I was a strange, ugly, possibly handicapped, totally insane pervert. I would rather be alone than have someone find out my true self. When I met girls, I was even more ill at ease and weird than usual. I was both nervous and excited. I found them sweet and charming, but also in a way unpleasant. It was simply better to be taking a bath or sniffing. Then everything was quiet and no one bothered me. If I felt the need to talk to someone I just went to the library and talked to the guy there about Bakunin or anarchism. He didn't know much about anarchism, so I could sometimes educate him. Then he was delighted and said:

"Oh, yeah, exactly. That's how it is."

Sometimes the phone rang at home. I avoided answering and usually let my mom take care of it. It was very rare that someone was calling me. When I was home alone, however, I had to answer the phone. Usually, it was some cousin or aunt who was trying to get hold of Mom. No one ever called for Dad. People would rather talk to my mom. Dad was even more annoying than usual when he spoke on the phone. He was all droll, worked up, talking loudly, and even shouting down the receiver as though people might struggle to hear him. He laughed a pretentious laugh, usually at something that wasn't funny.

"It's been rainy here all week. Ahahahahahaha."

The aunts were always glad to hear from me, even if they hadn't called for me.

"No, it's you, dearest Jón! How do you do? What's the news with you?"

"Yes, hi," I replied, although I didn't know who I was talking to. "All's well," I added, trying to sound happy.

"How is Núpur?"

"Yes, all well, really."

"Aren't there a lot of kids there?"

"Sure, simply loads, yeah."

"And how are you doing in school?"

"Just great, yeah."

I tried to answer all the questions as faithfully as I could, but as briefly as possible without being rude. If they didn't give up talking to me, I made up some lie to tell them. I told them my friend was waiting for me and I would have to go or that someone had rung the doorbell. Then they said to say hello to Mom and I had to let her know they'd called. When Mom came home, I said to her:

"Some old biddy called for you and asked you to ring her."

"Well, who was it?"

"I don't know."

"Was it my friend Siggi? Has she arrived in town?"

"Yes, I think that's it…"

Very rarely, the phone would be for me. Like when Alli called. I was inside my room reading when I heard the phone ring and my mother answered. She shouted for me and said:

"Jón Gunnar! Phone for you."

Who could be calling me? I went out and took the phone call.

"Hello?"

It was Alli, my childhood friend.

"Hi, it's Alli."

Alli lived in the next street over, but I had not spoken to him for a long time.

"What's up?"

"Eh, things are good. How are you?"

"Doing fine. You been in town long?"

"Er, no, no—or yes, I don't remember. What's up?"

"It's all good. Did you come for summer holidays?"

"Yes."

"I'm in the Youth Labor Program."

I had heard of this Youth Labor Program but didn't really know what it was. It was something to do with the city infrastructure. Teenagers could get jobs weeding and mowing fields, but it didn't pay very well. I was glad I didn't get in; I'd applied too late.

"Yeah, ok. How is Youth Labor?"

"Totally fine. You always get paid and you don't really need to do anything. Just show up and relax a bit. It's nice to get paid to relax."

Alli talked on and on, told me all kinds of stories about what took place in the Youth Labor Program. His supervisor was some idiot who was always ordering them to do something, but as soon as he was gone no one ever did anything. Then they all just lay on the grass and either slept or chatted together. It didn't sound bad.

"Are you doing anything tonight?"

"Nah, nothing much..."

"I'm totally home alone for the weekend."

"Seriously? You're home alone all weekend? Where are your mom and dad?"

"They've gone to their vacation home."

His parents had a summer house and had gone there and left Alli alone at home. It was probably all right because Alli was a good kid and always calm. It was obvious that his parents trusted him. My parents would never trust me to be home alone. But they would never take me with them on some holiday. They thought I was annoying and always a problem.

"So, I was thinking about having a little party."

"Yes, nice!"

"Would you want to come?"

I was absolutely interested in coming.

"Sure, who will be there?"

"Oh, just me and a few guys who are in the Youth Labor Program with me."

"Yes, anyone I know?"

"No, I don't think so. Do you know who Jói is?"

"Which Jói?"

"Ah, Jói. He was always called Jói Dwarf."

"Is he a dwarf?"

"No, he was just always called Jói Dwarf because he was so small."

I couldn't remember any Jói Dwarf.

"But he isn't small anymore," Alli added. "We sometimes hung out in Reykjavík and he always asks about you."

I couldn't recall him.

"We're planning to get together this evening and maybe watch a porno."

I froze. Porno? I had never watched a porn movie. I had heard of pornography and boys who had seen pornographic movies talked about them with great reverence. I didn't have to think about it at all.

"Yes, yes. I'd be happy to take a look. Where did you get it?"

I was trembling with excitement. I was going to watch a real porno! If Mom and Dad had invited me to choose between a whole weekend at Legoland or watching a porno, I would without hesitation have chosen the porno. I wouldn't want to watch it with them, though.

"From Ebba's brother, natch."

"Yes. And you've got a VCR?"

"Yes, Mom and Dad decided to buy a VCR, really."

"Yes. What time should I come?!"

"Around eight."

"Yes."

I looked at the clock: three.

"Looking forward to seeing you!"

"Me too," I replied, and hung up. I went straight into the gues-troom and sat on the bed. This was a big moment, a red-letter day in my life. I was going to watch a porno. This would probably be the best movie I had seen up until now. I had watched some movies that I really thought were good and some of them had had a profound effect on me.

For example, I found *The Wall* by Pink Floyd awesome. Pink Floyd weren't a really good band. They weren't punk, though they weren't new wave, and they didn't sing about anarchism. But there was still something cool about Pink Floyd. *The Wall* was an awesome movie because it was against the school system and kids being forced to go to school. That I could certainly get on board with. There was anarchy behind the message even though the word anarchy wasn't used. It was enough to say:

"Hey! Teachers! Leave them kids alone!"

Pink Floyd also said that you shouldn't participate in the system because if you did you were just like another brick being used. I could agree with that. I definitely wasn't going to be just another brick in some strange system. I was going to be free. I was dream-ing about the porn movie and counting down the minutes until I could go to Alli's.

I turned up at Alli's house at seven-thirty, extremely excited.

We said hello and chatted a bit. I had often been round to his before but always just inside his room. Now we went into the living room. Alli had a nice home. His Mom and Dad were young and they were professionals. His father was a teacher and his mother was a sort of engineer. The home showed the evidence of this; it was very different from my home. Then again, all homes were different from my home. But this home was somehow fashionable. My home was more outdated. I hadn't really noticed it until my friends mentioned it when they came to visit. Perhaps it was so outdated because my grandmother had lived with us and many things were hers, like the rocking chairs inside the living room. Maybe Mom and Dad had made an effort to make the home old-fashioned just for her.

"Want something to drink?"

"Uh, yeah, thanks."

Alli brought a Coke in a glass and gave it to me. I checked the room and looked wide-eyed at the spanking new VCR on a shelf below the TV. Hitachi. I was going to watch a porno on a Hitachi. I got goose bumps at the thought. This was incredibly exotic and exciting.

"Where's the tape?" I asked, excited. Alli smiled stealthily, reached behind the books in the bookshelf and pulled out the tape. The picture on the case was of a half-naked lady who was positioned like she was shouting something out. She was topless so you could see her breasts but down below she had on a short skirt. Under the picture was something written in Danish. This was clearly a Danish porno. I'd heard that Danish porno movies were the best in the world.

"I've only just got a glimpse of her and already she's totally sick!"

"Yeah…"

I couldn't wait to start watching it. Shortly, other kids drifted in. Everyone got a Coke, said hello to me, and asked if they could see the tape. They were clearly as excited as I was.

"Danish pornos are the absolute best pornos!" one boy said. I wondered what the other choices were. There weren't any Icelandic pornos. I'd certainly never heard of any. Wasn't all porn Danish? The porno mag I'd seen at Núpur was Danish. Maybe the Danes were somehow different from us. They were certainly more relaxed and definitely more globally aware. Perhaps they were also more liberal than Iceland. And maybe it was completely different being a teenager in Denmark than in Iceland. All the books I had read that had to do with teen sex were Danish. I had read *Wanna See My Sexy Belly Button?* It was about boys and girls sleeping together and it took place in Denmark. That happened to some teens in Iceland, but seemed to happen to all teens in Denmark. I'd also read *Catamaran*. I thought it was better than *Wanna See My Sexy Belly Button?*, but it was also pretty bad because the kid in *Catamaran* wasn't having sex with a girl, but instead he raped another boy.

We didn't have to wait any longer. Alli turned on the television, opened up the VCR, and put the tape in. I was totally focused on the porn movie and neither heard nor saw anyone else. I don't remember quite what the film dealt with and there wasn't actually a story line. It was about the woman who was on the front of the box. She was hanging out at home cleaning and tidying. However, she was dressed like she was working in a circus.

She had on a bright purple short skirt and a tight orange top and high heels. I thought it was very odd that any woman would walk around at home in high heels. I had seen, both in movies and at my sister's house, that when women got home they usually kicked off their heels to rest their feet. This woman, however, was wearing very high heels all around the house, and wearing a short skirt while she cleaned and watered the plants. And when she leaned over to water the plants, you could see she had no underwear on. This would definitely be an exciting movie.

Suddenly the doorbell rang, and the woman went to the door. Outside stood three craftsmen. They were topless but wearing overalls and carrying some tools. They said something to the woman in Danish and seemed to have come to repair something. Next, they were led into the kitchen. The guys were clearly going to fix the sink and one of them opened the cupboard under the sink. In order to continue cleaning, the lady sat at the kitchen table and spread her feet apart, so that you could see her pussy under her skirt. One guy noticed her pussy, asked about something and then they talked. The scene was done.

In the next scene, they were led into the bedroom. The woman was showing them her bed and telling them something about it. The guys said something in Danish and they all laughed. I was disappointed that it didn't have subtitles and so I understood little or nothing of what they were saying. Was she telling them where she had bought the bed or had these guys come to move her bed somewhere? Or were they perhaps come to fix it? Had they finished fixing the sink? While they went on about something among themselves and bent to examine the bed, the woman was smiling and flirting with them. She rubbed them on their chests and grabbed their crotches. She went back and forth and positioned herself now and then by putting a foot up on a bedside table or on a windowsill so that you could see her pussy. The woman was clearly very horny. The guys started to undress and she helped them rip off their clothes.

Suddenly they were all more or less naked. The little bit of plot that existed was now completely abandoned and a sex orgy began. This was clearly not the best movie in the world like I had thought. It wasn't exciting or funny or entertaining. At first I found it interesting and fun to see the woman's pussy, but it quickly became overwhelming and uncomfortable. And I felt really awkward seeing the guys all naked and I did what I could to avoid looking at their penises. I looked back and away again before and pretended to be examining the room so the other boys wouldn't notice. The guys were all taking turns fucking the woman and the camera work showed relentless close-ups, either of her face, pussy or their penises. They brayed and groaned. Sometimes the woman yelled and screamed something while they muttered in Danish. I was no longer turned on and thought it was disgusting. I found them all disgusting. Then there was a close-up of one of the guy's cocks sliding in and out of the woman's pussy, with the perspective somehow behind his ass and you could see his balls swinging back and forth. It reminded me of rams in the countryside. I was feeling distinctly ill. This wasn't as exciting and fun as I had thought and hoped it would be. On the contrary, I felt nothing but disgust.

Before the movie began, I had already gotten a hard-on but as the movie wore on, I felt it fade and vanish. I snuck eyes at the other boys and wondered if they were experiencing the same thing. But they seemed, however, consumed by the film, staring hypnotized at the TV with faint smiles playing on their lips. What should I do? I couldn't listen any longer to this sighing and muttering mixed with sloshing and splashing sounds which felt like it was merging into one long indescribably disgusting sound. I didn't want to watch this movie and felt terribly uncomfortable being there. I should never have come to this party. I realized I didn't want to watch people fuck any more than lie around peeping to watch people shit. I finished my Coke and scratched my head. Now it was time for a decent plan. What was I supposed to do? I looked at the clock: quarter to nine.

"Oh, I forgot! I promised my father to help him carry some stuff out of storage."

The boys sat glued to the movie and no one except Alli seemed to notice that I had said something. He mumbled "Uhu..." and remained gaping at the images, bewitched.

"Yes, I have to go."

"Aha..."

I stood up. The woman in the film cried out and the men growled something in Danish. I had to get out.

"Okay, bye!"

"Byeeee..." murmured some of the kids, distracted.

I slammed the door behind me and walked quickly away from the house. When I got home, I went into my room, sat down and did what I could to bring order and rule to my thoughts. This was a terrible disappointment. My expectations for the film had all failed. I had looked forward most of all to seeing a real pussy in a movie and not just a photo. When it loomed nearer, in close-up, I felt very uncomfortable and totally overwhelmed. Somehow it was too much, unpleasant in some odd way. This woman was disgusting, unattractive, and weird. The guys were twice as disgusting as she was. All hairy with pasty disgusting asses and their cocks up in the air and balls dangling in a ridiculous way. Who wanted to see that? This was certainly not anything I wanted to watch. But what had I expected? I thought maybe it would be more like *Wanna See My Sexy Belly Button?* where they were all really good friends and just had sex one at a time. In the porno they all were on the other hand doing everything at once. I would never watch a porno again.

After that, I no longer wanted to look at porn mags or watch pornographic movies. It was too disgusting and fake. The women in porn films had to be pretending. This couldn't be real. I didn't know exactly how it was meant to be, but it had to somehow be different, not so disgusting.

There had to be some romance in all this. People had to kiss and cuddle before fucking. What did I think about this? Why did I think about it at all? I wasn't going to do anything with any girl. I didn't dare: I was too shy, and afraid because I had a ridiculous penis. Wouldn't it be best to just forget everything that had to do with libido and sex? I had seen enough porn mags and I was totally done seeing what pussies looked like. Porn mags were lame and disgusting. It was all meaningless and hopeless. And this porno and everything that happened in it wasn't right. The movie was just a continuation of the bragging stories boys told at Núpur. Just stupid. No woman would act this way in reality.

And no normal people would start fucking an upset woman who was cleaning her home naked. They would just let her sit down and help her become calm.

My life is miserable and without purpose. I fear the future. I feel ugly and awkward. My face is ugly; I've got ugly hair and ugly hands. But I'm not just ugly on the outside; I'm ugly inside, too. I'm evil minded. There's something ugly living inside me. Maybe I'm simply an idiot. Things everyone else seems to know and understand I don't get; I find them hard to grasp. Even the easiest things, like shoelaces. Everyone can tie shoelaces—not me. I'm no good at handwriting, either. I feel bad being like this and I no longer have the excuse that I'm just a baby because I'm becoming an adult. There's something huge happening inside me. If you can't learn simple things like shoelaces then surely you're stupid. It's a terrible thought. And I try to hide it by being lively and entertaining, but I know I can't continue to do that throughout my whole life. My teacher in elementary school called it idiotic prattle and said I'd never get ahead in life with idiotic prattle. Mom and Dad have long since given up on me; everyone thinks I'm strange and weird. But maybe I'm just a fool, covering up his folly with prattle.

I'm stupid and ugly and unlucky. Everything I try to do fails. I screw up all the time. I'm not good at anything, except playing the fool. I try as best I can to dismiss these thoughts about myself and to think about something else. But at night, when I'm lying in bed and everything has gone quiet, my mind wanders instinctively to this and real life submerges me. I avoid looking at myself in the mirror; when I catch a glimpse of him there, I ask myself, but not out loud: "Why are you so ugly? You're ugly and stupid! Yes, I know." And when I think about it, I get angry. I think it's unfair. Why can't I learn to tie laces like other people? Why didn't someone teach me? Is it my fault? Aren't I good enough? I don't do well in school. I have no real family and I'm not doing well making friends. My only friends are guys who are even more freakish than me: Biggi.

If God exists, then this is his fault. He's a malicious and obnoxious villain who loves to create people like me, like Eiki, Biggi, and Sprelli. But maybe I inherited this from my Dad. Maybe I'm just like him. Perhaps Mom and Dad are to blame. Perhaps I can't do anything because they haven't taught me anything. If Óli's Mom and Dad were my parents, I would surely be able to tie shoelaces and use utensils. And then I'd I also know how to dance and to succeed at school.

I was already twelve years old by the time I learned to eat with a knife and fork. I was invited to dinner at a friend's house. Prior to that, I'd always used my knife to cut food into small pieces. Then I'd put down the knife, pick up a fork, and eat. I didn't know how to use cutlery at the same time, only separately. My friend's family laughed at this, and his mother asked me why I did it this way. I had never thought about it. I never really had to think about it because I usually always ate food my mother brought home from the city hospital. The few times the food was not already sliced, Mom cut it for me. My friend's mom took pity on me and showed me how to use a knife and fork at the same time. Prior to that, I'd used a fork like a spoon and kept it in my right hand the whole time. She taught me to put the fork in my left hand and the knife in my right.

And I got the hang of it with very little trouble. I was furious with my mother. She should have taught me. It was her responsibility. Why hadn't she ever taught me to eat with utensils? She thought that I couldn't learn? It was also her fault that I couldn't tie my shoes. It was all my mother's fault.

But it's not simply others' jobs to teach me. Some things are my fault. Mom has tried hard to teach me mathematics. I just can't learn it. I'm too stupid. But if God exists, he's a sadist. He's predetermined that I will be unsuccessful, that my life will be miserable. He's just playing about, making people who can't learn to tie shoes. Most people are dark- or blond-haired and don't wear glasses. Most are of average height. When God created me, he thought:

"Now I'm going to make Jón and I'll make him miserable. I'll start by making him ginger because there's no ginger in his family and it's going to confuse everyone. And I'm going to make him near-sighted and ugly. I'm going to make him really stupid so he can't learn the simplest things like tying his shoes and writing his name. And I'll make him always bite his nails; I'll make him absent-minded, too, so that people think he's even dumber than he really is."

Then God gloated, and he laughed to himself.

"And to crown this creation, next I'm going to make him really horny, but I'll put a curse on him and give him a penis so bent that he can never use it except to pee."

Then God gasped with joy and clapped his hands gleefully because He had managed to create the perfect idiot. Such a God cannot be good; a little Hitler up in the sky. Crass said so, too. God is not as good as he thinks he is. "Big A Little A," one of my favorite songs goes:

Hello, hello, hello, this is the Lord God, can you hear?
Hellfire and damnation's what I've got for you down there
On earth I have ambassadors, archbishops, vicar, pope
We'll blind you with morality, you'd best abandon any
  hope,
We're telling you you'd better pray cos you were born
  in sin
Right from the start we'll build you a cell and then we'll
  lock you in
We sit in holy judgment condemning those that stray
We offer our forgiveness, but first we'll make you pay

If God created everything, it's also his fault when things are miserable. If I make a game, like the Fisheries Game, which is so poor that you can't play it without the same people always losing no matter how often they play, it's not those people's fault. It's just a bad game. The more I thought about this, the more I realized God wasn't just evil to me. He was teasing me, but he was directly tormenting others. Why did God, for example, let children be born in places where they didn't have anything to eat? There was famine in Ethiopia. I had often seen pictures of little children there in the papers. They had scrawny feet, scrawny arms, distended stomachs, and flies in their eyes. And why did God create flies that wanted to get up in the eyes of hungry children? Why do we have to handle the great disgust that comes with such thoughts? These children don't have to worry about how to tie their laces because they don't even have shoes. Why did God decide to let them be born?

Grandma said that God was good and that I should always look to him and ask him to help me. For weeks I prayed fervently that God would allow my hair to be normal. But he never heard me. He doesn't listen to anyone. Case in point: the hungry people in Africa often prayed to God. But he never did shit. God allows children to be born only to suffer and die? And why did he do nothing to stop Hitler when he started killing innocent people? I guess the people in Auschwitz didn't ask God for help? Why did he never go to Auschwitz? Why he didn't he send Jesus to Auschwitz to drive the Nazis away? Crass said that Auschwitz was God's fault and that he should be ashamed of it. God didn't have time to listen to people imposing on him. I'd often asked God about all sorts of things and asked him to do things for me. I couldn't remember him ever lifting a finger, no more than for the people in Auschwitz. This meant that if God existed, then he thought everything was all right with him. And he wasn't good, but seriously crazy. He was clearly in agreement with Hitler. And now Hitler was up in heaven with God and they were really good pals. And if it was true what Grandma said, that God created everything, He also created Hitler and allowed him to do everything he did. It was he who created Hitler in his image.

It seemed obvious to me that God didn't exist. Any notion that he did must be a lie, created by people who enjoy tormenting and tricking others. I thought most priests I had met were dead dull, pretentious, and haughty. And because they were priests, they were pure and utter idiots. But people respected them because they thought they could connect to, and be in some special relationship with, God. And if God was so all knowing and wise, why would he choose so many morons to work for him? It was all nonsense. God wasn't good and if he wasn't good then I couldn't believe in him. It'd be like believing in Hitler. Yet Hitler was not nearly as much of a villain as God. Grandma might as well have told me:

"Jón, dear, just ask Hitler to help you. Hitler controls our whole life."

I never again asked God for anything. I was filled with frustration and anger towards everyone who had ever talked to me about the glory of God and Jesus. It was a pack of barefaced lies.

Poor Grandma had believed in God and put all her trust in him. But God had betrayed her. He had made her bear and birth stillborn children and children who died at birth or from some horrible disease when they were just two years old. He had let her be poor and he had caused Grandfather to drown. He created glaucoma and put it in Grandma's eyes and made her blind. There was nothing but hope and Grandma always being fearful of God and daring not to do anything but prostrate herself and bow before him. I wasn't going to follow suit. I wasn't going to believe in God. I hated God and I was in agreement with Crass and I joined them in saying "Jesus died for his own sins, not mine."

Hah! Take that, fuckfiend!

"Dear Jesus, disappear up your own ass; to Hell and the Devil with you!"

God cannot exist. Religion is just bullcrap that people say is true so everyone is afraid of divine punishment. And then other guys can get their own way and fondle girls' breasts just because they're priests. Priests are the worst people ever. They pretend to be holy but aren't. Under their robes they have erections and want to fuck all the girls. And while they are talking about Jesus and

God and the Bible, they're thinking about how much fun it would be to fuck all the women who look up to them. The priests are God's liars. They keep the lie alive and pretend to know everything about God and people trust them. The only thing they want is to dominate people. They like to have power over people. And when they are fondling girls they say that this is exactly what God wants. And God wants them to be allowed to fuck and it says so in the Bible. And that they can't be the ones to contradict God's will. They are all disgusting liars. All priests automatically hate me. I have no idea why. I think it's because they know I'm not afraid of them or their God. "I vomit for you, Jesus," I sing with Crass. The priest who confirmed me was like any other priest: also a liar. He told me and Eiki the Druggie that if we sat quietly in confirmation classes we'd get a hot dog party. It was just a lie. We were very well behaved the whole time, but never got hot dogs. He looked at the girls in disgusting ways and told them how beautiful and elegant they were. And when no one saw, he'd embrace them close to their breasts and rub his hard penis against them.

Everyone was ashamed of me. That was only natural: I'm slow, ugly and stupid. When confirmed children go up to the altar for First Communion, it's customary for their family and friends to stand up wherever they're sitting in church. Everyone clearly had lots of friends; there were lots of people who stood up as the confirmed went up. But when my name was called, only Ómar, my brother, and Rúna, my sister, stood up. Mom and Dad stayed seated and didn't budge. Mom told me they didn't want to stand up because they were ashamed of how old they were. But I knew that wasn't it. They were ashamed of me. Ashamed for having spawned this silly and ugly red-haired boy. And I understood completely. If I were my son, I would be embarrassed of me. I would be ashamed of me like I'm ashamed of my father. I don't know anything, can't use everyday utensils, don't know how to tie laces, can't add or write. I never know anything about anything, except for things that don't matter and that no one cares about. I don't know who I am or where I am. I don't know months and never remember the day. I'm always far behind everyone. I learn everything last.

All my friends had suddenly managed to learn how clocks worked so they always knew the time. I never did. Mom and Dad once gave me a wristwatch for my birthday. The face was like a soccer pitch. It was really cool, so I wore my watch but didn't know much about it and constantly got confused over the little and big hands. I recognized numbers like 1 and 6 and 12, but got confused where the hands were supposed to be when it was three or four o'clock. But I could use the watch to guess the time roughly. If both hands were down, it would soon be dinner. If they were both up, it was around noon. If someone asked me what time it was I tried to cover my ignorance by clowning around and joking.

"Jónsi, what's the time?"

I peered carefully at the clock and said, loud and clear:

"It's five minutes to one million."

This always earned a big laugh.

"No, really. What's the time?"

"Oh, right, of course!"

I looked back at the clock and said:

"It's a quarter to eternity."

When I was alone inside my room, I pored over the clock. I even went to the library and snuck out telling-the-time books for little kids. I copied down the pictures and wrote what time it was at each moment. But I didn't really know how to write. I wrote everything wrong and I often got things back to front. I was still teased at home for a letter I wrote Grandma from the countryside. Mom still remembered a whole sentence from it: "god bles you my grama," she said, and burst out laughing. It was totally miserable. I didn't want to give a shit about anything. To hell with all this fucking crap! To hell with the system. To hell with God. To hell with Jesus, too. To hell with school. To hell with this whole damn world. To hell with Núpur. And to hell with Ísafjörður and this whole fucking miserable Iceland.

But while I blamed others, I knew deep inside that really I had no one to blame but myself. I was wretched and I had failed. I was just stupid. Everything else was simply excuses: I couldn't tie my shoelaces because I was too dumb to learn. And that was why I couldn't learn division. As time went on, the more I studied math, the less I knew what was going on. And instead of admitting it and asking, I stayed silent because I didn't want everyone to see how stupid I was. Instead of revealing my idiocy, I hid it behind my clowning. I made it seem like I could learn math but chose not to. Not because I didn't understand it, but because I wasn't interested. I was able to mess about during math class, to joke and waste time. That's how it always went. It was all my fault. I couldn't blame someone else. It wasn't Mom or Dad or my teachers' fault that I didn't know math.

They had done nothing to me. I was just a fool who didn't know anything. That was the way it was. I thought it was just so awful that I avoided thinking about it.

It's terrible to be an idiot in this complex world and never be able to do anything in life. I won't have anything in the future because I can't learn anything. I won't even be able to get a driver's license. I will definitely become that guy who works shoveling with a spade while it's raining outside and everyone else sits inside drinking coffee. I alone will be outside, shoveling, covered in sloppy crappy mud, soaking wet, but still trying to be jolly. Then an excavator will fall on me while I'm down in some ditch and I'll die. Everyone will be unaffected; some will even be joyful. The priest who buries me will talk about how I was always healthy and industrious. Or I'll go to work on a fishing boat. Because I'm bound to mess something up, I'll fall into the sea and drown. Or I will be some kind of mobster. The police will catch me and put me in jail or in some loony bin with people who can't tie their shoelaces or only eat with forks because no one's allowed a knife. Maybe there will be some kind women who care for us and look at me with pity in their eyes and ask:

"Are you hungry, Jón, dear? Want to go out for a walk?"

Then we'll go for a walk and one of these kind women will tie my shoes because I can't. While I sit there, I'll look at her and think about how much fun it would be to fuck her.

When summer ended, I went back to Núpur. I enjoyed seeing my friends again. At one point in the summer, I had been hanging out downtown with some kids from Hlemmur. We ran into the evangelist who stood in Lækjartorg Square reading the Bible for passersby. He had a cardboard box full of cassettes he was selling; they featured recordings where he read things from the Bible. He was a very strange man; he stood at a weird angle and tilted his head. His voice screeched but was still soft; he always either screeched or muttered to himself. When people walked by, he asked them, "May I ask you to buy a cassette with Christian material on it?"

We really got very interested in this and stood a long time talking to the guy, teasing him and having a good time. We really wanted to buy a tape off him because we were certain that it would be really funny. We tried to make out we were true believers in the hope of getting a cassette for free. The guy was not up for it. When we next got together, we talked about the guy and remembered the conversation and laughed at the whole thing. I began to imitate him and managed to mimic his mannerisms and his voice quite well. I also remembered verbatim what he said. Between words, he would suck up saliva quickly and it made a very funny sound. Sliff.

"May I ask you–sliff–to buy a cassette with Christian material–sliff–on it?"

We thought this was impossibly funny so I kept on doing it. Then I walked around town, impersonating the guy, and screeching at strangers:

"May I ask you-sliff-to buy a cassette with Christian material-sliff-on it?"

We laughed at this. After I got home that night I kept thinking about the guy and mimicked him for my own amusement. I laughed myself to sleep. This guy was probably the most enjoyable thing to happen that summer.

I debuted my impression of the guy immediately on the plane on the way to Ísafjörður. As I walked between the seats, I shrieked:

"May I ask you-sliff-to buy a cassette with Christian material-sliff-on it?"

Even the flight attendants found this hilarious. I sat at the back of the plane and invited the other kids to come back to meet the guy. There, I was in my element. This was the social Jónsi. He was bringing joy and was proud of all the mirth: there was nothing better than being around others and blurting out something and messing about.

We landed in town. I looked neither right nor left but went straight to the bus and asked the bus driver to buy a cassette with Christian material on. Everyone laughed and I sat down. The bus was full of kids and it set off to Núpur. Things were even freer on the bus than the plane. We walked about, shouted and screamed, and threw rubbish everywhere. There were some new faces in the crowd, but I didn't pay them any special attention. Suddenly I noticed a girl I had not seen before. She was new. I thought she was amazing. That, though, wasn't unusual: I generally thought every girl was more amazing than the last. She had coal-black hair, a brooding appearance, and heavily made-up eyes. I noticed a striking resemblance to Nina Hagen. She was clearly a punk. She was dressed in black from head to toe, and wore military boots. This was exciting. Had another punk really come to Núpur? Maybe she listened to Crass? She seemed reserved but smiled and laughed when I mimicked the guy. That intrigued me and I could not help but sneak eyes at her and contemplate her. She was clearly an authentic punk and I really wanted to meet her. I watched her closely when the bus stopped and we got off. I looked specifically for badges on her clothes, band names or something like that. But nothing of the sort. Just black clothing, head to toe.

Zakarías the janitor greeted the bus and led us to our rooms. I had changed corridors and now went to the top corridor. When I had been to my new room, I went straight to the Smoker. It was the best place to hear stories, meet new kids, and hopefully this exciting girl. And not long after that, she came in, sat on the bench and lit a cigarette. She smiled friendly at me. Much to my delight, I noticed that she had dog collars around her neck.

"Are you a punk?" I asked her immediately.

"Yes."

"Yeah, I'm also a punk…so…"

"Yes, I can see that," she said, and smiled softly.

"I used to have dog collars."

"Yes, okay."

"I only really listen to Crass."

"Me too," she said, like it was normal. I thought this was really too good to be true. There was another punk at Núpur.

A girl, even! And she wasn't a fake punk or a new wave freak like so many girls but a Crass-punk! "Me too!" The answer echoed in my head. She was dressed in black and definitely an anarchist.

"Punk rock is dead, of course," I added. She nodded agreement.

"Yes, exactly, except Crass," she said, nodding toward my Crass logos. I almost choked with happiness. "Except Crass!" This girl was absolutely magnificent. For the second time in my life I was truly in love.

"I'm Kikka."

I had never heard this name before but it had to be the most beautiful woman's name ever. Kikka.

"I'm Jónsi. Nickname: Jónsi Punk."

From that moment, we hung out a lot together. We sought each other out, sat together in class, in the dining room and the Smoker, talked about punk, anarchism, and Crass. She was an anarchist like me and agreed it was by far the cleverest structure for society. We swapped tapes and I learned that she actually listened to much more than Crass. I was rather reluctant to listen to anything other than Crass, unless it was put out by Crass or somehow approved by Crass. I knew all the bands that Crass published but didn't enjoy most of them, and thought the lyrics weren't that good or objective. If songs discussed anything other than anarchy or war or nuclear weapons or the end of the world I wouldn't listen to them. What most got on my nerves were lyrics about going on a bender or getting hold of booze or crap about girls. I felt like it was a total waste of time and absolutely ludicrous to write songs about drinking or girls. It was unreasonable.

Kikka introduced me to John Lennon. One day when we were talking about punk and song lyrics, and I was explaining to her why I only listened on Crass, she asked out of the blue:

"But have you listened to John Lennon?"

This threw me. She didn't seem to be joking. John Lennon wasn't punk! Worse, he was a hippie. Even worse, he'd been in the Beatles, who were the worst of all the worst. The Beatles were bubblegum. All their tracks were totally peppy and their songs talked about how much fun dancing was and how nice it was to kiss girls! "Have you listened to John Lennon?" I didn't know how I was supposed to answer this ridiculous question. I had just explained to her why I only listened to Crass.

"Uhh, no, I don't listen to much of that hippie stuff."

"You're really going to enjoy the lyrics. You'd definitely get a lot out of his lyrics."

"Wasn't he in the Beatles…?" I asked, the way you'd ask if someone had been in jail for a horrible crime.

"Yes, but that was years ago. The Beatles are long gone, you see."

"Yeah."

"Haven't you listened to him?"

I shook my head awkwardly. I tried to recall whether Crass had ever said anything about John Lennon, but couldn't remember them doing so.

"So have you listened to any Marianne Faithful?"

I had no idea who that was.

"No. Is she a punk?"

"For sure she's a punk. She was Mick Jagger's lover."

Mick Jagger was to my mind the most jerk-off asshole ever. He was almost as ridiculous as Adam Ant. And, worse, he was an old man. He was so old he could even be Adam Ant's dad.

"Mick Jagger? From the Rolling Stones?"

I tried to put as much disapproval into my voice as I possibly could. This couldn't get much worse.

"Yes," she said, and nodded. "You mustn't judge her for it."

I didn't listen to anything connected with the Rolling Stones. They were the second worst band in the world, following close on the heels of The Beatles! What she was thinking of? The Rolling Stones were so bad that Mom and Dad could almost listen to them! Mom had indeed enjoyed a lot of Stones songs. I wasn't quite sure where this conversation was going, but I felt very uncomfortable. I just sighed and shook my head. I was speechless.

"Relax, Jónsi. I'll put on a song for you."

She reached for a tape and put it in the cassette player.

"So. This is a John Lennon song, sung by Marianne Faithful. Have you heard it?"

I knew nothing about it.

"It's a song about labor unions."

I knew a lot about labor unions. I had read both *The Struggle for Bread* and *Poor People* by Tryggvi Emilsson and *The Grapes of Wrath* by John Steinbeck. I also knew that anarchism was often closely linked to labor unions. I was very relieved to hear that the song wasn't about how John Lennon was really happy to go out dancing and meet some stupid girl. Kikka pressed play and the song came out the speakers. Marianne Faithful had this rough, masculine voice. I enjoyed the lyrics. I followed along with the melody:

They hurt you at home and they hit you at school.

They hate you if you're clever and they despise a fool.

Crass had also said this. The song was called "Working Class Hero" and was about being a trade union leader and helping other work-ers. It was something I could well imagine doing in future. I felt it was a massive song. He wasn't an utter idiot, John Lennon, after all. Perhaps he had been listening to Crass and maybe that was the reason he left the Beatles.

There were often times I'd be tempted to listen to something other than just Crass. Like when I went and saw *The Wall* by Pink Floyd. It was being shown at The New, the cinema, so I went with a friend. When I sat down, I noticed a purse lying on the floor. There was no money in it, but instead some hash crumbs. We ran back out and got to smoke a little pot before the movie started. I thought it was really good. I didn't really know what Pink Floyd was. I thought it was industrial rock. They weren't hippies, punks, or new wave. I thought the lyrics and the message of the film were very good. However, they made the mistake too many musicians make, which was having a long guitar solo in the middle of a song. Pink Floyd weren't punk, but they still wrote good lyrics.

"Hey! Teachers! Leave them kids alone!"

I had sung it loud when I burned my schoolbooks in front of the teachers' lounge at Fossvogur School. Maybe Pink Floyd and Crass were friends. They must be. Kikka looked at me, curious. When the song was done, she asked:

"Isn't it amazing?"

JÓN GNARR

I couldn't deny it. It was a cool song with an important message and good lyrics.

"Um, yeah. Very cool lyrics, yeah."

"Yes, John Lennon wrote it."

"Uhh, right. He stopped being a hippie? Is he an anarchist?"

"He's from the hippie generation, but he's gone his own way. You know, all the Beatles are his enemies, really."

I thought that was interesting.

"For ideological reasons?"

"Because he got with Yoko Ono."

I had no idea who that was.

"Who's that?"

"His girlfriend."

"Yes. And she's a hippie?"

"No. She's an artist."

I had very little knowledge about artists. Artists painted mountains and little birds. It didn't seem interesting to me.

"I have an album of theirs if you want to listen to it."

I felt I was already out on a limb in musical matters and didn't know if I was ready to take another step into the unknown. But this song was good and the lyrics, too, and she was certainly interesting, Marianne Faithful.

"So, John Lennon is now in a band with Yoko Ono called John Lennon/Plastic Ono Band."

"Okay?"

I had never heard of it. Kikka had a record player and a small collection of albums. She asked:

"Want to listen to an album of theirs?"

I couldn't say no. I was curious and trusted Kikka. She had taste. She put the album on the gramophone and handed me the sleeve. On the front were little pictures of John Lennon and some buck-naked people. I found this album art weird, unlike any I'd seen before. I examined it carefully and thought it resonated in some particular way with Crass. One picture was of John Lennon in bed with an acoustic guitar and a naked woman and above them, "Give Peace a Chance." Another picture was of a totally naked lady with her butt in the air and all around her were floating bullets. Above the figure it said, "Woman Is the Nigger of the World." In one corner was a picture of a military plane and above it was written "War is Over." That was like Crass's slogan, "Fight War Not Wars." Kikka continued to carefully watch me and scrutinize my reactions. She started the record player and the first song began to sound, "Give Peace a Chance." I'd heard that song before, it was often played on the radio, even. This was just a very typical, silly hippie tune. Hippies jumping about with some jingling and singing hippie songs all together like they were having fun at the Kópavogur Asylum. A silly hippie song. I smiled weakly to Kikka while I endured through the song. It was horrible.

I started wondering whether Kikka was trying to lead me astray. Maybe she wasn't a real punk? Was she perhaps just a punk on the surface, one who dressed like a punk but listened to all kinds of hippie crap? The songs rolled on. I found them all quite dull. But occasionally I heard something in the lyrics that struck me. The song "Mother" touched something inside me and I wanted to hear it again. "Woman Is the Nigger of the World" I also found very cool. This was a phrase Crass could have come up with.

Many of these songs could almost be songs by Poison Girls. In between were songs such as "Imagine" that I'd heard before. I thought the song okay and the lyrics good, but it was still a hippie song. I really wanted, however, to hear "Mother" again. Yet I dared not say so. The song was about a mom and dad and it reminded me of my parents. But it wasn't cool or tough.

"Yes, this is all good, fine. I think, for example, 'Woman Is the Nigger of the World' is really exactly what Crass is saying."

"Yes, exactly!" said Kikka, and beamed.

"But, in between, there's also quite a bit of hippie crap, honestly."

"Yes, he was still a hippie, but Yoko Ono managed to change him a lot."

"Yes, exactly."

I assumed it was a Chinese woman with him in the pictures. She also sometimes sang the songs.

"They're together in the Plastic Ono Band, the main figures in the band."

"Yes. Can I record the album on cassette so I can also listen to it in my room?"

"Yes, absolutely!"

Kikka was overjoyed by my words.

"I've got a blank cassette."

She set up her tape recorder to record from the record player and put on the album again. We listened to all the songs a second time, holding our breath and not saying a word so as not to damage the recording. Later that night, after the dorm was shut and everyone had gone to bed I listened to "Mother" again. I hid myself under the covers, spooled past all the songs and listened carefully.

251

And when the song was done I listened to it again. And once again. I began to cry.

So my attitude toward John Lennon changed. I thought he was an interesting guy and I wanted to know more about him. Kikka knew a lot and told me all kinds of stories about him and Yoko Ono and what they stood for and had done. They were pacifists and fought for peace. That was the gist of "Give Peace a Chance" and the message in "Imagine." And when I managed to overcome my prejudices against hippies and began to read the lyrics, I found they had a lot in common with what Crass said. If you imagined that there was no war, then the world would be better. It would be better, too, if there were no religion and no priests and none of this religious bullshit about heaven and that sort of nonsense. The confusion was only maintained to keep people quiet and so they weren't thinking much about their rights or wondering how the world could be so unjust. It was one big lie where the main idea was man's oppression. Robber barons oppressed people and religions were part of the oppression. John Lennon was against war and he was also against religion so he basically agreed with Crass, even though he said nothing about anarchism. But Kikka wanted to claim he was an anarchist, although he never said so. I was also sure he listened to Crass and felt I heard it in the lyrics. I found it really clear in "Working Class Hero." I wrote the lyrics carefully into my notebook and underlined what I found particularly inter-esting. I was used to doing this to learn Crass lyrics better. John Lennon had come into my life and I gave him a warm welcome.

I was taking a new step in my life and it made me happy and cheerful. I enjoyed discussing these topics with Kikka.

She was the first person at Núpur who liked talking to me about Crass and anarchism. But we could also talk about John Lennon and Pink Floyd. One day when we were sitting together inside her room and talking, she suddenly said:

"I've a little gift to give you."

"A gift to give me?"

She smiled shyly and handed me a folded piece of paper. When I opened it, I saw it was a poster of John Lennon. What a treasure! How could she have the heart to give me this splendid poster? It was a big moment in my life when I went into my Crass temple with my John Lennon poster. My room only had Crass posters and Crass images I'd put on the walls. Crass logos over the window. I felt shy: embarrassed but happy. Like I was telling Crass they were going to have a sibling, a little boy whose name was John Lennon. But I was quite confident they would welcome him. I hung it on the wall between Crass logos. Maybe I was growing up? Perhaps this was some sort of next step in something? I could certainly no longer solely listen to something no one else listened to. I had to share music with others. I was tired of having no one to talk to about Crass. No one knew Crass but everyone knew John Lennon and I felt good having him on my team. I tried mentioning Lennon's name many times and it did not matter who I was talking to or what the circumstances were. If I mentioned it, I always got a positive reaction. It seemed that somehow everyone was happy with John Lennon. Even people who agreed that the Beatles sucked, and the Rolling Stones too. John Lennon stood out as cool. He was not just a hippie, since he used his fame to fight for peace. That impressed me a lot. I would do that It was reasonable and logical and also trendy.

But could Kikka be my girlfriend? I was getting the hots for her. She was cute, funny, smart, and had a sense of punk music. I could not imagine that any girl could be as perfect as Kikka. She never said anything silly and never got on my nerves. We had become very good friends and were together most of the time. I decided to grow my hair and try to become more like John Lennon. Kikka found it very cool. She said I was like him and I thought it was the greatest compliment I'd ever got. There was now purpose in my otherwise directionless, contentless life. Now the days were oriented around Kikka. I hung out with her in class and we got together in the Smoker. We walked around together and sat side by side in the dining room. Then we got together inside one bedroom or other to listen to good music and read lyrics. Kikka was my best friend, my only real friend at Núpur. And she was a girl! Our relationship had never been difficult or uncomfortable; it had just developed by itself. She seemed to have as much fun being with me as I with her. She had beautiful hair, beautiful eyes, and beautiful hands. And when I thought about her, it warmed me inside. Even her army boots were beautiful. I had never before seen such beautiful army boots. I often wondered whether we could become a couple. Would she want that? Perhaps she wasn't interested in me that way. Maybe she just wanted us to be friends. Or were we already going out because we hung out so much with one another? Did it just happen automatically or did you have to do something? I had no idea about it and didn't dare ask anyone either. Sometimes the boys asked me:

"You going with Kikka?"

"Nah, we're just listening to music."

"Sure, she has totally great breasts."

I didn't quite know how to reply. I felt like I could neither deny not admit it. She was so awesome that I didn't really care about her breasts.

"So, why aren't you going with her?"

"Well, I don't know."

"She's shit-crazy for you, for sure."

Could that be? How did they know?

"No? How do you know?"

"Because you're always together and I see the way she looks at you and talks to you."

How she looked at me? What did they mean? Did Kikka talk about me? With who? What did she say? I didn't discuss her with the guys; I didn't know them well enough. There was no one I trusted. Óli the Stud was probably the only person I could possibly count on to talk about this with, but he wasn't there. I wouldn't call him up like some idiot.

Kids, however, were always going out and breaking up. In between, they were a couple for a long time and often cuddled and fondled on the sofas or on the benches in the Smoker. This world was foreign to me, and complicated, and I had felt sure I would never be a part of it.

I found no faults in Kikka's character. She was the first thing that came to mind when I woke up in the morning and the last thing I thought about before I fell asleep at night. I was no longer alone at Núpur. We were fellow punks. Some called us Sid and Nancy. When the dorm was locked at night and I was stuck in the boy's corridor and she in the girl's corridor, I was simply waiting to be able to see her again.

Should I be bold and ask her if she wanted to go out with me? But what if she didn't? What if she just laughed? Was I then maybe destroying our friendship? I had read in books how people sometimes sent a love letter or a declaration of love to the woman they had a crush on. Þórbergur Þórðarson did that. I struggled to write some kind of letter but didn't know what to say. Was I meant to write a long letter and say what I thought? I found that a bit silly and I was afraid she would think so too. I tried to write merely "Do you want to go out with me?" I still didn't think it worked. It wasn't a love letter. I wondered if I could ask her in a poem or lyrics. Kikka enjoyed poetry like me. She knew Steinn Steinarr's poems. I tried to write some fiery love poems in the spirit of Steinn. The results were silly and lame, and I ripped them up immediately and threw them in the trash.

For the first time in a long time, I began to think about my appearance. I started to wash. My hair was starting to grow longer. I tried to stop biting nails and to put on clean clothes. I'd previously let myself be dirty and disgusting, but now I stopped cold. Kikka used a hairbrush to brush her hair. I started to use a comb. I took my clothes to the laundry and washed them. It was something I had never done before. Mom had always seen to washing my clothes, but at Núpur I'd taken to just having dirty clothes. Now everything had changed. Though Kikka was a punk, she was tidy and thought about hygiene and I had to do that too. She had even two different types of shampoo: shampoo and conditioner. I knew what shampoo was, but I'd never heard of conditioner. I just washed with hand soap in the shower at Núpur and didn't think about anything else. And on the rare occasions when

I washed my clothes, I'd just get dressed in a lot of clothes and go in and get into the shower in them. When I was drenched, I smeared myself all over in hand soap and washed the clothes that way, and myself at the same time. But Kikka had conditioner. She told me that you put it in your hair when you were done washing it with shampoo and it made your hair soft. Sometimes she said things to me that sounded like suggestions but which immediately became decisions in my head:

"Perhaps you should walk around wearing socks."

And then she said:

"You might want to get yourself some new glasses, Jónsi. You'd definitely look totally cute with John Lennon-style glasses."

So it was decided. Next time I was in Reykjavík, I'd go straight to Mom and insist that she bought me socks and new glasses. Trendy glasses like John Lennon had.

One day a wonderful thing happened. A drama teacher came to Núpur. He was going to teach us drama and put on a play that we could act in. It was all very exciting. A notice appeared on the board outside the dining hall and said that the theatre club would have its first rehearsal in the gym. I was very excited and turned up at the appointed time with a group of other kids. The drama teacher was extremely dynamic and fun. The rehearsal began with a comic warm-up. He made us run around the room and gesticulate wildly and when he clapped his hands we had to freeze in the position we were in. We thought this was so much fun that we had a hard time not laughing. We had to speak, too. He made us whisper, talk, and yell. Finally, he brought us up to the stage one by one and had us read aloud some sentences from a script. We had to remember two or three sentences and speak them in various ways. He made us close our eyes and imagine that there were people around us that we were talking to. We also had to imagine that we were lost and there were other characters on stage who might help us find our way. I thought it was out-of-control fun and totally lost track of time and place. The drama teacher and the other kids were out in the gym and I was alone on stage—I was lost. I pretended to call out for someone and asked various questions and said things into thin air:

"I must get to Núpur!"

I could tell the drama teacher was pleased with my performance. I liked that. True, it had nothing to do with punk or Crass and the play wasn't about Crass or anarchism. To stand up on stage struck some strings inside me I did not know I had. I felt like I was in some kind of magic and I wanted it to last forever. I felt good on stage and in front of others. I wasn't afraid or insecure and did not feel inadequate, like when I was brought up to the desk in class or standing on stage with Runny Nose, my old band. I was good at this. And I was sure I could solve any task the drama teacher set me.

The next rehearsal was the very next day. The teacher had photocopied copies of the play. He made us sit on the floor and showed us the script.

"This is the play: *Unripe Fruit* by Pétur Gunnarsson. You know it?"

We all shook our heads. I didn't recognize the play, but I knew of Pétur Gunnarsson and had read two books by him. *Period period comma stroke* and *I and me and my and mine.*

"*Unripe Fruit* is one of the most wonderful teen dramas ever written."

Teen dramas? I had no idea teen drama existed. I knew there were children's plays and adult plays, but the existence of plays for teenagers was absolutely staggering. The teacher was going to give us different roles and have us read through the play together. We sat in a circle on the floor, each with our script. The play had many characters. Some weren't people, but a part of a group: "kids" or "girls." I hoped fervently that I would be a person, that I'd get a role, because I didn't want to just be part of a group. I would enjoy getting to be on stage and saying lines alone, rather than just with others. And I wasn't disappointed. The drama teacher had chosen me to play the lead. Waves of joy rippled my skin. The lead role! I was going to play the lead in the best teen drama in Iceland.

We did a substantial amount of rehearsing every day. There were other kids with big parts, but I was the main character. The play was about my coming of age. I was changing from a boy into a teenager. *Unripe Fruit* took over my life. Now I thought about the play as soon as I woke up in the morning and fell asleep to the script at night. Nothing else mattered. I spent every moment with my script and practiced my lines tirelessly. The play was fun and funny. But it was serious, too, and almost somehow sad. It talked about what it was like to be a teenager. It could be fun, but it could also be miserable and lame. It talked about what it was like to drink for the first time and what it felt like to have a crush. And so I discovered some of the magic of acting. As a character in the play, I could say things out loud on stage in front of hundreds of people that I myself had never dared say to anyone.

Acting opened a surprising world for me. It was not just this play or its words, but something far bigger. The language of theater was the language of another world. A language that was separate from, but connected to, normal language. It was like I'd discovered a new dimension where other principles applied than in the normal world. The world of acting was one world over from dreamland. And I couldn't remember having ever been so happy. Every day felt complete. The drama teacher taught me various techniques and tricks. He taught me, among other things, how to use my voice. When you talk on stage, you have to remember to tense your stomach muscles. Don't just speak your words form your throat, but your stomach. You'll be heard better and never get hoarse.

"You are an instrument, Jón; the body is your tool."

Then he explained how I should stand on stage. I always need to find the light so people could see me. Then he taught me how I'm supposed to move my body on stage.

"While you're talking to someone else on stage, then you still half-look in the direction of the audience because you're also talking to them."

I thought it all very logical. There was nothing in acting that I thought was nonsense or unnecessary like most of what they tried to teach me at school. Acting had a purpose. I felt the drama teacher was an angel sent from another dimension to save me. He was sent to take me from a boring country to the country of drama. And I felt that I was good at it. He often congratulated me and said I was a natural talent.

"You're a born actor, Jón!"

I'd never in my life received a compliment like it. "A born actor!" There was finally something I was good at. Until now I hadn't felt I was good at anything that mattered. I was not good at school or sports or music. I was just good at nonsense stuff, and things that didn't matter, like playing the Fisheries Game. Now I was an actor. Maybe it was something I could do in future? Maybe I could be an actor.

After a few weeks, the play was ready and we made a program. The drama teacher took pictures of us rehearsing and put them in the program to be printed. We made the scenery ourselves, but the drama teacher had fixed us up with costumes from Little Play House in Ísafjörður. We were in full costume, with scenery and props. I got bliss-chills from looking across the stage.

I felt like someone who has always been lost and wild, but was now finally home. And I forgot all my everyday concerns. I was happy and carefree and I felt myself flourish. It wasn't difficult to understand anything in acting and nothing stumped me. I looked forward more to each rehearsal than I had ever looked forward to Christmas. When acting, I wasn't stupid and I could remember everything and do everything right. And it was not difficult and boring; it was fun, and therefore effortless. I came to realize that what's meaningless isn't fun. If the drama teacher gave me new instructions, I listened to them without a fight and without effort. Sometimes he stopped me and said something I was doing was not good enough. Then I changed it immediately and fixed it. Sometimes he clapped his hands in admiration.

"You're absolutely fabulous, Jón!"

When that happened, I felt like I'd been injected with the most excellent drugs in the world. I had finally discovered something I was good at. I'd been chosen for the lead role. And it was because I was a good actor. I was also quick to know if someone went wrong with his lines because I had the whole play completely memorized. I often knew other kids' lines better than they did and had to make sure not to move my lips while they were talking. I could have played the play entirely alone. I would have run up and down the stage and played and talked to all the characters. I could be everyone and turn myself into any role there was. I was an actor.

All the kids at school, and the staff, too, were invited to the opening night. People from the surrounding area were also invited.

The audience came from all over and the crowd consisted of kids, teachers, farmers, and the local priest. It was a full house; the great hour had come. Klikki was really into acting, but hadn't been selected for a role. He couldn't learn lines and just said what he wanted to say. But Klikki got to be Stage Manager and compère. He set up the scenery and raised and lowered the curtain. But Klikki was odd and you never knew what he might do. Sometimes he just got the idea to do something no one expected. He liked to shock people and to disrupt things. And he did exactly that on opening night. At the start of the evening, he had to read a particular text welcoming everyone and introducing the play. When everyone was seated, the lights in the hall turned off, and the spotlight fell on the scenery, it was Klikki's part. He stepped out from among the scenery and into the spotlight. But instead of welcoming everyone and telling them about the play, he kept quiet and grinned slyly at the audience. The he turned his back to them. The cast watched him, peeping out from behind the scenery. He loosened his trousers so they fell down. Then he exposed his bare buttocks to the room and screamed from between his feet:

"I'm a compère-ass, I'm a compère-ass!"

There was hubbub in the room and some women covered their children's eyes. Someone shouted loudly: "Lout!"

But Klikki was amusing himself enormously and he giggled as he looked from between his feet and watched their reactions. The teachers jumped up on stage and dragged him off. There was grumbling around the hall. No one had expected this, least of all me. I was furious with Klikki. I didn't find it funny. He was ruining things. I was about to go on stage. I was going to act.

And Klikki was just an idiot who was disruptive, who got in the way, who was annoying. But after some fuss and agitation, the play began. The drama teacher took over stage management.

The curtain was raised and I stepped on stage. At that moment, I experienced an absolute exaltation of my soul. Instead of crumpled-up little Jón, who was always tripping himself up on something, there came an actor who seized my spirit. In a weird way, I filled the entire space. I filled myself and I filled the stage. I felt like I filled the whole room, every corner. It was like I held a huge energy balloon, which emerged from within me. It pushed outwards and enveloped everything and I could somehow control it. I could suck it inside myself and swallow it. And when I wanted to, I could push it slowly or quickly into the room. I could waft it gently across the room and I could play around with it on stage. Although it was invisible, it felt tangible to me. And the air in the balloon was my soul. It was like she moved through everything. I was huge. On stage, I became someone. It was magic. I saw and felt the way the audience felt it, too. They gasped and exploded in laughter. And it was I who controlled everything. Suddenly, the play was over. When the curtains had been closed and we stepped back on stage, the thunderous applause began. Some people whistled. Never, ever, had anyone clapped for anything I'd done ever before. I smiled proudly and earnestly out into the auditorium. Several people even rose from their seats because they were so happy. And I was the heartiest and most beautiful and most amazing kid in the whole world. I felt absolutely great and they were all happy with me. Even the teachers smiled. They who were almost always unhappy with me were now in ecstasy. Everyone wanted to come up to me and thank me.

"That was a great performance, Jón! You were so extraordinarily funny!"

People talked among themselves about the play. I got a buzzing in my ears from the flattery and praise. I felt light and weightless, like in a dream. When we walked back to the dormitory that evening I felt like my feet didn't even touch the ground. I was full of confidence and I felt invincible. And when I was in my room, my soul shone a wonderful light. I threw myself onto my bed, closed my eyes and returned to the theater in my mind to experience again the audience's reaction. Their applause and praise rang in my head. I had managed to do something unexpected and fun for everyone. And it was the most wonderful thing. Smiling, I passed into sleep, into a wonderful dreamland where I flew. I opened my arms and took off. Effortlessly, I flew over Núpur's gymnasium. I flew down to the shore, along the mountains and all the way up to the peaks. I flew high over the mountains and allowed myself to fall down behind them. I could fly to Núpur and I could fly away from Núpur. I could fly anywhere. I was free. As a bird.

It was the unanimous opinion of everyone that the play *Unripe Fruit* in the production of the Theater Club at Núpur was, clear and simple, a dramatic triumph. And everyone agreed that the performance of the lead actor, Jón Gunnar Kristinsson, was exceptional, that it was by far the best among equals. All around the region there was no other topic but this amazing youth.

"The boy's a born performer!"

Since the play was so good, it was decided we would go on a theater tour. We would get to stage the play in Þingeyri and Flateyri and there would be a final performance in the Little

Theater in Ísafjörður, which was practically a city and had a real theater! The performance in Þingeyri went off seamlessly. After the performance ended, the noise of the appreciation streaming from the applause seemed like it would never end. As with the premiere, the audience flocked around me and congratulated me. The whole cast was praised, but everyone specified how fabulous I had been in my role. Utter bliss. This was all absolutely wonderful. We'd been freed from school and were staying in Þingeyri. Then we took the bus over to Flateyri and our scenery was set up and made ready for the next show. The performance in Flateyri was even better than the one in Þingeyri. We had gained a better command of the lines, weren't nervous, and reacted better to the audience. I felt that I was growing with every show. Between performances, I had also given my fellow actors suggestions for improving their performances. I had even spotted things that the drama teacher had not commented on. I wasn't interfering or being difficult. I simply told them in order to help them do better. And once again, I experienced this lovely, dreamy euphoria from being on stage. I was looking forward to the moment when the curtains were drawn and I stood alone in front of everyone on stage. And instead of being small and hunched, I would get to expand and expand and expand in front of everyone. And the audience would enjoy it too. Because that's how it was: they expanded through me.

We stayed in the communal parish house in Flateyri. When the audience had gone we sat there alone and reflected on our theatrical triumph After the show at Þingeyri, we'd had trouble falling asleep; we'd shot the breeze and laughed long into the night. But what was different in Flateyri was that in the center of the parish house was a little convenience shop. And through the glass hatch we saw a bunch of candy, cigarettes, soda, and other treats. This was quite unlike the shop at Núpur, which was like a Russian deli. The little shop at Flateyri, by contrast, was like an American supermarket. Exotic and tempting. After having considered the splendor for a short time, I kicked open the door to the shop and tramped into its bounty. We looked about and grabbed candy, drank coke and chain-smoked until we emerged red-eyed right before sunrise.

The following morning, we were caught at the crime scene, sleeping beside one another in heaps of candy wrappers. We were hauled to our feet in disgrace and with quite the hullabaloo. I startled when someone grabbed my shoulder; suddenly the shop filled with strange kids. I tried to tell them that it was okay because it had been so much fun, but it did not matter.

"We thought it would be okay..."

We were driven into a closet and the lecture began.

"You are horrible, awful, vandals! Devils! Don't you dare move!"

We were all bewildered, confused and tired. The drama director came, as well as the teacher who had accompanied us. The teacher was angry, but the drama director was regretful and sad. That was painful to see.

"Get your woeful selves on the bus!" said the teacher and told us to leave. When we were sitting on the bus, the drama director stood up and told us that the trip had been canceled because of this incident, and we would not get to perform the play in Ísafjörður as planned, but were heading back to Núpur. I felt my eyes fill with tears; it was like my heart was pinched in two with tweezers.

I hadn't expected that. If I'd known this would happen, I would never have gone into the shop. In the euphoric high after the show, I had, however, felt invincible and thought nothing could stop my run. I felt like I deserved candy. I thought we all deserved it. And by virtue of who I was, I felt like I could kick open any doors and break into any kiosk. And I was certain that everyone thought it was just as obvious as I did. Clearly not.

Like a hand being waved, my career in drama ended as quickly as it had begun. There were no more performances of *Unripe Fruit* and the drama teacher vanished. After sitting through a scolding from all the teachers, being sent to the principal to listen to yet more scolding, and a call made to Mom and Dad, I was sent to my room. The principal said I was going to be expelled from school yet again and this might be the last time since they were all fed up with me and my shenanigans. I threw myself weeping into bed. I was nothing but a moron, a jackass, a halfwit. I played the fool for everyone and mostly for myself. I was more a clown than Klikki was. And I, who had previously been gliding in the mountains like a flying bird, now fell into the sea with a loud splash, sinking down to the bottom.

Kikka and I continued to be good friends and met daily, talking and listening to music. I was determined to go ahead and ask her to go out with me, but I always got discouraged and put it off. Time passed and it was spring. School was over and we were on our way back to town, and I still had not managed to make my proposal. I felt that it was now do or die, leap or retreat, and I was adamant that I would leap. I didn't have the guts to ask her to her face and maybe it would go better if I called her. If she laughed, I could always say I'd been joking. I'd already decided how I should act and had decided to just ask her straight up if she wanted to go out with me. After thinking about it carefully for a few days, I decided to take action. She answered:

"Hello?"

"Hi."

"Hi?"

"This is Jón."

"Hi. What's up?"

"All's good. And you?"

"Great, totally great."

"What's going on?"

"Things are just great, yeah."

"Yes."

An embarrassing silence took over. It was like she didn't know what to say and was waiting for me to say something.

That was entirely natural since I'd called. After we'd been silent a while into the phone, the tension began to get intolerable. There was no turning back. If I couldn't get the words out right now, I'd be the biggest loser in the world.

"So, I was just here thinking..."

"Yes?"

"Yes, whether you...yourself...that is, I wanted to say, to ask you..."

"Yes, what?"

"Just a thought, nothing, but..."

"Yes?"

"Whether you wanted to, perhaps, really...I would like to... or if you would like to really...uh, whether you want to go out with me?"

She said nothing. The silence was awkward and long. I heard her giggling. This was probably hopeless. Of course this was ridiculous.

"Is this a joke?"

Why would she think that? What did she mean?

"What?"

"Are you pranking me?"

This was deadly serious.

"No! I am asking sincerely."

"Okay. Yes! Of course I will."

My heart leapt with joy. I had a girlfriend. I was not a loser. I had asked a girl to go out with me, and she had said "yes, of course!" After this, we continued to meet daily. We were extremely shy with each other. When we met, we sat together and talked. When we went out, we held hands. I felt it was important.

It meant we were an authentic couple and everyone could see we were together. Sometimes we kissed and cuddled. I struggled with that. I was shy and timid. And something was up with my prick.

My anxiety about my prick weighed upon me. I was no longer able to play with it to my satisfaction. Every time I looked at it, I began to think that there was something wrong with it. Was I deformed? I hadn't told anyone. I had tried to find information in books but found little. What did this mean? What about that? I didn't trust myself to ask anyone or talk to anyone about it. I couldn't talk about it with Mom. I wouldn't talk to Óli. And I didn't want to discuss it with my girlfriend. Moreover, it was difficult to describe or explain. My prick was, on the whole, normal. It was only when I got a hard-on that the problem became apparent. And I didn't exactly show anyone that. I was afraid and ashamed. I avoided as far as possible having our relationship get too sexual, whether in words or acts. I accepted that we were a couple and often together and that we held hands out on the street. Sometimes we kissed. But nothing more. Perhaps it would change when we'd been together longer and I knew her better.

Her mother and I became good friends. I got on very well with her. She was a musician, but also ran a little wholesale business and imported stuff including animal feed. She had a small basement in Norðurmýri that she didn't live in, but used as a kind of warehouse for the products she imported. Although the apartment was full of dog and cat food, you could just about live in it. We wondered if we could possibly move in once we turned sixteen and weren't kids anymore. Kikka's mom agreed to it providing we were going strong and we paid a small rent. A few days later we moved in.

The apartment was equipped with simple furniture and furnishings. We came with clothes, records, and posters to hang on the walls, nothing else. We'd made a home.

I felt I like I'd really grown up and was well-set in life. I had gotten a girlfriend and I lived with her in an apartment. I felt I was on the right track and was doing what other people do. I had become a regular adult. And I felt like we were married. I talked to my father and asked him to help me find a good job. He spoke with a friend who was the Head Gardener in Reykjavík and as a result I got work. I was to go to the work camp on Klambratún early in the morning, and was added to the workforce. The work mainly involved driving a little pickup truck around town, weeding beds, cutting fields, planting trees, and fixing pavements. I enjoyed it and found it a fun job. I was happy to learn about gardening. I learned to recognize summer flowers and the various tree species. I learned to lay slabs and to plant plants. I could well imagine being a gardener. The workmen were pleased with me and I felt good. I was happy.

I had an apartment, a job, and a girlfriend. Possibly we would get married and go on a honeymoon. It could be a good idea to get married because that's when you get a lot of expensive and fancy gifts. Kikka had also found work. We hardly saw each other during the day and she was often working additional shifts at night and on weekends. I had no problem with that. I didn't miss her. Adults can't hang around each other all the time. We were quite good friends, but still had little communication. We continued to hold hands when we could. And working completely changed everything. I got money every week and suddenly could buy whatever the hell I wanted. That was entirely new. I'd become a sensible man, one who cohabited. I bought clothes and records. I bought shampoo and conditioner and sometimes even went to the store and bought food for the house.

The apartment was close to Hlemmur and we'd often go there after work in the evenings. I knew lots of people there and they were soon friends on both sides. More often than not, some of the kids came home with us; we talked, listened to music and smoked cannabis. One consequence of cannabis smoking is major hunger; cannabis feeds your appetite. People being treated for cancer often lose their appetites and get thin. They are sometimes given cannabis as it relieves the nausea and increases appetite. We weren't immune to that. After heavy smoking, our food supplies were often depleted. And when all the human food was gone, we turned to the dog and cat food. I opened a few cans and put them in a pan. With good spices, it made the finest food. It was an exciting change to eat cat food. I cooked it regularly when guests from Hlemmur came over. It was funny and entertaining and news got out. Some kids came over precisely in order to taste it. Only a few thought the food tasted bad; most thought it fine and were quite surprised at how good the food given to animals was. The secret lay in the spice blend I used. I had also tasted all the types and knew what was best. Cat food was better than dog food and looked better. Chicken was the best and actually tasted like regular chicken. Tuna was the worst. But, of course, most folk were generally high and willing to eat whatever. I set great pride in my cooking and worked to become the great punk who cooked pet food for my visitors. Sometimes I put "I Wanna Be Your Dog" by Iggy Pop on the turntable and we laughed. Then we smoked weed and needed to eat.

I knew we weren't like other couples. Sometimes couples went into a room and locked it behind them. We never did anything like that. We just kissed and held hands. We didn't sleep together, just side by side. I accepted it, but didn't know what she felt because we never discussed it. If she tried to talk to me about it, I turned the discussion to something else. But I thought about it and continued my search for information. One day I came across a book in a bookstore—a sex ed. book for women. I looked at everything written about penises; something caught my attention. It said that penises had all kinds of shapes and sizes, some straight and others bent. But sometimes the penis was so bent that it wasn't possible to have intercourse. If you were uncertain, you should seek out a urologist who should be able to advise.

I thought about it. It was time to consult a doctor. I had to get out of this rut. The doctor could tell me if it was something to worry about and what could be done to fix it. When I got home I immediately got out the phone book. I found the section for "Doctors" and went through the list until I found one with the title "urological surgeon." I wrote the name, address and phone number on a piece of paper and put it in my pocket. I carried around the piece of paper for a few days, until I had gathered the courage to call.

I was going to speak about it with someone who could tell me something. The one time I was alone at home, I decided to do it. With trembling hands, I dialed the number and took a deep breath.

"Medical Clinic," said the woman who answered the phone.

"Yes, good morning," I said in a trembling voice. "I'd like to make an appointment with Þorsteinn Gíslason."

The silence on the phone seemed to last forever. If she asked me what was wrong, I was going to hang up.

"Have you seen him before?"

"Eh, no," I murmured.

My mouth was so dry from the stress that I struggled to speak.

"I have a free appointment with Þorsteinn on Wednesday, the eighteenth at three o'clock."

A week away. That was a relief. I thought I might even have to wait months.

"Yes, that's fine."

"What's your name?"

It was time. When I had spoken my name, there was no going back. I would no longer be some anonymous guy downtown.

"Jón Gunnar Kristinsson."

A week later I turned up at the medical center in a timely fashion, checked in at reception, sat down, and waited. After a moment, the door opened and a doctor in a coat called my name. I stood up and he invited me into the doctor's office with him. He sat at his desk, greeted me, and told me to sit across from him.

"Well, what can I do for you?"

"Yeah, well, you see, I've just got some concerns about my prick..."

I half-expected that he would laugh at me, but he did not seem to find anything funny.

"And why are you worried about it?"

"It's bent."

"Yes, I see. Is it always bent or just when you get an erection?"

"Yes, I mean, no, or just…erect."

The doctor reached behind him, looked through some papers, found a piece of paper, and set it on the table. I leaned forward. On the paper there were drawings of different pricks.

"What of these here is like yours?"

I examined the paper carefully and pointed to the most bent one. The doctor nodded and wrote something down.

"Let's take a look." He stood up and said, "Lie here on the bench."

I took off my pants and underwear and lay on the bench. He examined my prick thoughtfully, touched it, poked, and pinched. I thought it was really very uncomfortable. I had never before shown another person my prick or discussed it with anyone. And here I was talking about it with a stranger while he looked at my prick.

"This looks fine, nothing abnormal."

"Yes, no, see, it's just…"

"Of course, it's just when you're erect. How old are you?"

"I'm, well… sixteen."

"Have you had sexual intercourse?"

"Eh, no."

"Have you ever tried it and not succeeded?"

"Eh, no…"

The doctor nodded. After examining my testicles and pinching something on my scrotum he said I could get dressed. I put my clothes on and sat back at the desk. I breathed easier and thought it was over.

"Tell me, Jón, have you begun to masturbate?"

I had to admit it.

"And how does that work?"

"Just fine..."

"And you can ejaculate?"

"Yes."

"Are there any aches and pains when you get an erection?"

"No."

"When you're playing with yourself... do you think about girls or boys?"

Did he think I was gay?

"Girls!"

He took some notes then looked at me.

"As you probably know, there are different penis sizes and shapes and no two are alike. It's not uncommon that they are bent up or down or to the side and there's nothing abnormal about that. But sometimes they are bent so much it inhibits sexual intercourse. And since you have never had sexual intercourse, it's difficult to assess. Well, I can't evaluate your case without seeing your penis fully erect, and I doubt you are going to do that standing here in front of me."

I nodded awkwardly.

"Isn't there something you can do?

"Well, what I suggest is that I book you some time under anesthesia in the operating room. Once you're under general anesthetic, I can stimulate an erection and then assess what the situation is. I'll see it right away."

"But if it's completely crooked?"

"Well, if I see nothing wrong after the inspection, we'll send you away and we'll have nothing more to do. But if it's abnormal then I can take action."

I wanted to know more about what might happen.

"What would you do then?"

"Of course, I can't tell you until I've seen it."

I nodded and gave my consent. He picked up the phone and made a call. He spoke to someone at the operating theater and made an appointment. I got an appointment at the National Hospital two weeks later. It was a huge relief to walk out of the medical center. I sat on a bench outside the house. I was totally exhausted. I felt like I had run continuously for two days; I shook and shook and had butterflies in my stomach.

Two weeks later, I went early in the morning to the National Hospital. I checked in at the reception desk and was told to sit and wait. After a while a fat nun came to get me. She was dressed in white from head to toe, with white shoes and a white scarf on her head. She was German and spoke heavily accented Icelandic.

"Vollow me," she commanded, and I ran after her. I vollowed her down a long hallway and up some stairs. We went into the operating theater.

"Leave all zur clothes and take a showver. Zair are clean clothes."

The nun pointed to some folded clothes on a chair. I nodded and waited for her to go out, but she just looked at me and was clearly not going anywhere. It was obvious that I had to do this in front of her. I undressed awkwardly, turning my back to her, then went into the shower and pulled the shower curtain. When I stepped out of the shower, I saw there was another nun in the room.

I dressed in the clothes that were on the chair. Underpants and some kind of paper dress. The nuns told me to lie on the hospital bed. They were absolutely expressionless and neither of them smiled at me or said anything to me; they just talked to each other in a foreign language. The second nun was slightly shorter and thinner than the first. When I was on the bed, she lifted up the gown and pulled my underwear down to my feet. Everything went black and a poisonous cocktail of feelings brewed inside me. I wanted to stop it all and run screaming out of the National Hospital in my new dress. Shockwaves of tension and terror shivered through me. The littler nun soaked a shaving brush in shaving foam. I pinched my eyes shut. She took my prick, lifted it up and daubed foam all around it. I thought in some other circumstances I might possibly find this sexy. I felt icy steel slide over my scrotum and around my prick. The nuns continued to talk in a foreign language. I thought of my mother when she made blood pudding. As suddenly as it started, it was over. The nun let go of my prick and it collapsed back down. Then she wiped the leftover shaving foam with a towel. I opened my eyes and saw the larger nun push a small plastic cup in my direction and I understood I should drink from it. I raised myself up and drank the liquid medication. It was a sweet flavor. I looked at my prick. The nun had shaved me clean down there. All the hair had gone and I was back the way I'd been as a child. This had such a profound effect on me that I was stunned and felt faint and fell powerless back down onto the bed. They pulled up my underwear and took the hospital bed safely between their hands and wheeled me away.

On the way, I wondered whether the hair would grow back at all around my balls. I thought it unlikely. Pubic hair was definitely different than the hair on your head. You're born with hair on your head; it's unstoppable and grows all your life, no matter how often you cut it. But pubic hairs are different. They only grow once. When you become sexually mature, and never again. They only grow to a certain length and don't cover anything more. You should never get a pubic haircut. I was confident that I would never again grow hair down there and I would always be like a child.

It was cold in the hallway. We went in the elevator and then out into another corridor and through some swing doors that swung open with a thundering noise when the bed was pushed into them. Suddenly we were in the operating theater. I was relieved to see the doctor. He was in a surgical gown with a green hairnet on his head. I felt a tingling in my head and smiled at the doctor. The mixture I'd drunk was beginning to affect me.

"Nice to see you," I said warmly to the doctor. Someone took my hand. I felt a sting and saw that a hellish needle was being stabbed in my arm. The syringe filled with blood. The hand took away the syringe and a blue plastic plug remained on my hand. Instead of the syringe a tube was inserted into the plastic plug. I saw the doctor walk away. Was he done? I wanted to cancel. Perhaps we could wait a little. I tried to speak, but no sound came out and I mumbled something incomprehensible. I tried to look at the people who were around me but they did not look up. Through the clear plastic tube, I saw a blue fluid flow into my hand. Everything went black.

When I came to, I was back in a hospital room. My sleep had

been dreamless; it was like no time had passed: just the moment before I had been inside the operating theater. Clearly they'd understood I wanted them to stop. I felt the syringe still in my hand. I was just going to lie there and rest. Then I was going to go back to work and think about it some more before I spoke to the doctor again. I wondered if it was possible to take hair from my head and fix my groin so that I was not bald down there. But I was relieved nothing had happened. I felt for my prick. I wanted to pat it in a reassuring way, as if to say it would be all right. It wasn't to blame. My prick couldn't think it was at fault. It hadn't done anything wrong. It couldn't help the way it had been born.

I could find my prick. My fingers only encountered bandages. I lifted the covers and checked. My prick was in a thick layer of bandages glued down with large Band-Aids. I poked the package but it was so numb and sensationless that I did not feel anything. When did this happen? Had the nuns put this on me when they were done shaving me? I didn't remember that. Why couldn't I feel my prick anymore? What had happened? Did I maybe no longer have a prick? I fell back on my pillow. I was still groggy and disoriented from the medication; my mouth was dry. The door opened and in came a nun in all white with a big steel jug and glass. She tipped the jug, poured juice into the glass, and handed it to me. I lifted myself up awkwardly and took the glass in a trembling hand. When I was done drinking, I handed her the glass. She immediately filled it again. I smiled politely to her and drank. She nodded her head but did not smile. She had a resolute face and it occurred to me that she had squeezed the juice herself and was asking me to taste it and let her know it was okay.

"This is very good," I said clearly when I had finished the glass; I smiled encouragingly. She really knew how to make juice. The nun didn't seem quite convinced and once again poured a full glass and handed it to me. I smiled awkwardly at her, nodded and drained the glass.

"Verrrrryyy good," I said again, even more clearly than before. She looked expressionlessly at me. Maybe she didn't talk Icelandic?

"Veeeery good," I tried, in English, and really emphasized "very." She seemed satisfied and put the jug and glass on my nightstand.

"Do you have to pee now?"

She was asking me whether I needed to pee. I didn't have to pee, that wasn't the issue. And if I had wanted to pee, I would not have been able to through the bandages. I lifted the covers and showed her the package by way of illustration. She nodded.

"If you need to pee, ring the bell," she said, pointing to the bell on the bedside table. What a decent, thoughtful woman, I said to myself. She knows I'm confused by the medicine I drank and she is going to help me to the bathroom. I smiled at her as nicely as I could.

"Thanks."

The nun went out and left the door open. I relaxed my eyes and fell asleep. When I woke up again, I needed to pee. I decided to get myself out of bed, but I was still too weak and muddled. Maybe I could just get her to support me into the bathroom. I rang the bell. The nun who made the juice came back and another was with her. They both had fixed expressions.

"Hi. Er, I think I need to pee."

"Yes, good," they answered and helped me to my feet. They each took me under their arms and helped me to the toilet. When I got to the toilet, they lifted up my paper dress. I looked in despair at the bandage package. It was the size of a beehive. How was I going to get my penis out of this? Then I noticed that there was a hole in the bandage. I looked questioningly at the nuns who stood on either side of me and held me up. They nodded their heads with fixed expressions. I understand that I should just let go and pee would flow out the hole. I relaxed and began to urinate. As soon as I let go, I experienced the greatest pain I'd ever felt. A sore, heavy pain, a stabbing pain. It was like many broken coke bottles were being expelled from my stomach out through my prick. I lost my footing and would have fallen forward into the toilet if the nuns had not held me up. My eyes went black and I was in tears. I tried to say something but could not bring up any words, nothing but a rattle and a pained moan. It was like I was bleeding out. I saw the packaging get wet and bloody. Blood-colored piss ran into the toilet and onto the floor and down my thighs. The pain flowed all over my body, permeating me. I felt my eyes blink repeatedly and then I fainted. The next time I came to, I was lying back in bed. Now I had a sharp pain in my genitals. Through the pain I could feel a piercing sensation. I was barely awake when the nun was back. She took the jug, poured juice into a glass and handed it to me. I shook my head. I didn't want to drink any more. I didn't want to have to pee. I never wanted to pee again. Ever. But the nun did not give up.

"Drink!" she commanded. I took the glass and had a sip. The nun nodded resolutely. I finished the glass. She filled it again and handed it to me. I started to cry. I cried great sucking sobs.

Between my weeping cries I drank juice under the commanding gaze of the nun. When I was done with the juice, I fell onto the bed, exhausted and bawling. The pain worsened and I groaned, screamed, and wept. The nun went away.

"Get the hell out and never come back!" I called after her. But soon after she returned, and another nun with her.

"Are you in pain?"

I nodded through clenched teeth. A great deal. She poured juice back into the glass and handed me a big white pill, which I swallowed and washed down with more juice.

"Do you need to pee more?"

I had to pee, but would not admit it and shook my head. They didn't believe me. The other nun took off my duvet. I tried to resist, but was too weak. They pulled me up, each took me under one arm, and dragged me to the toilet. I cried and cried and tried to resist. The robe was all stained and bloody. They lifted it and it was evident the bandages were soaked through with blood. I was sick at the sight and I gagged. I could not hold off. The splitting pain started again and through the pain I watched as if from a great distance as blood mixed with piss dripped into the toilet. I threw up and vomited juice on the wall. It was as if my whole body had sundered and come together again in involuntary spasms and everything flowed into one. Nausea, pain, and terrifying suffering. My eyes went black and they led me back.

For the whole next day this repeated again and again. Each time, however, was a little better than the last. Gradually the anesthesia faded and severe pain replaced it. The nuns regularly exchanged the bandages and gave me medicine for pain. What I found hardest was knowing nothing. What had been done to me? I tried to ask the nuns, but they were avoiding the subject and told me I would have to talk to my doctor. When he came, he told me that he had assessed the situation and deemed an intervention was necessary.

"It's what's called a birth defect or even a deformity."

"What did you do?"

"It's quite simple, really. I cut off your penis, removed a piece from the top half, and sewed it back on."

I looked at him appalled while I received this information. To explain it to me better he was sketching some careless drawings on paper. The words "birth defect" and "deformity" rang in my head.

"But did you fix it?"

"I hope so, but we won't know properly until you are healed."

"Will it be okay?"

"Yes, I don't expect any problems."

"How long will it take to heal?"

"Oh, it can take several years!"

My eyes widened and I felt like I'd been struck six ways from Sunday. Misery washed over me and I was seized by powerlessness. I felt humiliated and helpless.

"Several years?!"

"No, no. I'm just teasing you. This heals just like anything else."

There were no more words. The doctor turned and left. I only saw him once after that. I sat there confused and angry. No one knew why I was there except my mom. I had told everyone else that I had a hernia. I knew about that because I had a hernia a few times as a kid. I took time off work. I told my mom the truth and why I was going to be operated on.

"What now? What operation?"

"On my prick."

"What now?"

I stammered it out with difficulty, but didn't trust myself to explain it any further. Mom didn't seem at all eager to hear more about what was going on and what had to be done. She asked no questions and we discussed it no further. She never came to see me the ten days I was inside the hospital. No one came. The only people I saw were the nuns who attended to me.

I knew nothing about how I would heal or what my prick would look like. Would I have scars? I had understood from the doctor that he had cut around my foreskin and rolled down the skin before he cut off my penis. I found it hard to think about this and became dazed when I tried to see for myself. Would there be any sensation in my penis? Would it change anything? Would I always be in pain? I regretted immensely having taken this step, and wished I had never done so.

When the nuns changed the bandages, I seized the chance to evaluate the area. I was deadly sore, with unceasing pain, and could not look at it except for very briefly. There was no sign of my prick. The entire area around my groin was swollen and bruised and it difficult to work out what was what. The swelling ran over to my testicles, which were also bruised and blue. The nuns said little and there was little I could ask them or talk to them about. They gave me food to eat, regularly gave me glasses of juice, and encouraged me to pee. Gradually the swelling subsided and I saw a glimpse of my penis. It was swollen and black and full of protruding black stitches.

After a few days the doctor came back into my room. This time he was with a group of medical students. He didn't say anything to me, but was absorbed in talking to the class. He outlined my case for them in a medical language, which I didn't understand, using words and concepts that were foreign to me. I tried to act maturely and nodded to the students. He drew my blanket back and showed the students and explained to them the method involved in what he had done. It was not until he had put the bandage back and replaced my blanket that he first looked at me. I was so riled and angry, powerless and desperate, that I said the first thing that came to my mind:

"You're a Nazi!" I shouted at him. I saw that he was angry. He looked into my eyes. The medical students giggled timidly.

"No more out of you!"

He walked out with his students following him. I never saw him again and was discharged a few days later. I was able to piss for myself without pain and the swelling had subsided so much that I could clothe myself and totter about. I still had trouble walking because of the pain. I left the hospital alone and took a bus back home to my girlfriend.

Though I had gained some control, when I peed a cascade still flowed everywhere. My prick was so swollen and painful I couldn't hold it. Sometimes the spray of piss spurted into the toilet, but mostly the urine ran down to my feet, over the floor, and all around. I felt more comfortable just getting in the shower and peeing there. I always had to take a shower when I peed, anyway, because I was usually covered in piss. There was no longer blood in my urine. When the swelling subsided, I noticed that I no longer had a foreskin. it was gone and now there was nothing but black stitches all around where it had previously been.

I was supposed to return to the hospital a few days later to let them take out the stitches. I could not imagine going back to a medical institution and certainly not seeing the doctor. I took the stitches out myself. I cut them into pieces with nail clippers and pulled them out. All sexual thoughts related to my prick had disappeared. I had no thoughts of masturbation, not even whether I could masturbate. I was just happy to be able to piss without feeling it. Maybe it would always be like this. I had a whole bag of drugs with me from the hospital. Penicillin and painkillers. I was weakened by the drugs and mostly stayed in bed where I dozed and slept. I was alone in bed. My girlfriend had found a new boyfriend. He had even moved in. They were in the living room and I in the bedroom. I was waiting to get better so I could get out and leave her and the new boyfriend alone. A few days later I gathered up my stuff, went out and never came back.

I knocked round my mother's and got to stay in the guestroom, which was once my room. Mom asked no questions and we didn't talk about it. I began to be able to piss in the toilet without wetting my pants. A few days later I took a bath. It caused me so much pain it was like my prick was being torn off. I squeezed my eyes shut and waited for it to pass. After that, I wished fervently I could never again get an erection and I was careful to never think about anything sexual. I avoided as far as possible seeing anything that could turn me on. I didn't miss it. I had never imagined or fever dreamt a scenario like this. Lying alone in a hospital with a severed penis wrapped in a beehive had never occurred to me.

I had imagined that this operation would be little more than removing a mole or something similar. That some tiny piece of skin would be removed and it would perhaps just smart. But nothing more. I hated this doctor and all those fucking nuns could disappear up their own asses! I felt like an idiot.

A few weeks after I came out of hospital, I got in contact with Sprelli. I wanted drugs and knew that he had easy access to drugs through his brother. Sprelli had not changed and was as naive as he had been at Núpur. He lived with his brother in the tenement on Hverfisgata and I regularly went to see them. Sprelli's brother was considerably older and properly grown up. He was a drug dealer and had a lot of different kinds of drugs here and there around the apartment. He had a lot of cannabis and even grew cannabis inside the apartment. There was an entire room covered in cannabis plants. The plants were in flowerpots on the floor and from the ceiling hung large light lamps. I felt like a god walking into this room; it felt a bit like being abroad. Sprelli's brother made hash, grass, and hash oil. He cut the dope into portions and put hash oil in a small plastic cap. Sometimes when I came to visit them, I helped prepare the dope. The brother didn't only have cannabis; he had LSD, too, and large amounts of all kinds of pills. I was very keen to get dope off him; he would slip me some hash and grass and I could always get a smoke with him when he was smoking a pipe in the living room.

The brother cared about Sprelli and his friends. He told us that he thought it was okay if we smoked cannabis, but he would not give us anything stronger and he never let us have any pills or drugs that could be dangerous. I thought he was absolutely fantastic. But when he didn't see, I snuck pills and other things I could reach.

So I had gotten excellent access to various drugs and basically as much hash as I desired. I never had to pay for anything. I was Sprelli's friend and Sprelli's friends were his brother's friends. But Sprelli only had one friend, and that was me.

It was always a good time to smoke cannabis. It was good to start the day smoking. To get high for the day gave me a different view of reality. I also felt good smoking in the afternoon because it helped me relax and was a refreshing change. Life was just not as miserable when I was high; more things gave me joy. Mundane and boring things became almost funny. I found old women particularly funny. Sometimes when I was waiting for the bus, I would transfix on some old lady and giggle to myself. If they said something to me, it was all I could do not to burst out laughing. All old ladies were funny. They dressed in funny hats, their hair was funny, and they spoke with funny old lady voices.

"I sincerely hope this tiresome weather won't last."

"Yes," I said and giggled.

"Is there no sign of it easing up?"

I burst out laughing. The old ladies were oblivious to my being high and just thought that they were entertaining. They never worked out that I was laughing at them. They simply thought I was a really jolly and jovial boy.

"You're certainly in a summery mood."

I grinned and laughed as tears flowed down my cheeks. I felt happy, hanging out at the bus stop and chatting to old ladies. I cared about everyone and, when the bus came, I always thought about how buses were beautiful cars. Everything seemed so cool and well made on the bus.

I also found it good to smoke at night when I was going to sleep because it made it easier to fall asleep. I felt like hash was the perfect solution to all my problems. And when I became weary of hash and needed a change, then I either drank either alcohol or took pills.

All the same, I was always anxious. I regularly had the feeling that something was going to happen to me and I was often insecure and wary of myself.

When the high wore off, I got nervous again. I feared the police and feared they were watching me. If I had hash on me, I was particularly afraid. I tried my utmost to avoid it. I hid it in the attic or under a rock somewhere. But police were not the only thing I feared. I dreaded and dreaded above anything being beaten up. I feared the guys who beat me up at Rétto would start hitting me again. I started going about with a knife again and made sure to keep it where I could get to it quickly and efficiently. Sometimes I held it in my hand under the sleeve of my jacket. I used the knife like a superpower uses nuclear weapons: to show others more than to use. I wanted to create a reputation that I was crazy and armed with a knife. I wanted people to see that I was crazy and doped up and packing, too, and it would be best to leave me alone. When some kids were gathered around me, like at bus stops, I sometimes let them see the knife. I pulled the knife out of my sleeve and held it against me so they could see it and this would definitely get around. But I didn't wave it about because the police couldn't know about it.

I felt fairly well-oriented and didn't take so many pills and drugs that I got confused. But it would happen that I would lose track and get unsure about the amount I'd consumed.

Especially if I mixed my drugs. For example, when I drank on top of drugs. Then I'd have no memory of what had happened. Sometimes I wouldn't remember until the evening what had happened during the day before. One day I woke up, for example, in a prison cell on Hverfisgata but had no idea how I got there. The last thing I remembered was the day before I had been on the way to the Industrial Expo in Laugardalur. There was a lot to see and you got a lot of free samples of this and that. I had taken some pills, smoked cannabis, and drank and was planning to be in a great mood. I didn't remember anything else.

The Chief of Police came into my cell. He had an angry expression. I knew him because he was one of my dad's friends. I learned that the night before I had been in a fight outside Laugardalur Hall. The police had been told two men were fighting with knives. A police officer on a motorcycle was first on the scene and tried to intervene. I had responded by attacking the officer armed with a knife. That was unlike me. I had no memory of this. After the Chief had lectured me a while, I was released. I took the bus home.

The next day there was news of the incident in the newspapers under the heading "Knife Fight at Laugardalur Hall." With the story, there was a picture of me, in which you could see the police placing me in a police car. I thought it was exciting and funny, but also terrible. I felt bad for not recalling a thing, but I was grateful that I didn't hurt anyone. Because of my father and his relationship with the police, the case was dropped. The policeman I had attacked was his friend and did not file a complaint. I promised to change my behavior and never do anything like that again. The knife had been taken from me at the police station and I could not get it back.

But I had to have a knife, otherwise I could not have been safe around town. A few days later, I went into the shop Brynja on Laugavegur and found a cool knife I liked. When no one saw I slipped it onto my person, innocently looked around, and walked out. I felt confident and safe. If someone attacked me, I would have a knife. But I was still not going to attack anyone with it. I never again got in a knife fight with anyone.

If I smoked too much cannabis, I'd get sick. That was called a "whiteout." It felt worse than every other bad thing. It happened mainly when I smoked too much hash oil. Otherwise, hash was exceptionally good. It solved my anxiety, helped me relax and gave me the confidence and security in different situations. Hash also got rid of my discomfort and boredom. Mom even lost her threatening power over me. It was like hash formed a sort of wall around my heart so that things didn't touch me. Mom was always cross. She looked at me crossly with piercing eyes and spoke to me in a cross tone. But when I was high that didn't matter. Hash softened Dad, too. I thought he was not as annoying and I became relaxed in my dealings with him. When I had been smoking I thought it was almost fun to talk to my dad. He took my hand and held it firmly. I didn't feel anxious or tense. I thought it was just funny.

"Is everything okay, my boy?"

"Yesyesyes," I said reassuringly and smiled cheerfully at him.

"That's good. You know how it affects Mom and I when things are bad."

"Yes," I said and nodded my assent while I thought, "God, you're insane." And I thought it was so funny that I grinned. Dad thought I was smiling because I was such a healthy and happy young man and he smiled back in a friendly way.

The effect of hash also counteracted the everyday gray that characterized my life. There was nothing happening. If I wasn't inside my room or at Sprelli's home, I was either on the bus or waiting for the bus. There was never anything that enticed me, nothing I wanted. I didn't need friends, had no particular interest in music, and no hobbies except possibly reading or playing the Fisheries Game by myself. And I had no interest in girls anymore. I felt relieved at being free of them. There was nothing that piqued my curiosity or encouraged me. Except hashish. If I needed hashish, I headed over early to Sprelli's home. Hash gave me everything I needed. It ended my boredom and brought me joy. And old ladies continued to be funny and entertaining. One time, like before, I stood at the bus stop and waited for the bus. There was an old woman who did not understand the routes. She was waiting for the eleven. I told her the eleven had stopped going along Bústaðavegur and now went down Miklubrautina.

"It has become an express route."

"An express route?" she asked, surprised. She clearly had no idea what this meant. "Do they just keep changing the routes over and over again?!"

I nodded.

"Uhh, yeah..."

The woman shook her head and I watched her walk away. Her words echoed in my head and the woman's voice chanted again and again:

"Do they just keep changing the routes over and over again?! Do they just keep changing the routes over and over again?" I said it aloud, mimicking the lady. When the bus finally came and I got on, I asked the bus driver, "Do they just keep changing the routes over and over again?!"

He looked at me, surprised. I smiled at him and sat down. I relaxed my eyes and imagined that I was dressed like the old lady and was somehow always shocked by everything. I was Jónsi Punk except in tights and a cape with a perm and a plastic headscarf. So I walked around town with buttermilk in a plastic bag and asked everyone I met: "Well, do they just keep changing the routes over and over again?!"

I laughed and giggled to myself until I got tears in my eyes. It was warm and bright over Reykjavík and I smiled all the way down to Hlemmur.

I often smoked hash before I went to bed because I usually found it difficult to fall asleep. I was always apprehensive about lying down at night because worry poured over me at that time. Then the thoughts came thick and fast and I lost control of them. I was filled with anxiety, got a knot in my stomach, a weight across my chest. I tried and tried to drag it away until I was totally exhausted. Occasionally, I woke up rested in the morning and started the day by taking a deep breath. That, however, was short-lived; anxiety was usually quick to penetrate me. I felt bad about who I was and I felt bad in general. And soon I began to think about taking some stuff to beat the pain. Mom had also stopped checking up on me and watching me. Slowly but surely, she had given up. She had long since stopped asking me what I was doing or where I was headed. She never asked if I'd been smoking cannabis or taken any pills. She knew I was out and there was nothing she could do about it. She changed the way she treated me. When I didn't feel like hanging out inside my room any longer, I occasionally went to check on Dad. He was usually in front of the TV and watching some boring discussion show. I sat down with him. When I was high, I found my dad funny and entertaining. And boring discussion shows were like sitcoms. Credit terms, exchange rates, and inflation could make for amusing television. I found it awesome that there was some kind of ugly guy who bothered to think about such boring things and I sat with my dad and enthusiastically watched the debates. Dad enjoyed the company and spoke both to the men on TV and to me.

"Just answer the question!" he shouted at the guy on TV. Then he looked at me. "If this is so simple, why can't he explain it to us?!"

I smiled and shook my head. I didn't understand any more than he did. I found it cozy, sitting like this with my dad.

"Don't they know what they're doing?"

"Of course they know. They just pretend not to know. The leaders of the working class just need to speak more clearly."

"Uhmm."

Indeed. I totally agreed and nodded my head approvingly.

"They say it's not possible to raise wages because of inflation, but they can raise their own wages!"

Dad shook his head, shocked. I shook my head, too.

"This is ridiculous," I murmured. Hash united Dad and me. It was unlike alcohol in that you never got too high the way you could get too drunk. At worst, I got a whiteout. Dad never suspected anything.

Several times I went down to Hlemmur, where everything had changed. My old companions had all gone somewhere, ceased being punks, moved away, or started working. I had lost my position, didn't belong to any group, in fact didn't any longer know whether I was a true punk. I mostly mooched about town on my own.

I spent hours at the charity market for the Friends of Cats Society on Hafnarstræti; I liked to hang out there and dig through old clothes. It became a sort of hobby for me. The clothes cost almost nothing, but it was also very easy to steal them. I usually did. Occasionally, I even got gifts of clothes because the stall attendants felt sorry for me. They were usually clothes that people in the market thought were so ugly that they couldn't believe anyone would want to buy them. I, on the other hand, found them perfect and funny and loved to wear strange clothes. More often than not, I went about like a total scarecrow. My favorite jeans were orange and a little too short. I also wore canvas shoes and an overcoat. One day, I bought an old sailor's protective fishing coat, which was made from some sort of tar-covered sailcloth. I never had to hang it up because the material was so stiff that it stood up all by itself when I took it off. The tar stained the color of all my other clothes. When I was in the coat, I was shaped like a cone because the coat was so fat and wide. I thought it was high fashion and wore it at every opportunity and displayed it proudly with pink or orange jeans and canvas shoes. I also had some hand-knitted wool sweaters. The sweaters were mis-made and badly fashioned, unfortunate hobby products. There was something in this style that totally impressed me.

The days continued to pass uneventfully. I woke up, got high, took a bus into town, went to the flea market, found some old hippie polo-neck, stole it, put it on, put my overcoat on top, and walked out.

Wherever I was, I drew attention. People looked at me; small children even pointed in my direction. I got on the bus and started giggling to myself about what people must think seeing this teenager dressed in a hand-knitted wool sweater and old-lady pink jeans. By the time I got home, the sweater had done its job. As soon as the clothes stopped being funny, I lost interest in them.

I felt old. Like I'd lived a whole lifetime. I struggled to imagine the future. The weekdays all passed alike, but the weekends offered a slight variation because they offered a good chance of getting some booze and getting drunk. I usually drank alone. Usually I did not have much liquor, and would rather not share it with others. But when I was out of liquor, I began to take the bus into town and sometimes met kids who were with me at Núpur or who I'd hung around with in Reykjavík. Sometimes I went with the kids to their homes, but only if I was quite sure there would be alcohol or hash. I hung out while there was enough to drink, but when it was all over I was quick to disappear. There was nothing that held me there. I had no home; I was like a part of a world that once existed, but no longer. Through the years, something had always drawn my mind. But there was nothing now. Even my interest in girls had gone. I was bored of people, but most of all bored of myself. When someone tried to talk to me, I usually just said monosyllabic words, either yes or no. And I often wondered whether people found me incredibly boring. I had managed to lose an important part of myself, I thought, but didn't know when or where. Punk and anarchism were gone. I wasn't even Jónsi Punk any more.

I went back to Núpur. Mom didn't want me to just hang around town so I had to choose whether to go to school or work. I didn't feel like working. I managed to take some small amount of hash and pills with me. They didn't last long, however, they were quickly gone and daily life at Núpur became stark. I didn't have booze, hash, or anything else that made me feel good. I hadn't come to Núpur to do anything. I hadn't come to learn or to plan my future. I had just come to Núpur because I had nowhere else to go. Out of the many bad options, Núpur was the least bad. At least I had my own room, it was safe, and there were people I knew. But I didn't fit in there any better than elsewhere. Everyone was doing something, but I had no purpose. I didn't want to be there, but I preferred not to leave. Nothing felt possible. When I was in Reykjavík, I missed Núpur; now, when I was at Núpur, I missed Reykjavík.

The schoolwork was beyond me. I had to re-take the subjects I'd failed the tests in and had to learn the same math and Danish as the year before. I found it hopeless and was lost. I couldn't even mess about in class any more. My classmates were strangers, younger than me, and I felt my position had become a bit pitiful. I was no longer one of the group but I had a reputation. Everyone had heard of Jónsi Punk, the funny prankster. But I was no longer him. I was just a bewildered and confused tin pot. I could no longer pretend to be the witty guy who was everyone's friend.

It was not even funny anymore to get thrown out of class. I was no longer a rebel, just a drop out. I was merely a fool who could no longer hide that I was stupid. I was stupid, absolutely ridiculously stupid. No one but an absolute fool would have the idea of returning to Núpur. I puzzled over this and didn't understand a thing about myself.

A tradition had started where the older kids hazed the new students. I was called to a meeting with some older students to discuss the proposed hazing. I had never been involved in this before and found it exciting. Some of the boys had put sheep's' blood in bottles and smuggled it into the dorms. We were going to use the blood during the ceremony. We decided to consecrate the new kids in school on so-called hazing day. The day would be celebrated the Saturday after the first week; the containers of sheep blood were carefully hidden all about. When the day came, the blood had been stored at room temperature for ten days. None of us wondered whether it was a good storage method. We were just excited about the whole thing and there was a great atmosphere in the group.

We spent an entire day cutting and pasting all kinds of colorful signs. I took charge of what was written on them. "Hi! I'm an idiot—I'm a freshman." We fixed strings to the signs and then went about in groups and hung them on the new kids. We also had red markers to write on their foreheads: "freshman." We thought this was all just innocent fun. It never occurred to me that the freshmen might be afraid of us. If any of the kids put up a fuss, then we gave them a Pissed Ghost wedgie. Some of us held them still while someone else pulled his underwear up his ass. The day passed.

The ceremony was being held in the boy's dorm after locking-up time. We'd gone up quietly so as not to alert the teachers. We decided to collect all the freshmen boys in the toilets. We, the executioners, arranged ourselves on both sides of the corridor in front of the toilets so the freshmen went past us and inside. As they went in we sarcastically called out to them, laughed, and pointed at them.

"Freshman! Freshman!"

Some spat at them. When everybody was in the bathroom, I climbed up and settled myself on top of the wall that separated the sinks from the showers. Holding the sheep's blood containers. The high point of the ceremony was when the freshmen were driven into the shower cubicle. There were so many freshmen they barely fit inside the cubicle, and could hardly move for congestion. Well over twenty kids were gathered inside a shower intended for three. The older boys formed a wall at the exit to discourage any freshman from escaping; they pressed towards the crowd to further discomfort and confuse things. When I had done getting ready, I called out: "I'm ready!"

I twisted the cap off one bottle and went to pour sheep's blood on the group. But the blood didn't flow out. It was all semi-so-lidified and I had to squeeze the bottle. And instead of dripping the blood came out as a mucoid blob. It was disgusting; even worse was the smell. A concentrated decay smell instantly filled every inch of space and swamped everyone's organs. A fetid smell. I continued to squeeze bottles and blood congealed down in mucoid pellets and clots. A frenzy seized the freshmen crowd. They gasped for breath and began to struggle. It was more disgusting than we'd expected. When the smell hit me, I gagged and puked. As I sat on top of the wall above the freshman, I vomited down on them. My eyes went black and I dropped the bottles on the group. In terror, the freshmen tried their utmost to avoid the disgusting containers. The boys blocking the exit started to vomit, too. The containers fell among the kids and in the tumult they trampled on them so that even more disgusting stuff gunked out from them. I was now lying on my stomach on the dividing wall, gagging and vomiting. The room had a puke smell mixed with the decaying smell of blood. Still more kids started throwing up. Some puked on the shower walls and some puked over each other. Despair, chaos and total mayhem took over. A throng tried to push its way out, but most stopped on the way because they either retched or puked. The floor was completely soiled with the mess and they started to slip and fall. I couldn't move from where I lay vomiting down the wall. Some lay on the floor, retching and puking while other desperately climbed over them to try to get out. I gagged so much that I thought I would suffocate. The freshmen had gone totally out of control.

The corridor was not much nicer. The smell had reached the whole dormitory. The dormitory was locked and we could not get out. I clambered down from the wall, slipped in the crap, and fell to the floor. I was entirely soiled with the mess. With great effort I managed to drag myself out the doorway. Out along all the corridors you could see kids running amok in terror, nauseated boys retching and vomiting. Our panic had attracted the attention of the teachers who came running.

"What the hell are you up to, you damn idiots?!"

The teachers gave us orders, but kept themselves well away from us. They opened all the windows so that there was fresh air in the dormitory. They ordered me to go to the bathroom and clean it so that everyone could shower. I made many attempts to go inside the toilets but promptly had to leave because of the stench. I gagged just opening the door. I and two other boys stuffed toilet paper up our nostrils and so we managed to enter the toilets. It was a terrible sight. Slimy black blobs of blood lay scattered around the floor. The floor was covered with vomit and there was puke all up the walls. Even the ceiling had vomit stains. Others brought buckets and rags and threw them in to us and shut the door. We got started. We filled the buckets with water and splashed them in all directions. We turned on the showers to rinse the horror down the drain. We sprayed cleaning fluid in all directions, sloshed the buckets, dried with rags. It was about midnight before we were finally done.

The foul smell lingered in the dormitory and over the following days you could hardly distinguish between the temperature outside and inside since all the windows were open wide at all times. Freshman orientation was officially over; we had welcomed the new kids into the Núpur crowd. In retrospect, we found it funny. We had a lot to talk about and often sat for hours in the Smoker and told the girls about the amazing event. It was endless: you could always find a new angle, a fresh perspective, a new story:

"I upchucked only because you upchucked on me!"

"Yes, but I upchucked on you because you upchucked on me!"

"I upchucked on you?"

"Yes! Don't you remember? You upchucked right at me!"

"The hell!!"

The girls shuddered in horror, but still found it terribly exciting to listen to the stories.

After that, school and daily life went on. I finally realized that there was nothing for me there. My time at Núpur was simply over. I had no plan for going back home. Worse, I realized I didn't really have a home. My room at Núpur came closest to my home. I often pondered things and talked to other kids in the Smoker about what my options were. Most people's opinion was that I had to get a job. I'd been working as a gardener and enjoyed it. But it was winter, so no gardening. There was nothing exciting about laying paving slabs in the frost.

"Why don't you go to work as a fisherman?"

Many kids had worked in a fishing plant. There was something charming about it. Bubbi Morthens had also worked in fisheries and sung about a thousand cod on a conveyor belt. He had also sung about what it was like out at a fisherman's shack. There was plenty of money and hash. Those who worked in fishing always had plenty of money and a lot of hash. Bubbi also sang about having a kilo of hash out in nature, being really into grass where it grows, and having heaps of bills. I would be happy being in a fishing hut, pockets full of cash and a kilo of hash in my room. Perhaps the only intelligent thing was to go to a fisherman's hut. To travel around the country and encounter adventures instead of sitting somewhere in Núpur and learning Danish. But even though you got a lot of money from working in a fishery, you got even more money out at sea.

Several of the boys had been on fishing boats. If you got a good haul you could take home money beyond belief. But there was less hash at sea. Sailors also needed to work outside and it was always wet and cold. And although you were paid less in the fish processing plants, that was inside work and you could always smoke cannabis and drink booze.

I could well imagine going to a fisherman's hut. But I had been to a camp and knew that there were often a lot of fights. I didn't look forward to that. I also would much rather be in Reykjavík than Ísafjörður, Flateyri, or some other miserable shit place. But it was clear I needed to quit school and go to work. I saw my future in the labor market rather than in school. I had decided that I did not want to stay at Núpur but did not know how to achieve that. I knew for sure that it would not mean anything to call home and tell my mom that I was thinking about quitting school and going to work in fishing. She would just scream at me. I was no longer showing up to class. It led to nothing but humiliation. It was miserable to sit in front of strange kids and not know anything. They were learning algebra. I couldn't even do multiplication and division. I did plus and minus—but not really minus. Multiplication, fractions, and everything else, I was totally useless at. A hopeless case. And Danish was no better. Why did I have to learn Danish? I only wanted to learn English, but I knew it so didn't have to learn it.

I had completely stopped thinking about sex and had no inter-est in it anymore. I had stopped looking at girls' breasts. I didn't even think about my prick. I avoided it and didn't want to know whether it had healed. I never checked. I no longer got an erection in the morning. I didn't even get a piss feeling when I needed to pee really badly. Maybe my horniness had gone during the operation. Perhaps these were emotional or psychological consequences. But I didn't care. I was just glad to be asexual again and no longer needing to walk around with a burden on my back. I experienced a kind of return to childhood, to youth and innocence. I was no longer a hormonal teenager. I was a grown man, and yet also a vegetative child who had to learn Danish with kids who were even younger than him. I was a man-child who belonged nowhere.

There was always someone who was bullied the most in dorm life at Núpur. Previously, it was Biggi, but the kid who got the worst of it this year was called Quasimodo. He got the name because he was so ugly. The bullying mostly consisted of words that were constantly used to belittle him like his nickname. One of the boys was harsher in bullying than others. He was called Goggi and had been with me the winter before and we shared a room. It was as if he had a vendetta against Quasimodo. He raged at him at every opportunity, teased him, and pushed him. One day, Quasimodo had enough. He pushed back and that made Goggi angry and he attacked Quasimodo. This happened in the Smoker and the teacher who was on duty got wind of this and came running, saw what was happening, and stopped the fight that was beginning. Quasimodo went whimpering up to his room, but Goggi sat there fuming. This was not over.

"I fucking hate that dumbass moron!"

"Yeah, it was absolutely unnecessary for him..." I mumbled. "He just attacked you."

"Yes, shoved me! I fell backwards. I got a blow to my head because of him. I have a bad headache! I'm lucky if I don't have a concussion."

"Yes, he totally threw you into the wall..."

"Yeah, I'm going to kill that damn bastard."

I nodded. Such statements were not an unusual mode of speech at Núpur. It was often said that someone or other would knock someone else off. Boys just talked that way; they say all kinds of thing in the heat of the moment. Nothing ever really came of it. Goggi was in a similar place in life to me. He was behind in most subjects and struggling to find his footing in life.

Immediately, when evening arrived, I heard all around me that a fight was planned. Next Friday, Goggi and Quasimodo were going to meet and fight after the dormitory was shut. It was always exciting when there was a fight. It was fun entertainment and gave us something to look forward to. But the fight was almost always quite innocent. At most someone got punched on the mouth or put in a headlock until he gave up. It was more about the tension than the fight itself. Fights were usually quick. Usually only a few moments until someone was in a headlock and the other one yelled: "Give up? Give up?"

"Yes, I give up!"

And the fight was over. Very occasionally some blows were exchanged and then someone either got punched in the stomach or the mouth and then it was over. The only serious fight I remember was when Gaddi hit Kristinn. But that was one-of-a-kind.

After dinner on Friday, Goggi sat inside our room and prepared himself for the fight.

"Fuck! I'm going to destroy him. I'm going to pulverize him and beat him in such a way that he will always remember it."

"Yes, you're totally in the right. I mean, you barely touched him. I mean, he straight out pushed you."

"No, I didn't go near him! Is he somehow holy and you're not allowed near him? A guy has to be able to tease without getting himself pushed! I could have been knocked out!"

"Yeah, I mean, right. You totally could have been knocked out cold."

Goggi had elastic bindings like boxers wrap around their hands. He had been practicing boxing for a while and was very interested in it. He took the batteries out of his tape recorder, put them in each hand. Then he extended me his hands.

"Jónsi, wrap my hands."

"Uhh, with what?"

"With the bindings."

He nodded in the direction of the bindings lying on his bed.

"Yes, okay."

I took the elastic bandage and wrapped it around his clenched fists that each held a battery. The clock struck eight and the fight was about to begin. The boys had gathered in front of the toilets and waited. Quasimodo was also there, waiting with the others. When Goggi came walking down the hall, I felt like he was Rocky and I was coaching him.

"It's the eye of the tiger," I sang and laughed. Everyone clapped and laughed. I tapped on his shoulder and urged him forward. Despite the wrappings and the batteries, it hadn't occurred to me that he was really going to beat his opponent up. Before I could count down the contest, Goggi jumped forward and bombarded Quasimodo with blows. He beat him repeatedly in the face with closed fists. It happened so quickly that Quasimodo had no defense. I think he was even knocked out by one of the first punches. He fell to the ground, bloody. Goggi, however, wouldn't give up and continued to rain down blows at him while he shouted:

"You miserable fucking idiot! Take this, shithead! Think about that before you shove someone again. You disgusting waste of space."

The crowd fell silent. We were stone silent, watching. Then it was like the rage suddenly left Goggi and he stopped punching Quasimodo. He looked at us, surprised, and then at his bloodied hands. Nobody said anything; nothing could be heard except Goggi's labored breathing. None of really knew why Goggi was so angry and why Quasimodo didn't move. No one had expected this. I took off and ran to my room. I knew something terrible had happened, but had no idea what I should do. I didn't dare knock for the teacher because that was snitching. I didn't want to be a rat but I felt responsible. I had been involved in this. I was Goggi's friend, his roommate, I had urged him on. I hoped Quasimodo was not dead. I also hoped that someone else would do something.

The next day, Quasimodo wasn't in school. He'd been taken to the hospital in town. Goggi wasn't in school because he was with the principal. I was in absolute shock. I had been involved in this. Although I had not punched Quasimodo, I had encouraged it. I had been in league with Goggi. He was my friend and roommate and had also been with me before at Núpur. But I didn't know Quasimodo. I hadn't imagined Goggi would beat him to pieces. It caught me totally by surprise because I'd never see him as a guy who would really lash out and hurt someone. I thought he might be so afraid when he saw the wrappings that he would lift up his hands and say "I give up! I give up!"

After school, I sat in the Smoker and was smoking when a teacher came by with a serious expression.

"Jón. The principal wants to see you."

My blood ran cold. We walked out together to the principal's office.

"Well, once again you are standing here," said the school principal, looking severely at me.

"Yes, I think it is all just so upsetting."

"What happened?"

"Yes, you see, this started in the Smoker. The boy attacked Goggi by shoving him. And so they were going to have a fight. Is he okay?"

"Yes, he's fine, no thanks to you."

"Good."

"What is wrong with you? Where are you going in life?"

I was moved to tears. What were my aims in life? I didn't feel well and I had no idea where I was headed. Everything was so difficult and confusing. What everyone found simple, I felt was complicated. I started to sob in front of him. The principal looked impassively at me. Between choking sobs, I told him how I felt and how everything was miserable. I told him how confused I was and bewildered and I told him about the hash. He asked me if I had taken substances other than cannabis. I told him I had tried mushrooms, LSD, and amphetamines. But I also told him how I wanted to stop. I wanted to get to stay at Núpur.

"I'll talk to your teachers and then take a decision on what will be done."

I wiped my eyes and sucked up through my nose. It felt good to tell him this. I had never revealed this to any adult. Maybe he would tell Mom and Dad that they would come to some conclusion that would be for the best. I was going to apply myself. I was going to be good at studying and go to extra classes in math. I was going to write out my life principles. I was going to reduce my smoking. I was just going to smoke one cigarette in the morning, one at lunch, and one at night. I was going to let this be a lesson. And I was not going to smoke cannabis or take drugs, except only on weekends. I was going to stop lying awake at night and go to bed early. I was going to go to the pharmacy and buy something to put on my nails so I would stop biting them.

"I'm ready to turn myself around," I said candidly to the principal.

"We take what's happened very seriously."

"I didn't do anything."

"It's not just this issue, but other breaches of discipline, too. Any surprises here always seem in one way or another related to you. Many here believe that you're the moving spirit behind it all."

I felt that was unfair. Goggi was suspended for a week. He wasn't sent to Reykjavík, but went instead to a country farm. I was expelled from school permanently. I was sent away from Núpur and could never go back.

Mom yelled at me. She was sitting at the kitchen table. I was standing in the doorway. I had often I seen her angry, but never like this. She wanted to attack me and beat me. The principal had sent her a letter.

"It's not enough that you are so confused that it's impossible to talk to you, that you're up to your eyeballs in drugs, wandering about all night, but now you are getting violent! You've never been that. It's been the only positive thing I could say about you."

I had lied to her so often that I knew there was no point trying to explain that this wasn't right. Whatever I said would be doubted. She didn't believe anything I said, not even when I said I'd be going to the convenience store.

"You're just filth!" she screamed at me. She would not allow me to read the letter. But the principal seemed to have written that I alone bore the blame for this and that it had been me who beat the living daylights out of Quasimodo. That wasn't true. I hadn't touched him. The principal had also written to Mom about everything I'd confessed to him.

"You're just filth!"

She believed every word in the letter. She didn't believe me, so it didn't matter what I said. It was no surprise that I was expelled. Least of all to myself. I'd long been ready for it to be the last chance.

"I didn't hit that kid."

"Shut up! Shut up, you filthy boy! It says here in the letter how you described having repeatedly beat him."

Mom held up the letter and shook it at me. She was so angry and disappointed that she had tears in his eyes. My dear Mom. She did not deserve to have such a filthy and disgusting boy as me. If I didn't exist, she'd never be angry and sad. I'd done nothing but I was still a part of this. Confusion always reigned all around me. I was angry that the principal had lied about me and expelled me. But I was most angry with myself for being such an idiot.

Mom and Dad set down clear rules. If I was going to live with them, I either had to go to school or go to work and pay rent. There was no other choice. I would rather go to school than go to work, but it was impossible. I was many years behind my peers. The only school that I could possibly go to was some special school for the challenged. I didn't go out, just hung around inside my room, smoked out the window, and lay in bed. I was trapped. I couldn't keep on and couldn't go back, either. It would be better for everyone if I did not exist.

I began to think about what would happen if I killed myself and pondered ways to do it. I could eat so many pills that I died. I could hang myself. And I could slit my wrists. I got tears in my eyes at the thought. Self-contempt mixed with self-pity. If I killed myself, people would surely forgive me. They would not remember all the annoying things, just the positives. Mom would tell funny stories about me. Dad would be annoying. And the principal would be ashamed. He'd regret having written the letter and lying to Mom. Maybe he'd write another letter, admitting it and asking forgiveness. Mom would be so angry she'd call a meeting with him. She'd scream at him:

"Bastard! Liar!"

And he would start to cry; he'd regret it. I enjoyed that idea.

I couldn't talk to my parents; I couldn't talk to anyone. I was so isolated that I hardly had any friends and wasn't in communication with anyone. Who could be bothered to talk to me? I couldn't think of anyone. I had managed to paint myself into a corner.

Since I didn't want to go to school, I started to look for a job. Every morning I read job ads in Morgunblað and called the phone numbers for them. I got a job as a line-worker for Post and Phone. They were laying down a telephone line from Reykjavík to Mosfellsbær and I was supposed to help. I could start the next day. I took the bus to Höfði, where some guy in a tractor met me. It was pouring rain and freezing. I settled into the cab and we drove a ways out of town. The guy backed the tractor up to a huge electricity pylon. We got out of the tractor and fastened the harness to the winch. That was the phone line. He drove the tractor along a long trench that the wire had to go down into. My role was to walk along the canal after the wire and make sure that it was down in the canal and in the sand on the bottom. In the pouring rain, I walked along carrying a shovel and had to push away stones and other things from the cable and make sure that there was only sand around it. After a while, I was getting cold and wet to the bone. The worst thing was the sound of the bucket when it crashed against rocks and gravel. It gave me chills, like the sound when nails are scraped down a blackboard. The sound penetrated me to the bone.

My first job with Post and Phone lasted just over an hour. I had had enough. In that hour, we'd managed to lay about ten meters of the line. I saw it would take a lifetime to lay a phone line to Mosfellsbær. When the guy got out to check the spool, I seized the opportunity and excused myself by saying that I needed to go to the bathroom, which was in a nearby work shed. When I saw the guy wasn't watching me, I snuck behind the outhouse. From there, I ran bent double for cover, jumped a wall, and hitchhiked into town. A kind-hearted driver stopped for me.

"You're absolutely drenched."

"Yes, I've been walking for so long."

"You live over in Mosó?"

"Yes, I'm just headed to work."

"Where do you work?"

"Ah, for Post and Phone."

I'd told my parents that I had found work, but I didn't dare tell them I'd quit. I went out every morning to look for a new job.

After this, I was adamant that outdoor work was not for me and I needed to get some comfortable indoor job. I was fascinated with the idea of working in a factory. There, I would be working as part of a whole. Not alone in some trench in the middle of nowhere. In a factory, you're part of a group and like everyone else. People who work in a factory wear special work clothes, special gloves, and even a headset. I found that exciting. I did not want to work somewhere where I constantly had cold hands. I wanted to be inside in the warm with other people who were like me. In blue overalls and with headphones.

One morning I went to Hampiðjan and spoke to the foreman. I was lucky they were short of people; he told me to arrive promptly at eight o'clock the next day. It was shift work.

Sometimes you had to work in the morning and sometimes at night. If you were lucky you got to work at night. All the work was done inside and you never had to go out. I felt I had the heavens in my hands; I was extremely happy and excited. Not only because it was a factory, but because it was called Hampiðjan—like cannabis. Cannabis was hemp. I wonder if the staff got hash there. Perhaps the foreman at lunch would give everyone cannabis. I was becoming a character in a Bubbi song. Bubbi sang a lot about all kinds of jobs and when Bubbi was at work, he was also always smoking hash. Where else but in Hampiðjan would you grow a ton of grass and make all kinds of things from it? Maybe the staff got to take what wasn't used. I also knew of a book that taught you to cultivate cannabis; the book was called *Hampur*. And I was going to work in Hampiðjan. It all fit together.

I turned up at the stroke of eight. I got shiny blue work overalls and black headphones. A really smart uniform. When I didn't have the headphones on my head, I put them around my neck. My job was to stack the cord spools into the machine and thread the end of the cord into the hole. Then the machine spooled from the reel and wrapped it into a larger spool. I took down the empty roller and set a new one on the machine. This wasn't a complicated job. The headset was so high-tech that there were stations and it was possible to listen to Channel 1. Channel 2 had only just come on air and wasn't available on my headset. The programming on Channel 1 was simple. Every hour there was the news. Between it was strange music. Usually Icelandic songs.

"That concludes the news. And now we'll play a few easy-going tunes."

After midday was the lunch hour. They read some old Icelandic book. I found Channel 1 the most boring radio station in the world. It was as if it was station policy to be boring; all fun was banned. It never played rock or punk. Between songs there were sometimes announcements and shipping news.

"The Dettifoss will arrive at Siglufjörður at four o'clock today."

I clicked a new roller onto the machine.

"Departs from Siglufjörður at eight o'clock in the evening headed for Akureyri."

"Brynjólfur Jósepsson, a centennial remembrance. The Reverend Brynjólfur Jósepsson was born in Höllustaðir in 1821..."

There was nothing on the radio that interested me; I found it deathly dull. But I thought the people who worked with me were really intriguing. I paid attention to my work and was excited to get to know it well. At ten there was a coffee break where everyone met in the cafeteria. I looked carefully around the room, hoping to see some punks. I found none. It was also difficult to work out who was who in their work overalls. I tried hard to chat to my colleagues but they were not especially forthcoming and usually answered in short words, yes and no. I found many of them very odd and soon started to suspect they were all more or less mentally challenged. On closer examination, I found out that they were all weird. I did not have anything in common with these people. They were all older than me; there were no young people working in factories at this time. They were all in school. I found no one like Bubbi Morthens. There wasn't anything especially lively or fun. I made another attempt at social interaction at lunch and tried to strike up a conversation. It didn't happen.

There was no way to have a conversation with anyone about anything. Some of them were so strange that they didn't reply even when I spoke to them. I didn't see myself lasting long in the job. In many ways, however, I understood the work well. It was all logical and not particularly complex. When the roll was empty, I was supposed to put a new one on. I was completely in control of it. But the radio was awful and the working camaraderie hopeless.

Around two p.m. the next day, after having listened to the midday story, I went to the foreman and told him I had gotten something in my eye. Earlier that day, I had seen someone this had happened to, and the foreman had gone to get oxygen and water in a tube to inject into the eye. The employee in question had called out to foreman over the din of machines: "I got something in my eye!"

The foreman ran to some cabinet and reached for a tube with water in it and gave it to the worker who ran out with it. I played the same game. I called to the foreman, squinted one eye, and acted injured. He ran to the cabinet, handed me the tube, and I ran off. But instead of running straight out like the employee had done, I went into the locker room and did a lightning change of clothes. Then I ran as fast as my legs would go and did not stop until I got down to Hlemmur. There I could relax. There were a few people I knew there. I sat all day, told work stories, chain-smoked, and stared into the sky.

I knew I needed a job. I had to tell my mom I was working so I could live at home. And I also needed money for cigarettes and other small things. I didn't dare ask Mom for money. I thought of asking her to lend me money until I got my paycheck, but

I feared she'd see through me and find out I had nowhere to work. Mom was so angry, so tired of me, that I tried to have almost no interaction with her. I even feared she might attack me. Over the next few days, I acted like I was going to work every morning, but instead I took the bus down to Hlemmur where I hung out for the day. I hid in a corner where no one could see me and none of my parents' friends would recognize me. But I was also quite prepared with lies in the event that someone saw me and gossiped to Mom. Then I'd say I was on a break and had only been at Hlemmur to meet a friend who owed me money. But I was also searching for work, checking various job listings, and diligently asking the kids in Hlemmur where they worked. One evening I met an acquaintance I'd often hung around with at Hlemmur. He was totally changed, he'd gotten sensible and mature. He'd even gotten a wallet. He didn't put his bus ticket in his pocket any longer, but in a special compartment in his wallet. I had to get on that: my own wallet. I asked if he still came down to Hlemmur much, but he said he'd about stopped entirely since he was working so much. My eyes opened wide.

"Now? Where do you work?"

"In Plastos," he said, proudly

Plastos? It sounded exotic and exciting. Plastos. It was such a cool name that it could almost be the name of a band. Especially if you wrote the 's's as 'z's. The Plaztoz. That was exciting.

"What's that?"

"The new plastic factory over in Höfði."

I thought that was an immediately intriguing place. He was working there and he was practically a punk who hung at Hlemmur.

"Are there any mentally-handicapped people working there?"

"No, no. Just ordinary people like you and me."

"Yes, really?!"

"Yes. It's a great place to work."

A great place to work, and inside. That sounded good. I definitely would feel comfortable in a great workplace—inside.

"I'm looking for a job, you see."

"Right."

"I was working in Hampiðjan, but it was pretty dismal."

"Yes, my friend also worked there."

"Yes, everyone working there is handicapped. Even my foreman was handicapped."

We both laughed. I could see there would be no handicapped employees at Plastos.

"There was so much dust at Hampiðjan I was always getting something in my eye."

"Yes, totally, I know what you mean."

"Yes, do you think there is any way I could get a job at Plastos?"

"You can just try to come and talk to one of the foremen."

A few days later I took the bus not down to Hlemmur as usual, but up to Höfði to go to Plastos. It was a completely different factory from Hampiðjan. Plastos was a much more modern, clean, and vibrant company. Hampiðjan was a contaminated work environment compared to Plasto. All the machines were shiny and new and they were able to print all kinds of photos on plastic bags. I thought it was terribly cool. The bags bore the logos for Kjörgarður and Hagkaup and other Icelandic companies. I met the foreman in an office on the floor above the workspace.

I told him an acquaintance of mine worked there and he told me about the workplace and offered up some good stories. He looked at me, scoped me out, and I had a feeling not just anyone could work at Plastos.

"Why aren't you at school?"

"I was in school."

"Yeah?"

"Yes, I'm just not quite sure I want to go to university. I am really thinking more about going to the Technical College. Or maybe the Agricultural College."

"The Agricultural College, yes."

"Yes, I was working in horticulture before this, you see."

"So you're just deciding what it is you're going to study?"

"Yes, I want to think about it carefully before I start. I don't want to learn to be an electrician if I don't plan to get a job in that later."

There was a vacancy for me at Plastos and I could start the next day.

The next day, at exactly nine, I arrived in front of the punch clock. It felt like a really modern device. There'd been no punch clock at Hampiðjan. I got my own stamp card with my name on it. On the wall hung a container with a bunch of stamp cards and I put mine there when I was done stamping it. I felt great pride having my name there. It was almost like getting your name in the phone book. You totally become a real person when you had a stamp card. I was excited and happy on my first workday at Plastos. The foreman welcomed me and the employees seemed more interesting than Hampiðjan. There were even young guys close to my age. Everyone had a headset and music was played on the shop floor, too. Real rock music and not easy-going tunes. You couldn't really hear it because of the noise from the machines, but it was still something modern and fun.

"We put you on the Extruder," the foreman announced loudly. I thought that sounded good and imagined it was something I could say with pride. I imagined that when I was in my work clothes and carrying a plastic bag labeled Kjörgarður I had made myself, people would look at me and ask:

"Where do you work, young man?"

"I'm an employee of Plastos!"

I would answer with great pride because not just anybody worked there. People would smile happily because they'd heard such good things about Plastos.

"Yes, that's a great company! And what do you do there?"

"I'm on the Extruder."

It was something people didn't know about. I'd certainly never met anyone who worked on an Extruder. It sounded a bit like being a driver, almost a truck driver. Maybe I'd even qualify to take part in conversations between truck drivers and tractor drivers. All the drivers would listen with awe to me as they'd never worked on the Extruder and knew nothing about it.

The Extruder proved to be a huge machine that pumped out plastic bags. It was joined together by large plastic rollers. The machine made plastic bags from plastic. My job was to take the plastic bags once there were fifty and pack them in construction paper and tape the package. Very simple. I positioned myself in front of the machine. The plane began to pump out the bags and load them in a stack. On the front of the machine, a counter said exactly how many bags it had spit out. It turned out the job was not as easy as I had thought. It was a challenge to pack the bags. They were so staticky that they floated on top of each other rather than lying neatly together. I couldn't possibly pack them and they ran just hither and thither. Instead of gluing the construction paper, I caught the tape again and again on the bags. The tape was so sticky that there wasn't any way to free it without tearing the bags and then it was ruined. And before I knew it, the machine beeped at me to let me know it was releasing a new stack of fifty plastic bags that had accumulated while I tried to pack the previous stack. And before I got anything done, a third load had come out and bags lay everywhere like so many bodies. I could not handle anything at all and pushed the security button on the console. It stopped with a thud, gave a loud whine, and a red light began flashing on top. The foreman came running and shouted: "What is going on here?"

"Ah, you see, there's something wrong with this tape..."

"Yes, let's take a look. It's not complicated."

I tried to apologize. He showed me again what I had to do. Roll the machine paper, lay the roll of tape on top, and pull it so.

"It's not complicated."

Then he packed the three packages and I watched carefully so as to learn. This seemed incredibly simple. Occasionally he looked questioningly at me and I nodded as if I was totally on board. He turned away from the machine and went. The same routine began again. Plastic bags piled up in a stack and when the machine counted fifty it beeped and blinked. I got the machine paper and tried to do as the foreman had shown me. But it didn't happen. Bags piled up and the story repeated. Before I knew it, I was drowning in a pile of plastic bags all stuck together with tape. The foreman came running back and turned off the engine. This time he was a little frustrated.

The people who worked on the Extruder looked at me with pity. Now I was not the normal one working with handicapped colleagues, but the handicapped one and the others were normal. No one came over to me and said:

"It's not a problem. The first day is always a bit tricky."

It was plain people couldn't understand why I couldn't cope. For my part, I found it so complex and difficult that I didn't understand how anyone could do it. I tried to talk to colleagues at both coffee break and lunchtime.

"Well, it's a bit difficult out there with the bags as they slide about all the time."

"They're just staticky," one of the workers said.

"Yes, I know, sure, I just don't know what to do about it."

"You just keep them in place when you wrap them up. It's not complicated."

How could they say it wasn't complicated when it was complicated? No one told me anything important or offered to help me. That bothered me. I found the people at Plastos full of themselves and more arrogant than my colleagues at Hampiðjan. After a break, I tried to do what I could to hold onto the bags. I pushed them together forcefully, but that just made them run even more quickly away from my hands until they whipped into the air. There was no way I could learn this procedure. I thought I was just lacking a little practice and this afternoon or evening I would get much better. That wasn't the case and at the end of the day, I hadn't packed a single stack of plastic bags. The people who worked on the Extruders, however, had been obliging and raced between their machines and mine, packing them both. They seemed to do it effortlessly. Some had even become so good at it they could take a cigarette break while the machine was pumping out new bags. I was afraid for the life of me to light a cigarette. I would also undoubtedly set myself on fire because I was stuck together in plastic bags and glue.

The next day my disaster story continued. I began to suspect that I wasn't perhaps very well suited to packing plastic bags or working on the Extruder. No matter what I tried, I found it absolutely impossible to pack the damned bags. I just stood at the machine and scattered construction paper, crumpled plastic bags, and tape around me. And it wasn't enough that my nemeses the plastic bags crumpled together on the table in front of me, but they floated onto the floor where they stood thick at my feet. Sometimes I stepped on tape and glued bags to my feet but was so busy with the machine that I didn't have time to free them. The whole floor around me was covered with plastic bags and I was always tripping. Repeatedly, I stepped on top of a newly-made plastic bag and landed flat on my back. It was becoming dangerous. My reputation at Plastos rapidly deteriorated and my colleagues looked at me with pity. I couldn't seek reassurance or advice from my friend because he was on A-shifts while I was on B, so we never met; I was there alone.

The third day, I finally gave up. Either I must be an idiot or the machine broken. It was clearly not working. I found it frustrating because I had really put in some effort. I wanted to be a Plastos employee. I wanted to be part of the whole, one of them. I wanted to laugh along with them and to tell them that it wasn't complicated, just simple. But I had to accept that it wasn't. It was proven. This time I didn't want to run away like some miserable specimen, so I hauled myself upstairs to go talk to the boss. I told him I thought this job didn't suit me. I wasn't the right hire for this. I was expecting that he would try to dissuade me from this view and even give me a pep talk. Possibly he would offer me some other job than packing plastic bags. I was open to that. I was certain I could cope with all the other functions of the company. But instead of having a lively chat with me about the other options I had at Plastos he simply said, "Okay, buddy."

He did not even look at me once, but instead answered his phone and started talking. I stood like a clam for a few moments and waited. When the foreman had done talking on the phone he walked past me without speaking and left. That blew me away. I went into the locker room, put on my clothes and coat, and went out. I went onto the shop floor and stood in front of everyone and waited for people to notice me. Someone would definitely come and try to dissuade me from leaving. It didn't happen. No one showed any interest in me at all or seemed to care about whether I was coming or going. I didn't see the foreman anywhere. I slipped out and took the bus to Hlemmur.

I was ready to give up on my job search. The only work that I had enjoyed was with the Horticulture Department. I had understood it all quite nicely and it had gone so well I thought I could be a gardener. I was fine shoveling earth and being outside in a t-shirt in good weather. The problem with gardening was that you could only work for three months a year. There was no gardening this time of year.

Then my parents realized that I was no longer a line-man for Post and Phone. I tried to explain to my mother that I had really tried, but it just had not worked out as a line-man because it was totally unacceptable work. I told her that I had also tried elsewhere. I hadn't succeeded at anything, but I'd really put a lot of effort into finding a job. I had, for example, realized I would rather work inside than outside in this disgusting weather. It all fell on deaf ears. She sighed and merely said: "I can't be bothered to listen to this prattle."

"It's not prattle. I'm trying to tell you I would rather work inside... just not on the Extruder or with some handicapped people. Can't I just get a job with you?"

My mother worked in the kitchen at the City Hospital. It was inside work I could imagine doing. There you just put some food trays on a cart and then someone came and took the cart. There would be no slipping. Food trays all have these ridges so that they click well in the cart and nothing spills. Food trays are not staticky and you don't need to glue anything. I had often visited my mother at work and knew the people who were worked with her were lively and fun. I might have enjoyed my job there. Mom rolled her eyes.

"I don't know what the hell to do with you, child!"

There wasn't any point in my discussing this. I would just have to find a job. I continued to monitor the job advertisements but couldn't find a suitable match. I found all the jobs miserable and uninteresting. I was not going back to work at Hampiðjan. And the arrogant crowd at Plastos could jump up their own ass. Then my father announced to me one day that he had helped me get a job.

"Really, what?"

"Cleaning the timber joints for the new Central Bank."

I was totally unaware of any new Central Bank.

"Where is it?".

"On Arnarhóll."

I didn't know where Arnarhóll was.

"Up on Kjalarnes?"

"No, up on Arnarhóll, downtown."

"Yes," I replied, pretending to know where it was.

"I met with Anton yesterday and told him you were looking for work. He said that you should just come by."

I had never worked in construction but thought it sounded exciting. I had often seen guys building stuff and I had held a hammer before. There was something noble and exciting about building a house. The building of the Central Bank was hugely exciting. It was indeed an important building. I imagined that the Central Bank was going to be like a pyramid. I was enormously grateful to my father, glad he had got me this job. I was sure it would be a fun project. Maybe I'd wear an apron and got to walk around on the scaffolding. When I saw people I knew walking below, I would call out to them. I'd be very high up so they'd only see me if they squinted.

"What are you building?"

"I'm building a new Central Bank."

I arrived early in the morning. In front of me loomed a dark and scary scaffolding and rocks and backhoes all around. I went to a work shed and asked for Anton.

"That's me," said one guy, loud and clearly. "Are you Kidda's son?"

"Yes."

"And you're an extremely hard-working kid?"

"Yes—I'm always hard-working, for sure."

"Have you held a hammer before?"

"Yes. I once helped a man, my sister's husband's cousin, when he was constructing houses. He's a master builder."

"Okay, so you know the ins and outs."

"Yes. I've been on construction sites lots."

"Yeah, okay, great."

He clearly liked me. We walked out to a giant mountain of pieces of wood. Pieces of wood just lay in a heap full of iron pieces and nails. My job was to take each stick, place it on a trestle, beat the nails with a hammer, wrest the debris from the wood, and stack it. I could immediately see that this was unworkable for one person: it would never be over. It would take me months and even years to finish the whole mountain. Then there was the freezing cold and the snow showers. There would be sleet: snow which hasn't made up its mind whether to be snow or rain. Snowflakes fall to the ground and turn into water when they land on the street. Snowdrifts become puddles. I rubbed my hands together. What had given Dad the idea I'd enjoy this work? This wasn't a job I was prepared to spend a lot of time on. I hadn't even started working and I was already freezing. I didn't dare tell the guy; he thought he was taking good care of me so I allowed him to show

me what I had to do. He put a stick on the trestle and showed me. I nodded and said:

"Yes, no problem."

"And a coffee break at ten."

"Great, okay, I'll see you then."

I watched the man walk away and as soon as he disappeared round the corner of the work shed, I threw away the hammer and ran as fast as lightning down Lækjartorg. From there I took a bus to Hlemmur. I hung out in Reykjavík for the rest of the day and totally forgot about this awful job. It wasn't until I got home that night and my dad asked me how it went that I remembered.

"How was work?"

"Uh, work?"

"I thought you were working at the Central Bank today?"

"Yes, I went there, you see, but there was no work..."

"Is that so?"

"No, a guy told me that it was some mix-up and there was some other guy working there."

"That so? That's odd. He said you could come by."

"Yes, I don't know."

I shook my head helplessly. It was so much easier to lie to my dad than my mom. She never believed anything, but I could lie to him about anything. He never suspected me of untruths and it never seemed to occur to him that what I was saying might be false.

I was once more unemployed; it wasn't easy. I certainly appeared to be looking for a job, but the ones on offer were such lame and miserable jobs that it never once occurred to me to apply. A good friend in Reykjavík told me it would be a good idea to sign on for unemployment: you got money without having to do any work. That sounded good. I went that same day to the unemployment office in Reykjavík and signed up. I got an unemployment card and all I had to do was to go down to Borgartún once a week and let them stamp my card. If I didn't, I got no benefits. I dutifully caught the bus once a week and got a stamp on my card. I didn't get my benefit payments immediately, but had to wait six weeks. Someone in Reykjavík had told me that I could, however, request to get paid if I had worked somewhere for more than two and a half days. I had spent an hour at Post and Phone and one-and-a-half days at Hampiðjan. But I had spent two-and-a-half days at Plastos. I took the bus up to Höfði to the headquarters of Plastos to find out about my salary. I had certainly spent two-and-a-half days of my life there and so, of course, deserved to get paid for it. The work had been both difficult and boring. The people in the office didn't agree. I wasn't anywhere in their records, which had nothing to say about me. I told them I'd got a stamp card with my name on it, which I had dutifully put into the rack on the wall.

"I'm going to take this to the union!"

I don't know how I thought of threatening that; I'd probably seen it in some movie. But it worked. I was sent in to the cashier who handed me a small amount. Salary for two-and-a-half days. It wasn't much but enough for cigarettes and a sandwich from Sómastaðir. An absolute luxury of a meal, something I allowed myself only when I really could. A Sóma sandwich with ham and cheese heated in the microwave in the shop. It was the best, most adventurous food available in Iceland at the time. But with it began the worst period of unemployment in my life.

Mom and Dad didn't let me off the hook. I either had to go to school or to work.

"You can't hang around here every day!" Mom said resolutely. Neither of them had a formal education; in fact, no one in my family did. My parents had both started working when they were very young. Dad had been paid for his manual labor since the age of six and my mom started working once she was old enough for Confirmation. In my family, this was considered good: people had to be grateful to have a job and had to carry out their duties with humility and pride. Mom and Dad knew too well what it was like to be unemployed. They took their first steps into married life during a depression. In their minds, no jobs were boring or menial; they were just well or badly done.

The value of education was barely discussed in the home, except to say that I'd never amount to anything and would never get anywhere in life if I didn't educate myself. My parents, though, had both done well despite their lack of education. Mom had only passed her elementary school exams and my dad had spent just a single half-semester, under the tutelage of a priest, paid for with a lamb. That's how Dad learned to read, write and do sums, and how the priest got Christmas lunch after having held Christmas Mass, during which he told Dad that the poor are fortunate to be so poor and that it was much better to be poor than rich. While he preached, his wife cooked Dad's lamb.

I had long ago written off the possibility that I would ever educate myself. I knew I couldn't learn what you needed to get a college degree. I was witless. I sought comfort in Þórbergur's book The Prodigy and his trials studying in Reykjavík; I often flirted with the idea that I wasn't an idiot but a genius, like Þórbergur. We seemed so much alike, and he often put things just the way I would have. But no one ever told me so. There was never anyone who patted me on the back and said:

"Jón, you're a genius, pure and simple."

This was some weak hope. I found school remote, inaccessible, and somehow not for me. Probably it would be best for me to go do some vocational training. But there was nothing I particularly wanted to learn. I wanted to become a writer, actor, or artist. Þórbergur was a laborer before he became a poet. But after having tried that miserable job, I came to the conclusion that, of the two evils, it would be a bit nicer to be in school than in work. There was at least good company there and maybe something interesting would happen.

In the factories where I'd worked, we'd been given headset radios to shorten the working day. I found the radio, however, boring. I was totally bored by the unnecessary chatter and strange music on Channel 1. The sound was like if you were standing in the cultured home of some elderly couple, a home where everything was ironed and tidy, everyone was serious and quiet and talked about boring stuff. The radio stories were dull and pretentiously read. The radio plays were half as bad. Usually, they were Icelandic versions of some foreign crime drama that was meant to be tense. At best, they were comical and funny.

Sometimes people addressed each other very formally and said strange phrases like:

"Greetings to you, Mr. Higgins. I am Cliff Knowbells, a detective from Southampton."

"And greetings to you, too. Did you come by train this morning?" The police detective was surprised.

"No. I came on the riverboat from Barnesby Island."

I couldn't really follow them; I had no idea who these people were and why they spoke like that. What was the purpose of having people listen to this? It seemed astonishing that anyone could enjoy it. And what could be the benefit in it for anyone? When the radio plays were Icelandic, it was completely unbearable to listen to them because they were so staged, in both plot and dialogue. Instead of having a normal conversation, it was like people sat and yelled pretentiously at one another. But the music was the worst thing about the station. Icelandic songs— a women's choir from Selfoss, a men's choir from Húsavík, then those "easy-going tunes." Often a screeching Norwegian lady. And, worse, none of it was properly introduced. And they played classical music. I felt like all classical music was symphonic shit. I thought Channel 1 was definitely a decent radio station to die to. If you were on your deathbed, it would definitely be nice to have Channel 1 simmering somewhere in the background while you passed over to the other place.

Channel 2 was a little better. There was little talking, no radio plays or stuff. Channel 2 mostly played music and in between songs some announcer gave you some facts about the band playing the song. Where it was recorded, by whom, the name of the first album.

Then they played three songs from the album. Rarely any punk. I often wondered why there wasn't an entertaining station to which to listen, one that was informative, alternative, and surprising; one people would benefit from as well as enjoy. I thought it would need to be fun in order to made tedious work seem less dull for people.

On Channel 2, there was a program called *National Character*. It was an enormously popular program, remarkable for many reasons. I often enjoyed listening to it. *National Character* was hugely popular as soon as it began. It provided a platform for ordinary people to speak on the radio and to voice their interests. All kinds of eccentric and oddball people called in, usually to make comments about politics or current events, and discuss the things that were on the national agenda. Often the same people called again and again, becoming familiar to the program's hosts. It could be gripping entertainment. The more irritating and strange people were, the longer they were kept on the line. They got calls from screech-voiced men and furious ladies who wanted to complain about things. Occasionally people called in who were obviously drunk. And instead of making excuses for the listener and immediately getting them off the radio, the presenters kept going; they loved talking with these people. Frequent guests called so regularly that they became famous. These people often barely counted as normal, either because of their opinions about human affairs or due to their lifestyle or some association with alcohol or drugs. Some mumbled so much I hardly understood what they were saying. It was the best show on the radio and I always tried to listen to it.

Dad sometimes called *National Character*, I was sometimes listening when he called. He was usually complaining about language in the media and worrying that people would cease knowing Icelandic. Once he complained about something in that day's news: a plane that had made an emergency landing in a field. The aircraft had broken up and it was sheer fortune that the pilot wasn't hurt. The news said that the aircraft had flown oddly and eventually crashed in the fields. Dad read the news from the newspaper and the announcer repeated every word and said he'd read the story too.

"Yes, I have the paper here in front of me, Kristinn."

"The aircraft flew into the fjord," Dad read aloud.

"Yes, that's right."

"Isn't it the pilot who flies the plane?" asked Dad, decidedly.

"You'd think so, Kristinn."

"Yes, it's the pilot who flies the plane."

The host thanked Dad for pointing out this element of the story, which had been utterly overlooked, and thanked him very much for offering such an illuminating contribution.

"That's certainly right, Kristinn. The aircraft does not fly, it is flown by the pilot. It is the pilot flying the plane."

"I thought as much."

Dad was clearly relieved to have explained this. To reiterate his case, he noted, finally, that if no pilot were in the plane then it wouldn't fly anywhere. Instead, it would be perfectly still inside a hangar. The host repeated to Dad that he heartily agreed and they said goodbye warmly. I was deeply ashamed for Dad. Had it been any other guy, I would just have laughed.

Since I had not managed to complete my Standard Examinations, and passed only Icelandic and English, I couldn't go to any college. I asked other kids if I could go to school somewhere else and was told that the Comprehensive School in Ármúla would be most likely. Ármúla definitely looked past whether kids had achieved their examination scores or not, unlike other schools. I went to the Ármúla School, signed up, got a list of books, went to the school bookstore, and bought the books I had to read. They all seemed snoringly dull, weighty tomes. Every time I looked for a book from the list, I hoped it would be thin, less than fifty pages. But it never happened. These were all thick volumes. The mathematics book was over two hundred pages! Then I went over the schedule. I thought it looked quite demanding. The classes were long and there were many subjects. I would be attending classes all day and then have homework. I wasn't going there out of any desire to learn, but because I was forced to by my mother. I had neither interest nor ambition.

I knew some kids and could hang out with them and chat. Classes bored me. They weren't just boring in nature; I was also far behind the others. It was like discussing a book I had just begun to read: we were on the first page and now we were starting to discuss the end and the point of the story. I needed to know all the main points just to be able to understand the gist. And this happened in every subject. The terror of the past loomed before me in the form of tree diagrams, algebra, and spelling—things I had so often stood helpless against before. I felt tormented and lost, lost in a foreign land without a map. I wandered aimlessly, just keeping on. I realized that while I had let the time pass at Núpur, my peers had been taught things which seemed to have gone completely over my head. I had broken up with school before even starting.

I began to skip school lessons and stopped going to math. I found it useless. In other subjects, I simply believed that I could just study well for the tests and find, to my surprise, I knew every-thing. I told myself this as a way to mute my inferiority complex, to lessen the anxiety inside me.

Mom had taken it upon herself to carefully monitor what I did in school and asked me lots about schoolbooks and studies. It was obvious that this time she was going to follow up and make sure I hadn't dropped out of the system. There was nothing to do but to drag myself out in the morning and go to school with my full bag. Sometimes I'd not slept the night before because I was messing around reading or playing the Fisheries Game. When the other students went to class, I went to the toilets and locked myself in. Then I spread my coat on the floor, used my schoolbag for a pillow, and lay down. I often managed an excellent nap until someone had to use the bathroom and knocked violently on the door. There were usually some free minutes when I went out to smoke with the other kids. When teaching began again and the kids went back to class, I went back to the bathroom, and took a nap. It felt nice. I also found a boy at school who often had cannabis and could sometimes sell it to me. Hash made my schooling consider-ably more bearable. It helped me to sleep, relax, and pass the time.

When the mid-winter tests were over, things came crashing down.

"What the hell is this?!" Mom shouted, holding my report card in the air in front of me. I tried to seem just as surprised as she was.

"I just don't understand..."

"Three, two, zero, zero, five, three, six, five, zero, zero, three," she said, reading down the list of scores. "What the hell is going on with you, child?!"

"Well, like I say, see, I just don't understand..."

"Haven't you been attending school?"

"Sure."

"Haven't you learned anything?"

"Sure."

I always felt I had. Here and there I had even been doing quite well. Units completed per semester: zero. I had managed to go through an entire semester without completing a single unit.

"Why don't you have any score in Danish?"

I had a ready explanation. No point explaining to my mother how pointless learning Danish was.

"Now, that wasn't my fault. Er, see, the Danish test was advertised, sure... but then it was the wrong time advertised."

This wasn't entirely untrue. All I knew about the Danish test was that I'd heard some kids talking about how the test had been incorrectly advertised. Mom had, of course, long since ceased to believe anything I said and didn't listen to my excuses. She thought it was just laziness and folly. I threw out the idea that maybe the Comprehensive School in Ármúla wasn't the right school for me. I wondered if maybe I should go to vocational school.

"You're just lazy!"

I assured my mom that I would learn from this experience. And I would prove to her in the spring exams that I had totally turned the page.

One day I set eyes on an announcement on the board at school.

Drama Club
Ármúla's Drama Club will start its annual meetings.
Interested students should assemble in the hall, Wednesday at 4 p.m.

This caught my interest. I arrived promptly, along with several others. I was excited as I had had a good experience acting at Núpur. And though I couldn't study acting, I could take part in school plays. The drama teacher tested our acting and diction and chose me at once to play one of the main parts in the two one-acts he was planning to stage. I always looked forward to attending rehearsals, never slept through them, and had no difficulties learning my lines. I loved it all. When I acted, I was at home. I felt sure about things, I knew everything, and I could learn. And I had pride, joy, and satisfaction when it came to drama. I recited my lines and went over sentences, trying to say them in different ways. I studied at home. I had to find ways to emphasize each sentence and see how nuances changed with different emphases. The meaning wasn't only in the sentence, but also in how you said it.

The drama teacher taught me a lot and I was a model student. Once again I experienced joy, the love of the theater, and the happiness of standing on stage. When I wore a costume, I wore joy.

When we put on our costumes, everyday life became an adventure. As soon as the door had been shut and the lights turned off, I was no longer the red-haired troublemaker who couldn't learn because he was too stupid. I was a young Russian aristocrat coming home from war. And I didn't fail Danish or sit stunned by tree diagrams. I was going to get married. I wasn't going down, but rising up. I was in love with a young and beautiful woman and we had a future on a summer estate near the Black Sea. The first performance went great and everyone praised my acting in every respect.

"You're a born actor!"

People constantly asked if my parents were actors and if I was the son of this or that actor.

"You have acting in your blood."

When the play was done, I thought it was all over.

I knew that I was probably never going to be an actor because I could never get into drama school without first having taken my student examinations. And to get past those examinations, I had to learn tree diagrams and algebra and Danish. I would never be able to do that. I found it unfair and unnecessary. It made me angry. After Ármúla, I would give up acting. They can all go to hell. To hell with this school system that just wants to break people down and trample them into the same box. To hell with these stupid rules. The system was my enemy. The system thought it was on top because it had the power to give orders. And drama school couldn't be any different; it was also part of the system. So to hell with drama school. To hell with the theater. The devil take all of you.

When I was at Núpur, I'd met some kids from Hafnarfjörður. Until I went out west, I had no idea where Hafnarfjörður was and knew nothing about it except that my grandmother had lived there. And that, in my mind, was Hafnarfjörður: a collection of old people in old houses. I thought there were no streets, just farms called The Sands and The Bog and The City, and also a small fjord. But at Núpur, I learned that Hafnarfjörður was an entire town. I'd even gone there a few times to visit Biggi who was at Núpur with me. Biggi had started secondary school in a town called Flensborg. And I knew there were many interesting kids there. Through Biggi, I met Óttar Proppé, his friend. He was my age and lived in Hafnarfjörður. We immediately bonded and I found Óttar to be a very fun guy. There was also a strong connection between us and we thought the same in many ways, had the same views on many things. But Óttar did well in school. He came from a really cultured home and his parents were both teachers. At home he had a large, extensive library and all his family had an education. Óttar was like me, just much smarter. I thought that maybe if I went to the same school as Óttar he could perhaps help me and be my support so I could learn to learn. I decided to change schools in the middle of the semester and enroll at FNV Flensborg in Hafnarfjörður.

I had many interesting and enjoyable times in Flensborg, but none of that had anything to do with learning. My relationship to education didn't change, even when I went to another school. I was just as much off the map as I had been in Ármúla. My semester in Flensborg began in a similar way as my semester in Ármúla and at the end of I had completed three units. I did some loose calculations on paper and saw that the required units for matriculation were 150; if I finished zero to three units per semester,

I would probably be older than fifty when I finally finished school. After that, I gave up and admitted defeat. I was doomed to be a loser. I was like a lame man participating in a race or in some way trying to do something for which I was physically unable. All the doors seemed closed to me. I couldn't get asylum anywhere; everywhere I was an outsider.

I felt worse than awful. The summer came and everything blossomed, but inside me things were dead. Everything had failed. The
days merged into nights and I didn't want to do anything, I was
looking forward to nothing and nothing made any difference to
me. I isolated myself more than before; life was permanently stalled,
I felt. I didn't even care for movies. I had no peace of mind to read
or listen to anything. I didn't have anything in common with anyone: not with my family, not with the kids in the neighborhood.
I no longer knew the kids I'd been in touch with before. Óttar
had gone to the United States as an exchange student. Everyone
was going somewhere or had some task. I had no purpose and
was suffocating under my own weight. I didn't even have anything in common with the kids at Hlemmur anymore. They all
seemed to be doing much better than me. I didn't have anything
in common with anyone in the world or even with the world
itself. I just walked in circles in one big errand loop. I couldn't
find anything that gave me any reason to continue on into the
future. I had made so many mistakes in life and they were so far
back I could not return.

Things had evolved into the current situation slowly and surely.
I'd changed from wretched Jón to Jónsi Wretch. Whenever I met
other kids or old friends, I felt they looked at me with pity, like
they knew my deepest secrets. I was hopeless and everyone seemed
to know it and understand except me. I was never going to be

anything or make friends or do anything fun in life. This caused me great pain. I was ready to consider any options but found only a closed door before me. Everything was complicated, difficult and meaningless. I was simply ugly, a failure, witless, prickless. My prick had completely healed, but just lay there, emotionless, pointless. That's how I'd be forever.

I began to think actively about ways to put an end to my life. I thought about it daily. I felt creepy thinking about it, but maybe it was for the best. The days floated past and ran together. Sure, I had some pleasure drinking and if I got any booze I drank it down to the last drop, always alone. I was always more or less alone.

I saw before me the winos at Hlemmur. I had long been sure I would be just like them. I would be a funny, entertaining wino in Hlemmur. Sometimes I would be beaten up and the police would keep putting me in jail. Finally, I'd fall and injure myself. Guys were always coming to Hlemmur with a bandage on their head or a cast on their hand. They'd fallen. One came with casts on both legs, walking on crutches. He said he'd fallen in the shipyard. I had no idea what the shipyard was, but it had to be an absolutely terrible place so I would surely get to know it if I lived long enough. I would become known all over town as the idiot who, plastered, fell in the shipyard. But even the winos were better than me because they often had some girlfriend they got to sleep with. I would never get to try that. I contemplated this lonely, unforgiving thought. I could choose between killing myself like a man or becoming a wino out of gutlessness.

But how do you kill yourself? I'd tried to hang myself. It had failed and I felt I hadn't done it seriously. I didn't want to die in a painful, nasty way. I couldn't think of throwing myself off a roof because I didn't dare. I remembered, too, when my dad told me he had to clean up the parking lot in front of the City Hospital after some guy had thrown himself down from the top floor and landed on the pavement. I often wondered whether he hadn't been scared while falling. And perhaps he regretted it as he jumped? And wouldn't it hurt when you landed on the street? Gradually my mind gave birth to an idea. I often used to drink and wander about, hanging out downtown at night. I found it enjoyable. Maybe I could die like that. Wandering around in my own world and fading out until I didn't exist anymore. I could well imagine dying like that.

I often pissed myself and so I found it best to wear an overcoat. It was long, so you couldn't see anything. I wondered if I should try to talk to the doctor, but I dared not. I never wanted to see him again. Also, he would definitely not give a damn. There was no one to talk to about it. I knew for sure that there were many people who didn't really care about me, but I also felt uncomfortable talking about it. They began to ask me about things I felt uncomfortable to think about.

What helped me the most in getting some mental relief was going out for a walk. Sometimes when I was out walking alone at night, I played a game in which I tried to walk in front of cars. I did it when I'd been drinking. There weren't many cars on the road and I was totally prepared for the next car to run me down. I would suddenly go out into the street and hope a car would appear and run into me. This always took place at night. Because there weren't many cars about and I was probably easy to see in the middle of the road, I never got hit. They often honked me and shouted out the window. Eventually the police would come and grab me. Someone had complained about me.

"Do you like walking in the road?"

"No, no."

"Why are you walking in the path of the cars?"

"I don't know. I was just lost in thought."

"Have you been drinking?"

"No, no."

I'd carried a knife for years. I had often used it to cut myself, both at Núpur and in Reykjavík, on my own or with a group of kids. Sometimes we sat together in a circle and had to cut our hands and feet. There was no particular reason. It was just something we did. We burned ourselves sometimes, too. We'd heat the knife tip with a lighter and put it on our skin. We got a kick, a thrill, from it.

My knowledge of different suicide methods was mainly from books I'd read, from television shows and movies. I had sometimes talked to kids who had tried to kill themselves. The most common method was cutting one's wrists. I had often tried to put the knife on my pulse on the underside of my arm, but it was very difficult to cut your hand there because the skin was so sensitive. Cutting your wrist was still the best way to kill yourself. I thought a lot about this method. Touched my arm, examined the blood vessels, checked the pulse. There were arteries on your forearms. But if you cut your wrist, you had to make sure the blood didn't clot. Best to be in a hot bath or moving, for example, walking, so the blood flow continued. A good friend of mine had cut her wrists on both hands.

She had cut her hands with a razor blade. A waterfall bled from each hand but she still didn't die. She lost consciousness and woke up in the City Hospital. I visited her there.

I made the decision. I was going to cut my wrists. But I wasn't going to stay still. I'd walk around town until I fell down dead. I was going to take a lot of pills before I cut myself. Both to have the courage and also to numb the pain so I could cut deep enough. I started hoarding the pills I got either from other kids or from the winos at Hlemmur. I bought a bottle of spirits and hid it in my room. I decided to do it on a Sunday. It was so quiet in town then. I headed downtown and walked around, going to a few places I had enjoyed going, like the arcade, Magna, the central bus terminal in Lækjartorg, and finally the long walk to Hlemmur. There, I sat down in my favorite corner facing Laugavegur. There were many kids at Hlemmur. Without anyone seeing I had them, I snuck pills, one after the other. I'd gotten seasickness tablets from the pharmacy and had also stolen some pills from my mom—Valium and several other types I didn't recognize. Then I sipped liquor. That's how I spent the evening. When I felt I was getting properly light-headed, I got up.

It was past midnight. I felt dizzy and my head swam. I felt the knife in my right pocket. It was sharp-edged. I went off into a corner of Hlemmur, bit my bottom lip and clenched a fist with my left hand. And super-quick, without looking or letting anyone see, I took my hand from my pocket and cut with my right hand as forcefully as I could. I felt the knife tear apart the flesh and strike bone. This was definitely enough. I didn't want to see this, and without looking I put my hand in my pocket and walked off.

I still had a little booze left. I would walk around until I fell down and died. I wouldn't feel it and wouldn't think about it. I decided to walk down Hverfisgata then Laugavegur. I didn't meet anyone. Occasionally I had a sip of liquor. I waited to bleed out and faint. I was going to go into a corner and hide. I walked down Lækjartorg, down to the harbor, and around the Customs House. Then I walked back to Hverfisgata and up to Hlemmur. But Hlemmur was already closed. I finished the rest of the booze and took a turn on Öskjuhlíð. It would definitely be peaceful and quiet there.

The next thing I remembered was the hospital. I was in a lit room with a lot of people around me. A man who was apparently the doctor was scolding me.

"What's wrong with you, boy?!"

I'd done something to annoy the man, apparently, but didn't know what. What had I done? Someone pulled my hand all the way up and turned it over and smashed it down. Then I fell asleep. When I woke up again, I was in another room. The angry doctor was still with me. My hand lay under some green fabric. The doctor sat on a chair with my hand in his arms and worked on it through the fabric. He held a needle, which was bent like a hook.

"Who knows what you were thinking, boy?"

I smiled. I thought it was funny. Of course he didn't know what I was thinking. I didn't even know myself. I felt dizzy looking at him, lay back, closed my eyes and fell asleep. Next time I regained consciousness, I was lying in a hospital bed inside the hospital. I had a bandage around my hand from wrist to elbow. Shortly after, a nurse came into my room and asked loudly:

"How are you doing, Jón?"

She was friendly.

"Do you know what happened to me?"

She looked searchingly at me and smiled weakly.

"Don't you remember anything about what happened to you?"

"Noooo, I was just walking..."

"And you do not remember having come here yesterday?"

"No."

"You were brought to ER during the night. You had badly cut your hand. Don't you remember anything after that?"

I wasn't dead. I was very relieved. I knew exactly what had happened. Someone had found me or seen me. But I didn't want to talk about it. It's silly to try to kill yourself and fail. Later, the doctor came to check on me. It wasn't the same one who had scolded me during the night.

"Hey, Jón. How do you feel?"

"Fine, good."

"Do you remember anything from after you arrived here last night?"

"No, it's all kind of a haze."

"Yes, of course. You came here during the night with a serious injury to your left hand and were sent straight to surgery. We found a knife in your pocket we believe caused the injury. Did you cut yourself with a knife, Jón?"

"Yeah, that must be it," I mumbled and pretended to have a vague recollection of it.

"Do you remember why you did that?"

"Yes, I was just playing with some friends, see."

The doctor looked at me questioningly, like he didn't believe me.

"You'd also taken some pills. Do you remember which pills?"

"Uhmm, no. They were just some pills my friend had."

"Yes, yes. And do you remember which friend that was?"

"No, he wasn't really my friend. More just some kid I'd met before, but I don't really quite know what his name is, really."

The doctor nodded, but I saw that he didn't believe me in the slightest.

"We put a tube into your stomach and pumped it."

"Thank you."

"Can I see your hand?"

I lifted it up and he took it and touched it. He made me move my fingers and clench into a fist.

"It all works fine, really," I said and lifted my hand up and down.

"Yes, it was a considerably deep wound. You almost cut off your hand."

I nodded.

"It was a lot of surgery. We had to sew the muscle together."

"Were there many stitches?"

"Yes, 25 in all."

I nodded like this came as no surprise.

"We spent half the night patching you together."

"Yes, okay."

"But you don't remember why you cut your hand?"

"No, we were just cutting ourselves, that's all, really."

"You weren't trying to do something?"

"No."

"You weren't trying to kill yourself, Jón, were you?"

"No, not at all! I would never ever do that."

"Okay. Very well. We're going to have you stay here one more night then you should be able to go home. I talked to your GP and he will probably be in touch with you."

I nodded my head attentively.

"Thank you."

The doctor looked at me contemplatively. I smiled at him in a friendly way.

"Okay then. Take care, my friend."

"Yes, thank you."

Someone had seen me walking along Snorrabraut. I had gotten very wobbly and had been wandering in the road. A driver stopped his vehicle and intercepted me. He saw I was all bloody and drove me to the emergency room.

The next day I got to go home. I told my mother that I had fallen and sprained my wrist. A few days later, she let me know that the GP had called and I had an appointment with him. I found the doctor very nice. He had been told about my arrival in ER and asked me why I had cut myself and I told him I didn't know.

"Don't you feel well, Jón?"

I could have told him that I felt very well, but I began to think that maybe he could help me feel better.

"No, I often feel awful."

"And why do you feel so bad?"

I shrugged.

"I don't know. I just feel bad."

"And what form does that distress take?"

"I just always feel like I'm suffocating."

"Can you describe that in more detail?"

"I just always feel there's a great weight over my chest and I often find it difficult to catch my breath."

"Hmm... And have you discussed this with anyone?"

"No."

"But do you have any idea why you have this weight across your chest?"

"No, none at all."

The doctor told me it was a symptom of stress and said he wanted to put me on medication. He also thought I was depressed and what I had tried to do to myself would be called suicide and looked very serious.

"Well, I was just playing about, really."

He picked up a prescription and handed it to me.

"You should take two tablets daily, one in the morning and one at night. It says so on the package."

I was pleasantly surprised and thought it was fun to get drugs. I had brought some tablets home from the hospital. Pills were a convenient way to make yourself feel different. You didn't get a hangover from pills. Maybe these pills would make me feel good. It was with considerable anticipation and excitement that I went to the pharmacy in Austurbæjar and filled my first prescription. The product was named FLUANXOL. That was a cool name. Fluanxol could be the name of a band. I liked this doctor. He saw what was up with me and now I had drugs that would fix things. I was a bit crazy, a bit faulty, but it was possible to cure it with drugs. I would take Fluanxol and gradually change and feel better.

A few weeks later I went back and met the doctor. I didn't feel much had changed; the medication wasn't having any effect on me.

I felt no better; I felt stranger than before. I was experiencing a variety of physical discomforts, but I didn't associate them particularly with the medication. I had always had trouble sleeping, but now I felt it had deteriorated. I only managed to sleep for a moment. I had no idea why. I was tired during the day, lethargic and indifferent. Mom and Dad had completely stopped hassling me to go out to work or go to school. I felt I never saw them or talked to them. Mom had totally stopped talking to me; when we met, we just remained silent. I thought it was fine because I had no interest in talking to her. I had no interest in talking to anyone. On the rare occasion someone asked me about something I murmured something as a way to avoid the subject. "I don't know," was my answer to everything.

The doctor was interested.

"Hi, Jón. You've been taking Fluanxol for a month. Are you feeling any better?"

"I don't know," I muttered.

I felt the drugs weren't having any effect.

"I'm wondering whether we should increase the dose."

I nodded.

"Yes... I can't really sleep."

"You're having trouble sleeping?"

"I don't sleep at all, really... I'm always awake, see."

"And why do you have trouble falling asleep?"

"I just find it hard to breathe and always think about so many negative things."

"What are you thinking?"

"I don't know... all kinds of annoying things."

"Annoying in what way, Jón?"

I shrugged. "I don't know."

"Have you thought about repeating the experiment you did the other day with the knife?"

I shook my head.

"No, not really. I'll never do it again…"

"Well, that's good to hear."

Occasionally, he wrote something in his journal. I wondered what he was writing. Was he writing something about me? "Jón is a hopeless idiot and there's nothing you can do for him."

"I'm going to try to give you sleeping pills and see if they can help you sleep."

Sleeping pills. That sounded pleasant. I'd only heard good things about sleeping pills. I had taken sleeping pills before, and they made me feel good. Valium was a sleeping pill and it was great to take. It was very relaxing. If you're awake and uncomfortable then you just take a sleeping pill and you sleep at once. Then you wake up the next day refreshed, no longer tired, and joyful. You also aren't constantly waking up at night because you feel you're choking to death. I was looking forward to testing the sleeping pills. They would certainly fix things. Maybe they could also help me stop biting my nails. Sleeping pills would make me normal. Perhaps the root of the problem was insomnia. Maybe I always felt so bad because I slept so little. It was said that sleep was the best medicine. Mom said that many times when I was small and weak. I was looking forward to the sleeping pills. Perhaps I could sleep for days. I was no less excited this time when I went to the pharmacy to get the sleeping pills. ROHYPNOL.

Even the name was cool! A punk band could totally be called Rohypnol. There was something spiritual and alluring about the name. The name alone was even slightly hypnotic. Rowhypnol. Row. Row-hypnol would bring me peace. The tablets were very large and I found that comforting. The next night I slept like an angel. I took one tablet with food before sleep and had yoghurt or bananas with the pills. I couldn't remember having slept like this since I was a small child. Half an hour after I took the pill, I was full of warmth and ease. I stopped fretting about going to bed. Instead, eager to go to sleep, I began to look forward to lying down. I no longer felt wound-up and suffocated; instead, I was docile and calm. Then I just passed out of consciousness and slept a sound sleep until the next day. This was wonderful. I was immediately fond of Rohypnol.

The instructions with Rohypnol were that I should take one tablet at bedtime. But when I had done that for a few weeks, I started to experiment with taking different doses. I tried to take two tablets at bedtime. I felt like I slept even better than before. Then I tried to take three tablets. I managed to sleep uninterrupted all night and all the next day and woke up rested. I thought it was wonderful. I just lay in my bed and did not see any reason to do anything else, except go to the bathroom or get some water to drink. And though I had just slept for a whole day, I could go back to sleep when I wanted. I simply took more Rohypnol. I thought it best to take two at night. Two tablets completely knocked me out and I slept until noon the next day. I left my room and got something to eat. Buttermilk and banana or some hospital food my mother brought home. I had bread with cucumber and washed it down with cold mushroom soup. I had fruit cocktail for dessert. Then I went back to my room and scoffed down a third Rohypnol. I read until I passed out. I usually slept until midnight. Mom and Dad were asleep by then. I went out and got something else to eat. Then I killed time until the morning, messing about. I could totally control the timing of when I wanted to sleep and manage myself using drugs.

I only left the house to take the bus down to Borgartún to get my unemployment benefit. On the way home, I went to the pharmacy and got more drugs. I didn't spent money on anything but cigarettes. And for the first time in my life I had some savings. I was used to spending every cent, but now had pockets full of bills. I felt good. This was exactly what boys like me needed. Drugs. This had definitely always been the case. I was just missing these drugs. I had even stopped biting my nails. I was so much more relaxed and I felt better. I no longer thought about boring stuff and was not as worried as ever before. I loved sleeping. The most I took was five Rohypnol at once. I could sleep fifteen to twenty hours. I couldn't remember ever having slept so long.

The doctor had apparently been in communication with my mother. The next time we met, he expressed considerable concern. He knew I was not doing much and sleeping a lot. I told him that it was quite alright, I just enjoyed sleeping.

"So you're taking one Rohypnol at night and you feel it is doing you some good?"

"Yes, absolutely!"

I wasn't going to tell him that I was trying out increasing the dose.

"I was wondering if you wouldn't be better off having something to do. Have you ever thought about getting a job?"

I could not imagine going to work. I told him I had tried many jobs, but they were all awful and I was just not able to settle anywhere. I told him about the woodwork at the Central Bank and he agreed with me that it was neither an exciting nor fun job.

"I mean, can you imagine standing outside in the freezing cold all day cleaning wood?"

"No, it's not very exciting."

"No, exactly, I can't imagine it either."

We both agreed construction work suited neither of us.

"What are you doing during the day, Jon?"

"Just so much stuff, really..."

The truth, however, was that I was not doing anything. My life was mostly sleeping, urinating, and eating fruit cocktail.

The doctor wanted to give me a new drug, but he wanted me to still continue to take the other one. He wrote a prescription and once again I went to the pharmacy. This time to get an antidepressant, Tolvon. It would certainly help me feel even better. I felt my life now had a purpose that it had lacked before: it consisted of medications. Rohypnol was my favorite medicine. It calmed me and helped me to sleep and I was very grateful to have experienced it. I did not really know what effect the drugs were having on me. Fluanxol didn't seem to have any effect and it didn't matter if I took more or less. I tried sometimes necking some tablets to see if I could get high. Sometimes I even forgot to take it and it did not affect me. The same was true with Tolvon. I felt it had no effect. I tried to swallow several tablets at once, but it didn't change anything. I went up to ten tablets at once but to no avail. I felt no change and I didn't feel better. I didn't feel bad. It just didn't make a difference. But I took the pills faithfully.

And so several months passed where I floated on in a drug haze and slept more than I was awake. It had also become difficult to stir myself me because I was woozy and my balance was poor. If I stood up too quickly then my eyes went black and I often got dizzy if I went out for a walk. I found it best to stay home and remain in bed. I had stopped eating in the kitchen and just took food trays with me to bed. In one of my trips to the pharmacy, I had bought a pillbox. It was a small blue tray with compartments for each day. I allocated myself daily allowances in the chamber for a week at a time. I enjoyed arranging the pills in the pillbox and went over and over it to see if everything was not exactly as I arranged it. Sometimes I went into the pantry and raided the home-brewing bottles that contained homebrew my mom made. It was usually either rosé wine or beer. It felt extremely good to drink half a rosé with some Rohypnol. After that, I could sleep for twelve hours.

Sometimes I bumped into Mom in the corridor and she tried to chat with me, but without success because I could not keep the threads of the conversation straight. She sometimes asked me how I felt and I always told her I felt very well. I felt at ease because I did not feel bad. I was not worried. I liked to go to the pharmacy and I loved to fill my box full of pills and I loved to sleep. And though my mother had found me strange before, I reckoned she'd never found me as weird as now. I'd stopped wandering around at night and I had even stopped lying to her. I did not feel like lying anymore. I was calm and content. And I was always kind.

She did not have to worry about me. I was asleep when she went to work and I was usually still asleep when she came home. And when I was awake I stayed in my room until she went to work or to sleep. I just tried to avoid her.

But one day there was a hole in the bubble inside which I lived. It was over a year since I'd had penis surgery. I never thought about it and had not masturbated for over a year. I never thought about girls or sex and was indifferent to sexual content. In the months after the surgery, I had struggled with incontinence. Sometimes, my underwear got wet without my noticing, and sometimes I just peed myself. It took me a long time to control my urination, and it was like I had to learn all over again to control myself. And to begin with, I felt bad. But that had passed and now I had control of when I peed. The pain and the stinging had also gone, but it took a while for the numbness and lack of sensation, which I thought would last forever. It was like a piece had been cut off me and I didn't miss it at all. I was just grateful not to be in unceasing pain and peeing myself. I didn't expect any more than that. And then I had Rohypnol to help me to forget and to sleep.

When I was alone at home, I sometimes had a bath and lay there for hours. I found it reassuring and it broke up the monotony of the everyday. Sometimes I fell asleep but otherwise I just stared thoughtlessly into the air. And one day as I lay in the bath and stared thoughtlessly into the air, I suddenly felt blood flow into my prick and got hard for the first time in a year. I was so surprised that I stared open-mouthed as my prick rose up out of the water. This took me totally by surprise. I had not expected this. I was so astonished that I jumped out of the bath, ran to the mirror, and examined myself. I had a splendid prick that stood straight up in the air and neither bent down nor to the side. Mary Magdalene and the other women who met the angel at Jesus's tomb couldn't have been as surprised and delighted as I was. It was like an angel had whispered in my ear: See, your prick has risen. I was so happy that I wanted to run all over the place and show everyone my prick. And all the chemistry that had lain dormant now awakened inside me. I was filled with confidence and for the first time in my life I thought, "this prick is going places!" This prick has a purpose and goals and I need to find it a pussy and allow it to go inside. I seized this big, beautiful penis and I shivered blissfully.

The pills lost their magic. I no longer wanted to just sleep. I didn't want to sleep at all. I wanted to go out and I wanted to meet girls. They were the only people to whom I could show my prick. I had nothing to be ashamed of anymore. I also wanted to go to the doctor and to thank him. I didn't hate him anymore; I loved him with all my heart. I wanted to run up, grab his neck and kiss him. I was going to stop taking these pills. Maybe they were making me dull. I needed my full concentration to keep going; I didn't want to be overwhelmed and distracted. I felt like I was getting back a good friend who had died and been resurrected and returned to the realm of the living. It was a physical rebirth that hinged on my prick and my desire for sex, but it was no less spiritual for that. When my prick awoke, my soul woke too, and the life force and the inner will. The pills had lost all their charm. Girls certainly wouldn't crush on a boy who was on drugs. I didn't know what girls wanted but I needed to get it. Pills were just something for losers and fools. Not for cool, tough boys who had pricks which rose straight up in the air.

My life took on a new and unexpected direction. I had taken a life u-turn. I went from having nothing to live for to having everything to live for. Life loomed ahead, full of exciting adventures, challenges, and girls. I wanted to go meet girls. I didn't want to be unemployed any more. I had to get a job to earn some money and become independent. Instead of sleeping, I woke up early every morning, read job ads, made calls. The contractor Miðfell needed laborers. I looked up to laborers. Dad had told me many stories about labor heroes and I had read books by Tryggvi Emilsson, John Steinbeck, and Upton Sinclair. Laborers were the coolest people in the world. "A working class hero is something to be," said John Lennon. Laborers were elegant and strong because they worked so hard. They were broad shouldered and had huge muscles. Women liked that. Laborers were people you could look up to and who could hold their heads high. They were ordinary men who possessed great pride, like the people in *The Grapes of Wrath* by John Steinbeck. The thought of this was very romantic. I was brought up with great admiration for labor. Other people didn't actually do meaningful work and many were nothing but idlers who'd never given a handshake or pissed in the salt sea. They didn't know what life was for. My whole family were workers. My mom's brother worked on the sandbanks; grandfather was a bricklayer. He had arthritis, but he still laid walls because he was so hard working. I would be hard working like all my people. I would not be idle. I was a worker. I did not want the girls to look at me and feel sorry for me. I wanted them to look at me and find me attractive. I wanted to be like the communist heroes from the magazine *News from the Soviet Union*. The men were large and strong and all the women looked at them with admiration.

Dad had at one time taken me to the reading group of the Union of Revolutionary Communists because he thought it was something I would enjoy. We met twice a week in some room in Bolholt. There were a few kids and mostly grown men who taught us the basics of communist theory. There I learned that society was extremely simple. It consisted of the capitalist masters, who had all the money, and the rest of the working people. And it was the people who made everything of value. The capitalist overseers were slackers who'd never got their hands dirty but still had tons of money that they had stolen from the working class. The capitalist class was dependent on the working class and the proletariat was subject to the capitalist masters. Therefore, the proletariat had to rise up against capitalism and push it aside; it had to join hands and create a fair society where everyone was equal. That's communism. I thought it was very logical. If I work hard and make things of great value and am skilled in a craft and arrange everything carefully and graft, why am I not enjoying the fruits myself? Revolution is the ultimate goal of all labor unions. I wasn't a slacker but a revolutionary worker. Slackers are parasites like the capitalist masters. In all the pictures I had seen, the workers were always cool. They wore jeans and work shirts and rolled-up sleeves and sometimes had hats or scarves. All the workers were expressive and beautiful because they worked hard work and ate healthy food. But the capitalist guys were all fat with swollen faces and they were always sitting on their asses. They either sat on a heap of money or a pile of gold and looked like dying swine. It was as if they were collapsing under their own wealth and cor-pulence. It was so obvious that they were wrong; they were so obviously betraying and robbing everyone. This was unfair. Part of the exaltation of the spirit was to become a worker. I wasn't any longer going to tell people, "I don't know." I was going to speak loudly and with confidence: "I'm a worker!"

In the reading circle, we read the *Communist Manifesto* and Lenin's writings on dialectical materialism. And although I didn't really understand and didn't know, for example, what dialectical meant, I found it enticing, cool, and logical. Of course, the working people had to seize power. And when the communist revolution happened in Iceland it would be super cool to be a certified worker because then you'd be written into the new society. In a communist society there aren't false heroes like in a capitalist society. Pop stars, actors and people like that—slackers whose work was pure leisure. People who do not do any work and who never piss in the salt sea. Capitalism is an illusion, but communism is the truth, the only reasonable reality. I was heavily influenced by Communism so when I saw this ad in *Morgunblað* which advertised for workers, I was quick to pick up the phone and call. I wanted to become a worker and get to take part in the revolution from the beginning. I was so enthusiastic that I was hired over the phone. The guy I spoke to asked if I was hard-working.

"Yes, very hard-working!" I said, loud and clear.

"Where do you live?"

"Kúrlandi 1," I said proudly. And although my room was no longer my room but a guest room, it didn't matter; it just made me more proletarian.

"I'll be round at eight, make sure you're ready."

I'd become a worker. When Mom came home later that day,

she was surprised to see me because I was usually asleep when she came home. Now I was fully dressed, in the kitchen, drinking coffee.

"I made the coffee," I said with great pride.

"I'm shocked," she said, surprised.

"I've got a job!" I announced, proudly. That was a pleasant surprise for Mom.

"Yes, congratulations."

She had finally given up hope that I would ever leave my room. But there I stood, bright-eyed and full of expectation. But she did not know I had a brand new prick.

"That's good to hear. And when do you begin?"

"Well, they're coming for me tomorrow morning at eight."

"Yes. And don't you need some clothes to wear?"

"Yes, of course."

Mom was helpful, like always, going into the closet and finding me some of dad's work clothes: a checkered work shirt. A worker's uniform. I also got a wool sweater and coat. I had a reasonable pairs of jeans myself. I dressed in my uniform and looked at myself in the mirror. I was particularly stylish. Not unlike the images in communist books. Bright-eyed, honest, hard-working, and fair. My prick itched to be alive and I thrilled to watch myself. Inside the room, I had buttons that I had been given by the Association of Revolutionary Communists. Now would be the ideal time to use them. That way the workers would immediately see that I was not just a teenager or a slacker, but one of them, not only in appearance but also in ideology. I had read the theory and wanted to be in the revolution. We would create a fair land where everyone

would be equal and the slackers and exploiters wouldn't rob innocent people. I pinned the hammer and sickle to the breast of my
sweater. The next morning, I ate a worker's breakfast, the same
food as Dad always ate. I used to just have Cheerios, but now I ate
porridge and sour meat, and made myself a sandwich for lunch.
It's just children and losers who eat Cheerios. At quarter to eight
a white Lada station wagon slipped up to the house and I headed,
full of expectation and anticipation, towards my new adventures.

A chestnut-haired, lively, bright-eyed man stepped out of the
car. He was clearly a worker like me. He looked at me with a smile
and extended his hand:

"Matti."

"Hi. Jón."

He gestured to me to sit in the back. I opened the door and
saw that there were two boys inside.

"Good morning," I said, jauntily. They looked at me, tired and
disinterested.

"Hi."

I didn't know if they were slackers or real workers. We drove
off. Matti was very talkative and asked me endless questions.

"Were you born and raised here in Fossvogur?"

"Yes."

"Sure. My parents had a house in Hulduland."

"Oh..."

I couldn't imagine how old Matti was. He was of that ambig-
uous age which was older than twenty. Everyone over twenty
seemed to be the same age. I didn't see any difference in people
who were twenty-five years or fifty-five years old. They were all

somehow similar. I guessed Matti was somewhere between twenty-three and fifty-six years old. The boys were my age.

"What are your interests, Jón?

Interests? I had no interests. I was a worker.

"Uhhh, nothing, really."

"What? No hobbies? You don't play football, son?"

He looked at me in the rearview mirror.

"Uh, nah. Not so much."

"Right. You got a motorcycle?"

"No."

I didn't. I would have loved to own one, but it cost so much money and needed maintenance and parental support. I had no choice in any of that.

"Why aren't you in school?"

"Eh, I've gone to school for so long really, I was ready to take a break and get to know life."

"To know life!"

Matti laughed loudly. The boys giggled. He was laughing at me! What was so ridiculous? What was wrong with getting to know life?

"Sure, you're going to get to know life well around us."

The road was to Auðbrekka 10, the police headquarters in Kópavogur. Miðfell was contracted to build a new garage for the police. The workspace was a giant crater in the rock face. The challenge was to break the rocks so that it would be possible to build the garage. There were ten to fifteen men, most who struck me of being of an unfathomable age. When I greeted them, their eyes darted to the button on my chest.

"What's that, kid?"

"A hammer and sickle, the Communist logo."

"What, you a communist?"

How wouldn't I be?! Weren't all workers communists? Weren't we going to start the revolution?

"Yes!" I said with great pride. "I'm really a Leninist."

My words were rewarded with peals of laughter from the whole group.

"What did you say?" said an old worker who could have been cut from a book by Upton Sinclair.

"Are you a Leninist? That's a new one. And why are you a Leninist?"

"I just believe in equality for the proletariat and fair pay for work without exploitation."

The guys laughed even more. They found me amusing.

"Well, that's the ticket."

I didn't understand this reaction. The man from an Upton Sinclair book had to be a communist.

"Aren't you a communist?"

The guy roared with laughter.

"No, I'm no communist, not at all. I'm a die-hard Independent!"

Cold shivers ran down my spine. How could this be? The Independence Party was a group of exploiters. Reactionaries, my dad called them. They were conservative because they did not want revolution.

"Hafsteinn is the candidate for the Independent Party in Kópavogur."

I looked at Hafsteinn in amazement. He was clearly very proud to be a member of the Independence Party in Kópavogur.

He looked like a worker but he favored exploitation. The Independence Party was clearly the enemy. It was a fellowship for exploiters—that much I knew. I seemed to be the only communist in the group of workers. From that day on, I was never called anything but Lenin.

"Lenin! Go fetch the hammer!"

"Lenin, run to the shed and get some coffee."

"Uh, I'm really called Jón..."

It didn't matter what I said. I was Lenin. I was even Lenin when they were talking about me with each other.

"Matti, could you get here at eight o'clock tomorrow?"

"Yes. No, dammit, I need to pick up Lenin at eight."

"Ah, Lenin!"

"Yes," I answered, tentatively.

"Can you start at seven-thirty tomorrow?"

"Sure..."

"Great. Matti, you pick up Lenin at seven-thirty. You can get Lenin to help you carry the trestles."

"Yes, good idea."

I did what I could to get the guys above me to stop calling me Lenin and often talked to Matti about it when we were alone in the car. Sometimes it was too cold or too rainy and then we sat in the Lada for a bit. Matti turned on the central heating and switched on the radio. When some girl walked past, he'd say:

"Check it out, Lenin!"

"Er, yes... Would you be willing to stop calling me Lenin? I'm called Jón, see."

"Well... wouldn't be bad to cop a feel of that!"

He seemed to totally ignore my request. I was just Lenin. Discussion over.

And so the days passed. Matti came at eight a.m. and picked me up and we drove up to Auðbrekka. I worked mainly on the compressor. I began the day by finding some work gloves and putting on an orange protective jacket, then went out and shifted rocks with the compressor. I was pretty isolated and had little in common with my co-workers. I stopped wearing the communist logo and tried to keep a low profile. Most of their discussion consisted of teasing and I was almost invariably the butt of the workplace jokes. I did what I could when this happened. Sometimes the older guys talked about girls. Sometimes someone came to work on Monday full of self-confidence and everyone rushed to say that the guy had had sex with some girl over the weekend. More often than not, these stories were pretty crude. I had no idea if it was true or whether they were lying. There seemed to be a whole lot of lovers. Some were married, other had girlfriends, and still others seemed knee-deep in women and had many on the go at once. I didn't understand and thought they were all ugly, old, and silly. I didn't feel like listening to these stories and tried to pay attention to something else during these times.

"What about you, Lenin... Lenin got no girlfriend?"

"Nah, not right now..."

"Now? What, is Lenin a widower?"

They laughed. Not me. I looked seriously at them.

"I'm called Jón..."

"Hey, has Lenin lost his cherry?"

I didn't reply, irritated by this talk.

"Would you be willing to call me Jón?"

Sometimes the conversation turned to a guy who had worked there before me. He died. He had cancer. For me, the most terrible disease in the world was cancer. This guy had a pain in his leg and went to the doctor. A few days later he called the foreman, Matti, and told him he had been diagnosed with cancer. He never came back to work; five weeks later he was dead. It was not possible to imagine a fate worse than getting cancer. I wondered if I had walked into a curse that guy suffered from and which I'd taken and had after him. Maybe one day I would get a pain in my foot standing there working on the compressor? Was my work the root of the curse? I saw it clearly before me. After I'd had pain for a few days, I'd go to the doctor. He would examine it, bow his head, and say, sadly: "You have cancer, Jón." The guys changed when they talked about the kid; stopped laughing and became mournful. This had been a shock.

"Just awful when it happens like this. Such a young man..."

"Young man." The words rang in my head and a dagger pricked my heart. I was a young man. There could be no doubt. I'd gotten another man's curse; I'd taken up the invisible cross of cancer without knowing it. I was the condemned man on the compressor. I imagined how the older guys would talk about me.

"It was absolutely awful. He was such a fun guy. Just got a pain in his leg and a few weeks later, he was dead."

I was sick at the thought, and as I thought more about it,

I felt the cancer spreading through my body. I lamented my fate. Standing alone outside in the miserable cold, lonely, and chilly—and with cancer on top of it all. A more terrible fate was hardly imaginable.

"Terrible when young people get cancer," a guy said. I wondered what the boy looked like. I wondered if he was like me? Red-haired and odd. I wanted to ask about his appearance, but I dared not.

"How old was he?" I murmured.

"He was young," said one of them.

"Just a little over forty."

I gaped in wonder and relief. Forty! That's not young! How could they think that? This was a forty-year-old grown-up, not a young man. In my mind, a forty-year-old man already had one foot in the grave and was far from being young. I was very relieved. I hadn't walked into someone else's curse; I had nothing in common with such an old age as forty. "Young man!" These idiots didn't know anything! They were nothing but pseudo-communists who voted Independent. They were even members of the Independence Party in Kópavogur. They were just a lame group who'd given me a nickname and who thought forty-year-old men were young. I didn't have anything in common with these people. Moreover, they were annoying.

Matti was annoying although he was pretending to be nice. He even called me Lenin when we were alone, though multiple times I'd asked him to call me Jón. I'd never call him Snot, even though he was always picking his nose. I'd never say, "Well, Snotty, do you want to swallow that booger or blow it right out?"

I always called him Matti and hoped that he would call me Jón and stop calling me Lenin. I had gotten disillusioned with my colleagues. I had no interest in continuing to work with these men. They weren't my friends and it was terrible work. Outdoor work was clearly not for me. I was trying to find some inside work that wasn't complex, wasn't too noisy, where people talked to one another calmly and respectfully and didn't tease each other with nicknames. I wanted to be in a workplace where my colleagues were also my friends. Where people would talk about something that mattered, like books or movies. The guys at Miðfell had no sense of anything. They had bad musical taste and thought everything awful was good. Sometimes when we were all sitting in the Lada trying to warm up and we heard some pathetic song on the radio, like something by Björgvin Halldorsson, Matti turned up the radio. Then the guys came to life and sung the song:

> Through the years and centuries
> My love is always meant for you...

I was so ashamed, I blushed. I felt sorry for them. They were pathetic and didn't understand anything about life. They were worse than exploiters and slackers combined. They were Quislings who had betrayed their own class. They didn't even have taste in music, but just listened to lousy, lame-ass pop. I couldn't even look at them, so I just looked down. It reminded me of when I was watching a movie on TV with my dad and there was a love scene.

The day I got paid, I decided to quit. I had had enough of this. I had found that it was not for me to stay being a worker.

I wanted to do something else. I had no idea what I wanted to do, but I was adamant that I wouldn't work in a fishery. Fish were slimy, cold, and disgusting. You'd always be wet and have cold hands and you'd always cut your hands. People who worked in fisheries always had cuts in their hands. I'd developed a fear of knives and had stopped carrying one on me.

At midday, we went to the State Liquor Store. I asked one of the guys to buy for me and gave him money. When he got to the car he handed me a liquor bottle in a brown paper bag and gave me the change. No hassle. I'd become a real man. I'd been a worker doing miserable work and could now hold my head high. Moreover, I had a prick like the guys in the porn mags. I was a real man. I even had some booze. No one said, "Hey, you're just a kid, you can't drink liquor."

I opened the bottle in the car and drank from it. We went back to work. I snuck off regularly to the car to take more sips from the bottle in between working at the compressor. The booze had a good effect on me and cheered me up. It took away the mottled-looking everyday life and filled me with anticipation and energy and warmed me in the cold. It filled me with confidence, too: I didn't have anything in common with these people and was much better than them. They were all idiots—including Matti. This was a waste of my talents. I was worth much more than this. I needed to be surrounded by people who gave me intellectual stimulation. They didn't know anything, never listened to any albums, couldn't identify any paintings, had never read any important books, but anyway felt they knew everything. When Matti drove us home at the end of the day I was quite drunk so

I allowed myself to run my mouth and play around with his words.

"What's that you say, Snotty? Do you always eat snot?"

Matti looked at me in the mirror, surprised and not quite sure whether I was talking to him. I grinned at the boy who sat next to me. They just looked at me, surprised.

"What's that, Snotty? Are you a deaf halfwit?"

Matti looked back with a surprised expression and continued to drive.

"Are you talking to me, Lenin? Are you drunk?"

"Are you, Snotty?"

Matti smiled.

"I reckon that Lenin has gotten loaded."

That made me pissed. You couldn't even tease Matti, he was so dumb.

"Listen, I'm done with this awful job. I quit."

Matti didn't say anything, and the boys stared at me. I took a sip of my liquor.

"You're all idiots and I can't be bothered to be around you. You hear, Snotty?"

Matti looked questioningly at me in the mirror.

"I can't be bothered to be in this miserable silly ridiculous car of yours. It's just a Ladadadashit."

"What's up with Lenin, lad? Is he plastered or what?"

"I'm Jón! You damn idiotic dumbass. Simple Snotty."

Matti laughed loudly.

"Keep going, kid."

"Stop here," I said, pointing at a bus stop. "I don't want to stay in here any longer."

"Don't you want me to drive you home?"

"Let me out of the damn car!"

Matti stopped the vehicle at a bus stop on Miklabraut.

"Well, hurry up then."

I scrambled out of the car with my liquor bottle, mumbling, grumbling and cursing. Fucking idiots, all of them. Matti bid me farewell and said:

"We'll see you on Monday, friend."

"Shut up! We'll never see each other again!"

When I finished my last word I slammed the door with all my might behind me. I lifted the bottle of booze and took a swig. I was free. I was a folk hero. I walked home, singing loudly:

> They hurt you at home and they hate you at school.
> working class hero is something to be.

I realized the best way to get to know girls was going to be through clubbing, going out on the town. When clubbing, all kinds of adventures happened. You met girls and took them home. Clubbing was like a big party. I wanted to be cool, tough, and stylish. I began to tidy myself up. I started using conditioner, stole some Old Spice from Dad, and made sure my clothes were clean. I wanted to meet girls. I went downtown every day and tried to meet girls. I sometimes saw some, but didn't know who they were and had no idea how I was meant to talk to them. What could I say? Should I just walk up to them and say:

"Hey, girls, what do you make of the news?

I was shy, but I still believed that something could happen when you were clubbing. It was enough to just go out on the town. Then suddenly you'd were kissing some girl and starting to fondle her breasts. It occurred to me to ask about music. Sometimes I met girls in town and asked them what music they listened to.

"Hi."

"Hi."

"What sort of music do you listen to?"

"All kinds."

If they asked me, I told them what music I listened to.

"I listen to punk mainly, see. I've started to listen to more new wave."

Girls seemed to have little interest in punk, but tended to be fairly positive about new wave. But nothing else came to mind; I had no idea what else I should ask them about. I really just wanted to get them to sleep with me. I could always have asked them questions like "What's your name? Where are you from?"

I just didn't think to. Instead, I asked them what music they listened to. I didn't get anywhere and reckoned most of these girls thought I was a weirdo. I had to drink to give me the courage to dare talk to them. I also didn't quite know how to act. Should I be jolly, or serious and reserved? Sometimes they also said things to me I didn't expect and that threw me off. When it happened, I just smiled apologetically and vanished. If I met a girl who was really interested in discussing music, I got embarrassed. I found it hard to look at her and started to look down at the floor. Sometimes they said something or asked for something I didn't hear, so I just nodded my head and looked down. The atmosphere got awkward and there were embarrassing silences.

"Have you listened to any John Lennon?"

"No, not really," they usually said.

"There's some quite good lyrics really..."

"Oh, okay."

I often didn't understand what they said.

"I was here with my friend, she was so drunk that she gave me the slip." What could I say to that? I felt girls weren't interested in me. Maybe I was ugly and awkward. I knew they found me strange. I was strange and knew it, absolutely. These conversations were usually both awkward and uncomfortable. The girls I met didn't tend to say much, unless they were blind drunk, and then they just blurted out stuff. Otherwise, they said little without being asked.

I was always hoping to meet some girl who had questions for me about something she was itching to know. I was quite prepared to answer questions about punk or anarchism or Þórbergur Þórðarson. But they usually never asked me anything. At best, they asked me where I was from.

"Are you from Breiðholt?"

"No, Fossvogur."

"Do you have a brother called Kristján?"

"Kristján? No."

"Oh, you look so much like him."

Girls also seemed to have opinions I couldn't agree with at all. Like thinking ABBA was a good band or liking some lame movie. Usually these were even films that weren't just annoying but totally pathetic. Girls went to the movies to see films no one watched, not even old ladies, and they found them fun.

"Have you seen any good films?"

"Yes, I went to see *Splash* with my friend. It's awesome!"

"Oh, okay."

I tried to hide my disappointment. *Splash* was a lame picture about a man who fell into the sea and was rescued by a mermaid.

"Have you seen *1984*? It's awesome, really."

"Okay."

"It's based on a George Orwell book."

"Okay."

I found it totally hopeless to talk to some of them about music and found out everyone was just a musical whore. They had no loyalty to anything and it got on my nerves when kids said they listened to all kinds of music. That was almost worse than listening to disco.

Amid this fascinating nightlife, which took place mainly in the late evening and at night, it was a total drawback to live with your parents all the way out in Fossvogur. A definite hindrance. I couldn't imagine coming home with a girl and running into Mom and having to talk to her. Not to mention Dad! No girl would go to bed with me after a long time talking to my dad. Mom had also started to monitor me closely again, asking a lot about my trips out and what I was up to and whether I was looking for a job. I was a bit of an intruder in my home. I wanted to rent a place and so I needed money. Besides, I had to have money to buy conditioner and booze and go out into the world and meet girls. I read the for-rent columns in the classifieds in the newspaper. Sometimes I called to find out about some advertised apartment I liked, but the rent was always too high. Then one day I set eyes on an advertisement that caught my attention. "Room for rent. Only seven thousand per month." Seven thousand kronur. That was nothing! I immediately called the number. A friendly woman answered the phone.

"Yes, good morning. I'm calling about the room for rent."

"Yes, of course. It's a room with access to a shared bathroom located on Miðtún."

"Right."

I had no idea where Miðtún was but imagined it was in Reykjavík.

"Would you like to come and see the room?"

"Yes, it that possible?"

"Of course! Shall we say four o'clock today?"

"Yes..."

"See you then. Miðtún fourteen."

I looked at the maps in the phone book to find out where Miðtún was. To my delight it turned out to be close to Hlemmur. I took the bus down to Hlemmur and walked the last short distance. I arrived right at four. It was an old, two-story concrete house with a basement. The room to rent was at the end of the corridor in the basement, next to the toilet. It was big and spacious and I immediately liked it. It had a great energy. Out of the window you could see a garden of flowers. The basement had more rooms that the woman rented out and shared bathroom facilities.

"There's a man renting the room right next to yours. He's a bartender and extremely likeable."

"Great."

This was exciting. There would be other guys. I was looking forward to getting to know them. Seven thousand kronur was nothing! I'd have no problem paying it. I could easily bring all my stuff over.

"Yes, I'll take the room, if that's okay."

"Yes, that's fine. I like the look of you. Where do you work?"

It dawned on me. I didn't, of course, have a job and was back on unemployment.

"Uh, well... I'm between jobs. I stopped one and I'm beginning another."

"And where have you been working?"

"Well, I was first in horticulture and then in construction, you see."

"Well. You're quite the jack of all trades."

"Yeah," I said and smiled shyly. Now that I was renting, I definitely needed to get a job so I could pay the rent and buy booze.

We decided I would come to the woman's house the next day
to sign a lease. I went along, undeterred, signed a two-year lease,
and paid the first month in advance, seven thousand kronur. Now
I had my own apartment, or nearly so: a room, at least. That's how
Þórbergur began, too. He rented a room in Unuhús. And he liked
Unuhús so much he wrote a whole book about it. Maybe I would
eventually write a book about my adventures on Miðtún. I had
become my own boss, an independent man. And now I'd be able
to invite girls back without any risk they'd have to meet my father.
After I'd signed and paid, the woman said:

"There's actually one thing I wanted to mention to you..."

"What's that?"

"I just wanted to tell you my mother lives upstairs."

"Okay."

"Don't let it surprise you, but she's a bit special."

"No problem."

I couldn't fathom what she meant or what this woman was like.

"It's nothing serious. But she's just not like most folk."

"Yes, I'm not worried."

I didn't imagine this woman could surprise me in any way.
My family and I fell into the same category, or so I felt. We were
all people anyone could easily describe as "not like most folk."
I wasn't concerned.

I met her mother the day I moved into my room with several
boxes and a mattress. She was standing on the steps outside the
front door. She was probably around seventy, but I thought she
looked at least a hundred. She was short and wrinkly, with smooth
gray hair down to her rear. She was only wearing a threadbare

nightdress that was so transparent you could see her whole body. She was totally naked under her nightclothes. While I was carrying boxes to the house she ripped open the front door and jumped out, startling me.

"Good morning. I'm moving into your basement."

"Begone with the whores, begone with the soldiers. I am the princess Gullveig, gold stars, stars of gold and hallelujah!"

"I'm Jón," I murmured.

She raised her voice, shook her fists at me and yelled even louder:

"Begone with the whores, begone with the soldiers. I am the princess Gullveig, gold stars, stars of gold and hallelujah! And get lost. Get lost! Damn soldiers."

"Yes, I am, I'm definitely..."

"Begone with the whores, begone with the soldiers. I am the princess Gullveig, gold stars, stars of gold and hallelujah! Get lost. Get lost."

"I've recently signed a lease with your daughter."

I stood holding my box and trying to talk to her. But it didn't matter what I said. She just stood in the doorway and yelled at me, the same rigmarole over and over about how she was a princess and didn't want soldiers or whores. In the end, I gave up talking to her and took the box into the basement. She was still on the stairs when I went out and she continued to yell at me. I waited for someone to come and intervene or to look after her, but no one did. She was clearly a bit crazy. I just smiled at her in a friendly way as I got my stuff and she continued to yell at me.

"Begone with the whores, begone with the soldiers. I am the princess Gullveig, gold stars, stars of gold and hallelujah!"

After I left Miðfell, I once again had to register as unemployed at the Reykjavík Employment Office in Borgartún. Unemployment was comfortable in the sense that, although it wasn't much money, it came regularly. I always had a bit of money and found it a very agreeable arrangement. I was well positioned on Miðtún, in walking distance of Borgartún, which made my unemployment even more convenient. Now I simply had to stroll nonchalantly over and get my money. I could make the whole journey on foot. I padded from Miðtún down to Borgartún, received my check, and strolled into the Hlemmur branch of my bank, Búnaðar, to cash it. Then I could walk downtown or back to Miðtún. All within walking distance. A more comfortable life could not exist.

I arranged my things carefully in my room. I had a turntable, a mattress, some books, a bookshelf, and a desk. When I was all set up, I invited my mother over to visit. She'd supported me wholeheartedly in my apartment hunting. I think she was half-glad to get rid of me and the concerns that came with me. Mom brought me a house-warming gift. She gave me an egg cooker. I'd never seen such an appliance before. It was a kind of plate with a power cord you stuck in a socket. You arranged the eggs on a rack and set it on the plate, poured in some water and put the lid on. The egg cooker hard-boiled eggs within five minutes. I found it a fascinating gift, but I also wondered why my mom had decided to give me an egg cooker. I'd never especially cared for eggs and they hadn't often been served at home. I had a hunch it was something she'd been given and had put away in a closet. But the egg cooker was the first appliance I owned, and when I went to the store for the first time to buy food, I bought Coke and three packs of eggs. I was determined to have enough eggs to boil. It was so convenient. If I was hungry, I just stuffed a few eggs in the egg cooker. And that was the bulk of what I ate while I lived on Miðtún. Boiled eggs. When I went to the store I always bought several cartons of eggs. In the morning, I boiled myself eggs for breakfast. If I was hungry in the middle of the day, I threw some eggs in the egg cooker. I had four eggs for dinner. Sometimes, I found I was hungry when I was trying to go to sleep and needed something to snack on. Then I hard-boiled two or three eggs and munched on them while I read.

I didn't at first see much of the man who lived next to me and I only met him in passing because he was rarely at home. He was a bartender and worked a lot in the evenings and at night and slept during the day. I quickly surmised that he didn't live in the room, but used it mainly to store his clothes and stuff. Sometimes I saw him in a rush, dashing in super-quick to change clothes and run out again. These times we'd greet each other in the hallway. He was very likeable. He called me "friend."

"Cool stuff, friend. If you need any help, friend, don't hesitate to ask me."

He told me the woman upstairs was called Vigfúsína Engilberts-dóttir and she was crazy. I told him I'd met her when I moved in and how she'd acted and what she'd said. He knew what I was talking about; the same thing had happened to him.

"Nothing to worry about, friend. She won't do anything. She's completely harmless."

"Yes, it was mostly just awkward."

"Yeah. You'll get used to it, friend."

Vigfúsína shut herself inside her apartment, seldom left it, and then only ever as far as the stoop. She never wore anything other than see-through nightdress. The landlord, her daughter, brought her food and I sometimes saw her coming and going. Vigfúsína only ate singed sheep's head. She refused to let her daughter into the apartment, so she hung the food on the doorknob. Sometimes when she brought the sheep's heads, I heard the old woman yelling from behind the door:

"Trashlady! Trashlady!"

The daughter asked me how I was doing settling into my room.

"Fine, totally fine."

She didn't offer any comment on her mother's condition and acted as if it were the most natural of things. Sometimes when I ran into her on the sidewalk, she said: "I'm bringing food for Mom," and lifted up the bag with the sheep's heads. For the most part, Vigfúsína kept to herself and sat silently inside her apartment. But then she regularly had episodes where she screamed and cried. These episodes could last from several days to two to three weeks. I was curious to know what it was like inside Vigfúsína's apartment. One day I climbed up on a trashcan and spied through the kitchen window. I saw the kitchen and into the living room. There seemed to be no furniture in the apartment and I couldn't see any pictures on the walls. There were no chairs or tables; the apartment seemed totally empty apartment.

Occasionally, when I was coming or going from the house, I saw her shape in the window as she stood there, silent, staring out.

But when she had one of her fits, she changed. She screamed so loudly it echoed throughout the building. And if someone was coming or going from the house she'd come leaping towards them, ripping open the front door to yell:

"I am the princess Gullveig, gold stars, stars of gold, hallelujah! Begone with all soldiers and begone with all whores!"

Always the same nonsense, in the same voice. No point talking to her; I quickly learned that. I'd tried to explain to her that I wasn't a soldier, and that there were no whores here, but it didn't make a difference to Vigfúsína. She didn't even look at me, but somehow through me, and screamed and screamed. Gradually it just became ordinary.

When Vigfúsína was not there on the stairs screaming, she sometimes went howling around the apartment. Because the apartment was empty, she was especially audible, and the sounds thundered around everything. Her voice was high and clapped-out and sounded like a stabbed pig. One loud shriek of pain and tears. She also had a small stump of metal piping with which she beat the radiators as she cried and screamed. Initially, I had some difficulty falling asleep when she had her episodes, especially when she was hitting the radiators with the pipe. The heating system was interconnected so the noise crashed throughout the house. There were no rules when Vigfúsína had a fit. Sometimes she started in the morning or the afternoon, sometimes even in the middle of the night. And when she was in these episodes, she didn't seem to need sleep. Sometimes I jumped up in the middle of the night because she'd begun to scream and beat the radiators. At first, I felt very uncomfortable, but then I got used it. I went to the pharmacy and bought earplugs and when Vigfúsína screamed and raged violently, I stuffed the plugs in my ears and put my headphones on. I couldn't hear anything and was able to sleep. Little by little, however, her strength faded and her wails were less noticeable and less forceful and the knocking grew fainter. Finally, it fell silent. It was like Vigfúsína had fainted and was now comatose.

Between the stories there was a door locked from the inside. The first time I was aware of a fit, I went to the door, knocked and tried to call into the apartment:

"Are you all right?"

But she never said anything, just kept screaming and banging.

Once in a while, Vigfúsína came down to the basement through the door. Sometimes when I was going to the bathroom during the night, she was standing right outside my door armed with her pipe-stump. The old lady could have been cut from some American horror film. The first few times, she scared me witless and I yelled out in terror. She showed no expression, standing perfectly still in the sheer nightdress with the pipe-stump in her hand, staring at me. She was not at all prone to violence and never tried to attack me or beat me with the pipe. Sometimes she stood at one end of the corridor or even the front door.

Over time I got used to this and I stopped noticing her at night. I went to the bathroom and went back to my room without paying her particular attention. When she was yelling, and the breeze blew me away, I'd snap angrily back at her.

"I am the princess Gullveig, gold stars, stars of gold, hallelujah!

Begone with all soldiers and begone with all whores!"

"Oh, shut the fuck up, you damn crone!"

It had no effect on Vigfúsína. I slammed my door, put earplugs in my ears, put on my headphones, and went back to sleep. By the time I'd lived there for a few months, I'd entirely stopped noticing Vigfúsína and felt like I lived there alone, even when she screamed and beat the radiators.

When I was at Núpur, I'd become a subscriber to the British magazine, *Black Flag*. I'd gotten information about the magazine in some material that came with a Crass album. The magazine allowed me to follow the most important anarchist matters. I practiced my English, too, and found it a really fun pastime. Through *Black Flag*, I was put in contact with other organizations I saw advertised in the paper, like Greenpeace, Friends of the Earth, and CND—the Campaign for Nuclear Disarmament. It was great to write to those bodies and organizations that did so much good and ask them to send me stickers and labels and even posters. I always looked forward to getting letters from them. I could not, however, have any letters sent to Miðtún because of Vigfúsína. Once, I was waiting for the latest issue of *Black Flag*, which was published monthly. When I got home I saw that the magazine had arrived, but that someone had taken it, torn it to pieces, and scattered it along the corridor. I was so angry and disappointed that I was in tears. As I picked up the bits of paper and wondered if I could paste them together, I heard Vigfúsína screaming upstairs and beating her pipe-stump against the radiator. I went up and knocked on her door. Vigfúsína came to the door in a transparent nightdress; she stared fiercely at me as I stood there with tears in my eyes.

"Did you rip up my magazine?" I asked, holding out the pieces. She screamed:

"Begone with all soldiers! Begone with all whores! I am the princess Gullveig, gold stars. Stars of gold and hallelujah! And begone with all whores!"

"You're batshit crazy!"

"Begone with all whores!"

"Did you rip up my magazine?"

"Begone with all soldiers!"

"You're mental!"

"I'm the princess Gullveig, gold stars."

"It's my paper!"

"Stars of gold and hallelujah!"

You couldn't discuss anything with Vigfúsína. I called her daughter and complained. She was really understanding and said that her mother always did this, and so she got her mail at her own home. She told me she'd forgotten to let me know about this and apologized. I went to the post office at Hlemmur and explained the situation to the employee there. She advised me to just get a mailbox at the post office and get my mail sent there from now on.

My main occupations and hobbies involved getting letters from these sorts of places and participating in the work of these organizations. I wrote my name on petitions and corresponded with people who advertised for pen friends and for support in *Black Flag*. Sometimes there was a call in the paper to send letters of support to anarchists who were in prisons across the world. I wrote to many prisoners in Germany, Canada, and the United States. I sent a very touching and beautiful letter to Ulrike Meinhof, who was imprisoned in Germany. I encouraged her not to give up hope because there were people all over the world thinking positively about her. I wrote several letters to the terrorists in Canada called the Vancouver Five. These weren't complex or long letters, one page on average. I tried to be positive and supportive as I wanted to give these people hope and let them know they weren't alone. There were anarchists all over the world who cared about them. I also told them my news. I usually got no answer from these people, however. Ulrike Meinhof never wrote back, but *Black Flag* sent me a stack of photocopied letters she had written to others from prison. From Greenpeace and Friends of the Earth, I got sent lots of posters and postcards, so I decorated my room with them and felt it was a great privilege. I also really enjoyed making a show of my knowledge about these organizations. Greenpeace was fairly newly established and few people knew anything about it. In some ways, I looked at myself as their representative in Iceland. Sometimes I also got posters with my copy of *Black Flag*. I especially remember a poster of the British royal family as they stood waving on the balcony. Written over the image was "fuck'em." This poster hung in the center of my room. I dutifully bought envelopes, a notepad, and stamps; I loved to sit at my desk and write letters.

Slowly, the room in Miðtún took shape. I acquired furniture and household items. I went to the Army Surplus Store at Grensásvegi and bought a small American fridge to store my eggs and some milk for coffee. It was an easy, carefree life; I lived and existed in my own world. I had two good pen pals who always wrote me back. One was called Peter, a homeless man in the UK.

The other, Kathy Sparrow Aikman, was in a State penitentiary for women in Arizona. She'd been a member of the motorcycle organization Hells Angels. Her boyfriend had violently abused her until she saw no alternative but to shoot him dead. But she got life in prison, where she'd served twelve years of her sentence. She was studying leather-smithing and often sent me small objects she'd made. Her cell was extremely homey and she had a little lizard as a pet. One day I received a letter from her in which she informed me that she'd decided to become a lesbian and had gotten a girlfriend.

There were three rooms rented out in the cellar at Miðtún. The bartender who rented next to me was about ten years older than me. In his room there was a bed and a table and he mostly used the room for storing clothes and other personal items. He stole a lot of alcohol from work and sometimes came in late in the evening or at night, driving an American car; he stopped outside and ran in with a few boxes of liquor. But other times he had parties in his room and brought great joy to Miðtún. There were often a lot of people in the room and even in the corridor and the music was turned up high. Often these were people who had been enjoying themselves and needed some place to stay. More often than not, they had food with them, hamburgers and fries from Næturgrill. While the bartender was older than I was, he was extremely lovable. He treated me well, respected me as an equal, and I could always come into his room and have a hamburger. He thought I was an interesting guy and he had clearly told his friends stories about me.

I always liked to drop in on the parties. There were a lot of interesting people and many amazing stories got told. You'd chain smoke, eat fries, and you could have whatever you wanted to drink: an entire wall of the room was covered with bottles of alcohol. My neighbor occasionally had beer, which was banned in Iceland at the time, and he offered me one, prince that he was. It wasn't bad, sitting in that room chain-smoking, eating, drinking, and telling stories. His friends also seemed to like hearing me tell stories of my own. I was a good storyteller, and said fascinating stuff. Sometimes he specifically asked me to tell stories about the old lady on the upper floor. I was getting pretty clever at describing it; I could mimic her voice well and repeat verbatim what she said. I could describe it so well that people would fall about laughing. That felt good.

But sometimes I wasn't allowed to hang out with the bartender and his friends. Mostly when women were involved; those times, I had to keep to myself and stay in my room. These women were usually off-the-charts angry and would even scream at him. Things were pretty audible in the basement so I could understand most of what they were saying. Usually they were angry because they felt he wasn't being completely honest with them. They thought they were his girlfriend, but then found out he had other girlfriends and they got mad when they heard about each other. I'd always imagined he didn't have a girlfriend because whenever I saw him come home, he tended to have a new woman each time. Perhaps they all thought they were his girlfriend. He had a lot of irons in the fire, to say the least. Sometimes I tried to ask about his life, but he was the model of discretion when asked questions; he avoided giving any details away.

Sometimes at night he knocked on my window. He'd lost or forgotten his keys somewhere and needed me to let him in.

We'd sit down, sometimes in his room, and talk. He paid me back for this favor by giving me some white or red wine. I felt at home sitting and drinking red wine while I answered the latest letter from Friends of the Earth or wrote letters of encouragement and support to jailed terrorists.

In the room opposite mine, on the other side of the toilet, lived an intensely solitary and very particular individual. He was overweight, quiet, and mysterious. He worked in computer technology, which was then in its early stages. There were very few computers and they were huge and expensive. He had a massive computer called an Acorn Electron. I didn't really know what he did. When he was at home, he was invariably playing a computer game. He always played the same game, Elite. The game began nowhere, never ended, and took place in space. You were the captain of a large spaceship on a journey through the vast universe. Sometimes you met other spaceships or came across other planets and could buy yourself all sorts of accessories for the spacecraft like armor, guns, and missiles. It could, however, get difficult: if other spaceships were well armed, they might attack the spaceship rather than trade with it. From the outside, not much seemed to happen in this video game, for hours at time, and there was little to see, but the spacecraft was flying somewhere in some distant solar system. Nevertheless, I found video games a hugely intriguing phenomenon. I'd played both Atari and Space Invaders in arcades, but I'd never seen a desktop computer before. I enjoyed stopping by and watching him play. He wasn't that talkative. He didn't drink wine, just Tab, at all hours. He was considerably older than me and didn't care about me and my interests. After living there for a few months he moved out. He didn't say anything; one day, he just disappeared.

In his place, a Chinese guy named Nkava move in. He was an extremely likeable and lovable fellow. He was from Hong Kong and had a British passport. He'd originally come to Iceland because of some girl he was involved with. He had been a Kung Fu student at the Shaolin Monastery in China and had graduated with some degree in Kung Fu. He worked mainly as a Kung Fu teacher and traveled to different countries and ran workshops. He never tired of telling me about Kung Fu history and philosophy. I was really into *The Book of the Way*, which pleased him a lot. He introduced me to Bruce Lee, who was a hero to Nkava, the main model for his life. I thought Bruce was just a fighter, but Nkava taught me that wasn't the case. Bruce Lee was a hero and a philosopher. Nkava was doing so well he owned both a TV and a video player; we watched Bruce Lee films together while he explained the ideas behind each scene and how they related to Chinese philosophy and Taoism.

A great friendship blossomed between us. Nkava had all kinds of Kung Fu weapons and costumes and he gave me an excellent Kung Fu outfit. I enjoyed wearing the costume and I looked awesome in the black jacket, which was fastened with a white tie, and wide black trousers. With it I wore my canvas shoes. Nkava taught me the basic elements of Kung Fu: the grips, moves, and blows. Balance is everything: maintaining balance and inner calm. He told me that when he started Kung Fu study at Shaolin, he didn't do anything in the first year but squat, with his hands either held out or on his hips. A good Kung Fu champion has to have strong thigh muscles so he can sit on his haunches indefinitely, remaining calm. One day, Nkava vanished without saying goodbye and I never knew what became of him. But Bruce Lee stayed with me.

By this time, I'd somewhat lost interest in punk, reckoning it wouldn't help me with girls. I knew from past experience that they were generally skeptical of punk music and of punks unless they were themselves punk. There were, however, hardly any girl punks. Girls were very fond of new wave. As a real punk, I was always suspicious of new wave bands, but I now found that I enjoyed some songs. It had to be something serious, with a message. I tried hard to listen to the bands Joy Division and later New Order, but didn't really get into them. I was fascinated, though, by Bauhaus. They seemed like a cool band. They didn't just have cool lyrics—splendid artistic design was an important aspect of the band. Bauhaus was a sort of ideology. The albums had cool designs and they also had a cool logo and drawings. The music was gloomy and inspired by horror. I bought a few of their albums, and one day I realized I had changed fashion. I was no longer a Crass-punk. I had replaced Crass with Bauhaus. I'd become a new wave trendy.

I looked at photos of the band in *Melody Maker* and took a picture of the singer, Peter Murphy, to a barber; I asked for a haircut like his. A new wave cut. In order to keep the style, I had to buy hair gel. Until then I'd despised hair gel and everyone who used it. But not anymore. I'd become a new wave trendy and I wanted to meet a cute new wave girl who was similarly trendy. I got rid of my old shredded punk clothes, threw out my Sid Vicious t-shirt, and went to the store Flóna, where I bought real new wave clothes. I bought a two-tone sweater, black on one side and green on the other. I looked carefully at the images of Bauhaus and tried to imitate their dress code. So I bought two pairs of thick, black leggings. My army boots went out the window, and in their place I had pointed new wave shoes with zippers. I also bought a well-fitting suit, a white shirt, and a razor-thin, licorice-color tie. I'd use that sparingly. And though I totally bought the cheapest stuff, it still cost most of my unemployment benefit. The new wave shoes were cool to look at, but the sole was so thin that if I stepped on a pebble on the pavement, I got pain in my leg. I still put up with it. At Kattavinafélagið flea market, I bought a mid-length black coat with a large collar that I thought was extremely new wave. It was a woman's coat, but I didn't think that mattered. Other people, however, never tired of pointing that out to me.

"Hey ladies coat!"

"No, it's a new wave jacket."

"No, if the buttons fasten on the wrong side, it's women's clothing."

"That's how it used to be, but this is new wave..."

After having been repeatedly harassed, I admitted it had maybe been a mistake, so I got myself an overcoat. If I put the collar up, it was new wave-like, so it sufficed. To perfect my look, I went to a beauty salon and had my nose pierced. The woman set a simple stud in the nostril but as soon as the hole was healed, I straight-away put a ring through it. I'd morphed into a new wave trendy.

I was a new man. I was no longer Jónsi Punk. And I was no longer a kid. I was tired of always being the strange guy, always alone in a corner. A strange guy with no friends except other strange characters. I didn't want any more strange guys in my life. I wanted to meet cute girls. I no longer wanted to be the amazingly depressed kid who people looked at with pity and suspicion; I wanted to be the cool new wave stud who girls watched with admiration and interest. I imagined that this new style would lead to my first sexual experience. When I became a new wave trendy, that would somehow happen by itself. I'd been thinking a lot about it and imagining how it would happen. I was fairly certain what I would do and how I would do it.

But as so often, my first experience of sex was unexpected and not related to anything new wave. I was inside my room, sitting in my underwear and shirt at the desk, sipping white wine and writing my pen pal Peter a letter. It was an important letter because I was going to tell him about my transformation and change. "Dear Peter..."

The bartender came home with some people and there was a lot of noise from his room. He put on some music. He had terrible musical taste and played the sort of music I despised. Country jazz. He played songs like "Come Over, Girlfriend" and "Out All Night." Absolutely terrible music. I didn't enjoy his parties when they were nothing but benders. Those times, people were dead drunk and the music was so loud you couldn't talk or tell stories. To judge from the noise, they weren't just starting a bender but were well into it. I stayed in my room, keeping to myself and writing to Peter.

There was a knock on my door. I thought it was my neighbor, asking me to come over for a burger. I opened the door. Outside stood a fat older woman. She was strikingly drunk, pretty sloshed; it was clear she had been drinking and partying a long time. She had on a lot of makeup and her hair, which had once been styled, was now ruffled and went everywhere. She was wearing a skirt and t-shirt with a leather jacket over the top. She had a glass of wine in one hand.

"Hey," she said.

"Hey," I said, friendly.

"Are you Jón?"

"Yes."

I knew my neighbor sometimes told his companions stories about me and so she probably knew who I was. She was silent and looked at me. I didn't think of anything to say. I looked down the hall and noticed that my roommate's door was closed. I found that weird because usually there was no reason to shut the door. I looked awkwardly at the woman and smiled, friendly. She looked back, her eyes set.

"Do you have a pencil?" she asked, finally, and smiled.

"Yes, I think so..."

I went to my desk and looked through my pencil case until I found a pencil. The door closed and I looked over. She'd come into the room, closed the door, and now leaned up against it. She looked very strangely at me and smiled slyly. Suddenly everything became filled with intense excitement. I was in my underwear and a woman was standing by the door. I held the pencil in front of me and waited for her to say something. But she said nothing and looked at me, half-staring.

"Should I sharpen it for you?"

She tilted her head but did not look at me.

"Don't you have a bigger pencil than that?"

Suddenly I realized what was happening. There was an adult, totally drunk woman and she clearly wanted to sleep with me. This was such shocking news to me that it was like my thoughts froze and a paralyzing numbness came over my mind. I stood rigid as a pencil and did not know what to say. She took some firm steps towards me while she took off her leather jacket and threw it to the floor. She took the pencil from my hands and tossed it on the desk.

"Come on. You don't have to be afraid of me," she said, and pulled me down onto my bed mattress. We kissed. I closed my eyes and smelled her. The smell was a combination of perfume, alcohol, and stale smoke-breath. She pulled down my underwear.

"Come on," she whispered, and showed me the way. I clambered on top of her and she moved her legs apart. Amazement had now been defeated by resolute will. I was in this. She took my prick and I felt something soft. My eyes went black, and before I knew it, it was all over. The impression disappeared as suddenly as it had come. It was as if all strength had left me. I again felt uncomfortable, like when I'd held the pencil. I was lying on the floor in my room with a dead drunk woman and had no idea where my prick was and what had happened. What had happened? Had I managed to try sex? I didn't know if I had slipped my penis into her pussy, or just the fold of her thighs.

"What happened?" she said and looked questioningly at me. I couldn't speak and looked embarrassed at her. I felt my penis shrink and withdraw. I felt like I had been struck about the head with a sledgehammer.

"Keep going," she said and stroked me on the back. I was naked, but she was still dressed; evidently, she'd just pulled up her skirt. Perhaps she was still wearing her panties. I had no idea.

"I've got this incredibly sore stomach."

"Sure, but isn't this nice?"

"Oh, yeah, it's just…really…stomach."

"Want to try some more?"

"No, it's just this stomach, really."

She felt around down there.

"What's going on?"

"It's just this stomach, really."

I jumped up and turned around so we would not have to see each other. I dressed in a flash in my underwear and shirt and grabbed my jacket and leggings. I was embarrassed and hoped she wouldn't tell anybody. It was shameful to fuck some old lady, but it was twice as bad to come prematurely.

"Listen, lie down," she said in a drawling voice.

"Yes, I just remembered something. My friend might be coming over."

"Come and lie down beside me."

"Yes, but I really haven't eaten anything except eggs, see…"

When I'd got my clothes on, I had the courage to look at her. She lay still on the mattress, but had pulled the skirt down again. I laughed awkwardly. She didn't laugh back. She was so drunk and tired that she barely realized what was going on. Judging by her eyes, I imagined she might very well fall asleep in the middle of a sentence.

"Do you want to get up and move about?" I asked, encouragingly. I felt so bad that I wished I could sink into the floor.

I should not have opened the door. I should have thrown her out. But I had desired it and I felt ashamed. When she started to struggle to her feet, I made myself scarce. I ran into the bathroom and locked myself in, leaving my room door open. I sat on the toilet seat and listened to her moving about inside the room. I hoped she was getting dressed and hurrying away; I wished wholeheartedly that she would, and I would never see her or meet again.

I heard the door to the room open and the bartender enter; I listened.

"Something going on in here?" I heard the bartender say outside the toilet.

"No, no, I was just chatting with the kid."

I could tell from her voice she'd got up and was standing by the door.

"Right."

The knob to the toilet was turned.

"I'm on the toilet..."

They continued talking.

"We were thinking of heading to Nauthólsvík and then for breakfast at Loftleiðir."

"Yes, great."

I was relieved. They were going. I wasn't going to leave the toilet until they were totally gone. Occasionally, someone tried the knob. I didn't care what they thought of me. They could think I had diarrhea. I put my ear to the door and did not venture to open it until I heard the car drive away from the house. There was silence in the basement. I thought with terror that the woman might have been left inside my room. I slipped quietly out and checked.

The room was empty and the leather jacket was gone. I sighed in relief.

For weeks after, I lived in constant fear that this woman would pop up, in a shop, downtown, on a bus, even in a queue at the unemployment office. No matter what I was doing, suddenly and out of nowhere I was caught by this paralyzing fear. I was constantly on the alert and looked around. I was determined that if I saw her, I was going to run away and make myself disappear. If she tried to talk to me, I would pretend I'd never met her before. If she'd told my neighbors anything about it, I would angrily deny everything and say she was lying. I would forget all about it and pretend nothing had happened. I didn't really know what had happened. I hadn't even seen her tits. But she'd held my prick. Had we fucked? Was that it? Something soft, for a few seconds. Or had nothing happened? I had no idea. And who was this woman?

After this incident, I never went back to a party with the bartender, never ate fries, drank white wine, or told stories. Like when Vigfúsína had an episode, when he had a party, I started putting in my earplugs and wearing my headphones. And if someone knocked on the door then I made like I was sleeping. Luckily, I never met the woman again.

I stopped hanging around inside my room all evening and started making it my habit to go downtown. Though I wasn't yet eighteen, there were some places I could get in without being asked for ID. I could go to Safari, a nightclub on Skúlagata, and I could also go to Kaffi Gest on Laugavegur. I could get served there, and there was a lot going on. I'd start my evening by going to the coffee shop, Hressó.

Sometimes I met some friends there and smoked and drank coffee with them. I'd kept in contact with Biggi, who I'd known at Núpur, and sometimes visited him and Óttar further south in Hafnarfjörður. They also came to town a lot. It was really very enjoyable to talk crap and goof around with Óttar; we messed about and had a lot of fun together. The partying life was practically made for me; I felt I'd found my proper place in life. Wandering around, hanging out at some bar, shooting the breeze with some people, drinking, going to a club and staying until closing. Then following someone to a private home where the party continued: drinking, smoking, talking. This life was a dream.

Sometimes I also met a girl I fell in love with on the spot. It was always love at first sight. They were all absolutely lovely. The love affair began with kissing at Safari. You couldn't do more in a club and had to continue at home. After having been kissing the love of my life for hours, sometimes she started kissing someone else or just vanished. But I didn't care. Clubbing was about fluidity. You're not a performer when you're partying; you're part of a group that flows about, yet is still somehow always in the same place. Not unlike following a group around an airport at speed. You don't read the signs or know where you're going. You simply chase the group. The only difference is that party people are drunk, often kiss, and sometimes sleep together. I fell into this flow naturally. Sometimes I woke up at home and sometimes I woke up elsewhere. Usually on some sofa; sometimes in a room with some girl, and I could hardly remember how I'd gotten there or what had happened. First and foremost, I was enjoying myself and I could see myself spending my life this way. It was real happiness.

To kiss two girls in the same evening, maybe, and perhaps end it by sleeping with a third who I hadn't even been kissing. Having some drinks and staying up forever.

If you got tired or lost steam, there was usually someone nearby with amphetamine and you could take it up your nostril. A little speed in one nostril could ensure you had energy until the next afternoon. What beautiful circumstances. I didn't really choose my company; I just hung with the crowd that offered the most fun kids and the cutest girls at any given moment. And I became trendy. I was New Wave Jón. I was no longer lousy Jónsi Punk. Jón Gunnar Kristinsson with the bent penis and bitten nails had gone. I was cool, I listened to Bauhaus, I wore leggings, and I was able to kiss girls and sleep with them. I felt I could not wish for anything more in life than this.

Everything was absolutely without obligation. Even though I kissed some girl and slept with her did not mean that we would necessarily become a couple. We were just kids having fun. Sometimes the girls asked me if I had a condom. I never did. I no longer found it exciting to buy condoms. New wave trendies didn't use condoms. Bauhaus didn't use condoms. I thought condoms were lousy and had nothing to do with me. If girls wanted to use a condom, that was their problem. I was wearing leggings. There aren't even pockets on leggings! I had enough to do trying to make sure I had cigarettes and money. I had exactly zero responsibility for anything except paying the rent. And I imagined I was perhaps not unlike my neighbor. Maybe I was just the next generation of him. The thought filled me with ease and confidence. I could well imagine becoming a bartender in the future.

Maybe I would still be in my room on Miðtún in ten years. I would drink a lot of liquor that I'd stolen at work and occasionally do a bit of hash and I'd also have lots of girlfriends who I slept with alternately. They'd occasionally get angry and argue and embarrass me, but otherwise it would just be complete fun. I'd never eat anything but burgers and fries. Life would always be great, except when I was hungover—that wasn't fun. I was cool. I had a hairstyle, I wore gel, and cute girls wanted to talk to me and kiss me and sleep with me. People sought out my company. I almost felt like I was in a band. I looked the part and was the type in all respects—except I wasn't in a band.

This ideal life changed one cool fall day when I walked into Borgartún to get a stamp on my unemployment card, as normal. With the wave of a hand, everything changed. I stood in line in my new wave outfit with my styled hair, wearing leggings and my jacket and ready for anything. I needed money for the upcoming night of partying. The woman at the desk was waffling on about something. I didn't usually listen to what she said, just nodded my head, but this time she was telling me something. Work assignment?

"Wha-???"

"You need to take on a Work Assignment. You need to be in the City of Reykjavík's Work Assignment program."

I didn't understand what the woman was saying.

"I'm just here for a stamp. I'm unemployed, you see."

The woman looked at me fiercely and said, firmly:

"You don't get unemployment benefits unless you take part in Work Assignment."

I didn't understand what on earth she meant. I'd never heard of Work Assignment. Wasn't I going to get my benefits as usual?

"What's that?"

She gave a heavy sigh and looked at me.

"You have been unemployed for ten weeks and you cannot continue to receive unemployment benefits unless you accept the work that you are offered."

Work? What work? What was this woman talking about?

I was not going back to Hampiðjan or Plastos!

"Can't I just get stamped?"

She looked at me as if I were an idiot.

"No, you cannot! You've been allocated a job."

Working? A job, chosen for me? I hadn't applied for anything. What was going on?

"And I have to go do this work?"

"You have to accept the job allocated to you and you must show up. You will receive feedback from the foreman on how you conduct yourself and on your attendance."

"Oh… Where?"

"You've been allocated to work in the Reykjavík City Farm Garden and you should attend starting right away, on Monday; make yourself known on Klambratún."

"But I don't get my benefits now?"

"No. A young man like you should not be hanging around and accepting handouts. It'll be good for you to be outside in this nice weather."

It was a broken new wave trendy who walked out of the City of Reykjavík unemployment office that day. I was being forced to go to work. I found it pathetic and uninteresting.

Next Monday, I arrived at the work headquarters for the City of Reykjavík on Klambratún at the stroke of eight. I had worked there before going into surgery. Now it seemed far-off and unreal. As though I thought it had been some other person.

"Is Theódór here?" I asked a guy, who looked questioningly at me. He shouted out, loudly:

"Teddi!"

Theódór, a tall and powerful man, came over to me and I handed him my paper.

"I was told to show up here."

He took the paper and seemed not to acknowledge me. He clearly had nothing to do with me. He exchanged some words with some people standing there and vanished. I stood around in the parking lot like a lemon until a fat man called in my direction:

"Why don't we find you some overalls?"

"Sure..."

I followed the guy to a nearby work shed. Inside the shed hung orange work overalls along the walls. He groped about through the overalls and handed me pants and a jacket.

"These should fit you."

I put the clothes on and followed the guy back out. We went to a small four-door pickup truck and he told me to sit in the back. Inside the car were two men in orange overalls. The guy sat behind the wheel and we drove off.

The work involved running about the capital and emptying garbage bins using a special key. You opened the bin with the key, poured the trash into the black garbage bags, locked the bin again and threw the rubbish bag onto the truck bed, then drove to the next garbage bin. Sometimes we went out of our way and picked up trash piles people had left in the open country; we threw that trash onto the platform bed, too. After chatting a bit with my colleagues and getting to know about their circumstances, I concluded that they were developmentally challenged. I thought the same applied to the driver. There seemed to be little going on inside them; it was difficult to keep up a conversation.

For lunch, we went to the lunchroom. I noticed that our foreman swallowed one lump of sugar with every sip of coffee he took. That was evidently why he was called Lump. I'd become a city employee and was working with a group of people who were clearly backward. I tried to spend as little time as possible out of the car and when we drove around town I held my hand over my face. When I was forced to leave the car I looked down and hoped with all my heart that no one saw me. I put my hood over my head and hid under it.

I tried, however, to not let work interfere with clubbing; as soon as the workday ended, I went straight to Coffee Guest and didn't let on. Often, I went straight from clubbing to work the next day. On some occasions, I woke up somewhere in Breiðholt or in Hafnarfjörður and discovered I had to be at work in half-an-hour. Usually it worked out that I managed to trick someone into driving me. Often it was pretty difficult for me to last until midday in the pick-up truck. Sometimes I was even so hungover and tired that I vomited in the garbage bins as I emptied them. The combination of my physical condition and the incentive of the trashcans meant that I contributed a spurt of vomit into the plastic bag before I threw it on the bed. It wasn't easy to explain this to my co-workers; I just told them I was sick. They always treated it as a valid explanation.

One morning when we were about to leave and I was standing outside the headquarters smoking, a stately elderly man came up driving a Citroën. I'd never seen him there before and didn't know who he was. I watched as Theódór the foreman greeted the man and they chatted. When they said goodbye, the old man turned his eyes to me and asked Theódór, loud and clear:

"Can I take this one?"

Theodor looked indifferently at me and said:

"Sure, just take him. I'm not using him."

What this guy was going to use me for, I had no idea, and no one seemed to think it was worth taking the time to explain it to me first. They guy went back to the Citroën, stood there, and motioned for me to sit in the back. I sucked in my last cigarette smoke, threw the stub onto the parking lot, and got in the car. I had no clue where I was going or what I was going to do. As we talked in the car, it came out that we were on the way up to Arnarholt in Kjalarnes.

Arnarholt was a section of the City Hospital of Reykjavík; it was part of the state mental hospital. Psychotic individuals were kept there, diagnosed incurable and probably never able to live a normal life outside the institution. At Arnarholt they mixed together people with totally different diagnoses and conditions. There were several old schizophrenic patients, two or three with Down syndrome, and also a man who had a viral infection in his brain. Then there was a considerable group of misguided alcoholics who'd harmed themselves through years of drinking and debauchery.

I was in a team with some other kids. We had to trim the beds around the building and carry out minor maintenance to the outbuildings. This was a varied and enjoyable job. One week we painted a roof. The next week we went with a group of residents to the potato garden and planted potatoes. Sometimes we fixed a fence and sometimes we picked up trash. In between we weeded beds and planted plants.

The old man was called Guðbjörn Jóhannesson and he was our foreman. He had worked as a guard at the Correctional Facility on Skólavörðustígur for forty years and then went to work in gardening after he retired. Guðbjörn was a goldmine of stories. In his job as a warden, he'd often met many oddballs who'd made their mark in Reykjavík in the past—until the state built appropriate institutions for such people. Back then, those people had roamed the streets and roads of the city freely; some were infamous. Despite being well over seventy, Guðbjörn was an extremely dynamic person. He was hale and handsome. Guðbjörn was a ladies' man by nature and could never see a woman without addressing her, usually by flattering her appearance or asking a question. He used to come up with bizarre questions that made use of some fun wordplay. If a woman was fat or big, then he asked her what she was called.

"Are you called Broadwyn?"

I never understood the joke, nor did anyone else.

Guðbjörn also knew myriad poems and quatrains; he never tired of reciting them to us while we worked. He enjoyed asking us to finish a stanza or tell him the author's name. Sometimes he asked us about the context of a verse or to tell him how and why it came into existence. He told us many stories by Villi from Skálholt, about knowing him and about their friendship. He had most of Villi's verses memorized. He also knew Óli Maggadon, Dósóþeus Tímóteusson, and Steinn Steinarr; he knew tons of stories about them. I really enjoyed hearing stories about these guys. I'd heard of them before through my dad. From reading books of poetry, I'd developed a great love of Steinn Steinarr and thought him a remarkable poet. I was not at all bored to be around someone who'd met and known Steinn and knew stories about him. My co-workers didn't share this enthusiasm and found Guðbjörn boring. To a certain extent, he was. If the boys didn't show him or his verses any interest, he didn't have any particular reason to respect them. I quickly became a favorite of Guðbjörn, who treated me better than the other kids because I could sometimes recite verses. He was especially impressed when I could recite verses which he knew were by Steinn Steinarr but which hadn't ever been published.

> I earnt scant profit from wonder,
> from fields of learning and art,
> my seed sown in sleep departed
> that first day of the days of summer.

While my colleagues rolled their eyes, I talked tirelessly with Guðbjörn. The boys often asked me:

"How can you hang out with that guy? He is sooooo sickeningly boring, man!"

I tried to defend Guðbjörn and told them he wasn't so boring, he just knew a lot of poems and entertaining stories and the like. They sighed.

Along with our horticultural work, we sometimes had to deal with the residents. Sometimes the staff went out walking with a group and so were around where we were. Sometimes the residents were even sent out to help us. One of them was called Addi and he was damn crazy. No one seemed to know his background, why he was detained there, or what had happened to him.

Addi was extremely special. He was utterly quiet and only wanted to chain smoke all day. He was rationed cigarettes and he could smoke one every hour. If he chanced upon a packet, then he chain-smoked one after the other until the package was done. I had tremendous fun chatting with Addi, not least because of the fact that the conversation followed no particular thread, but went all over the place. He utterly charmed me.

"Did you live in Reykjavík, Addi?"

"Yes."

"And what did you do?"

"I played the harpsichord, you know. Harpsichord, you know. You know what a harpsichord is?"

I nodded.

"Yes, isn't it like a little piano?"

"Yes, that's a harpsichord, you see. Harpsichord."

"Yes. And where did you live in Reykjavík?"

"Yes. I lived in a house. House, you see. You know what a house is?"

"Er, yes, I know what a house is."

"Yes, it's a house, you see. House."

"Yes."

"It was a house and there was a range, you know. You know what a range is?"

I nodded and smiled.

"Sure, I know what a range is."

"Yes, there was a range and some stairs. And there was a woman. Woman. A woman who handed out her affection."

"Yes, okay. Above the range?

"Yes, it was a range, it was. You know what a range is?"

"Sure."

"Yes."

Then he went quiet, thought a while, then added, as if he had suddenly remembered something remarkable.

"Yes, and Jesus Christ rented the basement."

"Yes, okay..."

That's how all Addi's stories went. They were all different and he was always really careful that you could follow the elements of the story, that you knew what a range was and so on. He was particularly willing to tell a story if you gave him a cigarette. Invariably, the first thing he said when he came out was:

"Do you have a cigarette?"

"Yes, if you tell me a story."

"Story, yes, tell a story."

"Yes, I'll give you a cigarette if you tell me a story."

"Yes, tell you a story, yes."

"Yes. Have you ever been at sea, Addi?"

"Yes. Been at sea, yes. Was working for Coal and Salt."

"Coal and Salt, yes. Wait, is that a company?"

"It's a company, yes. You know what a company is?"

"Yes, I know what a company is."

"Yes. And we shoveled. Dug with a shovel."

"Yes, you were shoveling coal and salt?"

"I was shoveling. Dug with a shovel. You know what a shovel is?"

"Sure, I know what a shovel is."

"Yes. I was working with a man named Adolf Hitler. His name was Adolf Hitler, you see."

"Sure, he was working there with you at Coal and Salt?"

"Yes."

"Okay. And did you maybe sometimes play the harpsichord for him at work?"

"Yes. We had to drive the bus."

"So you might not have been able to play much while you were driving?"

"No. I was cleaning the bus. You know what a bus is?"

"I do. But Hitler: he was cleaning the bus with you or maybe he just played the harpsichord?"

"No, at Coal and Salt. Hitler worked with me."

"Ahhhhh, right."

I enjoyed talking with the residents about life and the world and I made many good friends at Arnarholt. I found many intriguing, but several were especially unusual. There was one very strange guy there who was always on the move. He never walked, only ran; he was always in a hurry. He reminded me of the rabbit in *Alice in Wonderland*. And if you stopped him, he became very agitated and was on tenterhooks. There was some tradition which involved getting the story of the day from him; he was always ready with some story he'd created specifically for the day. Whenever I came across him, I stopped him and said:

"Dóri! Tell me the story of the day."

"I'm in rather a hurry…"

"Stop for a moment and tell us the story of the day. You can't continue until you've finished telling us the story of the day."

He raised his voice and said loudly and clearly:

"The story of the day today is about a blue man on a yellow horse who went riding over green sand. Thank you. The story is over."

Then he ran off. But Dóri wasn't only a storyteller; he was also a singer. And often we didn't let him go until he had sung a song for us.

"You'll sing us a song, too, Dóri, get us in the mood for working."

Without any hesitation, he burst into song. He always sang the same song, "In Sun and Summer Warm." He had the pleasant habit of always placing special emphasis on the "s" so that it almost sounded like a "z," he pronounced it so softly:

"In zzun and zzzummer warmth, a zzzmall chiiiiild zzzhe played…"

He didn't say child but chiiiiild. There followed a brief artistic silence and then:

"…gently by a zzzmall laaaake. The story's over."

And then he made a break for it. He was one of many friendly fixtures at Arnarholt.

Some days were so strange that they were like myths or drug trips. Addi sometimes worked with us. He was a great bruiser and a vigorous worker. One time, I was especially impressed. An employee at the hospital came out with Addi and asked:

"Isn't there something Addi can do? He's dying to do something."

We were fencing the lawn and setting in fence posts. You dig a hole about a meter deep, fairly wide, then put a fence post into, pile some stones up by the pole so that it stands straight and shovel it down. Guðbjörn took the joyful Addi and set him to dig a hole. He put his shovel in the ground and said:

"Addi, my friend. You have to dig a hole right here."

"Yes. Dig a hole."

"Yes. Dig a hole here for fence posts."

"Yes. Digging holes for fence posts. Do you have a cigarette?"

"Dig a hole and you get a cigarette."

"Yes, dig a hole and I get a cigarette."

"Yes. It must be about a meter deep."

"Very well. A meter deep. Then I get a cigarette."

Addi was given a spade and shown where he should start shoveling. Guðbjörn said, loud and clear:

"Well, lads, now we are headed to do some weeding in the potato garden."

The potato garden was about a fifteen-minute drive from the institution if you went by tractor. Guðbjörn came over with the tractor; we jumped on the trailer and drove up to the park. We were busy weeding and cleaning out the bed, all the way up to afternoon coffee. When we came back and were riding down the slope to the place we had left Addi, we couldn't see him. Instead, there was a pile of soil rising up from the ground in front of us. We went silent and realized immediately what was happening. Hard worker that Addi was, he had shoveled himself really far down into the ground. We couldn't believe our eyes and sprang up from the trailer and ran to the hole. It was like we thought. Addi had managed to dig a huge crater and was standing down in the middle. The crater was so deep that Addi could not get himself back out and we had to climb in, helping to push and pull him up. We couldn't control our laughter when we were asking Addi about his shoveling. I couldn't even wipe the tears from my eyes because I was laughing so much.

"Do you have a cigarette?" Addi asked, as if nothing had happened.

"Yes, Addi, I've got a cigarette for you. You have very much earned one after shoveling such a wonderful crater."

"Yes."

Addi ecstatically got his cigarette and we went back home. The working day was over. The next morning the employee returned with Addi and asked if he couldn't help us. Guðbjörn gave him a warm welcome as usual.

"Of course, Addi is so efficient. He can help us, of course. Good morning, Addi."

"Good morning. Do you have a cigarette?"

"First you need to do something and then you get a cigarette."

"Yes, first do something and then get a cigarette."

"Yes. When you're done working, the cigarette."

"Yes, when I'm done working I get a cigarette."

"Yes, Addi, my friend."

Guðbjörn went over to the crater with him; it was not clear from Addi's expression whether he had ever seen it before. Guðbjörn handed him a shovel and said:

"You need to shovel the soil into this hole."

"Shovel soil into this hole. Then I get a cigarette?"

"Yes, when you are done with the hole you get a cigarette."

"Then I get a cigarette."

Addi didn't hesitate, but started powerfully shoveling the soil down into the hole as we walked to our work.

There were few inmates who had the physical capability or the minimum balance needed to help working outdoors.

In our breaks, I liked to stroll around inside Arnarholt and chat to the inmates. It was teeming with strange characters and I fell in love with many of them.

Old Konni was one of my favorite friends. He was an old man who was said to have lost himself to drink. He said he'd got liquor for a brain. He was neat and well-kempt in every way, always freshly combed and shaved and attired in well-tailored and elegant clothes. He had a meaningful expression and often thought and talked in riddles. I had great fun chatting to him. He must have thought I was fun because he always revived when he saw me. When I came into the lounge he patted the chair next to him in a friendly way and gave me a signal to come and sit. He usually spoke to me in a low voice to ensure others couldn't hear what we were saying. He always had some business with me, and asked me many questions.

"Have you started pinching the girls, Jon?"

"Ehh, sure, I just started pinching them."

"Yes. Will you do something for me?" he asked in a low voice.

"Yes, what is it?"

"Don't pinch these dark-haired ones," he whispered quietly.

"Oh? I'm not to pinch them?"

"No. They are highly dangerous. Pinch the blonde-haired ones instead."

"Sure, I'm to pinch these blonde-haired ones instead?"

"Shussh…" he said and placed a finger to his lips. He clearly didn't want this heard. This was two men talking, like the other things that passed between us.

"Tell me, Jón, do you have a radio?"

"Er, yes, I have a combined radio and cassette player."

"You can choose whether you listen to the radio or cassette on it?"

"Yes."

He nodded his head, a focused expression on his face, like he was reflecting thoughtfully about what I said. Then he leaned back towards me and asked:

"Do you sometimes bring your face right up to the radio?"

I thought a moment and said:

"I think I can say so, yes. I definitely have my face pretty close to the radio when I tune it."

"I suspected so," and he smiled a little. Then he leaned still closer to me and whispered:

"Watch out that it doesn't explode in your face, Jón."

I nodded.

"Sure, one must be careful."

Then he patted me on the back of my hand and said:

"I trust that you will do this."

I always liked having a short and decent chat with Konna.

All the inmates at Arnarholt were there because they were somehow peculiar. No one was outright dangerous, but Addi could come close. The employees inside always stressed to us when Addi came out to work that he mustn't hit anyone. He had a real temper and sometimes got fits of rage. I found it hard to imagine and struggled to believe them. I felt Addi was always so calm and collected, always just wanting a cigarette and chat. But one time when we were in the recreation room playing table tennis Addi came begging for cigarettes.

"Do you have a cigarette? Do you have a cigarette?"

We'd been asked by the staff not to give him cigarettes since he got one from them every hour. We didn't always do that, and gave him the occasional cigarette. It made it possible to have engaging talks with him and usually he'd tell us some funny stories. This time I was playing table tennis and Addi asked me repeatedly whether I had a cigarette. First I didn't answer him, because I was playing, but then I began to imitate him and repeat what he said in a deep voice:

"Do you have a cigarette? Do you have a cigarette?"

At first, he replied:

"I'd love to ask you whether you have a cigarette. Do you have a cigarette?"

"Do you have a cigarette?" I aped back, trying to imitate his voice and gestures. He looked expressionlessly at me and asked again:

"Do you have a cigarette?"

I mimicked him again:

"Do you have a cigarette?"

All at once I saw how he transformed. His eyes went black and shot sparks. I was so startled by this that I stepped back. With a penetrating gaze, he stared at me; he raised his hand super-quick and struck the table tennis so hard that he broke a piece off. He hissed at me:

"Are you making fun of me, you fuck?!"

I was terrified.

"No, no, no," I said, even as I escaped to the other end of the table tennis table. He rolled up the sleeves of his jacket and started walking towards me. It was obvious that he meant me no good. I ran lap after lap around the table tennis with him after me like a snorting bull. Suddenly it occurred to me that it would be an excellent plan to offer him a cigarette. I reached for a cigarette in my pocket and extended it towards him.

"Do you want a cigarette, Addi?"

It melted him in a flash.

"Cigarette, yes..."

His eyes were again calm and he was completely at ease. He looked alternately at me and cigarette and said:

"Yes, cigarette. Thanks for that."

He took the cigarette and lit it. I never ever teased Addi again.

I not only met the residents but also the staff. They were mainly women and there were a lot of cute girls. I always enjoyed going out to smoke and chat with them. I was no longer timid and shy with the opposite sex. I was even getting pretty good at keeping the conversation going, asking them about their lives and complimenting their appearance and stuff.

I thought at first they were all nurses, but then I found out that the girls, and indeed most people who worked there, were just ordinary, unqualified workers. It was clear anyone could get a job as a worker in a psychiatric ward. And when the Work Assignment scheme finished in the fall, I preferred to continue working with all these cute girls than return to unemployment benefits. This work fit me like a glove. I got paid well and didn't really have to do anything except talk to mental patients all day. I went to the office of the City Hospital and applied for a job as an employee of Arnarholt. I was hired on the spot and registered in the women's labor association, Sókn. I'd become a working woman. I'd become part of the Sisterhood, as became clear when I received the monthly newsletter.

Dear Sister Jón Gunnar Kristinsson.
The sisterhood shows solidarity!
Communicate your views to the health minister.

There weren't many men working in psychiatric wards at this time, but there was demand for them due to physical requirements. Sometimes patients got unsettled and you had to apply force to constrain them. In such circumstances, women were often scared and so the men on the ward were called on since they were often stronger than women. I enjoyed finding myself in this situation. I was surrounded by women all day and they praised me to the hilt. I had a fairly free hand with additional shifts and overtime and knew how good I had it. This quiet inside work was a fit for me. In my new job, dressed in a crisp white work uniform and white shoes, I went out with the girls to smoke just as the boys in gardening detail came inside to chat to us. I wasn't beyond feeling a little disdain. I pitied the poor guys. They were working in the mud and only had each other for company. I was working inside, surrounded by cute girls.

My work consisted primarily of following this one boy around, everywhere; two of us took turns, each having an hour with him at a time. The boy, who had the peculiar name Víðlyndur Víðlyndsson, had mental problems; he was brain damaged, too, and an obsessive compulsive. This led him to do his daily work at all times according to fixed routines. It took great patience to follow him about as he could often be really frustrating. For example, when he took a bath. It could take him well over a half-hour to put his clothes back on because he had to do it according to a predetermined routine, a fixed system. He began by standing on one foot for a few moments. Then he took one sock, put it over his shoulder, stepped into it with his bare foot, then finally lifted the other leg up and did the same thing again for the same length of time as before. Then he took the sock back off and repeated the same routine. Then he dressed in both socks and he was done. Next, he turned to his shirt. He put it on and took it off. He repeated the routine ten times. The eleventh time, he finally stopped taking the shirt off and turned to his pants. Same story. Everything had to happen ten times and if he messed something up, he had to start over. Stand on one leg... the routine began again. I sat with him and encouraged him but had to be careful not to push so much that he got distracted and started all over again and took even longer.

He was raised by his mother alone since they lived far away in the countryside. If I understood correctly, she'd always kept him hidden away at home. When the authorities entered the home, they found a dire spectacle. His mother had mental health problems and the boy had gone feral and behaved largely like an animal because he had never been taught anything. He was certainly mentally disabled, but he was also significantly damaged by his upbringing. He didn't, for example, know to use the toilet. At home he had bowel movements in flowerpots and drawers and anything else around.

The doctor told me that when he talked about it with the boy's mother she would burst out laughing and say:

"Oh, that's just a little human chocolate."

If the boy was left unattended, even if only for a few minutes, he usually pooped in the palm of his hand and made balls out of his shit. He'd find a place with a number of crannies, like the linen closet, and put the little poop balls in all the nooks. We didn't want this to happen because it involved so much extra work: we had to clean all over again the linen piled in the room, and clean all the corners, walls and the shelving, high and low. Besides which, the smell lingered in the air for ages, no matter how much we cleaned.

When I wasn't working, life was centered mostly around drinking and clubbing. I really enjoyed going to the Mál og Menning bookstore and leafing through newly published books or choosing some good pipe tobacco from the tobacco shop, Björk. But clubbing was what mattered. I continued to have fun with the people I met at Safari and downtown. But after I went to work on Arnarholt, a totally new way of entertaining myself had opened up. When I wasn't working, I was partying. I got dressed up, grabbed some money, and went to Coffee Guest. I had coffee, smoked and talked to some kids. Around ten, we went to Safari and I started drinking. I didn't dance, but I liked to sit and chat and drink. When Safari closed we went to a party. And I had my pick. I could go to any party taking place. I was welcome everywhere because I was fun. I was cool, I was a new wave trendy and many girls had a crush on me. I left my glasses at home. I'd started to wear contact lenses. Sometimes I was so drunk I lost them, but it didn't matter because I was usually with some girl and I just followed her.

The goal was always the same. I was out drinking and I was going to have fun. And I was always going to go home with some girl. I thought that was the ultimate fulfillment in life.

I never had time to sleep. To keep partying, I took speed. There was always someone who could get you speed. Speed was refreshing. It was like it got your drinking back under control. Although I'd been drinking a lot and for a long time, I wasn't drunk after just a little speed. When I'd drunk and done speed uninterrupted for several days and finally came home I was often so exhausted that I felt like my whole body trembled and shook. I often had exceptional trouble brushing my teeth because my hands trembled so much that I couldn't get to my mouth. That's when the Rohypnol came in handy. It was a savior in such situations. I was able to juice and party without sleeping, keeping myself going by taking speed. In between, I was able to bring myself down with Rohypnol, put in my earplugs and headphones, and sleep for twelve to fifteen hours.

I felt I had found a balance in life and thought I was happy. It was nothing more than what I wanted. To get drunk on booze and have sex without commitment. I'd always wanted this; it felt like it was the meaning and the goal of life. How could things be better? I never knew in advance what was going to happen and there was always a certain charge to things. The driving force and the purpose was always to get to sleep with some girl. Sometimes I slept with the same girl over and over again. We were just acquaintances who partied together but never discussed anything. It was totally free of obligation. We just wanted to try all sorts of stuff. I also enjoyed sleeping with girls I didn't know at all. Once I went home with a girl and we were kissing and cuddling, and she asked me:

"Why did you go home with me?"

"Because you've got a pussy," I said, half-joking and half-honest.

"Come on."

But that's what was happening. I didn't even know her name.

"If you took off your panties and I saw you were rounded down there like a Barbie doll, I'd just head back downtown."

She hit me lightly and said "I'm not rounded down there."

Then we laughed and kissed.

I had become a part of a crowd that many people wanted to be a part of. I sometimes met girls partying who showed an interest in me and I knew that they wanted to become part of the crowd. They wanted to be eligible for the gang. Perhaps they weren't quite as cute as the girls I could have got, but I wanted to fuck them anyway. I just liked seeing different bodies, breasts, and pussies. My interest in them was shaped primarily by sex and motivated by my prick. The sex was always both the intention and the ambition. Once we had slept together, fallen asleep, and woken up, I wanted badly to fuck them again. But they didn't seem to have the same interest in me. I soon discovered that the girls did not share this earnest interest in fucking me, but there was something more they were after. They wanted to listen to Joy Division, and they wanted to talk about stuff or ask about something or other.

I was not looking for any particular girl and I did not want anything as much as I wanted sex. If the girls did not share my interest in sex, we just didn't match up. And if they weren't interested in my prick, then they simply weren't interested in me. In truth, I wanted to know as little as possible about them.

It didn't make any difference to me what views or opinions they had on this or that. I was just so pleased and happy with my prick and I felt it deserved an endless variety of pussy.

But sometimes, when, glassesless and in dim light, I was feeling my way away from some girl that I'd gone home with, I'd run into part of her reality. I saw pictures on the walls and I saw her books. *Tao Te Ching*, Steinn Steinarr, and other books I thought remarkable. And I realized the girl breathing, asleep, in bed—she was not just a wrapping around a pussy, but a person like me, an entire solar system, a life. I was filled with emptiness and melancholy. And in some quite distinct way it reminded me of when I used to break into summer cottages. I didn't break anything, but I was, uninvited, inserting myself into others' lives, putting my fingerprints on their images. And that touched off in me the human rights of my prick and the human rights of the girls. I was a burglar, but I wasn't going to break anything and I didn't mean to hurt anyone. I just wanted to have fun.

One time, I went home with this girl. We were in bed and had started having sex when she passed out and fell asleep. I was filled with despair. Now I needed a plan. I'd been invited to an elegant party. I'd managed to open the door and there were delicacies on the table, and I wanted nothing more than to savor them. But everyone had gone. There was no one at home. It wasn't a party anymore. I stopped moving.

"Are you asleep?"

She didn't answer. I pushed her shoulder and patted her on the cheek.

"I do not believe this—are you asleep?"

She was totally unconscious. We'd been partying all night and had drunk a lot. There were two voices quarreling inside me. One said: "Finish it. It doesn't matter if she's asleep. She's not going to remember anything after this. It'll just take a few powerful thrusts and job done. She'll sleep just as she is, and you'll wake happy in the morning." But the other voice said: "No, this isn't good, Jón. You shouldn't fuck girls who don't know you're fucking them. And you know what's the right thing to do in this situation." And I did what I thought was right. The next day she asked me:

"Did we do it yesterday?"

I was at a loss.

"Yes, but you fell asleep in the middle of things…"

"Oh, I'm sorry. I was just so disgustingly tired. I was working all last week, you see, and perhaps had drunk a bit much too, hahaha."

She chuckled. I smiled.

"And what, you just stopped?

"Yes, of course."

"You didn't have to. You could have finished."

I was always running full speed. There was so much exciting happening, new places to go, new situations, new things about sex. I didn't want to sleep. I didn't want to miss a thing.

It had to be fun and you had to remember. And you couldn't live with your mother. It was better to hurry away than get stuck somewhere you didn't know you could escape. Don't get tied down, be free. Out all night, out in the city and alive. Out all night tra-la-la-la-la. Out all night, subject to no one. Oh-no, oh-no, oh-no. New wave trendy. With awesome hair, stylish clothes, a fantastic prick.

He never really eats anything but eggs because his mother gave him an egg cooker. He just goes to the store and buys a carton of eggs if he's hungry and he eats the eggs. He goes to work to keep up appearances, doesn't do anything, then clubbing, laughing, drinking, fucking—sometimes. Not going anywhere, not for anything, just being. A wrapper around a prick. Amphetamines, liquor, Rohypnol. I'm going to make a deal with myself. If I don't get to fuck then I can have Rohypnol. Either ensures a good and fair outcome. Gliding aimlessly onward; everyone's an idiot. No one gets me. No one gets anarchism. People don't even get new wave because they're not familiar with punk. New wave was born from punk. I never got enough. True of sex and of alcohol. I wasn't done and I already wanted more.

Arnarholt.

Sunday.

On weekends we sometimes went to the video rental store at Kjalarnes and rented a video we watched with the residents. That Sunday: *Conan the Barbarian*, with Arnold Schwarzenegger. Conan was put in captivity. He was a slave who turned the mill paddles. First with some others but, little by little, there were fewer and in the end he was alone. Walking the same ring turning the millstone. But he had bulked up and thickened out. He was a barbarian. I wasn't a barbarian. I was a new wave trendy. I'd settled myself in the most comfortable chair in the living room, a lounge chair that could be tilted back. I tilted my head, put my feet up, and got comfortable. Conan was a classy guy. Maybe I should go to the gym and become a muscle mountain like Arnold Schwarzenegger. I wouldn't just be a new wave trendy but a muscle-troll, too.

Darkness.

The End.

I woke up in a hospital bed in a hospital. What had happened? I'd forgotten all about Conan. The last thing I remembered was sitting in the kitchen with my mom and she was interrogating me.

"Where have you been? With whom? Why are you so skinny?" I was alone in the hospital room.

"Hello?" I called into the air. Why was I there? Had I taken some pills? I couldn't remember. A woman in a white gown came to the door and looked at me.

"Wait a moment," she said, and disappeared. I heard people outside. Shortly after, a doctor and a nurse came in, greeted me and asked how I felt.

"I feel very well," I replied and tried to act naturally. "Do you remember what happened?"

"Don't you remember when you came here yesterday?"

"I came in yesterday? Mom came with me?"

The nurse took my hand and took my pulse. The doctor was in a white gown with a shirt and tie underneath.

"Have you ever suffered from epilepsy, Jón?"

Epilepsy? I had epilepsy? I didn't remember ever having epilepsy. Maybe I had epilepsy when I was a kid? I didn't recall that.

"No, I don't think so."

"Do you remember what you were doing yesterday?"

"No, but maybe if you ask my mom..."

I didn't remember and, also, I wasn't entirely sure who I was. It was like I had come from nowhere and was suddenly there. I had an obscure past and couldn't remember any stories. It was just me and my mom at the kitchen table. If I thought of something else—but there was nothing, only a vacuum. Had I been born?

"Are you called Jón Gunnar Kristinsson?"

Jón Gunnar Kristinsson? I knew the name. I'd heard it before. I'd met the man, for sure. Jón Gunnar Kristinsson... I nodded.

"I know him."

Was this a trick question? Jón Gunnar Kristinsson? Was someone in the kitchen with my mother and I? Yes. He was in the living room. He sat at the dining table in the room but we didn't see him. But I knew he was listening to everything we said. He didn't let himself be heard and I didn't know who he was.

"Yes, isn't he the guy in the room? Did you already ask my mom?"

I looked around, searching for her.

"Where is she?"

The doctor looked at me thoughtfully. Okay. It was a trick question. He was clearly trying to trick me and wouldn't tell me what was going on. Why didn't he tell me? And why was he trying to trick me? The doctor turned to the nurse.

"Has he been in the scanner?"

She said no, but talked about brain scans and how they had been atypical. The doctor nodded. He looked back at me.

"How do you feel in your head?"

My head felt good.

"Good. I don't have a headache..."

He got up from my bed, and poked me here and there.

"Feel that?"

"Yes."

He grabbed my big toe and pulled it.

"Feel that?"

It was so funny that I couldn't help but laugh. This man was not a doctor. He was an actor pretending to be a doctor. I looked directly into his eyes, smiled and said: "Yes, I feel it."

This doctor was a funny guy. He went back to talking about Jón Gunnar Kristinsson and asked me when he was born.

I had no idea. The doctor told me what had happened to him. Jón Gunnar Kristinsson had been working in the psychiatric ward at Arnarholt up in Kjalarnes.

"Kjalarnes?"

I had never been to Arnarholt, but I suddenly remembered my sister, Rúna.

"My sister lives there."

In the lounge at Arnarholt, Jón Gunnar had had a raging seizure, resulting in his falling to the floor, injuring his head and losing consciousness. He was taken by ambulance to the city hospital.

"Okay."

I didn't quite see what it had to do with me. Why was the doctor telling me about this Jón Gunnar? We were clearly connected in some mysterious way.

"There are people here who want to meet you, Jón."

"Yes, okay."

"Do you trust yourself to do that?"

"Yes, of course."

The doctor went out to the corridor and I heard him talking to some people.

"You can see him now."

Three women entered the room. They all had worried expressions but they were trying to stay calm. One of them asked:

"Are you all right?"

I smiled at her in a reassuring way.

"Yes, I think so."

I had no idea who these women were. Perhaps they were some women who worked at the hospital? Maybe there was always some women in all hospitals who worked there being worried for the patients? Like in the movies. They asked if I knew where I was and what the doctor had said. I told them I was all right, but if they wanted any more information, they should just talk to my mom.

"It's best if you talk to Mom. She always knows something about everything. Mom knows quite unbelievable things and, what's more, she knows about all kinds of stuff she doesn't know anything about."

I thought it was a funny sentence but only I laughed. The same happened when I was joking with the doctors. I laughed, but they didn't smile back. Why so serious? I was all right. The women were immersed in their job and they did it very well. I smiled at them and looked into all their eyes to assure them I meant what I said, I was fine, I was happy, I was pleased with everything. I also wanted them to know I felt they were doing a good job.

"You can just ask my mom if there is anything more you want to know."

The rest of the day I was in all kinds of tests and was moved between departments in my bed. I went to the EEG for a brain scan. Sometimes doctors came and talked to me. That night I got to eat. People always asked me the same questions. Suddenly I remembered Vigfúsína Engilbertsdóttir.

"Have you met Vigfúsína Engilbertsdóttir?"

No one seemed to know her, so I told them about her.

"I'm the princess Gullveig, gold stars, gold stars and hallelujah! Begone with all soldiers! Begone with all whores!"

Then I laughed. They didn't laugh, and just looked at me seriously. But who was Vigfúsína again? Was she a friend of my mother?

Or perhaps my mom? Was I the son of Vigfúsína? Now I understood why they were so anxious. I stopped laughing and became worried.

"Is my mom called Vigfúsína?"

"Not according to my records, no."

"No, I thought not."

"Your mother is called Bjarney Ágústa Jónsdóttir," the doctor added, and looked searchingly at me.

"Yeah. And was that the woman who was in the kitchen asking me things?"

"What kitchen?"

"In Kúrland..."

I remembered. First I was in Kúrland and then at Núpur. And I was walking.

"I was going somewhere, I remember that."

"Where were you going?"

"Anywhere. I like to walk."

The doctor smiled back at meet for the first time. Good. We clearly both agreed it was good to walk.

Gradually I got my memory back. It was like my life had been covered with smoke, and then it disintegrated and dissipated. Suddenly I remembered everything. I was Jón and I lived on Miðtún and I worked at Arnarholt. I was the Jón Gunnar they were asking about. But still I didn't feel quite like him. In between things I fell asleep and when I woke up it was either day or night. By the next night I'd entirely recovered. I had been working at Arnarholt when the seizures started. They decided to take me to an EEG.

But I felt better. I was filled with an unprecedented calm. I felt reborn. I wasn't born, but I was somehow reborn. From now on I was going to change everything. I knew that nothing would ever be the way it had before. Everything would change because I had changed. My parents came to visit me. They were sad and annoyed. They both wept. Mom said repeatedly: "My cherished, cherished boy." I knew they loved me and I loved them. And I loved everyone. Everyone was trying to trouble themselves. Everyone was trying to do their best but they just did not always know what that was.

Everything has changed. There's nothing wrong with me. I have feelings in my body. I'm not a mistake. And I'm not an idiot. There's no curse on me. I'm just the way I am. I'm a child of nature like anyone else. She made me exactly as she wanted. She's my mother. From now on, I'm going to do everything in my power to make this mother of mine proud of me. I'll stop straining. I'm going to stop being angry. I'm going to stop constantly trying to succeed at things I can't do but which others somehow feel I should. I'm going to stop being ashamed of who I am and how I am. I'll be something. I'm going to be someone. I'm going to make up stories and I'm going to write poetry. I'm going to create and I'm going to reveal everything. I'm not going to allow anyone to stop me having the right to be me. And I'll never give up. I'm finally free.

JÓN GNARR was born in 1967 in Reykjavík. As a child, Gnarr was diagnosed with severe intellectual and developmental disabilities due to his emotional and learning differences, including dyslexia and ADHD, and spent much of his childhood receiving psychiatric treatment. He nevertheless overcame his hardships and went on to become one of Iceland's most popular actors and comedians. In the wake of the global economic crisis that devastated Iceland's economy, Gnarr, as a joke, formed the Best Party with friends, none of whom had a background in politics. His aim was to parody Icelandic politics and make life more fun for citizens. Gnarr's Best Party managed a plurality win in the 2010 municipal elections in Reykjavík, and as a result, Gnarr became major of Reykjavík. His term as mayor ended in June 2014, whereupon he served as artist-in-residence at Rice University's Center for Energy and Environmental Research in the Human Sciences in Houston. In his post-mayoral years he continues writing and speaking on the issues that are most important to him: freedom of speech, human rights, protecting the environment, tolerance, compassion, the importance of philosophy, and achieving world peace. Gnarr currently writes weekly columns for the newspaper *Fréttablaðið* and serves as the head of domestic content for 365 Media in Iceland, overseeing the production of original enter-tainment in the Icelandic language. His first big project was to produce the television show, "The Mayor", about a man who runs for mayor of Reykjavík as a joke—and wins. Filming began in the summer of 2016, and Gnarr, of course, stars as the mayor.

LYTTON SMITH is the award-winning author of two books of poetry from Nightboat Books and several translations from the Icelandic, including Jón Gnarr's childhood memoir trilogy, *The Indian, The Pirate,* and *The Outlaw* (Deep Vellum); *The Ambassador,* by Bragi Ólafsson (Open Letter); and *Children in Reindeer Woods* by Kristín Ómarsdóttir (Open Letter). His translations of Guðbergur Bergsson's *Tómas Jónsson—Bestseller* (Tómas Jónsson, metsölubók) and Ófeig Sigurðsson's *Öræfi: The Wasteland,* are forthcoming from Open Letter Books (2017) and Deep Vellum (2018) respectively. He is Assistant Professor of English at SUNY Geneseo in upstate New York.

Thank you all
for your support.
We do this for you,
and could not do
it without you.

DEEP
VELLUM

DEAR READERS,

Deep Vellum Publishing is a 501c3 nonprofit literary arts organization founded in 2013 with a threefold mission: to publish international literature in English translation; to foster the art and craft of translation; and to build a more vibrant book culture in Dallas and beyond. We are dedicated to broadening cultural connections across the English-reading world by connecting readers, in new and creative ways, with the work of international authors. We strive for diversity in publishing authors from various languages, viewpoints, genders, sexual orientations, countries, continents, and literary styles, whose works provide lasting cultural value and build bridges with foreign cultures while expanding our understanding of how the world thinks, feels, and experiences the human condition.

Operating as a nonprofit means that we rely on the generosity of tax-deductible donations from individual donors, cultural organizations, government institutions, and foundations. Your donations provide the basis of our operational budget as we seek out and publish exciting literary works from around the globe and build a vibrant and active literary arts community both locally and within the global society. Deep Vellum offers multiple donor levels, including LIGA DE ORO ($5,000+) and LIGA DEL SIGLO ($1,000+). Donors at various levels receive personalized benefits for their donations, including books and Deep Vellum merchandise, invitations to special events, and recognition in each book and on our website.

In addition to donations, we rely on subscriptions from readers like you to provide an invaluable ongoing investment in Deep Vellum that demonstrates a commitment to our editorial vision and mission. Subscribers are the bedrock of our support as we grow the readership for these amazing works of literature from every corner of the world. The investment our subscribers make allows us to demonstrate to potential donors and bookstores alike the support and demand for Deep Vellum's literature across a broad readership and gives us the ability to grow our mission in ever-new, ever-innovative ways.

In partnership with our sister company and bookstore, Deep Vellum Books, located in the historic cultural district of Deep Ellum in central Dallas, we organize and host literary programming such as author readings, translator workshops, creative writing classes, spoken word performances, and interdisciplinary arts events for writers, translators, and artists from across the globe. Our goal is to enrich and connect the world through the power of the written and spoken word, and we have been recognized for our efforts by being named one of the "Five Small Presses Changing the Face of the Industry" by *Flavorwire* and honored as Dallas's Best Publisher by *D Magazine*.

If you would like to get involved with Deep Vellum as a donor, subscriber, or volunteer, please contact us at deepvellum.org. We would love to hear from you.

Thank you all. Enjoy reading.
Will Evans Founder & Publisher Deep Vellum Publishing

LIGA DE ORO ($5,000+)

Anonymous (2)

LIGA DEL SIGLO ($1,000+)

Allred Capital Management
Ben & Sharon Fountain
David Tomlinson & Kathryn Berry
Judy Pollock
Life in Deep Ellum
Loretta Siciliano
Lori Feathers
Mary Ann Thompson-Frenk
& Joshua Frenk
Matthew Rittmayer
Meriwether Evans
Pixel and Texel
Nick Storch
Social Venture Partners Dallas
Stephen Bullock

DONORS

Adam Rekerdres
Alan Shockley
Amrit Dhir
Anonymous (4)
Andrew Yorke
Anthony Messenger
Bob Appel
Bob & Katherine Penn
Brandon Childress
Brandon Kennedy
Caitlin Baker
Caroline Casey
Charles Dee Mitchell

Charley Mitcherson
Cheryl Thompson
Christie Tull
CS Maynard
Cullen Schaar
Daniel J. Hale
Deborah Johnson
Dori Boone-Costantino
Ed Nawotka
Elizabeth Gillette
Rev. Elizabeth
  & Neil Moseley
Ester & Matt Harrison

Farley Houston
Garth Hallberg
Grace Kenney
Greg McConeghy
Jeff Waxman
JJ Italiano
Justin Childress
Kay Cattarulla
Kelly Falconer
Lea Courington
Leigh Ann Pike
Linda Nell Evans
Lissa Dunlay